CLOSE

Also by Martina Cole

Dangerous Lady

The Ladykiller

Goodnight Lady

The Jump

The Runaway

Two Women

Broken

Faceless

Maura's Game

The Know

The Graft

The Take

CLOSE

MARTINA COLE

GRAND CENTRAL
PUBLISHING

New York   Boston

Grand Central Publishing Edition
Copyright © 2006 by Martina Cole

This Grand Central Publishing edition is published by arrangement with Headline Publishing Group, 338 Euston Road, London NW1 3BH, UK.

Grand Central Publishing
Hachette Book Group USA
237 Park Avenue
New York, NY 10017

Visit our Web site at www.HachetteBookGroupUSA.com.

Printed in the United States of America

First Grand Central Publishing Edition: July 2008
10 9 8 7 6 5 4 3 2 1

Grand Central Publishing is a division of Hachette Book Group USA, Inc. The Grand Central Publishing name and logo is a trademark of Hachette Book Group USA, Inc.

Library of Congress Control Number: 2007937239
ISBN-10: 0-446-17996-5
ISBN-13: 978-0-446-17996-6

For my Peter, Mr. Peter Bates

CLOSE

Prologue

The pain was finally easing and the woman sighed with relief.

She glanced at the clock once more. Its ticking was heavy in the quiet of the room. Her long fingers picked at the candlewick bedspread, then the warmth of her bedding made her relax once more with the anticipation of the long sleep.

Her old granny had bragged about the long sleep, the only time a woman ever lay down without consequence, she said. Meaning that the grave alone could finally give you any kind of rest. It was a truth she had not understood for a long time. Had not wanted to believe that a time would come when you were so tired of living that death actually seemed inviting, so you didn't care about leaving the people you had spent your life looking out for, had spent your life taking care of. It had seemed almost unreal then, imagining herself with the criss-cross lines of old age, the paper-thin yellowed skin of regret, for a life lived without any kind of thought for the future when the future was important. The future was eventually all about what you had *really* done, not what you *wished* you had done. Then, to crown it all, the final realization that sex was nothing more than a primeval urge, an impulse, a bodily function like shitting or farting, not love.

She sighed again, heavily, the rattling of her bony frame reminding her how fleeting life really was.

Too much had happened in her life and it had finally tired her out; she was sick of fighting, she was ready to rest. She wanted to see her girl, her baby girl at last. See her Colleen. Take care of her.

It was time for her final sleep all right, she knew that much. But until she had seen all her children, made them understand her decision, she would wait until the time was right.

"I will break your fucking neck if you don't stop cunting me around."

The words were spoken quietly, not in anger, but they were laced with a malevolence that only a fool would choose to ignore. When Pat Brodie threatened, it was always done in an almost friendly fashion. It was his eyes that told the person he was talking to that he meant business. That he would destroy them without a second's thought, and smile while he did it.

Mikey Donovan kept his temper under control with difficulty; he was doing this man a favor and a half, and they both knew it. But cocaine was a firing offense for people who worked for the Home Office, especially prison wardens, and he had been supplying it for a while. Now there was a dearth of it and Brodie was not impressed. What did he expect him to do, magic it from thin air?

Pat Brodie was a handful, and although Mikey knew that he had a lot on his mind, his mother on the verge of snuffing it was affecting him badly, but even amiable and pleasant-natured Mikey had had enough. Brodie was one powerful man, built like the proverbial brick shithouse and he was also far above the intelligence levels of the usual bullshitters Mikey came across. Add to that a natural cunning and a psychotic personality, and you had one dangerous bastard to contend with. He was in for the alleged murder of his brother, and that alone spoke volumes.

Hard fuck did not even cover it, as far as Mikey was concerned, and he had seen his fair share of those over the years. No, Brodie was that totally unexpected quantity; he was an intelligent lunatic and they were as dangerous as they were rare.

"You had better have recommended me for a compassionate visit, Donovan, because I need out, and if I don't get bail, I am going to hold you personally responsible."

Mikey sighed, he had not expected any less.

Brodie knew he was pushing it and he knew that no matter how much Donovan might feel the urge to retaliate, he wouldn't. He was a warden, and like most wardens in hard prisons, he knew how far he could go.

The faint smell of cold tea and buttered bread reminded her of summer days long gone. She closed her eyes and allowed the memories to wash over her.

She could feel once more the oppressive summer heat of years gone by, a heat so intense that it had caused the petrol fumes to hang on the air. She could smell the different aromas of Sunday lunches cooking along the street. The roast was expected by the men, and no matter that the kitchens would all be as unbearably hot as her own and that stand-pipes were being used everywhere to keep water pressure during the usual summer drought, the women would still be expected to produce a huge meal for three o'clock on the dot. For after the pubs turned out the men would meander home in a state of inebriation and with a raging hunger brought on by drinking steadily from ten-thirty that morning.

She knew beef was the preferred meat of the day, but the smell of chicken and pork was just as popular when money was tight and some-one had ripped off someone else at an abattoir, making the meat avail-able when by rights they shouldn't have enough money to put a fucking sandwich together. It was all about paper, as her old man used to say. On paper things looked different, paper was just another excuse to scam, whether it was meat, clothes, whatever. Thanks to those little bits of paper no one went without. Except the people who owned the goods being bartered, of course, and they didn't count. After all, didn't they have enough?

She smiled then, remembering those lazy days. Then she remembered her husband had lived off paper and that it had caused a lot of aggra-vation when he had died, been murdered. In fact, she had been left penniless, and that had caused its own set of problems. She had ended up with two more kids, just to feed the ones she had already acquired. Her mother had made it her life's work telling her how she had fucked up. Then she had decided that she was the perfect daughter, but only because she had been scared of her own company. And that woman had loved Lance so much it had been almost a mania with her from his birth; she had adored him from the start. But *she* had never liked him, her own son, and she had always felt there was something sinister about him, even when he had been a baby. And she had been right.

She could hear her boys laughing as they kicked a football around the sparse grass of their backyard, see her daughters sitting on the back doorstep in their Sunday finery, pouring out imaginary cups of tea for their dolls and feeding them imaginary cakes made from dandelions and buttercups. Their thick blond hair brushed into tidy ponytails and their chubby childish knees scuffed with scabs that had been picked over leaving small bloodstains on their long white socks. The high-voiced laughter of her girls until the ball the boys were kicking would inevitably find its way over to them, knocking their carefully prepared picnic flying. She could remember the fat tears in her twin girls' eyes, her poor little daughters' bewilderment at the male presence that always managed to disturb the games, and her own relief at their brothers' hearty kindness as they picked up the brightly colored plastic tea set, and assorted dollies and tried, in their overly masculine way, to set it all right once more for them.

Pat Junior, the eldest, always the leader, his rough but kindly ministrations being copied by the other boys who knew it was expected of them. Pat loved those girls and he took great care of them, his brothers as well, in his own haphazard way. Colleen's death had taken him hard and she knew how he felt; it had nearly destroyed her, but she had learned a great lesson from it, they all had.

Poor Colleen had been far too good for this world; an old saying that had been proved only too true.

Kathleen and Eileen, the twins, adored their brother Pat, as had Colleen, and he would hug them and make them laugh once more, before going back to the game of football with the girls' adoring eyes turned to him as always. He was a good boy, and he was a good man, whatever anyone might try to say about him. He was his father's son all right, and for that she would always love him.

Now her Shawn was another good lad, as was Shamus, and she knew she would get a good look at them before she finally went for the long sleep.

The long sleep was such a wonderful thought; she was tired, bone weary in fact. Her mind was once more back in the present and now she could smell the faint odor of her own body; her sweat was sweet, almost like almonds. She knew it was the drugs she was on, the smell emanating from her pores a constant reminder of her old age and her pain-racked body.

There was nothing left of her now, the once voluptuous curves were nothing but bone and sagging skin. She smiled, she actually looked like her granny. Oh how history repeated itself.

She glanced at the photograph in a heavy silver frame that stood on her bedside table; in the photo she was a young woman with her eldest son in her arms, and a belly full of arms and legs. She knew now something she had never known back then.

She had been beautiful, really beautiful, and she had wasted it. Wasted the only thing she had ever really had going for her. Because in those days a woman's looks were all she had.

Her stepfather's rough, cigarette- and whisky-soaked voice came to her, laughing as he said, "You are sitting on a fucking goldmine, girl, remember that."

Her mother had gone off her head at him, screaming at him not to put those thoughts in her mind. She hated him, she realized now. Her mother had tied herself to a man who wasn't, as her granny would always say with a drink in her, worth a wank.

She tore her eyes away from the offending photo, unable to bear looking at the woman she had once been, and comparing her with the cancer-riddled wreck she was now.

But her life had been eventful, if nothing else.

She closed her eyes and retreated again into the past, which was becoming more and more real to her with every passing hour.

Patrick Brodie was still waiting patiently for word that he could visit his dying mother. He didn't hold out much hope, though his lawyer had pointed out that he was only on remand, even if they were making out like he was already sentenced. He would love to hold her in his arms once more. Feel her familiar embrace one last time.

She had been a game old bird, and a good mother, despite everything that had happened to her in her life.

He remembered her as he always did, in her heyday, shouting the odds, putting his father in his place. Cooking her gargantuan meals and always with a cigarette in her mouth.

She was such a character, and he had loved her more than anyone else, even after all the problems with her men after his father's untimely demise.

His father's murder had hit them hard, but his mother most of all. She had lost more than a husband, she had in effect lost the only person who had ever really valued her other than her kids.

His father's death had been the catalyst for all their problems and the hardships, and he saw that now. It had turned Pat into the man he was, made him the man he had become. The man who was awaiting trial for the murder of his brother, his own flesh and blood. A murder for which he had not one iota of remorse, only sorrow that he had not done it earlier. Got shot, got rid. Eradicated him as you would any kind of predatory vermin. They couldn't prove it, and no one was going to talk, he was as sure of that as he was sure of his own name. Everyone knew he had done the dirty deed, but no one could prove it. In this country you needed evidence, not circumstances, and he was confident of a "not guilty" verdict.

He had watched his dad die, seen it in glorious detail, and had learned very early in life that in this world, their world anyway, it was all about the survival of the fittest. His father had let his guard down, had not thought things through, a mistake he had never made himself. Seeing your old man's brains all over your mother's sweater tended to stay in your mind, and the reason for it happening tended to make you determined never to make the same mistake.

It had lodged in his head, it had made him wary, made him cold, but it had also made a child into a man well before his time. It had made him embrace skullduggery and chicanery with a fervor his father would have been proud of.

As a kid, he had only tried to help his mother look after his siblings, he had never realized then that it would become his way of life. A bit of hoisting here, a bit of burglary there, gravitating as the years went on to other kinds of illegal activities to keep them all clothed and fed, a roof over their heads, the bill collector off the doorstep, and a few pennies for his poor mum to go out and have a good time. It had been a means to an end, that was all.

That he would like the world he had been catapulted into, that he would rise in it and make a name for himself, had not been on the agenda. That he had eventually given his dead father's name some kind of meaning, after all that had happened, was just coincidence. How could he have known all that would happen?

His mother had tried to keep him in line, taken the strap to him, had threatened him and tried to keep him out of trouble. Even though she had inadvertently brought a lot of it on them all, with her choice of men, with her choice of lifestyle. She had been a girl though, there was no doubt about that. And, in fairness, she had traipsed around the prisons, visiting one or the other of them.

He sighed, he was only on remand in Belmarsh and they still had him locked up like a lifer. Double A grade, like some kind of fucking terrorist. How they had the nerve to sanction other countries about their penal laws when they treated their own as guilty before there was even a trial, he did not know. Innocent till proven guilty? A fucking joke or what?

There was no reason not to let him out to see his mother, but he knew they would find a way to keep him there if they could. They hated him, and they had good reason to. He hated the system, and whenever he had been in prison he had fought it with every bone in his body.

He breathed in deeply, feeling the familiar anger welling up inside him once more, the anger that had always been there, that had caused him to do terrible things, but he could also feel his determination not to let it spill over until he had seen the woman who had borne him, who had loved him.

Then he would let it explode once more, and feel the release wash over him and the peace descend as always.

Until the next time.

*　　*　　*

Eileen lit a cigarette and, taking a deep pull on it, she blinked back the tears that were threatening to spill over.

A few minutes earlier she had sponged down her mother's body and the sheer devastation of it had moved her profoundly.

She was like a skeleton, her poor arms and legs were sticklike, her chest was sunken and bruised all over from bleeding under her skin, and the scar from her mastectomy was vicious in the half-light.

She already looked dead and Eileen knew that it couldn't be long before she went. But even though she knew it would be a happy release for her mother, the thought of her never being there ever again was terrifying.

She depended on her so much, needed her so desperately that even though she knew it was selfish, she prayed her mother pulled through as she had before. Paulie, her husband, knew how hard this was for her. He alone knew she had come off the drink so she could nurse the woman who had cared for them all.

She watched through the kitchen window as her twin sister Kathleen made sandwiches and talked to anyone who would listen to her. Poor Kath, as she was known, it would hit her hard as well.

That bastard Lance was dead but would never be forgotten by any of them, no matter how hard they tried to push him from their thoughts.

His death had been the finish of their mother, even though Eileen knew she had hung on until she knew he was finally gone.

He was to be buried in a pauper's grave, no service arranged, no nothing, and she knew that everyone in their world would wonder why. They would be expecting pomp and circumstance, assuming he would be laid to rest like all the others. They would expect a big do, even though he had died, allegedly, at the hands of his older brother. Nothing had been proved yet, and she hoped that nothing ever was.

Lance had crossed the line, and the heinous nature of his offense had sent shock waves through the whole family. She also knew that the reason he had died would never be forthcoming from any of them. It was another secret, and they were used to secrets, being secretive was second nature to the Brodies.

Let people guess, let them wonder, she didn't care anymore.

It was over, it had happened, and it had been dealt with.

*　　*　　*

Christy, unlike his brother, Pat, was in a squad car being driven into London. He had been questioned about Lance's death as had the rest of his brothers and sisters. Too much had been swept under the carpet with his family, and even though he knew his mother thought it was all for the best, he also knew without a shadow of a doubt that old scores would soon need to be settled. Whatever she thought, and no matter how much she had begged them all not to react to circumstances and events. Once she was gone, it would be open season and they all knew that.

He expected the rows to start, though Patrick would probably put a block on them.

Shawn sipped at his tea and watched as his sister Kathleen made sandwiches with a speed that denoted years of practice. She had lived with their granny and Lance, and been used as a gofer for most of that time. Women were strange in that way, loyal but strange.

He smiled at her sadly and she stopped what she was doing to grab his hand and smile down at him. These two were close, even in a family as close as they all were.

His skin was so dark against hers, yet she never saw that, none of them did. He was the baby and they all doted on him. Most of them anyway.

His father had wandered into their lives and then wandered back out again, turning up periodically, not really a part of the family, but accepted all the same.

His earliest memory was of his mother's smiling face, and his brother Patrick taking him from her arms as she got herself ready for work. He had been about three years old, and he could still smell her particular smell. Cigarettes and Estée Lauder, he had never been able to forget the aroma of safety that smell had always engendered in him.

He wasn't silly, he knew it had been hard for her when she had produced him, but he also knew that she had never cared what anyone thought. His brothers and sisters had loved him more if anything, yet he had been conscious of his color from an early age, though mostly only when he left the comfort of his home. Now though, it didn't matter, times had changed, and things were different. And he was dreading the death of the woman he loved like he loved no other.

Lance was the only one in the family he had never cared for. He had been a bully and a vicious bully at that, but Shawn knew that his silence had been right and when it had finally come to a head, he was glad that he had not been the one to cause it.

Like his sister, he had suffered at his hands on more than one occasion.

He had seen him in the mortuary, identified the battered body that had not suffered enough, the sneaky bastard lying in peace, and he had finally relaxed knowing that his tormentor was gone forever.

He smiled as he remembered the scandalized expression on the faces around him as he had hawked in his throat and spat on the corpse of his older brother. "That's him, the rotten bastard."

He had said it with as much hatred as he could muster, and he had enjoyed the shock-horror it had caused. They were such a close family, put on such a united front, no one would have believed the under-currents and the feuds their closeness covered up. Now though, all his thoughts were with the woman upstairs in her bed, and he felt the wet-ness of his tears as they slid down his face and was amazed to realize he had been crying all along.

Kathleen held on to the hand that had steadied her as a child, that had washed her, brushed her hair and hugged her and the feel of its trembling and the warmth of the papery skin, were almost too much to bear.

This woman had given them life, had taken care of them all, visited the boys in every prison in the country come rain or shine, advised her daughters on every aspect of their lives and even when times were so hard there was hardly a bite to eat in the house, had provided them with a meal through the sale of the only asset she possessed. Her strength had communicated itself to them all at some time or another, she had solved her children's problems with a quiet dignity, or screaming anger, depending on the circumstances and her mood. She had stopped war from erupting, and welcomed back black sheep over and over again. She had held them together with the sheer force of her will and her overpowering love. What would happen to them all now? Who would keep them all together, make sure they didn't fall apart, didn't rake up the past and cause murders?

She had always been the voice of reason, had been the one who smoothed over quarrels and made sure that they remembered they were family. Stopped the fights before they began and reminded them that, at the end of the day, each other was all that any of them really had. As close as they were, they had all fallen out big time over the years.

She had been the voice of reason. She had stopped Patrick from murdering on more than one occasion. She had glossed over trouble with a smile, and she had forced them all to lie, if necessary, for the greater good of the family.

Now though she was dying, and none of them was going to find it easy to live without her.

Book One

O Lord, thou hast seen my wrong:
Judge thou my cause.

—Lamentations 3:59

Chapter One

"He's a loser, like his old man, but what can you do?" Barry Caldwell held out his arms in supplication and the men in the public house smiled with him. They were strained smiles though, and Barry observed that much and learned a valuable lesson. He had fucked with the wrong person.

Patrick Brodie, however, laughed heartily at the man's words.

It had been said about him in jest many times but he knew it was the truth. Barry had been well and truly ripped off and, like many a man before him, he was finding out that Patrick Brodie was not a man to cross.

Pat knew, better than any of them, what he was. But unlike the men around him, he knew exactly how far he was prepared to go to get what he wanted. All his life he had been looked down on, abused and treated like shit. This was in part because his father was a big, drunken Irishman with a mouth that ran away with him, and a gambling habit that he had never been able to afford. Consequently, his son, Pat Junior, was close-mouthed, hardly drank, and made his living from the bets amongst other things.

But it was also because he had been abandoned by his mother, had had no formal schooling, dodged the draft with a cheery smile and his natural ambivalence, that made him a law unto himself very early on in life.

He had no intention of fighting for a country that he saw as holding men down and offering them nothing except back-breaking work. He had said as much to his commanding officer. He had also robbed the army stores blind; the black market was still thriving at the time, and he had used that for his own ends.

They'd thrown him in the stockade for a year, and in that time he had learned a lot about life, the human condition, but most importantly, he had learned that you had no one to depend on in this life, except yourself.

He had inherited his father's fighting spirit and his absent mother's disregard for others, along with her knack of rewriting history when it suited her, and this had proved to be a winning combination on more than one occasion.

The army had finally waved him off with a sigh of relief and a dishonorable discharge because he fought anyone who disagreed with him about anything. And invariably, he won. He had been as relieved as they were, when they finally parted company.

Now, the last stage of this education was for him to make the final killing and set himself up for life. Barry had tried to rip him off, something he would never forgive or forget. Patrick was a force to be reckoned with, and this was made all the more amazing by the fact that he was basically a loner. He worked his scams himself, collected by himself alone, and had garnered a reputation as a man only a fool would cross.

But the main men were old now and, consequently, his job was getting harder and harder. They were like old women, dithering pimps, worried about getting busted because the judges were suddenly handing out great big sentences and making examples of people. This was now a world waiting to be taken, he was aware of that, and he reassessed his position as and when the occasion merited it.

His father had tolerated hangers-on, had bought himself flaky friendships with pints, with his stories and with his Irish charm. His son, however, trusted no one, needed no one, and his instincts had been proved right time and time again. He had no time for family, none of them had ever been anything except hangers-on, and he had ended their leeching. He was a one-man band, he could only trust himself and he accepted that and understood it.

He had a few young men working for him, but he had suddenly realized that after this debacle, he would need to recruit properly. The operation was getting too big for him to work alone. He was lucky that Barry had no serious backup; if he had, then this would end differently.

It was time to share his good fortune, he knew that, but at the moment he was collecting a debt that was long overdue. A debt that Barry had tried to ignore, believing that he would not have the nerve to come after him.

Brodie's name was synonymous with skulduggery, and he knew that only the rumors surrounding his dishonorable discharge and his phenomenal temper, coupled with the element of surprise, had stood between him and a firearm this night.

But there were others Barry dealt with, and they had their creds. Barry would be all over him like a rash once the shock wore off and he realized that he and his associates were more than capable of taking on a lone man with a large amount of cash.

He smiled and it occurred to him that whoever he decided to pal up with needed to be a new Face, an up-and-coming criminal like himself with the heart and the nerve to take on the more established of their counterparts. The world was changing, and the younger men were needing money and the older men were needing a lesson in the real world. The country was still rebuilding, not only buildings, but the economy, and the pickings were juicy enough to make Brodie not just a man of means, but also a man to be listened to, and more importantly, a man to respect.

Everything had changed with the war, and Patrick had seen that it was a new era coming, and that the new world they would finally inhabit was open to all sorts of moneymaking schemes. This meant a new criminal fraternity, and Brodie was determined that he would be a big part of that change. It was what he had worked towards, it was what made him the man he was, and it was why Barry was now awaiting his downfall.

It was the sixties, and life was sweet for anyone with a bit of street smarts and some dough to sweeten their journey through life.

Patrick was one of the first to challenge the likes of Barry Caldwell and his ilk. It was in with the young and out with the old.

They had all known this day was coming, they had just not had the foresight to make any kind of provision for when it all finally came to an end.

Well, fuck them. His rep would gather enough talk tonight to make him a household name in East London. The debt was large and had also been a long time coming, but when he actually went after Barry *and* his peers and took all their work off them they would understand that he was now not just their equal, but one of their betters. His rep would finally be strong enough for him to become the lynchpin of a new and exciting world that he would not only create, but also control.

The war had separated the men from the boys, and the old men who had ruled because the country's youth had been scattered to the ends of the earth, were now going to find out that it really was about the survival of the fittest.

Their days of being the top dogs were over, finished with, gone. This lot might have been the instigators of this brave new world way back, but they had no control over it any more. They were like fucking antiques, decrepit, and frightened of the new generation who had access to guns and no real fear of the filth. It was time to make his move all right, and he was ready to take the consequences of his actions.

His mind made up, he picked up his beer and, emptying the straight-lined Courage glass of its contents, he proceeded to smash it with all the force he could muster, into Barry Caldwell's chubby, pasty and comically surprised face.

Patrick had the psychological advantage, he had drawn first blood. He was quick to note that none of the men around him tried to intervene, and he knew then, without a shadow of a doubt, that his instincts, as usual, had been spot on.

They all looked defeated, they all looked shocked and they were all frightened that the next person on his agenda was going to be one of them. They were old, old before their time from drunken binges, chain-smoking and easy pickings. None of them had been seriously challenged since their draft notices; they were rejects, they were from the past, from a life that was grey and empty, and their antiquated moral code stifled younger men like himself. They were carrion, old, wizened bastards. They were finished and they all knew it.

Well, he was still young enough to make his mark, yet old enough to command respect. Pat Brodie was on his way up, and at twenty-nine, he was ready to put his money where his notoriously close mouth was.

The courts were handing out long sentences, and instead of that being a deterrent, it only made him and his counterparts more reckless, more violent, because if they were going to go down then they would make sure it was for a fucking good reason.

He looked down at Barry. Might as well be hung for a sheep as a lamb.

Lily Diamond was tired out. Her shift had been long and her legs were swelling from fourteen hours of standing in a freezing factory on a cold floor, and then waiting over an hour for the bus that dropped her off a ten-minute walk from her home.

As she went into her house, she was already yawning and her mother took her coat from her, hung it on the back of the door and poured her a cup of steaming black tea. Then, with her usual swiftness, she placed a plate of ham and eggs in front of her.

This was all done in silence so as not to wake the drunken man who was quietly snoring on the settee in the small parlor nearby.

Lily smiled at her mother but they both knew it meant nothing, these were two people who had realized that there was no real connection between them many years before.

Lily knew that she looked like her mother. They had the same thick hair and the same grey eyes, their builds were similar enough for people to mistake them for each other from the rear, and they were both blessed with a fantastic bone structure that belied her mother's advancing years, and reassured her daughter that her looks were probably going to last a lot longer than the majority of her friends. But other than that, they were as different in temperament as a dog and a cat.

They had only one thing in common and that was a hatred for the man who ruled their lives, and who terrorized their every waking moment.

Mick Diamond was not her father and she thanked God for that every day of her life, but he had married her mother when she was already pregnant with another man's child, made her respectable and then waited for the children of his own that had never arrived. Consequently, she had not only been resented by him, but also been a constant reminder that it was his fault there were no sons around his table, no children to look to in his old age and no other wages available to assuage his unhappiness by providing him with the alcohol he so desperately craved.

His name would live on through a bastard, through someone else's child. The fact she existed was proof positive that the blame for his wife's childless state must lie with him.

Lily had grown up in a household devoid of any kind of love, or any kind of normality. She had learned at an early age that keeping quiet, staying in the background and trying to be as invisible as possible, was the only way she could hope to survive.

She was a constant reminder to her mother of her shame and a constant reminder to her stepfather of his inability to sire any children of his own. By five, she was a diplomat, already understanding the need to keep both these unstable people happy by not ever making any noise, never demanding their time and most importantly, never bringing any attention to either them or herself from anyone outside their scuffed and well-worn front door.

Now, as a wage earner, she had gained a certain grudging respect, but it had been a long time coming. At fifteen, she understood her life better than people three times her age; she needed to keep the peace until she had enough money to set up on her own, or marry herself out of it all.

As Lily ate, she felt the oppressive atmosphere that always pervaded her home, and she swallowed quickly and quietly as she always had.

Meals were not something to be enjoyed in this house, they were just a necessary part of life, and the social element of eating had never been made apparent to her until she had gone to friends' homes. Seeing them eating leisurely whilst talking about their day or about what was in the newspaper, she had felt as if she was experiencing a revelation not unlike those of St John the Divine.

Until work had claimed her, she had never played outside her house, had never interacted with anyone, at school or otherwise, and she had never realized that her home life was so different to everyone else's.

At school she had been timid, and she had not made friends because her mother and stepfather had never seemed to make any friends either. It was a social skill she had only procured for herself since work had opened her eyes to a world she had never known existed.

At school she had been ridiculed, because of her clothes, her shyness and her terror of mixing with the other children. Her fear of them had given them all the power, but her greatest fear had been of bringing any kind of intrusion into the house she had been brought up in. The fear of someone knocking on the front door for her had caused her to almost faint with fright. Her loneliness had been so acute it had made her ache inside as if she were suffering from some kind of physical illness. Even the most hardened nun had been, to her, a contact with someone other than her parents, and she had relished even the wicked onslaughts of their tongues because at least someone was acknowledging that she existed.

Being part of a crowd was something she now understood, in fact now needed, and more than anything else, it was something she knew was actually keeping her sane. The "you never had it so good" era had come and gone without anyone in her household mentioning it. But then again, apparently her mother and granny had sat under the kitchen table or in the air-raid shelter in the small backyard and had not once made any kind of comment about the Germans, the war or Hitler himself; they were proud of that fact.

Nothing of note had ever been addressed in this house; it was as if the outside world didn't exist for them. Her granny had died suddenly one night and her mother had hardly mentioned it; she had been slid out of the front door in a wooden box and it had been just another day to them. But at least Lily's burden had been eased a little; her fatherless state had never failed to be mentioned at every available opportunity by her granny, so it was with relief that she mourned her passing.

Lily was scared, all the time she was terrified, but she had never really known what of. It was jumbled inside her head and as no one ever addressed her unless absolutely necessary, it had stayed there.

Her fear had been ignored in the same way she had, and not once had anyone tried to still the terrified beating of her heart, or explain to her that it would all be over soon. It was only at school, when she had eavesdropped on other kids' conversations, that she had an inkling of what other people's lives were about.

Now, the need to escape these people was all-encompassing. The need to cut herself off from them was so overpowering she wondered how they could not hear her thoughts, so loud were they at times, and so vicious, she was frightened of what she might be capable of doing to the pair of them while they slept.

Her mother cleared her plate away and refilled her cup without once speaking to her, and, as always, Lily took her cup of tea up to her tiny bedroom, undressed herself in the dark and lay down in the cold bed to sleep. She was shivering from the cold, and from her deep-seated fear of having to live a broken and lonely life like this for the rest of her days. So stunted were her emotions, though, that even now, at her lowest ebb, it did not occur to her to cry.

Crying had never gained Lily anything, even as a baby it had never brought her mother to her side, and so she did not understand that to most girls of her age it was a powerful weapon to be used, was a tool to be harnessed and eventually unleashed on the men in her life, both old and new, to guarantee that she got exactly what she wanted.

Her life was all wrong, and she knew it, had always known it deep inside, but her foray into the real world had made her not only aware of how it could, indeed should, be lived, it had also made her impatient to leave these two people in her past, and start living her own life in her own way. Without them.

The first thing she would do when she had enough money and confidence to branch out on her own, was to buy herself a radio.

She was going to surround herself with noise and with people, she was going to make her life mean something, if not to anyone else, then to herself. She wanted color and sound and laughter, she wanted to feel easy inside, wanted to experience the love of another human being and, most of all, she wanted peace of mind. She needed to feel a part of something bigger than her, bigger than the world that had been forced on her without her knowledge or her permission, wanted to be part of what was happening in the world. Lily Diamond had finally had a taste of reality and she was heady with the feeling of freedom it evoked inside her budding breasts, and she was suddenly beginning to understand just what life was really all about.

Lily Diamond had discovered boys or, more to the point, they had discovered her, and the exciting feelings they could engender inside her body amazed her. She had finally discovered freedom, the power to talk to people and to know they were listening to her. Lily was planning her escape, and it could not come soon enough for her.

She lay in the damp darkness and waited patiently for the sleep that would come because she was bone-weary. She welcomed it, sleep had always been her friend, sleep had been her only escape from a life that was as drab as the rain-sodden streets she walked, as drab as the woman who had borne her. Sleep had always been her only salvation; even God had abandoned her because her mother and father had also controlled what contact she had with him.

As her eyes closed, she was certain that, even though she had no idea what she was going to do when she left this house, once she was far away from the dragging dullness and the quiet desperation of these surroundings, she would miraculously know what to do with her life next.

She wondered if the man with the black car and the scar on his cheek would be there again tomorrow when she went for the bus. She hoped so. He excited her more than the pimply boys she worked alongside, or the clerks that gave her the once-over in the grubby factory offices when she picked up her pay packet.

This man somehow denoted a glamorous danger that, until now, she had only experienced on rare occasions in the lonely darkness of the movie theatre. She was, as the women she worked with would say, an accident waiting to happen.

Pat Brodie had been watching the girl for a while. She was young and that bothered him; he had always gone for brassy blondes with more mileage than an army truck and more carnal knowledge than was good for them. Talented, was how he described them to himself.

Those kind of women knew exactly what to expect from him, and they didn't harbor any illusions, had no foolish dreams of marriage, children or, God help him, love. They took what he was willing to give, the three Fs; a fuck, a fiver and some guaranteed fun. Until now, that was all he had wanted, needed.

Now, this young girl who worked in the Black Cat factory where he picked up cigarettes to sell in pubs and clubs for a fraction of their retail price, had got under his skin.

He was a lot older than her and she was far too young for him, but even knowing that, he still thought about her constantly and it was her obvious innocence that attracted him. Her scruffy clothes and defeated look only seemed to enhance her appeal. It was about more than looks, and this was what worried him the most. This young girl had somehow got under his skin. He had never even spoken to her, he did not know her name and he had no reason in the world to feel like he did.

Now, as he watched her walk to the bus stop once more, he saw the lean lines of her body under the shapeless coat, and appreciated the beauty of a face devoid of make-up and knew that the thing he had always dreaded had finally happened. He wanted her in more ways than just the biblical sense.

Getting out of his car, he followed her to the bus stop with a heavy heart and the hope that once she opened her mouth the illusion she created would disappear, that her allure would fade away because of her cockney accent and ignorant choice of vocabulary.

But under the weak light of the street lamp he found himself lost for words. She turned on hearing him approach, her eyes looked into his, and he saw mirrored there the same feelings and emotions as his own. Except her fear was real, he frightened her and this saddened him because he wanted to make her smile, to make her happy. That was his biggest fear: if he wanted to make her happy, he knew he needed her.

They stared at each other for long moments and he saw her physically relax as if he had told her she had nothing to be scared of, as if they had both agreed to become friends.

Her fear disappeared but his own seemed to increase along with his nervousness.

"Well?" Her voice was low, deep in fact, almost a whisper, and he heard the tremor of excitement the fear inside her caused. He knew then that she had been expecting him, that she welcomed his interest, understood somehow that he meant her no harm.

When she arched one well-plucked eyebrow in inquiry, he also knew then and there that he would never rest until she was his.

She suddenly had all the power and they both knew that, but he didn't care, he was just happy to be near her.

Mick Diamond looked at his stepdaughter in unconcealed disbelief and his wife Annie, he knew, was staring at him in exactly the same way.

"What did you say?" Lily's voice was as always low and respectful when talking to this huge mountain of red flesh and uncertain temper.

"I said, keep your money, girl . . ."

Lily Diamond had been trying to save her money for ages, but no matter where she hid it, this man found it and spent it without a second's thought. Her mother had no idea she had been given a raise and she had kept the few pennies aside, and because of that, she could never say out loud that this man had robbed her while she slept or while she worked. If her mother had known, she would not have had the money anyway, it would have been taken from her immediately.

Now he was standing before her and telling her, civilly mind, that she was not to hand over her few pennies. She was to keep it, and the most damaging and terrifying remark of all was that he had said she was to treat herself. This, she decided, had to be a new trick of some kind and she tensed up even more, waiting for the blow, the sarcastic remark or the derisory laughter that always made her feel like she was nothing.

She glanced at her mother and knew that she was waiting for the same reaction. What seemed like light-years passed by, each second dragged out almost tangibly in the heavy quiet of the kitchen. Still, it didn't come.

This was a new game then. She had survived worse so she stayed quiet and waited until she knew exactly what she was dealing with, her eyes trained on the money lying there so innocently on the tablecloth, her shoulders aching with the tension this house brought into her bones as soon as she entered the front door.

Mick Diamond looked at the girl and saw the attraction of her to a man like Brodie. He also saw his nemesis; this child could be the death of him with a careless word, because her name was now being coupled publicly and, he was amazed to hear, respectfully, with Patrick Brodie. The sweat was trickling down his face and dripping on to his vest, his hands were trembling and his wife was thankfully struck dumb at his demeanor and his words.

Lily herself, he saw, thought he was baiting her, and this fact worried him even more. It was obvious to him that she didn't know her strength yet, that she didn't understand the power she now wielded and he wanted to get on her good side before she did.

He only hoped it wasn't too late.

"Make the child some tea, woman, and some for meself and all. She's been working all day."

He smiled at Lily and she looked at her mother as if for guidance.

Annie looked as bewildered as Lily knew she did herself.

Her mother moved with her customary nervousness, the teacups clattering in her shaking hands. Both were wondering if this was a new game of his, a game where he pitted himself against the two of them. He was a bully and he knew his strengths.

He smiled as he lit a Senior Service and, pulling deeply on the cigarette, he held out his arm in a gesture of friendly amiability. He was, Lily realized, offering her a chair.

She sat, as always doing his bidding, even though her hatred of him was so acute she could taste it.

"So where did you meet Mr. Brodie then, eh?"

Then she understood, and for the first time ever, she knew how fear could bring you peace of mind, and how fear could change your life for the better. As long as it wasn't your own fear of course.

And as she had lived in abject terror for the best part of her young life, this feeling was wonderful, it was like being released from servitude; she knew that no matter what happened, this man would never frighten her again. He looked smaller already, somehow pathetic and old; his body was hunched over and she knew her own body was now straighter. Patrick had given her respect inside this house and for that alone she would love him to the day she died.

She had the power now, and it was all thanks to her Patrick, Patrick Brodie, the man she was going to marry.

She scooped up her wages from the kitchen table and placed them in her overall pocket. Then she took out her packet of cigarettes and dared to light one in front of her parents and, puffing deeply, she said quietly, "Tea would be lovely, thanks."

Her stepfather motioned to his wife and she actually poured the tea then, her mind racing on overtime at what had befallen her daughter and ultimately, she hoped, had befallen herself.

Patrick Brodie was a byword these days, and she knew that if her daughter had managed to snag a fine piece of manhood like him then she had to take the proverbial hat off to her.

Even as the jealousy kicked in, she was, like her husband, looking for ways to utilize the relationship for her own benefit.

This time the tea had sugar as well as milk, and as Lily Diamond lit another cigarette she hoped and prayed that Patrick didn't tire of her, because if he did, these two would slaughter her without a second's thought.

"You having me on?" Billy Spot was laughing, but the laughter was with the subject of his humor, definitely not against him, nor his notoriously flimsy pride.

Since taking out Barry Caldwell, this young man had become an overnight sensation and Billy, being Billy, was waiting to see if this lad's newfound status was going to be a fixture. He had seen them come and go over the years, he knew the score in their game. It was how you survived, you either outlived, or you out-boxed your opponents. At the moment, Pat was the top dog and he would worship at his altar if that was what it took to keep himself in the running. He was a follower, not a leader, he knew that better than anyone. But he knew Barry's death had caused ripples through their world and he also knew that retribution was on its way. He had funded it himself, along with a few other cronies.

He could afford to be friendly, but he had no intention of giving up his pavement without a fight.

"She seems a nice girl though." The laughter was gone now, he was all respect and feigned interest.

Pat smiled then. "She is."

Pat actually liked Billy and he saw his Lil as on a par with Billy's old woman. She was also a civilian and had never been inside any of her old man's clubs, and had no reputation to speak of. She produced children with the minimum of fuss and she lied to the police as and when the occasion warranted it. In short, she was a good bird and Billy worshipped the ground she walked on.

Like Billy, he too wanted the best of the best, a good girl. He wanted someone he could trust even if he got himself a twenty. And his instincts told him that all these attributes were possessed by the young girl he had become besotted with. And he was besotted. He had not wanted another woman for weeks, and for him that was like not wanting a drink or a deal.

In short, it was unheard of.

He had other things on his mind and once they were dealt with, he could relax and court his girl in peace. He was making himself a decent living so that once he was married he could live like a king.

Unfortunately, that involved stepping on more than a few toes, but he was prepared for the fallout and more than eager to take up any reins that might come his way.

He was a risktaker like his father, but unlike his father he liked to make sure that anything he accrued stayed close by. He guessed that Billy, like Barry, was not allowing for his acumen in this new world of skulduggery. Respecting your elders was a luxury these days, and the sooner the silly old fuckers realized that, the better off they would all be.

"Do you have a problem with me outing drugs, Bill?"

Billy shrugged, and Patrick was impressed at the way the man acted so nonchalantly when they both knew the score; he was taking Billy's businesses over gradually and irrevocably. Billy Spot's workforce were now all working in some way for him.

It was a checkmate situation and Patrick hoped that Billy would understand that and not grieve too much over times gone by.

He had heard the rumors about retribution for Barry and he watched his back, but he also accepted it as part and parcel of their choice of career.

Billy's day was long gone, he had made the mistake all powerful men make; he hadn't been on the actual street for years. He was told only what he wanted to hear and he couldn't cap anyone himself, relying on heavies to do his dirty work. He was an embarrassment to all and sundry.

Pat knew the man was waiting to see whether he could keep up this dangerous façade, and if he could, he knew he would have a partner, if not in crime, then at least at the local drinking establishments. He had been willing to use Billy even though he knew the man and his cronies were putting up pound notes to bring about his demise. None of them had liked Barry as such, but none of them wanted to be Barry.

He understood that, except if he had been in Billy's shoes he would have been dead by now.

"You jammy little mare!"

Constance White looked at the young girl packing cigarettes expertly into boxes beside her, and her grin was friendly and amiable. "Fuck me, girl, you got Pat Brodie! Most of his amours end up calling him Glenn Miller and that's because he normally goes on the missing list."

Everyone laughed, and Lily went bright red with embarrassment.

At twenty, Constance was already married and had two children; her husband was a no-neck with acne scars and the conversation of an African elephant. So she envied this little piece even as she admired her. Many women had tried to snag Brodie, herself included, but he had slipped away like an oily chain. Good-looking girl though, and men like Brodie liked the innocent look, in a wife anyway. Like all men he wanted to be sure that any children carrying his name were actually his. No cuckoos in the nest for him. He was thirty if he was a day and she was fifteen; he must think all his Christmases and birthdays had come at once.

But it was the change in Lily that amazed Constance. The girl had grown into herself overnight, had started walking tall, she spoke before she was spoken to and she had the flushed cheeks of a girl ripe for the marriage bed.

Connie, as she was called, knew that this child, and she was a child for all her mature looks, was not going to be one of Brodie's usual shack-ups. He wanted this one to breed with, and she had a feeling Lily would amaze them all.

Lily smiled happily; thanks to Pat she was set for life, and this factory and all it entailed would be a thing of the past soon. As soon as she hit sixteen she was gone.

Thunderclap Newman came on the radio and she sang along with her workmates; there definitely was something in the air.

Patrick affected her in so many ways, and as she packed her cigarettes she dreamed of his body touching hers, and longed for the kisses she was sure to get once the night drew in and they were alone in his car.

Billy Spot was standing outside his nightclub in Soho with his girlfriend on his arm. A redhead called Velma, she had all his usual prerequisites: big tits, nice teeth and long skinny legs. Billy was wearing his customary attire: black Crombie overcoat, pinstripe suit and an expensive cigar.

He was amazed to see his girlfriend start walking quickly away from him, extricating herself from his flabby arms even as he saw with his peripheral vision young Patrick Brodie pull a gun from underneath his coat. He was a dead man and he knew it.

He hit the floor with the minimum of fuss and Patrick was gone before anyone thought of calling in the law to make things look above-board, look normal. The gun was dispatched into the Thames, and Billy's associates were aware of his demise within hours. It made no odds to them; he was a nice bloke but as they all remarked in private, business was business.

It was out with the old and in with the new. Pat had decided, on the spur of the moment, to erase the older man and open up the streets properly. Spot had cunted him to a close associate, and that was something he was not about to allow. He was not going to screw around any more, he had Lil, and he wanted it all.

Pat bought the rest of the London consortium out with little fuss; he was too young and too dangerous for them and they all decided to retire from the game. He had everyone behind him and he had the edge because of that. This new generation were nutcases; they wanted it all and they wanted it as quickly as possible. Drugs had moved the goal posts and the old lot didn't want any part in it.

Billy should have seen that coming.

Chapter Two

Pat loved the docks at night. Even the stench of the river was something to be enjoyed. As a kid, after his mother had walked out, he had played here while waiting for his father to finish his fighting. A street fighter, he had sporadically made money with magnificent wins. As the drink got him though, he lost more often than not. Then the money had not been as plentiful and that had just made him drink all the more.

One of the reasons he had disappeared as well, Pat decided, was his gradual loss of face and reputation. He understood now how hard that must have been for him, but he still could find no forgiveness in his heart. He had dumped him without a by-your-leave and that alone had hardened him up, and it had also made him determined to always take care of his own, no matter what. Walking away was easy, it was staying around and sorting out your own shit that took guts, that made you a man.

Pat closed his eyes and forced all thoughts of his parents from his mind. They were over with, finished, gone. They were both the shit on his shoes, he had no care for either of them, and he certainly had no intentions of letting them encroach on his life any more than they already had. He had a coldness inside him, it had been there all his life, the fear of depending on another person, the fear of being soft, of being seen as a mark. Now though, with Lil, he felt in control because she needed him, it wasn't the other way around.

It hurt him to remember how he had been dragged up, how, like any child brought into the world of poverty, his life had been a lottery. He knew his parents wanted him now, shocked that their child had managed something neither of them had even dreamed of; they actually thought he would be cunt enough to take them on board. Like he was foolish enough to even entertain any of them. The only time in their life they had ever agreed on anything and it was too late. He would not piss on them if they burst into flames in front of his eyes. He was happy enough as he was. He had not needed anyone until his wife and she was all he needed, he respected her. Simple as that. Unlike his mother, she had not been round the turf more times than a fucking prize-winning greyhound. All his life he had been overlooked, thought a fool, and now he was making his mark, making people understand that he was a force to be reckoned with and he was enjoying every second of it. Not that he would ever admit that of course. Even to himself.

He stared up at the new moon and smiled to himself, enjoying his lonely vigil, enjoying his power over his past.

Under the cover of darkness, Custom House, like all the dock areas, was as alive at night as it was during the day. The difference being that the night-time deals were made by dark-clothed men with subdued voices and menacing reputations. The whores that walked the quays in the small hours were the older women, their best years behind them, the dim glow of the lampposts their only friend. They were used-up, weather-beaten, defeated-looking women. The dock dollies who frequented the wharfs with a determined stealth waited patiently for the johns they were now reduced to; the Chinamen, the Arabs and the Africans. Their bleached-blond hair and heavily made-up blue eyes were like beacons to these men, drawing them into their world with a slow smile, then finishing them off quickly and expertly with either a hand or their thighs.

The sex was quick, furtive, and unsatisfactory, not only for the men but also for their conquests. These hard women who only knew how to use, whose lives were lived in black and white, had no feeling any more for the reality they were unfortunate enough to charge money for. The darkness gave them a reason to ply the trade that had destroyed them; reduced to the lowest of humanity they embraced the night because it paid their rent. There were no pensions or savings for these women, easy money had ensured they were never off the pavement, and the money they were earning now was a pittance in comparison to their heydays.

This was another world, and it was a world that Pat Brodie hated and loved with equal passion. He had met his mother walking these very docks once, and her plight had not touched him one iota; he had enjoyed her embarrassment, enjoyed her demise. In his eyes she had hit rock-bottom when she had deserted him and he felt no allegiance to her at all. He didn't even mind if anyone knew about it: she was nothing to him, and he had no intentions of making her think otherwise.

Since his marriage he had found a renewed vigor for making money. Lil was everything to him and he found that his feelings for her seemed to grow on a daily basis. She was as astonished as he was to find that she had a very bad temper, which inflamed them both. She was passionate and she was funny.

Things that had either been hidden or had lain dormant inside her for years while tiptoeing round her mother's house trying to be invisible, had finally come to the surface. Pat's face hardened as he thought about the way she had been treated and he wondered for the millionth time why she still entertained her mother.

The fucking leech was never off the doorstep and she seemed to have a real affection for her grandchild, if not for her daughter, though she acted the concerned parent with a zeal that was as astounding as it was unbelievable. Money did that to people, he knew it better than anyone. He also knew Lil needed her, needed to believe that the woman who had birthed her, cared about her. She believed that it was her birth that had been the catalyst for her mother's unhappy marriage and was the reason for her own bullied and hated existence. Lil was too nice for her own good, and he swallowed it; if it made her happy then he was satisfied. But her mother was like his, a product of poverty and betrayal, the product of a man who had knocked her up and run away leaving her to make the best she could of her newfound circumstances. Lil forgave her for marrying a man who had tortured them both, and in a strange way he understood her forgiveness: at least this way she could pretend her life meant something. For himself, he couldn't wait until the old bag screwed up, and she would, her type always did, then he would take great pleasure in showing her the door. Until then, he would keep his mouth shut and smile when required.

Still, she helped out and that was something. Young Pat Junior was a handful, and he loved him with all his heart. He was his father's son all right; he only hoped that he didn't have anything of his paternal grand-father inside him. Only time would tell. Pat wanted a horde of children and he was shrewd enough to know that one of them would be likely to inherit not only the laziness, the bullshitting and lying that his father had been so good at, but also, the unconcerned demeanor of his mother. She would come out in one of them he knew, as would his father.

That man had been able to talk himself out of anything, and he would take the bread out of his child's mouth for a drink or a bet. It was Murphy's Law that a large family would throw up a loser but Pat prayed that he would recognize the traits early enough to stamp them out. Beat them out of the child, if that was what it took. Unlike his old man who beat him for no other reason than he wanted to.

And his mother. She had fucked off on a regular basis, left him there with a man who had no idea how to raise a child and no interest in anything except where the next drink was coming from. He had lived on and off with various relatives all his life, so his home with Lil was everything to him, as it was to her.

Although Lil tried to make excuses for her parents, well her mother anyway, he had no such illusions about his beginnings; all he knew was that he wanted to make a good life for his family and he wanted to make his wife feel needed, loved and respected for what she was.

He still took the occasional flier of course, but he was as faithful to her as he was ever going to be. It had been a voyage of discovery for both of them. But the bottom line was that they worked well together and they needed each other.

As he stamped out his cigarette, he looked around the warehouse and wondered at this cannabis that everyone seemed so mad about. He was a Scotch man himself, but if this was what would add to his fortunes, then he was happy enough to supply it. Times were changing and if you had any savvy at all, you changed with them.

He heard the low drone of an expensive car as it pulled up outside and he smiled once more. This was what life was all about, not just the skulduggery, but also the feeling of control skulduggery conferred on the likes of him. Money was everything, and anyone who pretended otherwise was either rich by birth or afflicted by a mental ague. Too stupid to see what was around them.

Dicky Williams walked into the warehouse, as always surrounded by his brothers. They were like clones of one another, all short, stocky and with crew cuts. They all favored tonic suits, shirts and ties. This was one of the reasons Pat liked doing business with them; they were smart, both in their minds and their appearance.

They were funny as well and this went a long way in their world. A sense of humor could be the deciding factor in many aspects of their business. Especially the debts; a first call with a smiling face and a few quips could garner more money than all the baseball bats and tire irons in the vicinity. It was more about getting your point across to begin with; if no one took that on board then anything that might happen after the initial warning was just classed as gravy. A warning was, after all, a warning.

Why borrow money if you had no intentions of paying it back? The people who approached them knew they were not the fucking bank. If they had been welcome there in the first place they would not be asking them as an alternative, would they? So, ergo, they had to understand that, unlike dealing with the banks, they would be expected to pay the amount back not only quickly and expensively, but with a cheery smile and a promise to pass on their good fortune to friends and associates.

They were the last resort for the people who borrowed from them and they provided the money when no one else would take the chance. Shame this was what gave them a bad name in society.

Dicky came in, rubbing his hands together like Uriah Heep on Dexedrine. "Froze me cods off, Pat. How the fuck do you stand it?"

Pat laughed.

Dicky had been to see the man they were dealing with for some clothes that had mysteriously disappeared from a large storage depot in Whitechapel. The man rummaged from a huge old house, and even if there was six feet of snow on the ground, the place was never heated and the guy never wore a coat. Consequently, he was known as Freezing Freddie Dwyer or Fucking Freezing Freddie Dwyer.

"He is off his fucking nut. You should have seen him, Pat. He was popping pills like there was no tomorrow."

The Williams brothers all nodded in unison and this made Pat want to laugh at *them* now. He had more sense than to give in to the urge though.

"It's the purple hearts, see, he can't get on without them."

Pat nodded sagely as they lit cigarettes, and then he poured them out large Scotches. This had become a ritual.

The smell of whisky and cigarette smoke still couldn't cover the stench of dirt and blood that seemed to permeate the place. The warehouses had witnessed many deaths over the years and the bodies thrown into the Thames had either made their way to Tilbury or out to the open sea depending on the tides. Either way, they were gone, and that was all that mattered to these men and their earlier counterparts.

As they sipped their drinks and chatted, money exchanged hands and the bags of green, sweet-smelling herb were put into the trunks of cars.

Dicky and Pat went back years and had an easy camaraderie. They were both products of their environment and knew the pavements better than they knew their own families. It was home to them and they were comfortable with it.

Lately, they had entered into a partnership of sorts that had been as enjoyable as it had been lucrative. Between them, they had sewn up most of the main scams and, even though no one had named them outright as Faces—the new gangsters on the block—people were approaching them and asking their permission before undertaking any kind of skullduggery on their streets.

They found this amusing, as well as indicative of the way they were now being regarded by the main players in their fields. If the average man on the street was giving them their due, it meant Lily Law would not be far behind them. They acknowledged this as part of the price they paid for their lifestyles and both wanted to make sure they stayed this side of the visiting room. They loved the notoriety, but they also had no intention of being five-minute wonders. Here today, going down tomorrow, was not in their plans. They wanted to be around for many years to come and they wanted to maximize their potential. In short, they thought, like many a man before them, that they were too clever to be caught.

"One thing about that freezing fucker though, he loves a gossip and he hears everything. He told me a little old bloke has been bandying our names about."

Pat nodded. This was, it seemed, old news to him. He didn't say a word and eventually the silence was too heavy for the brothers.

"So what do we do now?" Dicky sounded stressed, unsure of himself.

Pat shrugged.

It was a statement not a question, and Dicky was more than aware of the underlying menace in Pat's voice as he snapped, "We do what we always do: keep it fucking quiet. That is what gets people's collars felt, too much fucking talk. Remember the old adage, careless talk and all that." His eyes were cold, dead. His voice was without any kind of inflection at all.

Dicky grinned. His smile was, like a lot of his contemporaries', ruined by a combination of bad diet and missing teeth. In Dicky's case though, it made him look amiable, foolish even. A mistake many men had made over the years. His demeanor hid a vicious and vengeful personality that came to the fore whenever he felt he was not being given his due. This was another thing he had in common with Pat Brodie: neither of them looked the least bit capable of the violence that bubbled away under the surface of their friendly, smiling faces.

Dicky though, brought up in a family of thirteen, was a pack-fighter. Like dogs, if one of the Williams brothers went off, the others followed suit. Pat was a loner, a dirty fighter who would use anything that came to hand, be it a bottle, bicycle chain or gun. He had no preference as long as whatever it was would cause untold pain.

"I think it's time we gave everyone a fright, Pat, you know, talked to a few old Faces and reminded them about what can happen when someone speaks out of turn."

Pat had heard this from Dicky a lot over the last year or so and he knew that he could not hold him back indefinitely. He had a point though, so he sighed gently and nodded his agreement.

The fact that Dicky consulted him before he did anything of import spoke volumes, not just to Patrick Brodie, but also to Dicky's numerous siblings and their hangers-on. Pat had no hangers-on, he had people who *worked* for him and he kept them, for the most part, at arm's length. A few were invited into his inner sanctum, but even they had no real knowledge of the man they professed to know.

He had no actual friends though, not in the real sense. Dicky was the nearest person to have earned that title. But Pat had a lot of acquaintances and he also had the knack of making people feel that they had his full attention, even though he rarely listened to anything unless it benefited him or his family.

He knew it was this aloofness that was the key to his success and he found that now he actually cultivated it. Used it to his advantage.

"Soon, OK? Give me a few days to think about it."

Dicky knew he was in and he pushed it as Pat had known he would from the outset. He waited patiently for him to get to the crux of his conversation.

"Come and meet this tame cop I've found, eh, mouthy little ponce he is, always shooting his mouth off and chancing his arm. Now we own him, well you do actually, it's your club he fucked up in. Though he don't realize that yet, of course, he thought Lenny Donnelly owned it. He is a bit of a lad, typical cop, more mouth than cows got cunt, and a personality like a pair of nylon socks. However, he is also on his way to what he perceives as greatness, mainly through the pursuit of promotion in the police force. In short, Pat, he is a cunt with an earhole in the right places, and a knob that rises on a regular basis. Know what I mean?"

Pat nodded. Poor Dicky was telling him nothing he did not already know. He had been one step ahead of everyone all his life, had had to be, but as always he kept his own counsel. People only know what you tell them. And it was true. People gave out their whole life stories to anyone and everyone without a second's thought. Stand at a bus stop, sit in a strange pub, get locked up, and someone would always give you their life story. It was as if they were trying to prove they existed.

Dicky smiled nervously, the silence as always making him slightly uneasy, and Pat refilled their glasses without uttering a word.

"We'll keep our traps shut as always, Pat, keep our business to ourselves, but this way, we can also get a bit of insurance for the future."

Pat grinned.

The point had been taken but the subject was now closed.

Detective Inspector Harry Lomond was drunk. Really drunk, and his stomach was just about to vacate its contents.

He was in a hostess club in Soho, he was without his trousers, and he was also convinced that the walls were breathing. LSD would do that to a body. Dilys Crawford, known as Sabina while at work, was sitting beside him, bored out of her brains.

An unnatural redhead, she had small breasts, large thighs and a mouth that was legendary. She had three kids, a husband doing a ten-stretch in Dartmoor and more varicose veins than the Michelin man. Still, men sought her out, and stone-cold sober she sorted them out quickly and efficiently. She would never have full sex with a john, only a blow job. A bit of tit and a laugh was about as far as she would go with them. Most men were happy with that, and as for her, she would slip under the table and do it, so even paying for a hotel room was not part of the equation.

Tonight though, she was not even bothering to pour the champagne on the floor, a ruse many hostesses used so they didn't get drunk and ripped off. This loser was so far gone, fucking Donald Campbell would have trouble keeping up with him.

A stripper came on the stage and she sighed in relief. Candy did an act with a snake and a trilby hat that was so outrageous it left all the hostesses free to relax, have a cigarette and work out their next moves.

Her next move was to pass this cop on to Dicky, the sooner the better as far as she was concerned. When she saw Pat walk in with the Williams brothers, she sighed with relief. She would suck off a fucking tramp if he had the money, but she balked at touching the police. They were about as much use as a handbrake on the proverbial canoe. She had done her bit for England, she just wanted her cash and a cab home. Harry was still smiling drunkenly when she dumped him in the basement of the club.

*   *   *

Lil settled the child once more, and sitting down at the kitchen table she yawned noisily.

As tired as she was, she loved every second of her life so much that even a fractious child was bearable. As she looked around the kitchen she sighed with sheer contentment. Her life was so different and she thanked God for that every minute of every day.

Even though it was three-thirty in the morning and she had no idea where her husband was, or what he was doing, she didn't fret. The life that she now lived was what she classified as normal. It had been like this since day one. Naturally close-mouthed, she didn't question Pat and he didn't expect her to. It was a perfect arrangement for them both.

He would turn up at some point, he always did, and she would cook for him, chat to him and make love to him. It had never occurred to her that the life she lived was not the norm for most young women; she never questioned him about his whereabouts as any other young wife would.

All she understood was that he was out grafting for her, and because of that, she had everything a girl could want, from a twin-tub washing machine to a set of Carmen hair rollers. Never in her life had she been so cared for, or felt so safe. She depended on him for everything, from the food she ate to the light she read by. He provided for her and their son, more than provided, and she was happy enough with that. Since her marriage she had money coming out of her ears and she spent it like it was going out of fashion. The best of everything was Pat's mantra and she enjoyed having just that.

It all seemed very fragile at times, precarious even, but she put that down to the way she had been brought up. The fear of her life collapsing around her was never far from her mind, and she struggled to stop the fear enveloping her. All her life she had felt as if she had been waiting for something good to happen, and now it had, the feeling was still there, but it was mixed with a frightening dread that sometimes felt stronger and more real than anything else.

*   *   *

Dicky was laughing. Pat had beaten the cop until he had passed out. Whether that was through the drink or the ministrations of the prostitute combined with the alcohol, or Pat's bruised knuckles, no one was sure. The lesson had been duly administered. From a friendly drinking session, it had eventually deteriorated into a drunken beating. Lomond was now theirs and he would realize it as soon as he sobered up.

On the cold floor, Harry Lomond was having trouble breathing, although no one in the room was worried. In the hostess club they had seen so many cops gasping for breath it was a running joke.

Cops like Lomond were renowned skirt chasers, he was typical of his ilk. A bully, a bruiser, and ultimately a coward. The strange thing was, no one minded an arrest off a straight cop. It was expected if not welcomed, but it was a *pure* collar. Everyone was generous if it occurred, inasmuch as they had a mutual respect for each other. A bust off a dirty cop, however, was a different story, it was a complete and utter blow. Corrupt cops convicted anyone they were asked to, or paid to, depending on whether they *owed* money, or *needed* money. No one wanted the aggravation or indeed humiliation of being locked up by someone they had no respect for or, worse still, for something they didn't do. Honest cops feeling your collar at least afforded you the respect you were due. Bang to rights, it was a fair arrest. A changeling on your case, though, told you and all your contemporaries that you had been framed for a crime you never committed, to get you out of the way usually, so that whatever skulduggery you might actually be involved in would now be taken over by a different Face. Or you had been well and truly snitched on by someone close to you, not even an enemy. Either way, this was seen by police and criminals alike as an unsafe conviction. Especially for the person who brought it about in the first place.

For a judicial system to work, it had to be adhered to by the people who had sworn to uphold it. Criminals broke the law, the boys in blue busted them, that was how the world worked. No one liked it, but it was accepted. Once that all broke down of course, it was a different ball game. A corrupt judge was a menace to society in far more ways than the man he relegated to prison. If they put away a body that they knew was innocent then it stood to reason that they knew the real villain was still walking the streets. It also cast aspersions on every case they had ever been in contact with: if they set up one person, how many more could be in the frame?

To uphold the law the judge had to be beyond reproach, something that did not apply, of course, to the men they were not only judging, but sentencing to prison. They were expected to lie and cheat, that was all part of the game. There was nothing worse than being lectured in a courtroom by someone who you knew to be morally bankrupt. A jury trial was about the police making sure that they had enough evidence to convict the accused; the jury had to have enough facts presented to them to convince them of their guilt. These laws were brought about to safeguard innocent people who, through no fault of their own, may have been in the wrong place at the wrong time. The police had to establish not only a motive but also gather enough evidence to put the person on trial in that right place at that right time.

Just because someone might look good for a conviction didn't mean they deserved one. The law was there to give them a fair trial. You expected the alleged criminals to lie, you did not expect the trial judge to already have reached a verdict before the evidence was shown or for a policeman to take an oath yet lie, knowing that the job they held made people assume they were telling the truth.

Honesty was supposed to be their forte. Unfortunately, the consumer society they inhabited and the relaxing of the gambling laws had soon put an end to that. This was one of the main reasons why the police and judges were being sought out and bought up, not only as an early-warning system in the case of the police, but also to even out some of the judicial playing fields when court appearances could not be avoided and bail was a necessity.

Lomond was about to find out that, like any snitch, cop or criminal, once you perverted the course of justice for your own ends, *no one* wanted you. *No one* trusted you and *no one* cared what happened to you. By the very nature of your dual lifestyle you were well and truly on your own. Lomond was now neither fish nor fowl. The strength of his position had overnight become his biggest weakness. He was now like a tame guard dog. If he worked well enough, he might get fed. But he would also be made to realize that there were plenty more puppies from the litter he came from.

"You don't think he is gonna die, do you?" Dicky said.

Lomond was breathing with difficulty now.

Pat shrugged. The man on the dirt-strewn floor disgusted him. "Who cares."

Lily walked into the prison and felt her stomach heave.

She hated the smell of the place and she hated the feeling of confinement. The walls were grimy, the aroma was putrid and to crown it all, she was here to pass on a message to someone she didn't even like. Kevin Craig was a man with little imagination, a vicious temper and a vindictive personality.

He suited his surroundings as far as Lil was concerned. Wormwood Scrubs was a shithouse although Du Cane Road had been a nice place in its day. Hammersmith Hospital was next door and there were still some nice houses around and about. She liked the area but hated the prison. Every time she stepped inside she felt as if the walls were coming in on her and she wondered how anyone stood it.

To be locked up was, to her, the worst thing that could happen to anyone. To have no say whatsoever over your life was a terrifying thought, and she should know, her home life had been the same.

The whole place stank of despair and front. The front most people put on for family and friends when they were looking at a long sentence. Front was how you coped with being told by a judge that you were being locked away for the best years of your life, that you were a menace to society and prison was all you would know from now on. Front was pretending that you accepted what had happened. Front was what made you get up in the morning after such an abomination, and was what made you carry on through every day after that. Front was, in the end, all you had to rely on.

Front was also, unfortunately, more often than not what had put the majority of the convicts there in the first place.

*   *   *

Kevin Craig sat down and Lil smiled at him tremulously.

"Thanks for coming." He afforded her the respect her husband's reputation automatically afforded her.

"That's all right, mate."

Her smile was wide, but her nerves were making her feel faint. She
was heavily pregnant once more and her huge belly was evident as she
sat down and tried to make herself comfortable.

As she looked around the visiting room she felt the fear once more.
She looked at the women with their kids; dilapidated, scruffy, trying to
be cheerful, trying to make some kind of connection with the men who
had fathered their children and who might not hold any of them close
again for years.

This was all her nightmares come to life, losing her Pat to the prison
system. Seeing him locked up and vulnerable and watching him shrink
a bit more as every year passed, she knew that her physical make-up
would make her seek solace elsewhere even though the man would not,
could not, ever match up to the man she had lost through no fault of
her own.

Kevin smiled at her then as if reading her mind. "Tell Pat and Dicky
that I have put me hand up, wiped me mouth and took the onus off
them. But my old woman *has* to be taken care of. I am only a bagman, I
collected the rents, that's all. Make sure the protection is paid; they owe
me, they owe me big time."

Lil didn't hear the underlying threat in his voice, she just felt relieved;
this was something she could cope with, something she knew all about.
He was telling her what she was supposed to be telling him. Keep your
trap shut, your head down and your arse up and everything would be
all right.

Kevin's wife, Amy, was a mate of sorts. They lived near each other
and they talked if they met in the market. She knew his kids by sight
and she talked to him about them, assuring him that they would be well
taken care of. That they would not go without, even though she knew
that they would be going without the most important person in their
life after their mother.

Although, from what she had heard from Amy, she wasn't so sure about that now. But she knew better than to say these thoughts out loud.

Instead, she told this troubled man that he was not to worry, his family was safe, and at the same time she was praying that she would never have to visit her husband or children in a place like this.

Lil hated the whole depressing aura of prison. It was like a living tomb to her. People lived inside the prison walls, but they might as well have been long dead because they were only existing, and that was not what life was supposed to be about.

"Lil is handling it, relax." Patrick sounded far more confident than he felt, but he knew that Dicky would not pick up on that. Kevin had been nabbed completely by accident, and they were all still trying to clear up the mess.

Pat was shrewd enough to know that Kevin had been served up, and he would be very interested to know who the culprit was. It had to be someone close, because he kept his business dealings quiet; even Dicky didn't have any real idea of how enormous his empire had become. But then again, no one did. He used different people for different things. Never telling his right hand what the left hand was doing.

It worked better that way. People only know what you tell them. Well, if you didn't tell them anything then you were safe.

So whoever had put Kevin away had either a working knowledge of his business practices, or a vested interest in seeing Kevin Craig off the pavement. The former he doubted, the latter he suspected.

Kevin had never had the gift of friendship. He was like a fucking old woman, looking for slights everywhere, taking offense at nothing and, worst of all, he thought he was the lynchpin of the protection business.

People amazed him: if they were so fucking clever why were they on a wage? Why depend on someone else for their daily bread? So he had once had affiliations with Barry Caldwell, why would he think that gave him any street credibility? Barry had been taken for a fool, he was yesterday's news. He would see about bailing Kevin out if he could, he would concentrate on lessening the blow of his sentence, and finally he would take care of his family until such time as the courts saw fit to release him back into society. It was the usual, it was what anyone could expect in his employ and it wasn't fucking rocket science. It also meant he was about two grand down a week, and that was the real priority here; when all was said and done, he wasn't about to lose any income. Still, he would find out the score soon enough, and like any problem, the sooner it was dealt with, the better.

Lil was still nervous after her prison visit. The place made her nerves bad, undermined her life in every way imaginable. Reminded her of what could happen, reminded her of how difficult her life could easily become.

But it also reminded her of how she had to keep these thoughts to herself. All her life she had felt as if she was walking on quicksand and that feeling overwhelmed her every time she walked through the prison doors.

It was an ending, a big lump, it was society's way of telling people they were being excluded, it was also like a time warp. All her life she had heard the phrase "let the punishment fit the crime," and she was agreeable to that.

Money and property were what got people locked up for years, and as her husband now fell into that category, it bothered her. Especially as she knew that the prison lifestyle would kill him.

But it was so true, crimes against money and property guaranteed a seriously long sentence, murder and sex crimes guaranteed a much lesser sentence. It was to her, at first, an unbelievable truth. She had believed it, because it had been explained to her by her husband. Now though, the papers had proved the case in point, and it scared her. That her husband would do less time for murdering a complete stranger on the street than for robbing a bank was outrageous. He was breaking the law of course, but how was that a worse offense than a murder or a rape? It was these thoughts that were stopping her from sleeping at night.

It did occur to her that he might be a murderer, but she forced those thoughts away. If he did murder someone there would have to be a good reason for it, she was convinced. It was like her mother had said, it would be like an occupational hazard to him. But he wouldn't do that, she knew he wouldn't do anything like that.

As she poured out a cup of tea, she looked around her kitchen and tried to take in everything about it. Compared to her upbringing, this place was luxury, yet even she was now aware that they did not live within her husband's means. They lived well but not excessively so. Pat always said that the first interest from the police was if there was a nice house and a decent car and no real means of employment. His legal business would have provided this standard of living so that is how they lived. It was still a better lifestyle than most people's.

If she was to be taken away from here at a moment's notice, what would she really remember? What would she miss? Like her husband, she lived for the moment. If it all came to an end, she would pack a bag and walk away from here without a backward glance. Somewhere in her head she knew that was wrong. She had a child, another on the way, she should feel settled here instead of feeling like this was just another stop. Somewhere to sit and wait for the man who dominated her existence. Yet she knew she wasn't alone, that a lot of the women in her position lived their lives in exactly the same way.

For the first time though, she was really worried about what the future might bring. Pat wasn't a fool, he would dodge the law as best he could, but, pregnant once more, she was terrified of being alone. Seeing the prisons up close and personal, she was frightened of the power the thought of them had over her. As she looked at her little son playing with his toys on the linoleum floor, she felt the familiar sickness wash over her. Patrick said it was just the baby; once the new one arrived she would be OK, but she wasn't so sure.

She had the same feelings in the prison as she had felt as a child growing up. The utter loneliness that pervaded the place was bad enough, but to then be told when to eat, sleep and even shit, was terrifying. To live your whole life on a schedule, even worse, a schedule planned and executed by people you would cross the road to avoid, was to her the worst thing she could ever imagine.

Being at the mercy of other people was something she understood very well, and it was something she hated with a passion that surprised her.

She picked up Pat Junior and held him close, even though he wriggled to get away from her to continue his playing. She needed bodily contact constantly: after being starved of affection for so long, she now craved it desperately. Her husband's arm across her belly was like her life's blood, a necessity.

Since Pat had started using her to visit and relay messages, she was now frighteningly aware of just how precarious her life actually was. She put the squealing child down and lit a cigarette with trembling hands. Needing people brought its own set of problems; at times like this she wondered if she had been better off as she was before. Then she had felt she was missing out on something, she just had not known what that something was. Now she knew, it was even worse.

She took a deep breath and sighed once more.

Life, after all, was what you made it, and Pat was making sure her life was wonderful. Even to her own ears that sounded hollow.

Chapter Three

Everyone, especially the police, knew that Pat had taken out his arch rivals. And as luck would have it, nobody, including the police, cared. Billy Spot's demise had been on the cards for a while, it was just a case of who would be responsible, as opposed to when it would happen. Pat Brodie had been a contender for a while and the sensible money had been on him.

When he had wiped out Spot he had opened up the West End for everyone. Unlike Spot and his cronies, though, Pat and his cohorts were quite happy to let people work their trades in relative peace and tranquility. Providing they made sure that a percentage of the money earned made its way into their pockets they were happy. Life was good for everyone; Pat was fair, and the numerous Williams brothers who were on his leash were amicable and easy enough to get along with. Business thrived for everyone, from the street vendors to the club owners. Life was easier than it had been for years and, as Pat and his cohorts made a point of being seen on the very streets they policed, no one was worried about late-night visits and protection money being demanded twice in one night. Spot had not watched over his troops and that had been when the rot had set in. So now, everyone was earning, and everyone was feeling relaxed enough to unload the shotguns they kept under their bars and hide away the handguns they might have kept in their cars.

Until, that is, they had all been brought to the notice of the local cops by a disgruntled hustler. Kevin Craig had been served up by a man called Denny Harris and, even though it had been a worry at the time, it had ended up being a blessing in disguise.

Denny had a grievance, a fair grievance as it turned out, because Kevin was a greedy crook who was taking more than he was entitled to. He was in effect shaking him down twice, something that normally would have been frowned upon by everyone concerned. That, however, was another story. The main thrust of the whole saga was that Denny had snitched, and even though Kevin was out of order, there was still no justifiable reason in their world for Denny's outrageous actions. Snitching anyone up to the police was tantamount to treason, and Denny's mistake came at a time when a well-earned lesson was not only needed, but was also welcomed by the powers that be.

Pat and the Williams brothers knew that in order to cement their newfound notoriety, they would need to make an example of someone. In short, Billy Spot and Barry Caldwell had been big fish, and big fish expected to be challenged eventually. Now they needed to show the smaller fish, the hustlers, the pimps, the bookies and the club owners, the people who would ultimately be their bread and butter, that they had their fingers on every pulse in the city, and would know immediately if anyone was trying to hold back any of their earnings. Pat knew that anyone who was waltzing through life without paying their due was going to brag about it eventually, and because they had had a touch without any kind of redress, they would not see them as a real threat. Instead, they would eventually take on more businesses without consulting anyone about it first, and that would be how the rot could set in. The first serious offense had to be sorted quickly, violently and with the maximum of fuss. If they let it go, people would soon notice, and that was how you lost face, because it was the smaller businesses that were the staple of any empire. The rents, as they were known, were what kept everyone on their toes. If you would go to war for a few pounds, it was assumed you would be capable of murder for the larger amounts. This was a natural dilemma for anyone who was in control of any business, legit or otherwise.

So Denny, by rights, should have brought his problem to them, and they would have sorted it out. Everyone would have been a winner,

Kevin would have had his wrist slapped and it would have been a five-minute wonder and of no consequence to anyone. Instead, Denny had actually had the gall to overlook them, to try to sort it out with Kevin, who was a bona fide arsehole at the best of times, and so far down the pecking order he was virtually classed as a serf. And when that had failed and knowing he had messed himself up with Kevin's bosses, he had then had the audacity to go to the police. Unbelievable as it was, this had been what had happened.

So, all in all, what was an abortion had actually ended up working in everyone's favor. Denny had been outed as the treacherous bastard he was, and had been the recipient of a world-class hammering. If he walked again it would be a miracle, and on top of that, as a known snitch, he was also off everyone's Christmas card list for the foreseeable future.

The Williamses had let it be known that the cop involved was, as luck would have it, one of theirs, and Pat had ostentatiously given Denny's business interests over to a local firm who were known to make themselves busy and earn a few pounds, but who would never be a contender for anyone's crown because they were not the sharpest knives in the drawer. All in all, it had been perfect PR.

Taking their due was one thing, and they knew that, keeping it, though, was another story entirely. Now the word was out that they had a finger in all the main pies, life was easier than ever.

Snitches had to be dealt with severely because they did not just affect people's livelihoods, they could also be the reason why men were separated from their families for years. Children lost their fathers, wives lost their husbands, mothers lost their sons. It was the ultimate prank, the ultimate double-cross.

Consequently, a clear message had to be sent out; the culprit had to bear the scars of their treachery for everyone to see. It was unacceptable behavior, all the more heinous because they were people that had been trusted, had been allowed access to the world of the very people they had betrayed. In short, they had to be trounced publicly and with the maximum of pain and humiliation, so anyone else harboring thoughts of the big time would take a step back and have a serious rethink of their situation.

Denny now bore the mark of the snitch, otherwise known as the permanent grin. It was a throwback from the fifties, but even twenty years later it still did its job. His mouth had been opened from ear to ear with a boxcutter's knife. Every time Denny looked in the mirror he would be reminded of what he had done.

The scars would also guarantee that he would be shunned by anyone in the life, no matter how far he tried to roam. He was a pariah, an outcast, but more importantly he was a fool to himself. Even his brothers had turned their back on him, as would his sons eventually.

Pat was still riding the crest of his own wave. The Williams brothers were his partners and they were all earning serious dough. They had plenty of people working the pavements for them and plenty of time now for leisure pursuits, and as the owners of massage parlors, gambling dens and hostess clubs, their leisure time and their business meetings tended to be held in these places.

Pat, though, made a point of going home, unlike the Williamses who felt they had their own personal playgrounds. It was hard for any man to live their kind of lives and still want to go home to the little woman. The wife was respected, loved even, but her main attraction was that she would not put herself about. The men, however, did not see that as any kind of barrier to enjoying themselves. It was the nature of their very lifestyles; women and sex were everywhere they turned. Even for the men who were not exactly the answer to a maiden's prayer.

Girls lined up to be with them and the men chose to believe that it was because of their handsome faces and sparkling personalities. They forgot that these were women who were already predisposed to sleeping with any man for financial gain. That these were women who were better actresses in bed than the cream of the Hollywood divas. These were women and girls who saw sleeping with one man, whoever he might be, as a better deal than trying their luck every night with whoever wandered into their very limited orbit. With a Face, a criminal, they at least had some respect, and they also had regular money and a proper in, say

if a new club opened and a head girl might be needed. They were someone already in the foreground, they knew the ropes, were trustworthy
and above all, would keep any secrets that might emerge. They would
also keep quiet if one of the newer, fresher, younger girls caught their
man's eye. They had what they wanted, why would they care?

They were perfect mistresses, their whole lifestyle stopped them ever
getting above their station, and it also guaranteed an affection and loyalty that would last them for years. The wives, however, had something
these women would never have; they had their husbands' respect and
because of that they were safe even if they put on weight, lost interest
in sex or became a religious fanatic. The legal always had the edge, and
a sensible legal used that to her advantage, turned a blind eye to her
husband's sexual gymnastics and enjoyed the fruits of her husband's en-
deavors. It was nothing personal, it was just an occupational hazard.

Even Pat took a flier occasionally; a bit of sex on the side was on most
men's agenda and he was no different, he just had more access to it than
the average guy. But that was as far as it went with him, the odd flier.
Never the same bird and always without any kind of wooing. No drink
bought, no meal provided, and definitely no offer of a lift home. He did
not want a repeat performance, and he did not want to get involved in
their lives in any way, shape or form. He got a blow job and that was it.
Something he would never have asked of, or expected from, his Lil. And
nine times out of ten, only then when Lil was indisposed through pregnancy or after a birth. It was nothing more than an urge. It had nothing
to do with his life, or his family.

This was another reason he was respected by his peers. There was no
real talk about him, in fact no one really knew *anything* about him. Even
the Williamses had to admit that much.

As for Lil, she attended church regularly, she was still young enough
to hold his interest and he loved her and what she represented to him.
And in her own way she was now a lynchpin in his organization. He
used her and she was shrewd enough to understand that. She was the
only person he could really trust.

Lil still visited the prisons and passed on information; it had never occurred to her not to do it, her husband expected it and she did as he asked. It made her feel needed, a part of it all.

She also felt that, at nineteen with two handsome sons, and enough money to keep her in a way that most people only dreamed about, she could turn a blind eye to any rumors or suspicions she might harbor about her husband.

Lily Brodie, née Diamond, was a great believer in what you didn't know could not hurt you. She had known instinctively when he had been unfaithful to her the first time. She had felt his shame, had breathed in his treachery, yet at the same time she had always known that the day would come. She didn't know how she knew that; she had been so naïve sexually, still was in many ways, but somewhere in the back of her mind she had registered that fact.

She also knew that only a complete fool would cause an international incident over it. On some level she knew without a doubt that it meant nothing to him, and she also knew that it must therefore mean *nothing* to her. He was not like the average man, and if she tried to make him like that, she would only set herself up for failure. She had seen the consequences of the women who had tried to tame their mates and it had always ended in tears. The men eventually divorced even the most virginal of wives, the mothers of their legal children, because the women had been too much like hard work. No woman, no matter who they were, could compete with youth and the mystery of a silky pair of drawers and a lusty laugh. So she decided early on in her marriage to overlook his other life; it was the only way she could even hope to survive it.

No matter how much her mother tried to poison her mind, she knew that the woman who could lure Pat away from her for any length of time had not been born yet.

When they went out together she saw the way he was treated and she knew the temptation that was under his nose on a daily basis. Lily had the same sexual drive as her husband and so she appreciated that he had the opportunity to take advantage of it by the very nature of his business commitments. Men like Pat Brodie needed to take advantage of their freedom because they never knew when it was going to be taken away from them.

Ignoring it all was, she knew, a mindset. She just had to accept it as something that was part and parcel of his lifestyle and she was not about to throw away the best thing that had ever happened to her over something that was so trivial to her, and so unimportant to him that he forgot about it within minutes of it happening.

She had decided that she would rather live with him, and all that entailed, than be without him. She had also realized that she had to be more to him than just his wife, than just the mother of his children. She had to make a connection with him that would give them something other than their shared children in common. She was determined to become an important part of his life in her own right.

He was going to be unfaithful to her, it was something she expected and accepted. It was inevitable. She was a realist, and she hoped that her honesty would not be rewarded by her breaking her heart over his disloyalty. At least his forays into the world of other women were not a regular occurrence; unlike most of his contemporaries.

The first time it happened she had felt as if her heart had been ripped out of her chest; now she felt contempt for a woman who would allow herself to be used like that, even as she pitied her, because the life the girl lived ensured that encounters with men like her husband were a foregone conclusion.

Lily had an innate kindness that allowed her to see everyone in the best possible light. Once she had seen the inside of a club she had not seen the women as whores, or rivals in any way. Instead, she had seen them as victims. Victims of men in that they were forced by circumstances to utilize the only asset they possessed. If she had daughters, she was determined that they would be educated enough to make different choices if their life went pear-shaped.

She had once gone to one of the hostess clubs to relay a message after one of her prison visits and been witness to a customer causing World War Three over a bill. She had watched as the doorman tried to calm the situation and seen how the bill had finally been paid in full, without the hostess getting her fee. She had stepped in, and before the john had left the premises she had seen to it that the girl was also paid in full. The doorman was left in no doubt that the hostesses were to be his priority in future as they were the ones who brought the men into the club in the first place.

Without the girls, why would the men pay the inflated prices? Why should a girl spend the best part of the night talking the man out of his money for the club and then be left out when the john was asked to pay at the end of the night?

To Lil, it was ludicrous, but then she was too young to realize that the girls in the clubs were ten a penny. Pretty girls were commonplace and women willing to sit on the meat seats were legion. Men walked away from their kids without a backward glance; women, however, were not afforded that luxury, nor would they want to anyway. But they still had to earn a living so they could feed and clothe their kids, which was why the clubs were inundated with women.

The doorman, however, had humored her that night and the girls had fallen in love with her.

It had been a difficult situation for Patrick Brodie when he listened to Lil; he had never in his life been expected to see a hooker all right. But the hooker in question had been an acquaintance of Lil's in the cigarette factory. Seeing her reduced to hostessing because her husband had run off, leaving her with three kids and a mountain of debt, had made the now-powerful and fair-minded Lily Brodie angry. And she let Patrick know it in no uncertain terms.

She liked the feel of the clubs anyway; she enjoyed the camaraderie of the girls, it reminded her of the cigarette factory and how she had finally felt a part of something. She found that she liked being outside the home with other women, and it brought her closer to her husband. Like any young girl, Lily craved excitement and suddenly she had it in abundance.

Now that Pat wanted her to do more in the clubs she was realizing just how hard the life was for the women who had to live it. She didn't yet understand that it was the kindness inside her that her husband was exploiting because he saw the way the girls reacted to her, and how she dealt with them. Lil was a natural leader, and she was not averse to see-ing a john slaughtered if he was not feeling inclined to pay his hugely inflated bill.

Pat was thrilled that his Lily, his heart, was willing to work for him and take the burden of the girls off his shoulders. She was now going from club to club, keeping an eye out and making sure that things were run in an orderly fashion. She had a knack for it and she also had a nose for troublemakers, both male and female. She was good with money and tallied the takings up quicker than he ever could. She was an asset and he was pleased and amazed that she was willing to work with him, even after finding out firsthand what he was involved in. Unlike the other wives, Lily was a real asset; in the days when women were either used or exploited, she was making use of her acumen for both their benefits.

He had thought that the prostitution would have gone against the grain, she was so prim and proper in many ways. But she seemed to understand better than he did what made the women tick, and what made them sell themselves on a daily basis.

She was making her mark and she was also making sure that the clubs ran smoothly and that gave him more time for his other businesses. Some of the people he dealt with were not impressed. They saw him as being pussy-whipped but he always pointed out, when they dared say so to his face, that at the end of the day, if he couldn't trust her, who the fuck could he trust?

Lil was putting the boys to bed. She was already dressed up to go out and she was trying unsuccessfully to blot out her mother's voice.

Since her marriage, her mother had made herself busy. At first, she had been a dream, although it had taken Lily a while before she had trusted her enough to let her into her new life.

After the birth of Lance though, her second son, her mother had reverted back to her old ways. Finding fault, making remarks and it was getting more and more difficult to pretend that all was well with them.

Annie loved her first grandson, Patrick Junior, but Lance, she was absolutely besotted with him. Since the day he had emerged from her womb, a month early, kicking and screaming, she had been like a woman demented. It was as if she had birthed him herself.

Now, as Lil looked down at her boys, she wondered why she didn't feel the same way. She loved her second son, but he was such a strange child, he stared at her as if he was sizing her up. Waiting for her to make a fuss of some sort. He was a handsome child, with a shock of dark hair like his father, and with Annie's pale-grey eyes. He was striking, and people had remarked on his coloring since the day he was born. But Lil's guilt over this child stemmed from the fact that she found touching him slightly distasteful. She had stopped breast-feeding him as soon as she could, reverting to the bottle with what her mother saw as unseemly haste, even though it meant she could nurse him for hours on end. Lance's skin always felt clammy to the touch, and unlike young Pat, he had a big-boned feel to him that made her uncomfortable. He was also very well endowed, which gave his father cause for ribald comments, yet made her feel uncomfortable with him. He lay there at three years old, legs splayed and still in diapers, making her mother comment that here was a boy who would do things in his own time. But Lil thought it was laziness that kept him in diapers, nothing more. Lance let Pat Junior do everything for him, and it felt wrong. He manipulated everyone around him, especially Annie. And he did it without any effort on his part at all. Even Patrick was enamored of him but, as bad as it made her feel, and no matter how much the guilt ate at her, she couldn't see this child as everyone else did.

Yet she loved him, and in her own way she protected him, because he was hers, she had birthed him. He was her responsibility and, unlike her mother who had left her to her own devices, she was determined that none of her children would ever feel abandoned, unwanted or unloved. They were hers, and she would die for them.

As she bent to kiss Lance's head, his peculiar smell of baby sweat and urine once more made her shudder. She couldn't figure out why he made her feel so uncomfortable and the feelings that he engendered made her question her role as a mother.

Pat Junior was lying in the other bed smiling at her, and his smile lifted her heart. This was a child she could really love. He was happy, healthy and, unlike Lance, he talked to her and reacted with her. Lance said few words, and it wasn't because he couldn't, he just didn't want to.

"Night, Mum."

She smiled at her eldest child, and her heart swelled with pride. His dark good looks and startling blue eyes marked a winning combination. He looked Irish, and he had the blarney, as Pat was always joking.

He was all for cuddling his sweet-smelling mother and she, as always, obliged.

"Off to sleep now, baby, and I'll bring you back a Caramac."

He was thrilled, his sweets were assured and his eyes were already closing as she snuck from the room.

Annie was making a cup of tea and Lil, as always, felt the burden of her. She felt responsible for people, even though she knew in her heart of hearts that it wasn't her job. Her mother had treated her worse than a dog all her life. Pat questioned her about it constantly but, as she tried to explain, her mother was the only mother she was ever going to get. Like with Lance, no matter what she felt inside, they were her family and she would never ever let them down. No one really guessed about her feelings for her younger son and if it was left to her no one ever would.

As Annie laced her tea liberally with a bottle of Bushmills whiskey, Lil forced a smile and said gaily, "I'm off, Mum."

"You're looking more and more like the women you are supposed to be earning from." It was supposed to be funny, but the underlying sarcasm was there all the same.

Lil looked into the faded eyes so like her own and felt a sudden urge to scream. She felt stifled, suffocated and, like Patrick Brodie, she wondered why she put herself through all this day after day. Her mother was like a snake, dripping her venom into her sons' ears. Guilt was a strange thing, a destructive thing.

As Lil walked from the house, the silence was deafening and the atmosphere was heavy with unspoken thoughts and unwanted emotions.

In the cool evening air, she was finally able to breathe easily once more. She gulped it into her lungs as if her life depended on it.

Ruby Tyler smiled at Pat as he looked over the club; he was searching for someone in particular though no one would have guessed that from his demeanor.

He saw Ruby's eyes on him and he wished he had not been so drunk the night before. Ruby had ambitions for the big time, and now she had serviced him she was expecting some kind of reward. She saw him as a step-up, as a wage packet for the foreseeable future. She was not, he realized, a woman who would be shrugged off easily; in fact, she was already looking decidedly piqued at his lack of interest in her. Ruby, unfortunately for them both, had a very high opinion of herself.

As Pat walked through the club into his small office, he knew she would not be far behind him.

He was pouring himself a Scotch when he heard her enter the room: the door closed quietly and he took a deep breath before saying, "What can I do you for?"

As he turned to face her, he marveled at the stupidity of women. Especially women like Ruby. She was an attractive woman, an earner. That was her prerogative of course, but it was also a good reason for her to realize that he wouldn't be looking for a long relationship with her just because she had blown him off once.

Ruby, for her part, was well aware that she was a good-looking girl, but she also saw herself as a bit of a shrewdie. She thought she had enough street smarts and enough body to tame the wildest of men. Patrick Brodie was a prize by anyone's estimation and she saw herself as the new contender for his affections. He had a couple of kids with his wife so he must be getting bored, and he was a Face. In her book, he was in line for the full Ruby Tyler treatment. She wanted the notoriety that being his girl would bring, and she wanted an easy ride in the club as would be her right as his girlfriend. Ruby saw herself as a realist: she knew he would never marry her, or live with her. She would be strictly his outside girl. And she was content with that and all it would bring her. He had singled her out, she had obliged and now she was determined to make the most of the opportunity he had afforded her. As she had remarked to her best friend, she was not letting this one go without a fucking good fight.

Patrick stared at her for long moments and she felt the sheer magnetism that dangerous men seemed to have in abundance. He was a handsome fuck, no doubt about that and, coupled with his rep and his financial status, he was the answer to every hostess's dreams. A man with a bit of clout was what she wanted; she had no interest in his loyalty, no interest in anything pertaining to him and his married life. Not yet anyway. All she wanted was a piece of the action, her fifteen minutes of fame.

"Well?"

His blue eyes were cold and for a split second she faltered.

She smiled then, showing her perfect teeth. Ruby had a lovely smile and she had paid a fortune to guarantee that it stayed that way. All her body maintenance was about the long term and making sure she didn't end up like her mother. Old before her time and acting twenty years older than she actually was because her life had ended abruptly with the unfortunate acceptance of a plain gold wedding band.

"Are you a bit fucking thick?"

Ruby stared at him, unsure what to say, the smile still on her thickly painted face.

He walked towards her: he wasn't rushing, he didn't seem angry so she wasn't too bothered until he grabbed her around the throat and pushed her up against the door. "You listen to me and you listen good. If I ever see you within three foot of me again I'll break your fucking neck. Now, do you understand me or shall I tattoo it on your fucking fat arse?"

Pat's voice was low, and she realized then that she had completely misread the situation.

Ruby Tyler was now terrified of the man she had so recently seen as an easy mark.

He looked into her eyes and then, hawking deeply in his throat, he spat into her face. The globule of phlegm hit her on the cheek, the residue sprayed her eyes and she closed them instinctively, expecting the worst.

"You ever fucking come near me again, girl, and you'll regret it for the rest of your life. A blow job gains you nothing from me except my disgust. Now *out*! Get your coat and anything else you have here and don't come back, you hear me?"

She nodded, her perfectly backcombed hair unmoving even with the violence of his attack. He loosened his grip on her throat and she instinctively leaned back further on to the door, her breath coming in short and painful gasps.

He turned back to his desk and started tidying his papers, and she made her escape as quietly and as quickly as she could.

Patrick was controlling his anger with difficulty; a cunt like her could ruin his whole way of life. As easy-going as Lil was, a tart like that sleeping with her man would guarantee Lil having to do something about it, if just to save face. He had to make sure that never happened again; what the eye don't see, the heart don't grieve over, that had been his mantra all his life and he saw no reason to change it just because some cunt with a cleavage and a friendly mouth had got too big for her boots.

Trouble looked for him, as it did most people, and he had no intention of bringing it to his own front door because some hooker didn't understand the ways of the world.

Annie Diamond went to the front door, her steps light and easy on the thick carpet that she marveled at every day. That Lil, the neuter, the runt, had managed to get herself this far on in life irked her, even though her daughter's circumstances gained her not only respect but a decent roof over her head and the added bonus of serious money regularly. Annie's jealousy of her daughter knew no bounds.

As she opened the door, she smiled craftily, and Mick Diamond slipped inside without a sound.

The terror of her life, the man she had shackled herself to because a name for her child had been more important than anything else, was once more a fixture. Only this time, he needed her more than she needed him.

For Annie though, his main appeal these days was the fact that she could sit with him and criticize her daughter without worrying that it would get back to her or indeed that husband of hers.

Mick and Annie finally had a common goal; they were both determined to make the most of Lil's good fortune, and they were even more determined to wait patiently until the day Patrick Brodie got fed up with her and pushed her aside for a newer model. Although that would signal the end of any money that came their way, they were both agreed that she was getting far too big for her boots.

Mick had been overlooked by Lil and her new husband; he had been ignored and humiliated by Pat more than once. The first time he had approached him and Lil as they sat in the pub chatting. Patrick had acted like he was invisible and he had stood there all nice and friendly while his cronies had looked knowingly at each other. Lil had glanced at him and he had been gratified to see a flicker of fear in her large grey eyes.

The second time, he had waited until Pat was leaving his house and he had hailed him, introducing himself with a flourish and acting the concerned parent. He had then been told in no uncertain terms by Brodie that he knew he was a bullying punk who had given his Lil a bastard of a life and if he thought her alliance with him was going to bring any kind of rewards then he was obviously a fucking nutcase. He also made it very clear that if he ever approached him again he would make sure that he spent the remainder of his miserable life as a cripple.

Mick had swallowed though, and when his wife had also gone AWOL he had learned a hard and bitter lesson. The survival of the fittest was an act of nature and he was now so far down the food chain that he was practically human plankton. His reign of terror was over and his daughter's wages were well out of his reach. His wife had left him without a backward glance and ingratiated herself with her daughter and her new beau. She had signed the papers that guaranteed their marriage could go ahead and she had made herself indispensable into the bargain.

She had one thing he didn't; she was blood and blood went a long way in the East End. It took a lot for anyone to turn their backs on it, and Lil was no different to anyone else in that respect. Bolting the door on a parent, no matter what they had done, would have been seen as an outrageous act of arrogance. The only way you could have got away with that was if your mother or father was proved to be either a snitch or a child molester. Anything else was expected to be overlooked, and taken into consideration when the parent in question was housed and fed. Inside the front door you could do what you liked, beat the shit out of them, whatever; outside the front door though, it had to look like you were doing your duty.

Now, here he was, dependent on the woman who he felt had tricked him into marriage and then produced a child by someone else, without ever giving him a child he could call his own. But thanks to Annie's naturally antagonistic personality, he had finally got his in, even if it was only by sneaking around when Lil and Pat were both out and then having to listen to his wife's litany of complaints until she slipped him some cash and hurried him out lest they got caught together.

He also learned a lot about Brodie and his business dealings, and the more he heard, the more his anger swelled up inside him.

Annie opened the bedroom door as always, and he looked down at the two sleeping boys, all the while wanting to wring his wife's neck for rubbing in the fact that he had no real kin of his own. But he admired them as always, and waited for her to lead him through to the kitchen and pour him a large drink.

Annie, for her part, loved the hold she now had over this man. Marriage to Mick Diamond had been a constant battle of nerves and she had been left bitter. Her daughter had been the cause of all the strife and, until Lance had been produced one sunny afternoon, she had never understood what other women seemed to take for granted. The pure unadulterated love for a child, a baby.

She had glanced at her grandson and it had been as if a bolt had been shot through her heart. From his first breath he had been to her like a young god, and the strength of her emotions concerning him had frightened her. She loved him with a passion that she had not believed she was capable of. He ate at her like a cancer, and when his mother had been nursing him she had felt an almost murderous rage that the child had not been born to her. She had convinced herself that if he had, Mick would have treated her properly, would have been proud of the child she had produced. She wasn't taunting him as he thought when she showed him her grandsons, she was trying to make him see what might have been. She had produced a child after all, he had not, and that bastard had ridden her hard for many years in the hope of making her pregnant and the more disappointed he had become, the worse her life had become. He had seen to that, blaming her for her barrenness, and begrudging the few shillings he had to provide for a child who, through no fault of her own, reminded him of his own shortcomings.

Like Mick, Annie was a person with a chip on her shoulder bigger than the San Andreas fault. They both resented Lil because she had fallen into a wonderful life and there was nothing they could do to control it. Annie lived on her son-in-law's largesse and she was sensible enough to know that if it had been left to him, she would have been aimed out of the front door without a second's thought and with his boot in her arse.

This was how these two people had ended up back together again; no one else wanted them, and that knowledge guaranteed that they would have to stick together. But for now, Annie had the upper hand and she relished it because she was shrewd enough to know that circumstances could change overnight. Lil had proved the truth of that old chestnut, as they both knew to their detriment.

Mick Diamond looked around his stepdaughter's lovely home and marveled at what a pair of tits and a nice smile could accomplish. Women had it easy really, he was convinced of that. His treatment of his own wife was, as always, forgotten when he came here. All he saw was the benefits that Lily's comely figure had accrued and the way she had spurned the man who had given her not only his name but her respectability. God was good though; he knew that without a doubt his time would come with her. Lily Brodie would eventually fall from grace and when she did, he would be waiting.

Brodie might be the big man now, but things changed and always when people least expected it. Death crept up, illness, all manner of things were waiting to jump out and tear a lump out of the arse of people who thought they were immune to the trials and tribulations of real life.

Brodie would eventually get his collar felt or his stomach shot out like Billy Spot; it was the way of their world and patience would reward him, he was sure. And he had patience, he had it in abundance.

Chapter Four

James Curtis had run a bookies in Ilford High Street for over twenty years and, even though betting had only been legal for some of that time, people still referred to him as Jamie the Book. The shop he owned had once sold haberdashery, but it had in fact been a front for the bets, a nice little earner in its own way. On weekends he would be seen paying out in the pubs around East London and Essex with a smile and his self-deprecating wit. He was a funny man and people liked him; he always paid out without a murmur of discontent. You won fair and square with Jamie and people trusted him. He paid you with a grin, a joke and a story about how hard-up you had made him. People liked that, it made the win feel extra special.

He was sitting now behind the polished walnut counter, perched precariously as always on his high leather stool, the usual cigarette dangling from his thick lips, working out the odds and taking only the serious bets himself. His balding head was glistening with sweat and his shirt sleeves were rolled up showing his heavily tattooed arms. The door opened and a young man with short blond hair and a sawed-off shotgun nonchalantly strolled in and, taking aim, shot Jamie the Book in the chest.

The regular gamblers watched in shock as the man they liked and respected was lifted bodily off his stool before landing heavily against his office door, blood pouring from his nose and mouth.

The short-haired man then walked out of the shop without uttering a word. The gamblers picked up the pieces of paper with their bets written neatly down and hastily beat their retreat. The two girls who worked there were left screaming their heads off in terror, their noise guaranteeing the presence of the police at some point and thereby saving them the job of making the call themselves.

That was how come the police had arrived with no backup and, as luck would have it, no witnesses. The two girls had by that time decided between themselves to say that they had been in the back making tea when it had all gone down.

No one actually realized for a long time that no money had been taken, so it was not technically a robbery as such. It was murder.

It was this fact that made everyone involved so nervous.

Jamie was liked; he was honest, in his game you *had* to be. People did not like losing money at the best of times, especially through their own foolishness, let alone because someone had ripped them off. A bet was a personal thing, it was a wager made in good faith and the bettors were more than aware that the wager could go either way; they would win and then pat themselves on the back for their cleverness or they would lose and the bookies patted themselves on the back. The bookies, as everyone knew, did the majority of the back-patting.

Most of the clients were betting for a sporting chance and a bit of excitement, a few of the customers were professional gamblers and they, by their very nature, were suspicious, greedy and notoriously bad losers.

Because of this, the betting industry was a very small world. Because of the professional gamblers, people like Jamie had to rely on the backing of the Brodies and the Williamses of the world. They needed a backup more than anyone else. A big loss could make the mildest of men capable of extreme violence. The loss of a week's wages and the knowledge that a family were now unable to eat could turn the quietest of men into a rampaging lunatic. The thought of Pat or the Williams brothers was what guaranteed that this would only be a passing fancy. No one who bet was willing to take on the big boys. Jamie was good anyway, he was always a fair man and understood the devastation that his line of business depended on. He was well liked by bettors, even the serious ones respected him. He would only take a big bet if he knew the client was genuinely up for it.

The bets were the straightest of all dodgy dealings really, by their very nature, trust was important to keep the customers coming back. In fact, a good bookie would offer a regular bettor a half a point more than the going price, would make it worth people's while to bet in their shops, as opposed to someone else's. The winners were paid out with a smile and a cheery wave; after all, the money would be winging its way back to him soon anyway.

So, as there were no big races on, no big bets had been placed, and no money removed from the premises, the reason for Jamie's shooting was already being speculated on by all and sundry. The fact the police had wandered in without any kind of haste added to the mystery. Something was happening, but what, no one seemed to know.

Terry Williams was twenty-three and looked like his brothers had at his age. All brawn and no real brain. But he was an amiable lad with a kind heart and his first serious girlfriend.

Although Pat respected the Williams brothers as businessmen and counterparts, he was more than aware that he was the one people wanted to deal with. The Williamses were also aware of that fact but they did not let it bother them at all. They were happy enough with the way things were because it meant that Pat dealt with the minutiae of their daily lives. Which left them to get on with what they did best, strong-arming. Shrewd enough, they had no finesse, they didn't want it; fear of them was more than adequate recompense. They were hard nuts, and they had their place in the world.

Terry was collecting rents in and around Custom House when he was shot in the face. He took the full force of the bullet as well as the glass from his driver's-side window; this left him a bloody wreck and guaranteed a closed coffin for his expensive and lavish funeral. He was still alive when the ambulance arrived, but he drowned in his own blood on his way to the hospital, something his mother would have nightmares about and would never come to terms with.

He was calling out for her as he died, by all accounts, but this in no way diminished his credibility or his standing in their community. Everyone wanted their mums when life threw them a curve. They were often the only people who stood by you no matter what you had done or, more to the point, been accused of. Men had been given life sentences and the only person to visit for the duration of their sentence on a regular basis was their mother. All the time you had a mother you had somewhere to go and someone to care.

Terry had died calling out for his mother. That alone would have to be addressed by his brothers, let alone the sheer fucking nerve of the perpetrator thinking they could get away with such a heinous act. Their mother was in absolute bits and that was something none of them could bear to see. This whole debacle was an outrageous and diabolical liberty, mainly because no one could find any reason for it. There was no one in the frame, no enemies wandering abroad and no grudges that warranted such extreme action. It was a complete and utter head-scratcher. Terry wasn't even trumping someone else's old woman, he was on a fucking love job. There was no reason whatsoever for his murder and the sheer senselessness of it only made his brothers all the more determined to get their revenge.

But the one thing they were agreed on was that when they found out who had been the perpetrator of such a daring and needless killing, the woman who had given birth to them would get that person back bit by bit through the post. For every hurt their mother experienced, they would pay it back tenfold.

Pat was sitting with an old friend in a drinking club he had recently acquired when he heard the news about young Terry.

The murder of the bookie Jamie Curtis had not really affected him; he had put it down to a grudge of some description, personal maybe, or a private bet that had gone wrong. James would not be the first bookmaker to take on a few private bets. The trouble with private bets was that the bookie had no redress if it all fell apart. As the bets were not accountable to people like himself, meaning they did not go through the books he earned from, meaning he earned fuck all off them, Pat had no reason to make sure they were paid in full. Why would he? A big debt could turn nasty, everyone knew that; gamblers were like junkies, once they were given their fun upfront with no money changing hands, they had a tendency to be a trifle lax when the bills started rolling in.

They were more inclined to look elsewhere to spend the money they had left.

Most bookies would sell a debt like that and take whatever they could get for it, leaving the bettor to take his chances with whatever lunatic eventually came after them. And make no mistake, someone would come after them. Pat bought a debt occasionally, for a favor, and collected it quickly and efficiently.

So Pat assumed that Jamie had made a complete fuck up; it was not, after all, a robbery. So it had to be a score being settled, or someone who had decided it was cheaper for them if Jamie was off the scene once and for all.

Either way, Pat wasn't too worried. It had nothing to do with him and anyway, he was confident he would know the reason sooner rather than later. He was sorry, of course. Jamie was all right, and whoever did it was on a fucking death wish because they must know that Jamie paid them protection money, and so this was a double insult. What kind of an advert was this for the firm? Naturally, someone would have to pay for that. But if it was a private bet, they would not step in, so he was happy enough to wait until he had the full story and take it from there.

Now though, young Terry's demise within hours of Jamie's, put a different complexion on it completely. This felt personal, was personal, Pat would lay money on it, even though the irony of that thought nearly made him smile. He still wasn't too worried though because he was confident in his role as a man to be reckoned with. There had to be a logical explanation, he was sure. He needed to see Dicky and find out what he knew about the situation. Young Terry had to have been up to a bit of private skulduggery.

A chill passed through his body all the same and he ordered a large brandy to counteract it. He was suddenly very uneasy. Paranoia went with the territory, he had known that when he took all this on, it was what kept them on their toes and was part and parcel of their lives. When evil whispered there was always someone willing to take heed. He knew that, trouble was how they earned a living after all. But now he had a feeling that this was not just the usual one-up, this was real trouble, serious trouble.

No one watching Patrick would ever have guessed his thoughts in a million years. He looked relaxed and untroubled. Like a politician caught with his cock in his hand and a friend's son naked beside him, he was bluffing it out. No one watching him could see him question or ponder on anything that had occurred; as he was hearing about the afternoon's atrocities, so were they. He was bluffing all right, but he was also watching everyone around him carefully in case they might be involved in some way. In case he picked up a nuance, or a vibe.

In Pat's world you were guilty until proven otherwise and, even then, he would keep an open mind.

Dicky Williams was angry. He knew it was a fruitless anger though, because there was nothing he could do about it. Terry was dead and nothing would bring him back, but he was still reeling from the realization that his little brother had been murdered.

It had not been what he would call a happy or even productive few hours. In fact, it had made him feel so vulnerable and so convinced that there was more serious skulduggery afoot that he was on the verge of harming someone just to vent his colossal anger and therefore get some respite. Pat had explained on the phone that the only relevant thing he had heard was concerning Freezing Freddie, and he had no real proof that it had anything to do with the day's events. Dicky was convinced though that Pat knew more than he was letting on.

It seemed that Fucking Freddie Dwyer, the cold and callous piece of shit, had managed to get himself a serious capture. He had been caught, so the word on the street had it, with a large amount of money and drugs. The house he scavenged from had been overrun at daybreak by a crowd of cops who hailed from New Scotland Yard and went under the name of the Flying Squad. The Flying Squad had actually been around since 1919 and no one had given a flying fuck about them until the early seventies when they were suddenly in everyone's faces. They were as bent as a barrister's cock and about as effective on serious crime as Germolene ointment on an amputated leg.

The Sweeney, as they were known, were not averse to setting someone up, that was public knowledge, and they were also loath to strike unless they had the person bang to rights in their minds, meaning the setup was watertight. Sometimes they had a genuine capture, which was less often than they let the public and their bosses believe. Dicky knew for a fact that Freddie had been in possession of enough amphetamines to keep the whole of London up for a week and still have enough left over to do the same again in Glasgow. He should know, he had supplied them to him in the first place.

So how was it that they were hearing that Freddie had got bail? Was it because he had been overzealous with his explanations to the police? Being overly helpful with the cops was becoming more and more acceptable these days, at least that is how it looked at the moment to Dicky Williams. Especially where a dealer like Dwyer was concerned. The courts had started handing out such outrageous sentences that some of the members of their world were unwilling, or more pointedly, unable to cope with that amount of time in prison. He was convinced that Dwyer was one of those people. The dirty, filthy, two-faced fucking rat.

In short, he now strongly suspected Dwyer had offered up some choice information in exchange for a guaranteed sentence and if that was the case, what the fuck had he said? And, even more to the point, how much of his chatter involved him and Pat? If Terry had been taken out and Jamie the Book, then the police were obviously using old scores to take the onus off Freddie's snitching. The Flying Squad often used old scores to take out people they knew they had no chance of arresting.

Freddie was a useless hustler, everyone knew that. But he was also a necessary evil where they were concerned because he made sure that any contacts he managed to secure were guaranteed earners. But, no matter what anyone said about crooked cops, you had to procure them long before you finally used them with any degree of confidence, and the fact that they were selling out their own mates and colleagues spoke volumes. With crooked cops it was all about baiting the trap and making sure you grabbed the fucker painfully and with malice aforethought by their gonads, therefore ensuring their full and frank cooperation. Freddie had no cops in his pocket; he relied on Pat and the Williamses to smooth out anything that might cause him aggravation. But the amount of speed he had in his possession would have been the collar of the year to Lily Law and they would have locked him up and thrown away the key before he had even seen his arrest report. His sojourn in whatever prison they decided to bury him in should have been a foregone conclusion; it was too many drugs to even contemplate getting any kind of result, let alone fucking bail. This was fucking freaky, there was no doubt about that.

As Dicky Williams had pointed out to Patrick not an hour ago, if Fucking Freddie Dwyer had snitched on him or anyone close to him, he was a fucking dead man. Because Terry's demise was such an affront none of them could believe it was to do with business. Who would be mad enough to take them on?

Patrick's car pulled up outside Dicky's house in Bow and he was already in possession of a large Scotch before he had even walked inside. It was placed in his hand as he stood on the doorstep.

Like Dicky Williams, Pat was also going over the events in his mind once more. And he had to agree with Dicky. Who would be mad enough to take them on? Pat had sighed to himself when he had heard that gem of wisdom, there was nothing like stating the bleeding obvious, but then the Williamses were not renowned for their command of the English language or their intelligence, even as a group, so Pat had overlooked the idiocy of Dicky's words and instead decided to concentrate on finding out what the fuck had gone down. Terry's death had to be avenged and he wanted that vengeance as much as they did, even if it was for a different reason. Dwyer was not a big enough fish for them to bother about; he was a dealer, no more and no less, and he had no real muscle or respect except what he garnered through his relationship with them.

Pat believed that Dwyer was the catalyst for this day's work, but whoever else the police had brought on board obviously thought they were beyond reproach, and for that reason alone, Pat wanted to obliterate them. He had to think this through and he had to make sure that no one was topped off before they had some idea of what this was all about. Everyone was a suspect now, but he wanted the real suspect not a phony one. The brothers, however, were on red alert; anyone could be wiped out on the smallest piece of evidence.

Like any soldier, Pat wanted a strategy and you couldn't work one out until you knew exactly what you were dealing with. He would find out if it was the last thing he did on this earth and, the way things were going, that could be exactly his fate before this day was out.

"Look, Dicky, no disrespect, but we need to find out who took out poor Terry, right? Find out the score."

Dicky nodded solemnly. "They are fucking amateurs. I mean, think about it: if they had half a fucking brain the whole mess would have come after us."

Pat looked into Dicky's open face and saw the pain and the uncertainty there. "I think Jamie the Book was a red herring. I think whoever did it wanted us wondering what the fuck was going on. What we need to do now is open this fucking town up and get the answers we need. I have a few Faces I can talk to, you start getting everyone together, then wait till I come back and we'll have a plan of action, all right?"

Dicky nodded once more, relieved that Pat was taking it all over. The reason the Williamses were happier working with Pat was because he was a rational thinker and they were unable to think beyond the last thought that might have invaded their heads, even collectively. They were shrewd enough when it came to earning a crust, no one disputed that, but Pat was the real brains of the outfit and he knew he had to try to sort this out before the Williams brothers started shooting first and asking questions later. Much later.

Lil was happy. Pregnant again, she was happier than she had ever been. Her life was everything she could have hoped for, and more. Patrick was fussing over her as always and, like her, his children were the focal point of his existence. Both had experienced such neglect and utter misery in their own childhoods that they wanted to make sure their children were happy and cared for. They were united in making their children the mainstay of their whole lives. Pat, thanks to his erratic working hours, was able to spend a lot of time with the boys and it showed. Pat Junior was his double; he emulated everything his father did, and at eight years old he was already a force to be reckoned with. His Holy Communion had ensured his place in local folklore because it had been such an event.

No one had ever seen the like of it, before or since, and Pat Junior had been like a little angel throughout. The party afterwards had gone on long into the night, and people had talked about it for weeks afterwards. Pat was a happy, popular child who was already showing signs of his father's fighting spirit and his mother's determination to get what he wanted. But his strength was tempered with an innate kindness that she knew his father saw as a flaw, even though deep inside he was pleased that such a generous and big-hearted boy had sprung from his loins. In their world men could not be soft, it was seen as a weakness and Pat wanted his sons to be seen as being strong and as reflections of himself.

Lance, however, was another story. At six he was a big boy for his age and he was still not what she would call normal. He was quiet and surly and he was also very temperamental, causing untold problems when the mood was upon him. He would argue black was white and her mother, as always, would back him to the hilt.

Lily had regretted having her mother back in her life many times, and always because of Lance. Annie had been a pain in the neck where he was concerned and Lil was constantly on the verge of fighting with her, but her mother had always seemed to sense when she had gone too far, making sure her daughter had nothing to complain about. Annie also knew that her babysitting was appreciated by her daughter who, if nothing else, trusted her with her grandsons.

Pat, however, was a different kettle of fish. He had put her mother in her place when he had seen his son in bed with her, asleep in her arms. Lance had been naked and, for some reason, this had sent Patrick off on a roaring diatribe that had raised the roof and also ensured that her mother was no longer encouraged to stay the night. Now that she was big with her pregnancy, her mother's uses were limited as Lil wasn't working the clubs any more. Her sons were therefore benefiting from her being home of an evening insomuch as their behavior was being monitored more than usual. Lance hated it, of course, because he couldn't get away with anything and he couldn't stay up with his granny, while his older brother was left to his own devices. Lil was shocked at just how much sway her mother had over Lance. Seeing him perform when he didn't get his own way had been an eye-opener and she regretted letting her mother have such autonomy over him; it wasn't healthy.

They had a way of looking at each other that excluded everyone around them, but what really bothered her was that if *she*, his mother, asked him to do something, he looked first at Annie for confirmation before undertaking the task. It sounded so trivial and unbelievable when said out loud, yet when she saw it happening between them it was almost sinister. She consoled herself that she was home now, and she would keep everyone on an even keel.

Pat Junior, on the other hand, loved having her home all the time. In fact, she felt his relief when the nights drew in because she realized just how much of a hold her mother had over her younger son. She was almost pleased to learn that the school felt pretty much the same way as she did about Lance. They told her that he was not a sociable child and she had smiled and interpreted the words as they were meant to be interpreted. He was a bully and, if his father had been anyone else, he would have been taken properly in hand. Pat Junior, God love him, had been pushed aside to make way for Lance, the golden boy, the child she knew Annie saw as her own. The child her mother seemed to think was more important than anyone else in the world.

Yet no matter what happened, Lil couldn't find it in her heart to push her mother away completely. Somehow she knew that the woman was experiencing love for the first time in her life and as she had such difficulty loving Lance herself, she knew she was guilty of letting her mother give it to him instead. Lance, God love him, gave her the creeps and the guilt she felt because of this was what kept her mother in her life. The new child would be born soon and she would reassess the situation then. At the moment though, she was tired and out of sorts. Lance and his problems would have to wait.

Annie placed a glass of milk beside her, and Lil smiled her thanks, noticing that her mother was being much more civil since Pat had taken her in hand.

The shriek that came from the bedroom brought both women running. It was high-pitched and terrifying; as they burst through the bedroom door they saw Lance cowering on the floor with Patrick leaning over him. It was a scene that neither mother nor daughter had ever experienced before. Pat was always the peacemaker, the good boy. Annie immediately shot across the room and slapped Patrick hard across the face. Lil, for the first time in weeks, found the energy returning to her body. As heavy as she was with the pregnancy, she walked purposely over to her mother who was now kneeling on the linoleum hugging a screeching Lance and, taking back her fist, Lil slammed it with all her might into the side of her mother's head.

Lance screamed even louder and, without thinking, she slapped him too, a stinging blow across his face. "Get out of my sight before I do for you, boy!"

Lil's voice was deep and resonant, the force of the words penetrated the child's brain and he ran from the room, the shock of the slap quieting him.

Lil pulled Patrick into her arms, hugging him to her. He still wasn't crying, even though the blow from her mother must have been painful.

"You and all, Mother, out."

Annie looked into the face so like her own and knew that her reign in this house had come to an end. In just a few seconds all the good things she'd had while under her daughter's protection flew into her mind. Money, prestige, warmth and companionship. She would rather lick this bitch's boots than be parted from the child she adored.

"Calm yourself down, Lil, think of the baby." Her voice was low, her face a travesty of hurt and sorrow.

"Get the fuck out of my house." Lil was talking through her teeth, her anger causing her to pant, and it was this more than anything that warned Annie she was skating on very thin ice.

"I am sorry. Lil, will you please calm down, love?"

Annie was pulling herself up off the floor by leaning on Pat's bed, and Lil saw that she was a woman aged before her time, from her severe, pulled-back hair to the deep grooves around her eyes and mouth. She was mean; her eyes told the truth of her real feelings and, once more, Lil felt the urge to murder her where she stood.

"Go home, Mother, before I do something I regret."

Annie walked slowly from the room then and Lil didn't expel the breath she was holding until she heard the front door downstairs close behind her.

Patrick stared up at her and said sadly, "It weren't my fault, Mum."

She squeezed him to her once more, realizing how big he was growing and how sturdy he was.

"What did he do, Pat?"

"He hurt me, he grabbed me and he hurt me."

He indicated his groin as he spoke and Lil didn't question what he said, as most women would after hearing that said about their child; she knew Pat Junior was telling the truth.

"Go and get yourself a treat and send your brother in."

She sat herself on the bed and waited until her younger son slipped into the room. "Why did you grab him there? What have you been told about that?"

He stared into her eyes and, for the first time ever, she saw wariness and fear.

"I didn't . . ." The whine was in his voice now. The poor-me whine that had Annie running around like a blue-arsed fly.

She pushed her face close to his and had the satisfaction of seeing him flinch. "Don't you lie to me, boy. Now, get the belt."

"Please, Mum, please." He was shaking his head, the shock and terror evident from the whiteness of his face.

She slapped him once more across his cheek, the force snapping his head to the side with a sickening crunch. "Get the belt, boy, and get it now."

Lance stumbled from the room, his face already awash with tears.

She watched him go. He was heavier than Pat, similar-looking, but with a tendency to flabbiness. It was because her mother gave him whatever he asked for. Well, he was going to get what he was asking for today, she was determined on that much.

Pat was in Brixton. He pulled up outside a terraced house in Ballater Road and, before turning off the engine, he sat back on the plush leather seats and listened to the radio for a few minutes. He needed a second to calm himself down before he went inside.

The house was small, a three-bedroom duplex, nothing to write home about; it blended in with the other dilapidated properties in the road. But Pat knew that inside this house was the information he needed.

As he walked up the small pathway, the door was discreetly opened by a tall black man with dreadlocks and bloodshot eyes. Spider Block was a mate, and they nodded to each other cautiously. "He expecting you, man."

Pat grinned then. "He fucking better be, Spider."

As Pat slipped inside the small hallway, he nodded a greeting to another large black man and walked straight into the parlor. The place was as dilapidated inside as it was on the outside. There were a few bits of furniture, no floor covering, not even linoleum; just brown tiles caked with years of grime and paint drips. The smell consisted mainly of Dwyer's body odor and mouse droppings; the decay and stench of neglect was a familiar odor to Patrick Brodie. It was what he had grown up with, and it was for that reason he loathed it so much. It reminded him of what he had come from, reminded him of the hunger and the despair that had spurred him on to make something of himself. He breathed it in deeply to make sure he never forgot it because if he ever did, he would be finished in his world and he knew that. These people smelled weakness like other people smelled their own shit; it wasn't nice, but it was a necessary part of life.

Dwyer had come from the same background so Pat had no respect for him still choosing to live like an animal. Pat knew his own children would never know this stench, and never know the shame of having to live like it.

At a scuffed wooden table sat three men. Patrick knew only one of them and, standing stiffly in the doorway of the room, he said harshly, "I take it you were expecting me then?"

Freddie nodded and sighed in a very nervous and exaggerated manner.

Pat decided he really did look like a rat; he had the long nose of his Jewish mother and the shifty mud-brown eyes of his Welsh father. Freddie was an ugly bastard, and, until now, that had not mattered one iota, but suddenly his ugliness spelled out treachery, hate, and underlying all that emotion was fear. Not just Freddie's, that was hanging in the room like a net curtain; for Pat it was the fear of what Freddie knew, what Freddie could use against him if cornered.

Patrick's head was reeling with all the information he had gathered in the last four hours. Some he knew to be true, some he guessed was gossip, gossip that had gained momentum as the day's events had been discussed and dissected by the common herd. There was always an element of truth in gossip though, and he had tried to ferret it out as best he could. He also knew for a fact that at least one of the men at the table was a cop, and he decided to wait and hear what Freddie had to say before committing himself.

No one was more surprised than Lil when the police had knocked at her door. They were warrantless, aggressive, and they turned the whole place over in a matter of minutes.

She sat on her black and orange PVC sofa with the boys either side of her and watched as her beautiful home was systematically ripped apart before her eyes. As drawers were pulled out and emptied on to the beige carpet, she lit a cigarette with shaking hands and acted as if this was a normal day. She chatted to her two wide-eyed children and listened to the police conversations all at the same time.

"Are there any guns in the house?"

DCI Kent was a tall, thin man with halitosis and stooped shoulders. He had his usual comb-over hairdo and a cigarette constantly on the go. His grubby raincoat had a fine layer of dandruff all over the shoulders and Lil hated him.

"What are you on about? Why would we have guns?" She sounded scandalized and angry; she knew how to play the game. "Look at my house, you rotten bastards, what the fuck you got to wreck it for?"

"This is nothing, Lil, this is just the start."

She didn't answer him, she just pulled the children closer to her as if protecting them from an invisible force.

Kent lit a new cigarette from the butt of the old one, breathing clouds of smoke over the boys. Lil looked wary and worried, and he noticed the brightness of the kids' eyes as they watched the commotion around them. Already they were street-smart and the knowledge depressed him for some reason. He knew he was looking at the next generation of lunatics and psychopaths. This scene would become a normal occurrence to them; one day it would all be re-enacted with their own kids and so the cycle would go on. He had seen it so many times over the years and, the older he got, the more he noticed how futile it all was. Young Pat Junior had his father's craggy good looks, he was also well set-up; even for a small boy he had the look of a fighter. He would be a lump in a few years and it went without saying that he would be a fighter.

The bigger of the boys though, Lance, would run to fat, he was already too chubby to be comfortable. He also had the furtive look that would mark him all his life; it was the same look the little bastards who were already hanging around the estates causing trouble had.

Yet he had to admit that, in fairness to Patrick, he had provided for his family handsomely. But, as his father used to say, blood will out.

He smiled at Lil and said gently, "You better sort your old man out, Lil, he is making a lot of enemies lately."

"Get out and leave me and my children alone."

Kent looked at her then and she saw the sadness in his eyes as he shook his head slowly.

"You're a fool, Lil, that old man of yours is living on borrowed time. If I don't get him, then his so-called mates will; at least with me he is in with a chance of seeing his babies grow up."

He nodded towards her belly and she felt the truth of what he was saying; this was not the usual cop bullshit. Her old man paid out too much money to get turned over without fair warning. This was serious all right.

But she kept her own counsel.

Chapter Five

Lil was bone-weary, but she tidied the place up anyway. Her home was everything to her; it made her feel safe, it was the place she felt she could finally relax in. It was important to her that it was a calm, clean and quiet oasis, especially now that she was pregnant. Even more so when her old man was on the missing list.

She tried to phone through to all his known haunts, and once again she was met with either a continuous ringtone or an engaged signal, which told her the phone in question was off the hook. She knew better than to phone certain pubs and watering-holes because it would then have alerted people to what could be a serious situation. Until she knew the score, she knew she had to be circumspect.

His silence though, and the fact that no one seemed to know his whereabouts, was making her feel ill with worry, and she forced herself to calm down once more. Her belly was heavy, dragging at her whole being. Her fear and tiredness was making her movements sluggish, her back was aching and her eyes were red-rimmed with tiredness. She had straightened up the boys' room first, making it like a game, encouraging them to help and then settling them into their beds, all the time feeling the bewilderment and fright coming off them in waves. As young as they were though, they knew to keep their traps shut in front of the police. In a strange way she was proud of that. Pat Junior knew where his father's gun was, he could have tracked it down like a bloodhound if the fancy took him. They often joked between themselves about how many times it had been hidden away and how many times young Pat had found it. The cops had got nowhere near it tonight, and this was a small victory for her. It gave her spirits a little boost, made her feel they were still in control. The frightening thing was, until the police turned your place over in front of your kids, and more importantly with what seemed like a good reason, you never really quite understood just how precarious your life actually was. Being left without a breadwinner and a father for your children, a protector, never crossed your mind. When the cops showed up, the precariousness of your situation hit you in the face with the force of a speeding car.

Now, with a belly full of arms and legs, two boys dependent on her, and an old man she loved so much it hurt her, Lil felt the cold hand of fear patting her on her back. It was warning her, making her start questioning all the things she had taken for granted. Like all villains' wives, she had received her first real wake-up call. Tonight wasn't the usual half-hearted assault by the cops to make it all look good on paper, this was serious. Her husband, the father of her kids, was likely on the wrong end of a capture; if it all went pear-shaped he could go away for so long he would be a grandfather before he came home. Judges were handing out outrageous sentences these days, the short sharp shock was a thing of the past; this new government was all for burying the fuckers and forgetting them.

Once more Lil was reminded of the fact that she had no real money, no hard cash, nothing to call her own. Pat controlled it all, as he should. But the seed was sown now, and that would have to be addressed sooner rather than later. When, and if, he came home, she was going to make sure she was never left in this position again.

She kissed her boys and watched as they settled themselves down in their now tidy bedroom. They were calmer now, drinking their drinks and chatting between themselves as usual. The first shock was over with, normality was gradually being reinstated. Something inside was telling her that they should have been more bothered by the night's events, but she pushed these thoughts away. Kids were resilient.

If Pat had been arrested, he had been arrested. There was nothing she could do about it, but the thought terrified her. Her heart was racing at that thought and she breathed in deeply, knowing that she could easily dissolve into hysterics at any moment.

She forced herself to concentrate on the job in hand. The sitting room was destroyed. They had even taken the seat cushions off the sofa and split them open with a knife; the stuffing was everywhere and the tears stung her eyes as she cleared it all away.

She still had not heard a word from Pat and she was getting more and more agitated by the minute. She checked her purse and realized that she had less than eight pounds to her name. If Pat was nabbed, or worse, she had no access to his money at all. Her mother's voice came back to her and, as much as she hated to admit it, the old bitch was right. Pat should have set her straight in case he was arrested. She needed access to money, not just for his lawyer, but for the daily business of living with a young family and the expense that children brought with them. These were desperate times, and desperate times meant desperate measures.

A little voice, though, was telling her that she was entitled to his money anyway, she had eight fucking pounds and a family to feed. Why didn't she have a stash? Why was she dependent on him for everything when she had a fucking growing family? More to the point, why hadn't Pat thought to make provision for them? Plan fucking B was what he always referred to when discussing work, it was for when Plan A fell apart. And here she was with nothing, not a Plan A, let alone a Plan B. Not a brass razoo to her bastard name. She was shaking with fear for him and fear for herself and her family. Anger kept her going. She was still cleaning up when her mother arrived, all brown teeth, lavender cologne and pretending a concern she was not capable of feeling.

She let Annie give the boys their breakfast because she had no heart to do anything except sit and feel her baby kicking as if it was reminding her that it was there. Another mouth to feed on eight pathetic pounds. Throughout the day young Pat stuck to her like shit to a blanket but Lance acted as if nothing was amiss.

Annie had the sense to keep her nose out and silence the questions that were hurling themselves around her head. The neighbors were vocal about the raid; speculation was rife as always and the dolt she called a daughter had not uttered one word about any of it. She could see that her daughter was not in the mood for a full and frank discussion of any description. Her daughter's plight affected her not one iota; she was there for no other reason than accruing some Brownie points. With them she could gain access to her Lance. Without that child her life was meaningless; her feelings for him were so strong she felt them as a physical force. She would endure anything to be near him, and do anything to keep others away from him.

Love was a strange emotion. It was something she had never felt before, or felt the need to express in any way. She saw herself in him, and that was enough to make her feel that finally her life was worth living.

Dwyer was trembling so much that he couldn't light his cigarette. Pat leaned over and struck a match, holding it out for him, watching him trying to inhale and make the cigarette work at last. His three attempts left them all embarrassed and the room was heavy with tension. Dwyer's breathing was loud, even to his own ears, and his actions were unnatural and overly dramatic. He looked what he was.

Patrick grinned at him in a friendly manner. "You all right, mate? You on the gear as usual?"

Dwyer smiled then. His wrinkled face was suddenly familiar, his hangdog look back, he could have been a favorite uncle. Pat felt a smidgen of sorrow for him. He was a product of circumstances, as they all were. The bloke Pat thought was a cop was watching them nervously, but in fairness he was calm enough to get away with it. Patrick, however, was relaxed. Sitting back in the chair, he waited until Dwyer was puffing away on his Embassy before he spoke. "Who are this lot? I think an introduction is on the cards, don't you?"

The suspect cop looked him in the face then and Pat smiled gently once more.

"We're friends of Freddie's . . ."

Pat pointed a finger at the suspect cop without looking at him directly, he was now leaning once more across the table staring into Freddie's eyes, but talking to the other man. "Who gave you permission to address me, you cheeky cunt?"

Freddie was terrified again, this was not what was supposed to happen. Pat wasn't supposed to be like this, cocky and spoiling for a fight. It was Pat who was supposed to be caught asleep at the wheel. Freddie was not geared up for this behavior at all.

"You shut the fuck up until I speak to you directly, OK? You are a no-neck, a fucking ice-cream, a nothing." The violence behind Pat's eyes was barely hidden, everyone was reminded of just how slippery he could be, especially when he thought he was being made a fool of.

Pat had a reputation and the people in the room had conveniently forgotten it because as a collective they had assumed they would be the stronger. Pat had just reminded them of how big a mistake an assumption could turn out to be.

The cop was unsure how to react to Brodie. He knew though that he had been discovered. Pat snapped his head round to look at the man, his eyes were dead now, he was in work mode and anyone who really knew him would be seriously worried. Pat was capable of anything when he felt even remotely threatened, extreme violence was how he had attained his position in the first place. Tonight he was not going down without taking this lot with him, and they were now all aware of that. He planned ahead and he thought on his feet; he was ready for whatever these pieces of shit were intending to lay on him. So when he smiled once more it was with a chilling certainty that he would be the victor no matter what happened.

"Two fucking deaths and you are here with strangers, Fred, fucking *strangers*. Suspect strangers at that." He looked at Dwyer again, his voice high with utter contempt, not only for them but for the situation they had all found themselves in.

"Have I got cunt tattooed on my fucking forehead or what?" Pat held his arms up in a gesture of supplication. It was overly dramatic, and it was also a warning that he was playing with them, enjoying the moment.

Dwyer puffed furiously on his cigarette, not even attempting to justify himself and, more to the point, not trying to even introduce his newfound friends. He knew it was over, he knew they were finished. His terror was now communicating itself to the other men in the room.

Patrick started to laugh. He could feel the power flowing into him, knew he had them on edge. He was an unknown quantity, all they knew of him was his reputation, none of them had experienced him first-hand. Pat was more than a handful when the fancy took him, and the fancy was on him tonight, he could feel the menace inside him desperate to be unleashed. He was actually enjoying himself. He was willing to go away to avenge this fucking atrocity, and go away for a long time. This was an out-and-out fucking liberty of Olympian standards and, because of that, he was not going to keep quiet. He wanted blood and retribution and he was determined to get it, no matter what the personal cost might be.

"I came here to try and make some kind of fucking sense out of the deliberate and willful dereliction of your fucking duties. *You* had a tug and *you* fucking sold us down the river, you treacherous cunt. You are the cause of two good men being outed, and the most heinous crime of all is that none of you thought that I might have cottoned on, that you thought I was too thick to suss this lot out? Is this the best you could fucking do, the best you could come up with?"

He laughed once more, and pointed at Dwyer. "Him? You relied on him? Fucking Freezing Freddie? And you are the so-called Sweeney Todd, the scourge of the criminal classes? Oh fuck off!"

There was no anger in his voice now, just righteous indignation, sarcasm and a smattering of honest disbelief. "You're a fucking joke."

The suspect cop was a big lad, he had broad shoulders, but the soft, pudgy body of a lazy man. Like most plainclothes cops he had never really worked at anything since promotion; he relied on other people to make his cases for him. He was dependent on snitches like Dwyer and statements from the general public. In short, he chased rumors, gossip and idle chit-chat. His mentality was such that he actually thought that a man like Pat Brodie could be collared. Would roll over because they might have garnered some information that could put him away. He did not have the experience or intelligence to see that a man like Brodie would go down for a twenty-stretch without letting them hear one of his farts, let alone anything that would incriminate anyone else.

"Look, Pat, you got this all wrong . . . We want you with us . . ."

The suspect cop had finally spoken, was trying to get him onside, actually thought he would roll over and snitch on his mates. The man had a deep voice, a pleasing voice in fact; it had an underlying lilt to it, Welsh maybe. He was playing at the London accent though, so many CID and Flying Squad were guilty of that. They thought it made them seem harder and more on the ball. These upper working-class boys from the Home Counties now saw themselves as the new and improved Z Cars. Patrick looked around the table and sighed in disappointment. This was the legendary Sweeney? He had seen harder nuts in his Christmas stocking. There was even a television program about them and, after tonight, he could only assume it was a fucking comedy.

Too late, the suspect cop realized he had said the wrong thing. He was still secure enough in his job to believe that even if Brodie didn't play the game he would not have the nerve to do any real damage to them; after all they were Lily Law, when all was said and done. He was wondering, though, if Brodie might be tempted to wallop one of them, just to prove a point.

"Who're you calling Pat? How dare you attempt any kind of familiarity with me?"

The room was now steeped in animosity and righteous indignation; Patrick's natural-born hatred of any kind of authority was in evidence and he was offended, really offended. Then, from underneath his coat, he produced a machete. He brandished it with relish, watching the men around him as the realization of their situation dawned on them. Spider and his Jamaican cousin were standing in the doorway, their own weapons, a scythe and a Japanese samurai sword, clearly visible.

The three men at the table finally understood that they were in grave danger and the fact that they were part of the establishment guaranteed them nothing from the bunch of psychopaths looking at them with excitement in their eyes and malice in their hearts.

Standing up, Patrick brought the machete down with all the force he could muster, on to Freddie Dwyer's head. Spider and Pat laughed out loud as they systematically hacked him to pieces, the blood splattering on to the scandalized faces of the police as they awaited their turn, making it all the more hilarious.

A lesson was administered swiftly and with the maximum of brutality. It was a lesson well learned by everyone who had to deal with Patrick Brodie from that day on.

He had gone from hard nut to headcase overnight, and it was a well-planned, well-executed and deliberate ploy to ensure that anyone who had dreams of snitching on him would remember that Dwyer, and the cop he had been fool enough to associate with, had been sentenced to death without any repercussions whatsoever.

Lil was lying on the sofa trying to get comfortable. Her belly was tight once more, and the devastation of her home was still in evidence. She had put everything back as neatly as she could, but the police had done a thorough job inasmuch as most of the soft furnishings would have to be replaced.

She took a few deep breaths and tried to calm the beating of her heart, which was pounding inside her breast with such force it was almost painful. She still had not heard anything from Pat and the time was crawling by. Every time she looked at the clock on her mantelpiece it seemed that an hour had passed, but in fact it had been only minutes. Her mother was still in with the boys and she blocked out the thoughts that were crowding her mind. Her belly was tightening once more and she knew on some level that she was in labor.

However, the pain was nothing she couldn't handle and her mind was still racing and reliving the last few hours. She lit a cigarette and pulled on it deeply, the nicotine hitting her brain and making her feel dizzy. The second draw was better and the third eased her nerves. She looked down at herself and saw the movement of her belly that she knew heralded the arrival of a new person into the world. It was early and she was too tired to make a fuss.

If Patrick had been arrested it might be eight or even ten years before he came home to her and his kids; it was a sobering and frightening thought. She felt so alone and so vulnerable, and all she kept focusing on was the fact she had only eight pounds to her name.

Eight lousy pounds and a new child fighting for its place in the world. What the fuck was she going to do?

*   *   *

Spider and Pat were in a house just off the Railton Road. They were soaked with blood and still on the high that often followed a bout of extreme violence.

Dicky and the Williams brothers were over the moon at the retribution Pat had doled out in their names. Dicky had been disappointed that he had missed out on the shenanigans but he was also secretly pleased that no one could put him or his brothers anywhere near the crime scene. Dead cops tended to cause serious aggravation, even crooked dead cops. His brother's untimely demise had hit them all hard and he knew that Pat's logic for keeping this away from them was the act of a good mate. Their faces would be the first in the frame and they had genuinely been somewhere else, so they had the perfect alibi.

They were now pouring drinks and assuring each other that if the cops had any intention of feeling their collars it would have happened already. Pat knew, as Spider knew, that the cops were taking time to lick their wounds, especially the ones they had something on. They would regroup at some point, that was human nature, but at this particular moment in time the police felt it was better to retreat, smile and nod, wait till the time was right then, when they were at their weakest, they would come for them en masse. Until then, fuck them! The murder of young Terry Williams had not been a smart move and the up-and-coming young Face they had bought with promises of aggrandizement was now the most wanted Face in London, for all the wrong reasons, running scared and, suddenly, without any protection whatsoever. Jamie the Book's death had barely registered on the Richter scale of criminal London, so even that had not given the Flying Squad anything that they could use against the Williamses or Brodie. It was a catastrophic fuck up but lessons had been learned.

In reality, anything that had been gained from the whole sorry business was in Brodie's favor; he was the new king of the swingers and the crooked police he had gathered made him a no-go because he had been astute enough to buy only the best. As his mum had always told him, you get what you pay for and how true those words had turned out to be.

Spider had been a good mate to Pat over the years but he had made a life-changing choice this night: he had chosen Pat over the guaranteed protection of the police. If he had gone along with Dwyer, he would have been given a free rein to serve up his cannabis with no hassle whatsoever. But, like Patrick Brodie, he would rather take his chances in their world than live under the protective umbrella and sickening stench of the police.

Patrick was filled with enthusiasm now: as he had showered the blood from his body he had relived the feelings of excitement that the night had created inside him. That he had enjoyed the violence so much made him question everything about himself; he had watched Dwyer die slowly and painfully and he had been fascinated by it. As the others had waited for their turn, he had observed their absolute terror, could smell the fear emanating from their pores. As he had remarked to Spider, it was absolute power; the knowledge that you chose whether someone lived or died was the greatest buzz of all. It was their horror and the realization that they were in over their heads that had made him feel so good, that had made him prolong the agony of Dwyer so he could enjoy their fear, feed off it and make it work for him, for his benefit.

Now he was calming down he waited for the feelings to disappear, but they didn't, and he knew that he had awakened something inside himself that had been waiting to escape for years. He was his father's son, his mother's child and he knew now that he had a hard streak running through him that made him immune to other people's suffering; at least the people who thwarted him.

He was determined to use that to his advantage. After this little debacle he was going to make sure he was never again in a position of weakness; if extreme fear kept him safe then that was fine by him.

He had put the word out for information on the whereabouts of the shooter. Once he had a reliable lead and wiped him out, the whole episode would be closed once and for all. He was sending out more messages than the post office, and anyone with half a brain would take heed. Patrick Brodie was not a man to cross, even cops had learned that lesson the hard way.

Lil opened her eyes and quickly closed them again. It was early in the evening and the sun was bright in the hospital room. She was still unable to relax, still worried about Patrick. Not a word, and no one seemed able to track him down. All through the delivery she had been on red alert for a message to say he was outside, a word from someone, anyone, to tell her that he was OK and still on the outside. But no one seemed to have heard from him and no one seemed bothered about his disappearance.

A thin mewling brought her bolt upright and she smiled into the cot placed beside her bed; two perfectly formed little girls lay side by side, identical in every way. Despite being early, they were healthy, robust children with well-rounded limbs and thick curly hair.

Twins. The sheer enormity of their birth was overwhelming her. No one had detected a second baby, no one had been prepared for the second birth and no one could love them more than she did. It was a revelation that, even in her terror of what the next few hours might bring, a fierce determination to protect them was foremost in her mind.

Pat would be over the moon, she knew, when he eventually found out about them. It had been the most eventful night of her life and having to keep up the pretense that everything was OK, lying that her husband was working away and couldn't be contacted, was taking its toll on her.

She had to spend ten days in this small bed but until she knew what was going on with her old man, she knew that the sleep her body was crying out for would not come. If and when he finally turned up she was going to launch him into outer space. That thought made her feel better for a while.

Laina Dawson was seventy-two years old and had moved out to Southend fifteen years earlier with the Greater London Council and the slum clearance. Her two daughters and her youngest son were still in the city and she saw them often, but to have her grandson, her Leonard, named for his dead grandfather, living with her was as close to heaven as she thought she was ever going to get.

His nerves seemed to be getting the better of him though and she believed, as did his mother, that the sea air would soon have him back on his feet. Good home cooking and a few weeks' watching telly with his old nana would soon put the color back into his cheeks.

"Fancy coming to bingo, love?"

Lenny forced a smile and shook his head, his resemblance to his errant father all the more striking since he had shaved his hair off.

It was the only thing about this boy she found difficult to like, his looks; he was his father's son in that department. He was that two-faced loser all over again but, as luck would have it, that was where the similarity between them ended. Unlike his old man, he was a kind, decent lad with good manners and an amiable way about him.

The rumors going round that he was involved with criminals she shrugged off as nonsense. He wasn't a violent thug and anyone who said otherwise was a liar; as she was always telling him, people were jealous. What they had to be jealous of she had never explained, but that had been her answer to all her children's complaints since they were babies. It never occurred to her that they might have been at fault, it was always everyone's jealousy of her perfect brood.

Now she had her grandson here, only because he was in some kind of trouble, and she was once more making up excuses for him. He was young and foolish, he would learn. The pungent tobacco he smoked made him almost catatonic and if it had been anyone else's grandson, she would have sworn it was that new cannabis stuff she had read about in the papers. Not her boy though, he was above all that.

As she got ready to go to bingo she chatted to him, ignoring the fact that he hardly registered her existence. She was lonely since her old man had passed and even though she would die before admitting it, she was making the most of having someone to prattle on to. The boy did look rough though. He was white-faced, and he was sporting bags under his eyes large enough to fetch her shopping in. He was caught up in some kind of fuckery, she would swear to that, but what it was, she would not ask.

Overwork, that was his mother's explanation for his condition and Laina had not questioned the fact that, to her knowledge, Lenny had never actually had a job. They must think she was in her dotage. For all her talk about how good they were to her, Laina knew that she only saw her kids or their offspring when there was aggravation afoot or money was needed.

Lenny was a bright boy though, he made a few quid and had slipped her a ton for his little sojourn with her, so that wasn't too bad, was it? As her old man had always said, it would all come out in the wash.

As she bowled down Progress Road on her way to bingo she heard the screech of tires that was becoming more and more prevalent in the area. Southend was going to the dogs, and she didn't mean the kind that raced at Walthamstow either.

As she crossed the road, Laina didn't see the three men slip up her pathway and enter her home without even having the decency to knock.

And she didn't see her grandson's face as he heard a familiar voice say quietly, "Hello, Lenny."

Even though he had known that this moment was inevitable, the shock still rendered Lenny speechless.

"Nothing like a bit of sea air, a nice little holiday."

Lenny looked into the eyes of Pat Brodie and knew without a doubt that all that was left for him now was to die with some dignity about him, with a bit of self-respect.

When they told the story of his demise, as he knew they would, in their cups, boys together, he wanted them to say that he took it like a man. That he had held his hand up, wiped his mouth and accepted the inevitable. He wanted them to give him credit for his bravery, talk about him with respect. He knew that a good death would earn him some kudos for the future, even though he would not be there to hear about it. He wanted his friends to know that he had not begged for his life or tried to talk his way out of it; he wanted to go with his pride intact, no matter how ruthlessly Brodie decided to eliminate him. This was what was left for him now: Brodie saying that he died like a man, and Brodie would say it, would give him his due, and in their world that meant a lot. The fact that he was thinking about how he would be perceived after his death at twenty-five years old did not enter his mind; the fact that it was that kind of warped thinking that had brought about his early demise, did not enter it either. He had gambled, and he had lost. If he had won, he would not have any sympathy as the victor, consequently he expected no less for himself. He smiled half-heartedly, still the hard nut, the Face. He swallowed down his fear, a small part of him relieved that he would not have to wait for the knock on the door any more; the door had finally been opened and a peace was descending over him.

"Not here, mate, me nan . . ."

The boy looked like a child, his chubby face was open and he was more than aware of his fate.

Pat grinned and said jovially, "What do you think we are, Lenny, fucking animals?"

"Fuck me, Lil, a pair of beauties there, girl." Her stepfather's voice dragged her from the sleep that complete exhaustion and two tranquilizers from a worried nurse had finally given to her.

Lil looked at him with dark-rimmed, tired eyes and Mick knew that she wished him as far away as was physically possible. He felt the urge to smack her across her smug face, but he didn't, he was still playing the game. Still acting as if she was his daughter and he was a doting grandfather.

The twins, though, they were beauties; even he was touched by their good looks and the perfect symmetry of their features. They were two peas in a pod all right, and he envied Brodie his family more at this moment than ever before.

The word had hit the street that Brodie had out-gunned the pretenders to his throne, hence this very public appearance at the hospital to welcome his new granddaughters. But as the man of the moment was nowhere to be seen, maybe the pavement talk was a bit premature.

"You need anything, love?"

She barely moved her head in denial and the disrespect was not lost on him and he grinned.

"I bet Pat is over the moon, eh, love?"

This was said with the confidence of someone who knew that her husband had not been anywhere near and Lil could feel the animosity coming off her stepfather in waves. There was an underlying sarcasm in his voice that told her he had heard something about her old man's whereabouts. He was aware of the police turning the house over; her mother would have seen to that, so she kept her expression blank, unwilling to give him the satisfaction of knowing he had rattled her.

The silence between them was finally broken by Mick's harsh cough. He broke eye contact and dropped his head on to his chest in a shamefaced manner and Lil knew she had unnerved him; for all his hatred and his bravado he was a coward, and like all cowards, he was also treacherous. She knew he would sell every one of them down the river without a second's thought if it gained him anything.

"Fuck off and leave me be." Her voice was deep from a lack of sleep and emotion, and she was pleased to note that he left without a word. She was shaking again. It was over forty-eight hours and she had still not heard from Pat. That in itself was not unusual, he often disappeared, but he had to have known that they had been turned over. That she had been left to handle it while her belly was nearly dragging on the floor. He had to have thought of her condition and his boys, surely? The fact he had not contacted her made her feel abandoned, frightened and lonely.

No one seemed to be answering their phones either, and that alone told her that something was wrong, very wrong. Even the club phones were off the hook, so she had nothing and no one to allay her fears. Once more she felt the enormous weight of her worries lying heavy on her shoulders as she wondered where the fuck her old man was and why he had not been in touch. The ache in her breasts was nothing to the tight band of tension that was slowly squeezing her head until she felt as if it was going to explode. In a strange way, she hoped he was locked up, because if he was still at large it meant that he had not been bothered about them all; that they had not even entered his head.

Dicky Williams was getting out of his car with his usual jaunty air when he was shot repeatedly in the head and body. Lenny was obviously not the culprit, and no one seemed any the wiser about who it might have been. It was a head-scratcher all right.

It was too late for his death, that was the sad part, because the whole debacle was over and poor Dicky had been taken out after everything had been sorted, but no one seemed to have any knowledge about it whatsoever.

It was a tragedy, more so because the other Williamses were not capable of keeping themselves together without his strength of character. It would soon become apparent that Dicky's death, not Terry's, would be the catalyst that would bring the whole lot of them down.

Chapter Six

Kathleen and Eileen were toddling around the room and Pat was laughing at their antics. They were his heart and everyone, including the boys, accepted that fact. The girls, as they were always referred to, were gorgeous; blond-haired, blue-eyed beauties who had never in their life been subject to anything except love and spoiling. At three, they were a mirror image of each other. They were also bright; early talkers, early walkers and they were already ruined by their parents and brothers.

Patrick watched his wife as she wiped noses, tidied up the house and cooked the dinner. Lil was a strong girl and she was still the only woman for him. As his daughters held out their arms to her and she reached down to hug them, he smiled at the picture they created and felt a lump in his throat.

She was a beautiful woman and four children had not diminished her allure in his eyes. If anything it had made her more attractive to him. But with the birth of the twins she had been forced to give up working with him, and even though she loved being a mother to them all, he knew she missed the excitement of being a part of his working life. She glanced at him and smiled sadly; she could see through him as if he was a pane of glass and they both knew it.

Guilt ate away at him. He had been on the missing list for two days when the girls were born, and the fact that his wife, his Lil, had not even mentioned it, spoke volumes. She had stopped asking him questions a long time ago, didn't want to know where he had been, she no longer cared. All she seemed interested in was money, she was obsessed with money. She demanded it as her right and how could he deny her? Four kids cost money, a lot of money, but sometimes he felt that was all he was to her, a meal ticket, a pay packet, even though he knew that was unfair.

He was turning into his father and he hated himself for that. But the clubs called to him, he got a few drinks inside him, started talking crap and, before he knew it, the night was over and the morning was there. The girl he had spent the day and night with wasn't fit to clean Lil's shoes, yet he had not cared about that. She had been young, available and fresh-looking. She had also been as thick as shit and up for anything. He had fucked her rigid in the back of his car and he couldn't even remember her name. She had been in possession of a pair of firm tits and a nice smile and that had been criteria enough for what he had wanted at that particular moment in time. He had used her, as he always used the girls who hung around him, and who made him more grateful than ever that he had his Lil waiting for him at home. As soon as it was over and the drink wore off, he wanted rid of them and he was disgusted with himself, swearing it would be the last time.

However, it was becoming a frequent occurrence, even though it meant nothing. He stayed out even when there was no actual work involved, nothing to do, no reason not to go home to his family, and he felt a right scumbag. He was disrespecting Lily and he knew it. More to the point, she knew it. If Lil had been out all night carousing he would have caused a fucking riot. If anyone even looked at her sideways, he felt a jealousy that was capable of causing him to murder. As she always pointed out, you judged people by your own standards. Because he was capable of taking a flier, he assumed she was, even though he knew she was better than that. The worst thing was that she had a natural, built-in shit detector that told her when he was pulling a fast one.

Patrick was the king of the hill now, he had made himself a rep that was so solid, so concrete, that no one in their right mind would challenge him. In a strange way, this disappointed him. Patrick knew that to keep on top you had to put on a show of strength on a regular basis, not only to warn off any pretenders, but to keep your workforce in line. He had a lot of people working for him now, and a few of them were capable of being contenders if he was fool enough to give them too much leeway.

Even Dave and the other Williams brothers were pushing their luck lately, and it was getting to the stage where a fight might very well be on the cards.

Spider and his cronies were still on his payroll, but as the Williamses and the blacks had never really mixed, it was causing aggravation. The Williamses resented the money that was going their way, not understanding that Spider was a good mate and that he earned fortunes off the blues, the grass and the firearms that he had a knack of sniffing out. Times were changing and the Jamaicans were the future for them. If Dave could only get his thick head around that fact, they would all have been the better for it. They had been offered a chance and they had knocked it back long ago. Now the money was rolling in and resentments were surfacing because of that.

Spider worked the front line and ran the whole shebang, from blues to birds. Blues were parties that went on for days; a derelict property was located, boarded up, cleared of debris, then a sound system would be installed and a bar erected. The party could go on for days and the money collected off the door and the bar was astronomical. The grass sales were always good and the police kept well away. All in all, it was a good earner and Spider had it sewn up. No one could have a blues, sell a bit of grass or pimp a woman without Spider's express say-so. That meant of course, without *his* say-so. Spider didn't care about that, he and Patrick had gone into it as a team, but it seemed that suddenly Dave and his brothers did mind. They had no foothold in south London and resented the money that Patrick was creaming off, but they had originally been offered an in and refused it. They had not seen Brixton and its potential, they had not paid for any of the original deals and they were going to have to swallow the fact they had made a big fuck up. There was no way at this late stage that anyone was going to cut the profits three ways just to keep the peace.

Spider was shifting Dexedrine at fifty quid a thousand and the kids wanted them. Amphetamine was the new drug of choice, whether in pill form or powder, and it was making shitloads of money for them.

Spider ran the business with military precision and he was adamant that south London was his and Pat had to stand by him on that.

Pat looked around the house he had recently purchased and a sense of pride washed over him once more; no one in his family had ever bought their own home before. It was a strange feeling, owning something so significant. It was a commitment, it was the roof over his family's head. It was an asset as well, he was aware of that. He had paid cash, that had been another of Lil's demands. Until now he had not thought of putting money into anything tangible, had steered clear of anything that could be investigated by the tax or the police. But Lily had pointed out that the turnover from his legit businesses was more than ample for a purchase of this size and as usual she had been right.

The house was in her name and she held the deeds to it. It was the least he could do. He owned other houses, but they were business properties and they were in his name; he could walk away from them at any time. This place felt solid though, it was his home; his family's home. He liked the feeling of belonging somewhere, of having a base. And he loved the fact that his Lil was happy here, that she felt safe knowing it was hers no matter what.

His boys started fighting, they were watching Tom and Jerry on TV and arguing over who should be the cat and who the mouse. His daughters went over to them and, as always, Kathy sat with Pat Junior and Eileen sat with Lance. The girls' presence stopped the fighting in its tracks and he was proud of his boys and their gentle way with their sisters.

He was exhausted and as he sat back on the sofa and relaxed, Lil brought him in a cup of strong, sweet tea. He pulled her down beside him, kissing her hard, slipping his tongue into her mouth and he felt her responding as she always did. She could never be angry with him for long. As angry as she got, she needed him like other women needed to eat and drink. Without him, she was nothing. Without him, her life was empty, even with four children to occupy her time. She hated herself for it, but she accepted it as part of her life.

The awkwardness between them was over once more, until the next time. But the accusation was still behind her eyes, as was the tired acceptance of his lifestyle and the effect it had on her and their family.

He was a man and, in their world, that meant he could do what he wanted. She didn't like it, but she dealt with it. It was this he found so hard to cope with. She was worth better than that and they both knew it.

Spider was drinking white rum and smoking a twist; the scent of cannabis was heavy on the air. His girlfriend, a young Jamaican woman with braided hair and almond-shaped eyes, was nursing her baby son while listening to Peter Tosh on the sound system.

Spider watched Rochelle lazily, his thick dreadlocked hair hanging over his face, his eyes closing with tiredness. Like Patrick, he had been out on the lam for a few days; unlike Patrick, his girlfriend had eaten his face off when he had come home. Finally, and with much persuasion on his part, she had calmed down enough to nurse their baby. He knew he was going to have to do some serious groveling over the next few days to get her back onside. She was a good girl and he loved her; she was fiery, too young for him really, but she had heart and he respected that.

There was a knock on his front door and Spider had to shake himself awake to answer it. He was seriously stoned and he opened the front door with difficulty. The house was like a fortress and he took his time unbolting the front door. He knew who was behind it and he was smiling genially when he finally slid the last lock.

"Fucking hell, man, this place is like Fort Knox." Spider's younger brother, Cain, was standing there, grinning.

Cain was the antithesis of Spider in that he had short, cropped hair and he favored tailored trousers and understated shirts. Spider was a larger-than-life character and his apparel reflected that. He was wearing baggy tracksuit bottoms and a pure-cotton embroidered overshirt that looked tight on his heavy frame. With his dreads and his moccasins, he looked every inch the Rasta dealer. Cain was an up-and-coming young blood; at twenty-one he had the nerve and the street smarts to make his mark on his community. He had an easy way about him that belied the strength and single-mindedness that was only evident to the people who knew him. Spider was twelve years older than him and proud of the young man he was grooming for the future and for his eventual retirement.

"You got my money?"

Cain laughed, his white, even teeth glinting in the sunlight. "Shut the fucking door. You the one who told me never to talk business in the street or me own backyard!"

As he locked up once more, Spider could hear his brother chatting about his nephew's good looks and flirting with Rochelle. The boy was a natural-born womanizer and, listening to him talking and joking with his Rochelle, he felt the love that many men reserved for their children. He loved his life. It was times like this that made him realize just how lucky he was.

"They are coining it in and walking all over us, Dave, and we are being fucking mugged-off."

Dave Williams sighed as he listened once more to his brother Dennis's usual litany of perceived wrongs. Since Dicky had been murdered he had taken on the mantle of the older brother and it was hard. Dicky had been the main man; he had always known what to do and how to do it. Dave tried and Patrick gave him his due, but he was always worried that he would get it wrong. Dicky's death had left a hole that Dave knew he wasn't able to fill, and he had the distinct impression his brothers felt the same way as he did. They were grown men now, and he knew they were itching to get a few pounds off their own backs. He was now the eldest and they respected him, but they were not boys any more. They were a handful, and he knew that better than *anyone*.

"Relax, for fuck's sake! You're like an old woman."

"Fucking relax? You have the audacity to tell me to relax?"

Dennis had his usual petulant look; he had a temper and it was not easily kept under control. He had always kicked off at the slightest thing; he saw insults where none were forthcoming and he heard conversations that had never taken place. He was an angry fucker and he was getting harder and harder to control.

"No one can get a fucking foot on the front line and that is what's giving me the fucking hump. Spider and his brother have sewn it all up."

Dave sipped his coffee in silence and waited for the rant to continue as he knew it would. This had been a daily occurrence since Dennis had tried to shift some speed in south London; he had sold enough for a small profit, but he had not sold enough for his liking. He had also been warned off; in a nice way, with respect, but to be warned off was something that had never happened to any of them in living memory. They were the ones who did the warning and they were not about to step back and watch others get a serious graft without them even having a touch. It had caused a lot of upset and a lot of bad feeling towards Patrick Brodie, who was being seen more and more as a traitor by his own workforce.

Dennis was stalking around the room. His broad shoulders were stiff with the anger he was feeling and his moonface was screwed up with hatred and humiliation.

"To add insult to fucking injury, Dave, that black cunt and his cohorts are dealing all over the show. They are in every nook and cranny; the pavement stinks of them, so where does that leave us? Fucking Brodie is all right, ain't he? He is in league with them, he fucking owns them. He is raking it in, but what about us, Dave? I was told to fuck off last night, as if I was a fucking ice-cream, a cunt. I was told that Ilford and Barking were no-go areas because that lot were already dealing out of Celebrities nightclub in Forest Gate." Dennis shook his head in bewilderment.

"We have nowhere to peddle anything. They've sewn up the Lacy Lady, Room at the Top and the fucking Tavern. Lautrec's is already part of their domain and Southend is sewn up tighter than a nun's crack. It's everywhere we go; Raquel's in Basildon, the fucking Roxy, the Vortex, Dingwall's in Camden. There is not a pub or a club left that we can call our own, from the Old Rose to the Dean Swift, and that even includes The Green Man, *my* watering-hole. They have Callie Road, the fucking main pubs, the fucking docks and all the poxy local boozers. They are like fucking leeches taking the food out of my kid's mouth." He spat into the fireplace for maximum effect.

"We have got fuck all left, their boys are even selling speed in the fucking Beehive on Brixton Road and they are, by nature, puffers. The West End and Islington are overrun with that smooth-talking ponce's fucking minions and I ain't swallowing no more. We either have a touch or we take it over once and for all."

"Will you fucking calm down?"

"Calm down? You want me to calm down? Who are you, the fucking yoga king of East London? Up yours, Dave. I want this fucking sorted, and I want it sorted soon. Spider and his brother are riding around in fucking flash cars with all sorts of fucking weapons. They are kinging it up like they own the fucking show and we are expected to just fucking tug our forelocks and not say a word? We can't even shift anything in Manchester, Liverpool or fucking Scotland. We have been frozen out, fucked off like recalcitrant school boys and all you can say is *calm down*? Are you stuck up Brodie's arse or what?"

Dave didn't answer, it was pointless, but he was digesting the information. He knew that he was going to have to sort this out sooner rather than later, because his brothers were on his case now. Drugs, speed in particular, was big business and they had invested a lot of money into it. The problem was that Pat was not only a good mate but he was also their biggest rival and, short of selling to him personally at a loss, they were in real trouble. Pat wasn't going to pay over the odds for the drugs and who could blame him?

But he was out of order to assume that they wouldn't want a bite of what was a fucking lucrative business. Just because they had not bothered with it in the beginning did not mean they were going to walk away from an earner now the product was in such high demand. If Spider had stuck to his own turf, none of this would have happened. Everyone could have had a bite, and everyone would have been happy.

Dave chose to ignore the fact that Pat Brodie was running the show and that anything outside south London was his domain. He conveniently forgot that Pat had offered them an in many times and they had been too busy chasing the dollar in other areas. He also chose to disregard the warnings that Pat had given him in a very gentle but firm way; they were free to pursue their dealings as long as it didn't encroach on any existing businesses he had already put in place. Basically, he had insinuated that they had missed the boat and it was too late now to start complaining about it.

But, as Dennis had pointed out, if they were dealing out of all the nightclubs and they had a monopoly, then a talk was definitely in order. He was aware that most of the little firms could only deal because they had Pat's permission to do so and that they were only answerable to Spider, who was universally acknowledged as Pat's front man where the Persian Rugs were concerned. This, of course, was the problem where his brothers were concerned.

They were feeling left out, feeling that they were being overlooked, insulted even. The boys were men and, like all up-and-coming young-sters, they were ripe for an excuse to flex their muscles, to make their mark. They were greedy little fuckers, and they were dangerous because of that. The only reason they had been given such a ride over the last couple of years was because of Patrick Brodie, but they were not intel-ligent enough to suss that out and he was not about to mention that fact just yet. Dennis was their spokesman, the only one with the guts to come into his home and air his grievances. The others would follow, he knew, but only when they were assured they would have a friendly reception.

They were conveniently forgetting all the graft they had because of Pat, all the money they were raking in with him on other businesses. The speed was making them greedy; the money to be earned was astro-nomical and naturally they wanted in on it. The groundwork had been done, as it had always been done for them, though they couldn't see that of course. They were heavies, no more and no less, and their egos were bigger than King Kong's cock, but they were adamant they were not going to take "no" for an answer.

Dave *was* starting to see his brother's point of view; that they *were* being treated like second-class citizens and that they would be better off without Brodie.

He was honest enough, at times, to admit to himself that Pat had overtaken him; he saw an opportunity and he went for it, taking Dave and his brothers along with him. It irked Dave at times because he not only wanted to have the respect Brodie commanded; he also wanted to be seen as a vital link in the criminal chain that ruled London.

The fact that people were relaxed enough to tell his brothers that they were not going to deal with them, thank you very much, because they were already being served up by Spider, was another reminder that they were, and always would be, only foot soldiers to Brodie. This was a melon-scratcher all right, and he needed to think about it long and hard before he did anything of any substance. Once something like this was put into words and thereby into the public domain, there was no going back. He needed to seriously consider their options and the best way to approach the problem in hand.

"Let me think about it, all right?"

Dennis nodded imperceptibly. He was halfway home and he knew it; he had given his brother the bullets, now it was up to him to fire them.

Annie was putting the children to bed and, as usual, Lance was playing her up. She pulled him on to her lap and whispered in his ear as she always did. "Once the others drop off, come out to your nana, darling."

This was despite the fact that Pat had made a point of telling her that the children were to go to bed at the same time, and if he did find out that she had been favoring Lance, she was out for good. She and Pat had an uneasy alliance in that she made sure she didn't antagonize him and he made sure she spent as little time with the kids as possible.

"I don't want to sit with you, Nana."

Lance's petulant face was beginning to irritate her and she took a deep breath before saying quietly, "I have a few sweeties for you, and you can watch TV." Her voice was soft and the other children watched the little tableau with interest.

"Come on, darling. Nana has missed you, give me a hug?" The yearning was in her voice and the child picked up on it, knew he had the upper hand, and used it to his advantage.

"No, Nana. I'm tired." Lance pulled away from her, his thickset body almost knocking her off the chair with its strength. He hated the feel of her rough hands on him, the way she pulled him about, kissed him all the time and squeezed him into her body, nearly suffocating him. But he loved the power he had over her, and because of that, he had power over his brother and sisters. His nana adored him and tolerated them, they all knew that. Because it had always been like that none of them questioned it; they were just glad she didn't feel the same way about them.

It was the first time in ages that Annie had babysat. Pat made sure she spent as little time as possible with the kids and she knew she was on borrowed time. Lil was not enamored of her any more either, so she had to sit it out and wait until they were desperate before she got access to the one thing that made her life bearable.

"Kiss your poor old nana and we'll play games; whatever you like."

Lance shook his head and said loudly and with force, "I don't want to, Nana. I don't like you any more."

The hurt in her faded eyes made him feel a moment's sadness, but she made him feel uncomfortable and he had realized, as young as he was, that her feelings for him were not healthy. His mother had no real time for him; he knew that she didn't love him like she did the others. But his nana, who worshipped him, just made him want to hurt her. She smelled awful and she made him feel like he was being suffocated.

The smack was loud in the room and all four children jumped with fright. Lance had a red mark on his face and he stared at Annie with defiance and hatred as she started to berate him.

Pat Junior pushed his sisters from the untidy living room and walked back towards his brother. He grabbed his arm and started to pull him from the room, all the time Annie's screaming and swearing was ringing in their ears.

"You two-faced little fucker, all I've done for you . . ."

It was the usual litany of complaints and both boys closed their ears to it.

Lance watched helplessly as Pat Junior was dragged back into the middle of the room by his hair. All his power was gone now, and he knew it. His nana was off on one of her rants and no one could calm her down. He ran from the room and went up the stairs to his sisters, settling them into their beds and listening to the commotion below him.

Pat Junior felt her nails in his scalp and, turning towards his grandmother, he landed a hefty kick on to her shins, making her let go of him, and also making her curse louder than ever. He was eight years old and he pushed her forcefully and shouted, "I am telling my dad about you."

Annie knew she had gone too far and forced herself to calm down.

She looked at the boy in front of her and, smiling tremulously, she did what she always did. With eyes full of tears and a broken voice she said sadly, "I am so sorry, child, but I miss you all so much, and you are all so horrible to me . . ."

Pat Junior stood there without any expression on his face and after a few seconds he said with quiet dignity, "We are never rude to anyone. My sisters need a drink of hot milk and a story and I am telling my mum that we don't want you looking after us any more."

Annie was in bits at his words. If the kids mentioned what had happened she would be relegated to the wilderness once more and she needed to be around Lance like other people needed water or food.

As Annie tidied the room, she felt the jealousy that ate at her like a cancer once more. The house was large, beautifully decorated and peopled by a family who loved and cared for one another; Patrick and Lance had proved that much this night. Her daughter and her lifestyle was like a thorn in her side. She produced children with ease and kept a man in her bed without even trying. She was everything that Annie Diamond had wanted to be and more. People actually liked Lil, she still had her friends from the factory and she attracted new friends. She was a naturally happy person and, other than Pat's sojourns every now and then, she loved her life. It was all this that made Annie resent her only daughter so much: that *her* child could have made something of her life without even trying, galled. That she was dependent on her daughter for the very bread she ate was something she would never be able to forgive, even though she had been living off her only child since the day she had started work. Sighing heavily, she made the hot milk Pat Junior had requested for his sisters. Then she placed cookies and cake on to a tray and went up to her grandchildren to attempt to repair the damage she had caused earlier.

She smiled when she saw the twins asleep in their brothers' arms, even though the urge to batter Lance was so overwhelming that she had to breathe in deeply to calm herself down. But instinctively she knew it was Patrick Junior who was the dangerous one, the one who she needed on her side, so she concentrated her efforts on him.

Like his father, you couldn't fathom what was going on behind his deep-set blue eyes. And like his father, she knew he was going to become one dangerous fucker in the future; he had the same arrogance, the same blank stare and, uncannily, the same presence that had made his father a man to be wary of. He was still only a lad, but the coldness in his expression was enough to make anyone uneasy if they found it directed at them.

Cain was smiling as Dennis Williams bought him another drink.

They were in the Burford Arms in east London; it was a predominantly black pub, but Dennis was a frequent, if not exactly welcome, visitor. He had a few of the boys around Stratford on his payroll and he paid them out there. Cain was often in there having a drink while he sorted out business and the two men had always had a good rapport until recently. Cain could not say exactly when the dynamics of the relationship between them had changed, but he knew it had now gone too far to attempt any kind of reconciliation. He knew it was over the drugs and he was not about to climb down or give this fucker an inch. This was personal now; it was about territory and making sure no one took what was rightfully yours.

He was secure enough while Dennis was alone; the brothers did give him pause for thought though. But he was relaxed enough knowing that Brodie was behind them. He reasoned that the Williamses had enough going on without pulling Brodie and his businesses into the limelight with public aggravation. Cain had a crew that stayed close and watched over him at all times. The Williamses were not people to take lightly or to overlook; they were dangerous fucks and he knew that he needed to watch his back. He was sorry though, because he had always liked Dave and his family. It was a shame that it was going wrong now, but that was the times they were living in.

Cain knew that Dennis and his younger brothers, Bernie and Tommy, had attempted to muscle in on his operation but he was wise enough to keep that gem of wisdom to himself; once they showed their hand, he would show his. He always had a contingency plan; Brodie had taught him that much.

Chapter Seven

"He walks all over you and you are too stupid to see it."

Lil was pregnant again and this time it was not easy for her. She was constantly sick and her body didn't feel like her own any more. She felt exhausted, couldn't keep anything down and, worst of all, as far as she was concerned, she couldn't even face a cigarette or a cup of tea, which was her usual pregnancy staple diet. She knew her mother was taking advantage of her but she felt so ill with this baby that she didn't have the energy to argue with her. She watched as Annie busied herself, her slim back stiff with indignation, and marveled, as she always did, that one person could hold so much animosity inside without exploding in some way. She was determined never to let anything in life make her as bitter and twisted as Annie Diamond. She couldn't remember a time when she was growing up that her mother had not worn a frown and when she saw her smiling at her grandchildren, especially the twins, it hurt her deeply. She still made Lily feel inadequate, unloved, and she undermined the very structure of the life that the daughter she loathed, provided for her. A better life than she could ever have dreamed of. Lily always treated her mother well, made sure she had a few quid in her pocket and saw to it that her bills were taken care of.

"Out till all hours, whoring, I should imagine. It's a wonder you ain't caught nothing from him, especially in your condition."

"Stop it, Mum. He'll be in any minute and you know he can't stand it when you're here anyway, so don't fucking antagonize him."

The fact that Lily swore at Annie showed just how far they had actually come over the years. Annie had to toe the line if she wanted any kind of access to her daughter or her daughter's family. Even Pat had to admit that the twins had melted Annie's hard heart. They were gorgeous, and Annie, against her will, had fallen in love with them like everyone else. They were little cases and when they ran into Annie's open arms she felt the love that they seemed to have in abundance. Lance would always be her Golden Boy, but the girls were a close second and Lil watched them charm the woman she alternately loved and hated in equal measure.

That she was trying to cause more fights than John Wayne because of Pat's nights on the town was a bone of contention between them. Lil knew that her mother was stirring it, wanted them to fall out because with Pat out of the way she would get a far better stranglehold on her daughter and the children. Pat hated Annie and made no secret of that fact. He would insult her to her face and she would take it, amazingly often, in really good part. In fairness to Patrick, he could be funny, and he was fast with a quip. He slaughtered his mother-in-law with a malicious humor that caused belly laughs to anyone in earshot.

That her mother continued to come around was a constant source of amazement to Lil. Anyone else would have beaten a retreat long ago, but in a strange way she was glad, and she relied on her because she was always exhausted. Annie made her life easier and she was almost lovable at times, if they were not discussing her husband of course. She knew her stepfather was somewhere in the background and she accepted that. As long as he kept away from her she didn't give a damn.

"I'm just saying that you should put your bleeding foot down, love, four kids and he still thinks he's a fucking teenager."

Lil sighed. "Put a sock in it; he is all right. I know he wouldn't do anything to hurt me or the kids so let it go, will you?"

This time her voice had an edge to it and Annie knew that she had gone as far as she could. Lil was still protective over her husband and even in the club and feeling like shit she would only take so much.

"Where is he anyway?"

Annie always wanted to know Pat's movements and Lil rarely obliged her by explaining where he was supposed to be. There was something about Annie that told her daughter not to trust her with any information whatsoever, no matter how innocent that information might be. Even her stepfather had an unhealthy interest in what was going on. She wondered once more why she needed her mother so much when the woman had never given her an ounce of loyalty or care. Annie Diamond had treated her with utter contempt all her life, even as a small child, and yet she still felt the need to be near her. As she watched her mother wipe down the kitchen worktops and rinse out the cloths, she once again questioned her own motives for keeping the woman who had despised her in her life.

The children were playing in the parlor and their voices drifted into the kitchen. She could hear Pat Junior telling the girls to keep quiet so they didn't disturb their mummy and she loved her eldest child for his kindness and his thoughtfulness. Then she heard Lance telling them to piss off and his voice grated on her like scratching on a blackboard. His voice set her teeth on edge and she knew her mother was aware of that and used it against her. There was the same whine in it that her mother had; it was a nasal kind of voice that had no real inflection to it. Just a flat and constant drone that made Lil feel like punching his lights out at times. Especially now, at five months pregnant and feeling seriously under the weather.

She wished that she could take to her younger son, but it had never happened and she knew it was too late now to do anything about it. She pretended a love she didn't feel and this made her so ashamed. She knew it was also partly the reason her mother was still in her life but she could never admit all this out loud; especially not to her husband who doted on the twins and loved his two boys with a passion. Both of them.

"There will be ambulances arriving, Pat, and you know it."

Spider said the words without passion and Patrick knew that what he was saying was true. The situation was becoming unbearable for them all and the atmosphere was starting to make everyone nervous. In some ways he wanted it to go off so they could finally bring it to an end. Resolve it once and for all; it would be a bloody and vengeful affair but at least it would be over. Patrick could hear the want in Spider's voice and knew that he had to sort this out sooner rather than later.

Spider was oozing menace and hatred; he was old school like himself and he was on the verge of total annihilation. Despite himself, Patrick Brodie was also getting caught up in his excitement.

"I am telling you that we can't swallow this any more; if we carve this lot up, what's next? The clubs, the pubs, the fucking cab ranks, what?"

Patrick shrugged. "I'll talk to Dave. He ain't a cunt, he'll understand the seriousness of the situation and sort it out."

Spider rubbed his large hands over his dreadlocks in agitation. "He won't, Pat, he is as bad as them now. He asked me how much I was going to pass on to him not an hour ago, as if it was his fucking birthright or something. Like we were doing them out of a wage. They are in the fucking bar now, acting like they own the fucking place and making snide remarks. This is our boozer, we bought it fair and square. Fuck them, fuck them all. I ain't fucking swallowing this in front of everyone."

Spider was spoiling for a fight and Pat knew he had every right to feel that way but he was also confident that this could all be sorted amicably. He didn't want to take sides but if he did, he knew it would be Spider's, and he had a gut feeling that the Williams brothers knew that too. They owed him; he had paid out for their brother's death and given them a living the likes of which they could only have dreamed of. They were flexing their muscles and he was beginning to feel that a lesson might need to be distributed. If that was the case, he was going to enjoy doling it out himself. They were starting to get on his nerves and that was never a good idea where he was concerned.

They needed to be put in their place, that was all. No one in their right mind seriously expected a drink off work they had not taken any part in either creating or, more to the point, working up from scratch. The Williams brothers were pushing their luck and he knew that, as much as he didn't really want to admit it out loud, Spider had a valid and honest beef with them. Pat also knew it was Spider's hold over the London drug scene that was the bone of contention; the fact was that they had overlooked a fucking serious pile of money because deep down inside they had not wanted to work with the blacks.

No one had ever said any of this out loud, but it was glaringly obvious to him, so he knew that it had to be obvious to Spider as well. Spider was one of the most astute people he had ever come across in his life so he had to have figured that much out from the start.

Dave and his brothers were bully boys, no more and no less. They were basically muscle and, without Pat, they would have been scratching a living debt-collecting or bouncing. An original thought in any of their heads would die of fucking loneliness and they had the nerve to try to cause aggravation when they had their very livelihoods to thank him for in the first place. Spider and himself had made all the connections needed, paid out where necessary and strong-armed anyone who had been averse to their having control over the merchandise that hit the streets. There was no way Pat would carve that up to keep a few bullies in place; it was a ridiculous thing to expect and the Williams brothers had gone down in his estimation because of it.

Without him, and without Spider, they were nothing. He had tried to bring them up in the firm and it had been a fucking waste of time, so if they needed that pointed out to them then he knew it was up to him to do it. Spider and his opinions would not go down well with the Williams boys. He was going to have to sort this out himself.

Lisa Callard was tired and as she pulled on her underwear, she was attempting to stifle a yawn. She had a thin body, boyish almost, and her feather-cut hair gave her the look of a very pretty elf. She had small breasts and a tight behind which made most men give her a second glance. She was on the ball enough to put out only for men who could either give her a few pounds or enhance her reputation, and as Dennis Williams could do both these things for her, she was more than happy to let him have carte blanche over her adolescent body. At a very young age she had understood the power that youth had over men and she had exploited it ever since. Her mother had wasted too much of her youth and looks on the loser who had fathered her and Lisa had decided early on that the pill and opening her legs would gain her what her mother had never had: a few pounds in her purse, a nice car and peace of mind. That she was also seeing Brixton Cain was not on her mind, though she knew it was part of her charm as far as Dennis was concerned.

Dave and Dennis Williams watched Lisa lazily; she was only a kid really, but she was a game girl for all that. Earlier, Dave had walked into the bedroom and sat down quietly on the small white wicker chair his mother had purchased on the Portobello Road and watched his brother finish his usiness. As Lisa pulled on her skirt she said hoarsely, "Am I staying?"

Dennis shook his head, and leaning over the side of the bed picked up his trousers off the floor and took out a small roll of money and gave it to her. Kissing him gently, Lisa grabbed the rest of her clothes and walked from the room. She nearly collided with Doris Williams who had a tray of teas and a plate of cookies.

"You off, love." It was statement, not a question.

Doris placed the tray on the small dressing table noisily and her sons watched her with wary eyes.

She looked at Dave then, and her eyes were like ice. "You got my money?"

Dave sighed. "Leave it out, Mother. You know the score where that cunt is concerned. Tell him to pay his own fucking debts."

The words had a finality about them that anyone else would have picked up on but his mother had no intention of letting this go. "What's a couple of grand to you two?"

She sat on the crumpled bed and, picking up Dennis's pack of cigarettes, she lit one with a slow deliberation that told her sons she was willing to sit this one out for the night. Doris Williams was a fighter, had always been a fighter and would continue to be a fighter. Since her husband's death two years previously, she had gone through a series of men; men her sons saw as either scumbags, or right fucking scumbags, depending. There was no way anyone was going to take their father's place and she understood and respected that, but now she had been given a taste of freedom and she liked it. Her boys were not going to change that fact.

Her new beau was a gambler ten years her junior with long black hair, sad blue eyes and a cock that was so big it could easily get its own postal code. She had put in her time with her old man and now she was having a bit of fun. Even though her sons knew the life she had led with their father, they still thought she was too old and too stupid to know her own mind.

"Don't fucking start lecturing me either, I ain't in the mood. I want the poke; it was me as well as him having a flutter and, let's face it, you lot fucking owe me."

There was truth in that statement. She always spoke in statements somehow, she was a very dramatic woman, much taken to brightly colored clothes and too tight skirts. In their hearts they knew the truth of it, but she was still their mum when all was said and done, and she was an embarrassment.

"I just want me due, that's all."

Dennis was covered by the blanket but now he wanted to get up and go to the toilet and his mother sitting on the bed was making that impossible.

"I know everything about you lot and you better remember that, boys. I stood between you and your old man when he was giving you a hiding and took the brunt of it meself. I have provided an alibi for every one of you at some time or another, as I am sure I will in the future, and now I am asking you lot to let me have a bit of life."

In the harsh light of the naked bulb, Dave could make out the scars around his mother's mouth from his father's fists, the lines around her eyes that they had all helped put there over the years and the thick eye make-up that she had taken to wearing because her husband would have scrubbed it off with a Brillo pad had he still been alive. She was in her second childhood and, in fairness to her, she deserved a bit of excitement. She had been chained to this house all her married life; his father had been a hard man who had been quick with his fists and even quicker with a leather belt. But she was going through money like it was water and they were not actually as well-heeled as everyone seemed to think. They lived well and spent well and even though they earned a decent amount, the money was going out as fast as it was coming in.

Dave had also made a lot of bad business decisions over the last year and he had lost a small fortune on dope deals that had not come to fruition. The trouble with the weed was that the money was always paid out upfront and if the merchandise was intercepted before it arrived at the correct destination, everyone lost their initial investment. The police had been waiting at the last three drops, two at airfields and one on the Thames estuary. It had been no one's fault, even though that fucking Spider and his brother seemed to produce cannabis out of thin air and his brothers had questioned why they never had a fucking arrest of any kind. In his heart he knew that the underlying accusations were not only unfair, but complete rubbish.

Spider had sewn it all up a long time before they had decided to try to get an in themselves. Spider's stuff came straight out of the docks and it was good dope; the stuff they managed to procure was low-grade and had more seeds in it than a packet of Trill. The reality was that they had been ripped off, not once but many times, and without going to Patrick Brodie and asking him to step in and sort it out, there was not a lot they could do about it.

The realization that they were only regarded as part of his workforce bothered them more than any of them cared to admit. It seemed that the truth did indeed hurt, and Spider's growing place in Patrick's heart had not only been observed, but acknowledged, by all the powers that be.

Basically, they had been shown up for the motley crew they actually were and without any real money to spread around they were in danger of going broke.

Dave had lost over two hundred grand in the last ten months, and his brothers had lost a similar amount between them as well. It was a lot of money. Money they didn't have any more and money they were not in a position to replace any time in the near future. They were all broke and they were starting to panic; they owed money all over London and they knew it was only a matter of time before the creditors started whispering to Patrick.

Bank robbery was on the cards; it was the only earner left to them. The problem with that though, was that they would need to run it by Patrick first and give him a taste of whatever they managed to get.

"You'll get your money, Mum, but fucking go easy on it this time, OK?"

Doris nodded, pleased the conversation was over.

"Bacon sandwich, anyone?"

*   *   *

"Here, Annie, I got you a part-time job, love, haunting fucking houses!"

Pat Junior and Lance laughed out loud; their laughter tinged with shock, as always, that their father dared to talk to their granny like that. The girls, happily ensconced in their father's arms, were laughing because everyone else was laughing.

Annie carried on smiling her martyr smile as her son-inlaw bellowed, "Get off your cross, woman, we need the fucking wood!"

Lil smiled too and Pat looked at her for long seconds before saying seriously, "You all right, girl, need the quack?"

Lil shook her head and Pat looked into her eyes. He worshipped her and lately the thought of her going through another pregnancy worried him. She wasn't right this time and she looked dreadful; even her lovely thick hair looked lank and her face was drawn.

"I'm OK. Fancy a cuppa?"

Pat looked at the boys as he shouted irreverently, "Let Attila the fucking Hun make it!"

Pat sat beside Lil and pulled her into his arms. "You look whacked-out, girl."

"I am a bit. Look at your gorgeous daughters."

Lil always changed the subject if it was about the way she looked or felt; she continued to collect certain rents for her husband and did the prison visits when they were needed. She didn't want him to see her as weak, even though that was how she felt lately. She wanted him to trust her and rely on her. Lily knew almost as much about the businesses as he did, and although he was only trying to save her energy by giving her a break, she wasn't happy about it.

"My pair of beauties." Pat grinned once more. He was ageing fast but she still felt the pull of him when he looked at her full-on. She grinned too, her perfect white teeth at odds with her white face.

"The girls look at you with such love, Pat."

He opened his arms in a gesture of understanding. "All women look at me like that."

This was said arrogantly and, too late, he saw the way she was staring at him. He saw the fear and the loneliness inside her, the sadness his silly words had caused, and he cursed women and their bloody moods.

"I was only joking, darling."

But the moment was gone again. This was happening a lot lately and it was starting to get on his nerves; he had enough on his mind without her looking for petty rows as well.

"Why do you wind yourself up, Lil? It was a joke, that's all. Look at the kids' faces."

Lil could see the exasperation in his eyes and the children watching their parents with worried expressions, and she saw then that they picked up on everything around them and it wasn't healthy. She knew it was her, her feeling so rough, her worry that Pat was going to either get arrested or go off with a newer model. The latter was the biggest fear of all; there was an old saying about how if a wandering old man got his collar felt, at least you knew where they were. She now knew how true that was.

"Go and play upstairs, kids. Mummy's feeling a bit tired."

Pat Junior and Lance picked up a sister each and left the warmth of the room without question. Annie, Lil knew, had her ears on red alert as she listened to everything that was being said between them.

"I'm sorry, Pat. I just feel so rough all the time . . ."

He cuddled her into him again and she could smell cigarettes and the lingering aroma of cheap perfume.

"You've got to stop this, Lil. You are me girl, always will be. You're the mother of me children for fuck's sake." His voice was earnest and she wished with all her heart that she could believe him, but she knew him better than he knew himself. She forced a smile as she answered him.

"I look like a bloody cow. Don't take no notice, it's just me hormones talking."

"More like your fucking mother talking." Pat pulled her face up to his and kissed her on the lips.

"You're my wife and you're the world to me. I am out collaring every day to provide for you all, OK?"

Lil nodded again and he felt the strength of his love for her. Why couldn't she believe that even at her heaviest, with her belly hanging down to her knees, she could never look more beautiful to him than when she was carrying his children. Fuck knows, he had made enough of them with her. Now he had the unenviable task of telling her he was going out again tonight.

That little gem was going to go down like a two-ton tart in the back of a Mini.

Cain and Spider were stoned and as the night drew in, they settled down to watch some TV while they waited for people to collect their dope. They doled out anything over 2.2 lb themselves. It didn't matter whether it was pot or speed; they wanted to see who was new to the game and find out their connections. It was a point of honor now that the Williams brothers didn't score from them by any means. They had a good rapport with the people they sold to, and any new faces brought in had to be referenced by at least two of their trusted dealers. Especially if they were white.

Skinheads were smoking grass like there was no tomorrow and so were the middle-class white boys. It was becoming the drug of choice for a whole generation. Together with the new seventies music scene and the opening up of so many clubs all over London and the Home Counties, speed was also an earner. Pills were still going strong, but the preference was for the white powder.

Nineteen seventy-six was the year of the snort with punks desperate to stay up all night, the rude boys wanting the blues that lasted for days on end and the casuals with their Depeche Mode and asymmetric haircuts. Selling speed was like printing money and that was why they changed flops every few months; no reason to ask for trouble. By five in the morning they would have about eighty grand in the room with them and that was a temptation to anyone, let alone the people they dealt with on a daily basis.

This flop was new and they had made a point of making it habitable. Hence the TV and the comfortable sofa. It was a large property in Clapham and it was rented out by the room. The place stank of goat meat and sweat and there were people in and out at all hours of the day and night which was a bonus as far as they were concerned. It was owned through a holding company that had its annual general meeting in Jamaica. By the time the tax man finally worked out who actually owned the place they would be retired and living in Montego Bay.

All in all, it was a good flop and it was also worth a few pennies from the rents. It was full of black men and white girls, it always had music blaring and, in that respect, it was no different to any other house in the street.

They felt safe there and so they only had two guns with them, both ex-army-issue pistols. One was a thirty-eight and the other was a forty-five, which was enough firepower to do real damage, yet small enough to tuck into a waistband and hide from prying eyes. But they weren't too bothered about security, in fact they were overconfident. Outside, in a Ford Zodiac, sat three Rastas who had not yet embraced the beautiful meaning of their religion. They would shoot their own mothers if they tried to rip any of them off.

They had also clocked Dennis Williams and his little crew when they had driven by not ten minutes before. Dennis had looked them over as if they were so much shit on his shoes and the Rastas had taken it; give the boys a false sense of security, that was their motto. Anyone who listened to music that had words like Ballroom Blitz in it deserved all they got. The Rastas had guns and machetes and they were ready for anything the white boys had to offer them. In fact, they were looking forward to a real fight; it would sort out the men from the white boys once and for all.

Dennis was rocking. He had been drinking steadily all day and he was up for a fight. The Rastas in the car earlier had really given him the taste for a violent confrontation; it was only his baby brother, Ricky, driving them to the pub, that had stopped anything from occurring.

"Calm down, for fuck's sake."

Ricky was a little hard nut, not as big as his brothers, but he had a quick wit and an even quicker temper. But he was also sensible enough to know that Dave would have their balls for breakfast if anything happened without his express say-so or knowledge. Dave was still sucking Brodie's cock and as much as that annoyed him, Dave was still the driving force of the family and Ricky respected that.

He knew that Dave was trying to stop this going off. But even he was beginning to see why the others were getting the serious ache. The blacks were fucking all over the place and, no matter how much the Williams boys were told they had missed their chance, it was fucking out of order that they were practically paupers in the grand scheme of things.

Ricky had just gotten his latest girl pregnant and he needed some money to pay for the new arrival. It was therefore a matter of grave importance to him that he was broker than a striking miner. By the time he pulled up outside the Beckton club they ran, Ricky was already spoiling for the fight he had prevented.

It took him, Bernie and Dave five minutes to get Dennis inside, on account of the fact that there were three girls outside with schoolie written all over them, wearing skirts shorter than a traffic warden's attention span.

"Come on darlings, show us your tits."

The girls were scandalized and thrilled at the same time but they were also relieved when the other men finally dragged Dennis into the pub.

The brothers made their way to the back room, acknowledging people as they went. Dave looked around him as he half-carried, half-dragged Dennis to safety. The place was packed as always, and most of the clientele were mates or associates. He knew that not much money would go over the bar; they had made a big fuck up on the Grand Opening night when they had let people have a drink on the house. It was expected now, they could never ask for payment and they were finding it hard to make ends meet. Even robbing the Cash and Carry was out of the question because they were supposed to be above all that petty fucking shit.

He only hoped that his meeting with Patrick later on in the evening would bring about a solution to their problems. They had spunked money up the wall left, right and centre and now there was hardly any left. They worked for Patrick Brodie and no matter how much his brothers tried to talk him into retaliation, Dave had to remember that Patrick Brodie was a bad man to fuck with. Maybe he should come clean, tell him the truth of their situation; it was no shame to lose your money where the grass was concerned. Lily Law were always in the running to get to it first and it was a chance everyone took: you paid out knowing you would either make a real profit on your investment or lose the fucking lot. This was not, after all, legitimate business. Still, they had lost more than most and it was embarrassing to have to go to the man they depended on for their daily bread and admit that they had fucked up so phenomenally. Like Spider and his cronies, Pat was coining it in; they were like the Keystone Cops in comparison, and it was this that was causing all the bad feeling.

They were amateurs and any kudos they possessed was because Patrick Brodie was their boss. It had been a harsh lesson for them and, as usual, he now had to try to sort it all out without any help from his brothers whatsoever.

Dennis was sitting slumped in the chair by the doorway, Bernie next to him, and little Ricky had brought them all drinks from the bar. As they sat and chatted, Dennis finally sobered up enough to make relative sense; he was still off his face but the pills he had been given by Ricky seemed to be doing the job. He was now speeding out of his nut, the blue ones he had taken were making him dry-mouthed and paranoid, not a good idea for Dennis at any time. He was a violent man by nature, and with alcohol and narcotics in his system, he was not easily controllable.

As they waited for the others to arrive, Dennis heard the loud voice of their cousin, Vincent Williams. Vince and Dennis had been rivals since boys; of a similar build and with strikingly similar looks, they had been natural antagonists.

Now Vince was buying into the pill business with Brodie and Spider, the relationship had soured even more. Dennis saw him as a traitor. He couldn't see that it suited Vince to make a few quid with guaranteed protection, he just saw his cousin raking it in and, worse than that, spending it wisely. There was a family joke that Vince was so tight even the Queen came to the opening of his wallet, but that was not really the case. Vince wasn't tight, he was simply a shrewdie. He didn't countenance hangers-on and he saw no reason to spend money unless it was to make more money. Dave and the others loved him but Dennis had always had a problem with him and the feeling was, unfortunately, mutual.

If it came to an out-and-out tumble, everyone's money was on Vince. Vince drank moderately and resisted drugs. He had two lovely kids, a wife with an arse to die for and a nice mock-Tudor house in Essex. Vince had made his fortune on the horses; as a professional gambler he had books all over the place and he offered a point or two more than the legal bookies. He had a big clientele who had money they wanted to spend without too many questions asked about where it had come from.

Vince also paid for his drinks, never expecting anything for nothing, even from his family. He was hailing everyone with his usual camaraderie when Dennis shot out of the back room and attacked him with a length of metal pipe he always carried with him, for what he jokingly called emergencies.

As Vince went down, Dave and Ricky grabbed Dennis and dragged him off. The place was suddenly quiet and Dave looked around at the faces of his regulars: hustlers and hangers-on, all drinking for free and waiting with bated breath and eyes alight with excitement for the cabaret to start. There wasn't one real mate in the whole place and even his brother didn't have enough loyalty to wish one of his own well or toast their success and good fortune.

Dave had learned nothing from his years with Patrick Brodie but it was as if someone had turned a light on in his brain. He was suddenly seeing himself and what he had achieved with a stunning clarity that was as enlightening as it was terrifying. A room full of no-necks and empty pockets did not augur well for his peace of mind or his brothers' safety. The tatty furnishings, the over-the-hill barmaids and the fug of cigarette smoke showed him the reality of what he had allowed to happen to what had once been a promising young life.

Vince was kneeling up on one knee, his head was bleeding profusely and his arm was groping about for the bar so he could hoist himself upright. He was obviously concussed and Dave felt the anger rising up inside him. He picked up the metal pipe from the floor where Dennis had dropped it and laid into his brother with all the strength he possessed. No one attempted to stop him, not even Ricky, and that spoke volumes as far as Dave was concerned.

Chapter Eight

"You nearly killed your own brother." Dave was still covered in his brother's blood and as he listened to Patrick's shocked voice, he could smell his own sweat and vomit; it made him start to heave. Patrick stepped away from him quickly, expecting him to spew up again at any moment.

Patrick looked at the man before him and despaired of what he had been reduced to. In the years he had known Dave, he had watched as the promise he had seen in the beginning had been proved to be nothing more than youthful ambition. He had not cut it in the real world and though it had never been said out loud, it had been there between them for a long time.

He had had a lot of time for Dave and he cared about him, but he had passed him over many times because he had not had any faith left in him. Patrick had tried to help him, tried to give him advice, but it was like talking to a brick wall. With Dave, all the lights were on but no one actually seemed to live there a lot of the time. He didn't have the staying power you needed to keep shady businesses afloat. He was a risktaker by nature, like them all. Dave would be better off as a con man; a quick scam, a good payout.

"You all right, son?" Patrick's voice was sad and he was sorry that it had come to this.

He was also relieved that the struggle between the Williams brothers and Spider's graft had not had to be resolved by him. He liked this boy and he liked his brothers; they were useful if not indispensable. They had a history together and that meant a lot to him. He knew it was

Dennis who was the driving force for most of the aggravation the family encountered and he also knew that Vince Williams, being a decent bloke, would not exact any kind of retribution. At least, he wouldn't once Pat had talked to him. This was an unfortunate turn of events and the best way to deal with it was to settle it sooner rather than later. This meet they were supposed to have had with Dave was not exactly what he had had in mind, but if it kept a turf war at bay then it could only be a good thing.

Cain and Spider were laughing as James McMullen, a large Jamaican with a permanent smile and an erratic dress sense, filled them in on what had happened to Dennis Williams.

James was feeling the buzz of the grass acutely and was in the process of building another joint of Olympian standards. The men fell quiet as the enormity of what had happened sank in.

Cain shook his head sadly, wondering what had caused the Williams family to implode so violently. "Poor old Vince, he is a really nice bloke. A really trustworthy geezer; what was that fucking Dennis thinking about?"

Spider shrugged. "Fucking scum, the lot of them. They think they're better than everyone else. That Dennis would take out his mother if he thought a few pennies would come his way. They are sixpenny killers, they ain't in the real world. Cheap and fucking nasty, the whole lot of them. No loyalty, no fucking respect for themselves or anyone around them."

Cain nodded at the truth of his brother's statement. "Imagine going for your own family though, your own flesh and blood."

James licked the big bamboo papers he had rolled so expertly and said, matter-of-factly, "Jealousy, man. Plain and simple jealousy. Vince is still in the game, big time, has made a few quid and continues to make a few quid. That lot owe money everywhere and the fact they are under Brodie's umbrella is the only reason they ain't been forced to cough it up yet. Debts are mounting; I heard they can't get any more credit from the fucking Cash and Carry, let alone anywhere else."

Cain digested this bit of logic. "Dave should have finished him off.

Dennis won't let this go, he ain't got the fucking brains of a lab rat. Dave would be well advised to watch his back."

"Where does that leave us though?" Spider asked. "They want what we got and they will still be wanting it. It might take them a while to regroup, get back on track but, mind my words, they will still need money. I think we should go in and finish them off, once and for all."

James nodded in agreement but Cain wasn't so sure. He honestly believed that this was a classic case of feuding and that the Williams brothers would be too busy infighting in the future to do anything else and he said as much.

"I don't know. They will be taking sides even as we are talking about it; Vince will want redress at some point, he ain't a cunt. He must know that if he lets this go, he will lose respect. Dave will be fighting to keep his position as head of the family because who's gonna trust him now? It's over for them, finished."

James and Spider grinned at each other at the naivety of youth.

"Listen, boy, when something like this happens you can only do one thing in their position. And that is to bounce back bigger and better than before. It's like when the police get caught taking money; the others feel it as badly as their mates so they posse up and go out and feel everyone's collars, whether they be guilty or not, to make the public respect them once more. We all the same, we need to overcome fuck-ups by making a show of strength. We haven't seen the last of those fuckers, especially that Dennis. He is a hot-headed prick looking for something he ain't got the fucking brains to see if it was lying in the gutter and whistling at him."

Spider laughed at James's words. "Wisdom like that is something you gather with age, Cain. You can't buy it, no more than the Williams brothers can buy business sense or outside friendship. James be right, it's not a matter of when they will be back, it's more a matter of how. They are going to have to do something pretty spectacular to get the attention of everyone; they will need to be a talking point to regain their respect and, worst of all for us, it will entail stealing someone's livelihood. So you watch your back, they still want what we got and we still got to protect our assets."

James nodded sagely, his big, powerful body moving gracefully with the grass he had smoked. He was mellowing out by the second, but he was still capable of keeping his reputation intact, no matter how much dope he smoked. He was a big man who was stronger than the average, both mentally and physically. He was a strategist by nature and a womanizer through choice. He was about as dangerous as any one person could be.

He pointed a large and calloused finger at Cain; he tried to teach the boy about their way of life at every opportunity. "They be more dangerous to us now than ever before. Now they got to prove something to themselves as well as everyone else. You watch your back and you up your personal security, they be coming for us *all*, Brodie included. And they be coming sooner rather than later."

Dennis was in agony. As he lay in the hospital bed he wondered at a brother who could have committed such a barbaric act against one of his own. The fact that he had attacked his cousin, a man who had stood by them in the past and lent them money on a regular basis, meant nothing to him. Dennis had always made a point of adjusting his morals to suit himself.

As he lay there, he could only think about how other people would react to what had happened, what other people would think of him, and the damage that had been done to his reputation.

That it should be a talking point, something to joke about, was driving him nearly insane. He would be discussed like a fool; he had done enough man talking to know exactly what the reception to his troubles would be in the pubs and clubs he frequented. He would be laughed at, stupid jokes would be made up at his expense and no matter how hard or how fast he sprang back, it would always be out there in the public domain. Whispered about, maybe, but still ingrained into the folklore of their world. It would have been bad enough to be trounced by a stranger, or someone he had a genuine fucking beef with, but to be humiliated by his own brother? The one person in the world he would have trusted above all others?

This was tantamount to mutiny as far as he was concerned and Dave would be made to pay for that: made to pay for his public humiliation and his loss of face. He was not going to rest until Dave had paid out for every fucking slight, real or imagined, that came his way over this debacle.

Dennis had already requested a mirror and as he looked at his badly swollen and stitched face and head, the anger once more overwhelmed him. Dave, his older brother, the person he looked up to and admired, had beaten him to within an inch of his life and he was not going to let that go.

And the fact that no one had been in to see him was also something to be addressed in the near future. His mother, the fucking poncing cunt she was, had obviously decided to take the side of who she thought was the victor. His brothers could fuck off as well, they should have been by his side, making sure that it never happened. Well, his memory was long and his temper was short, and he would pay them back with such fucking force they would think Hitler had been reincarnated and was back among them all, bombing the East End once again. Only this time, south London was going to get a turn.

Dennis knew how to play the long game and that is exactly what he was going to do. He was going to make a comeback that would shame Henry Cooper; he was going to bide his time and then, when it was all quiet and everyone thought it had blown over, he would strike with all the force he could muster.

He could hear his own breathing now; it was labored and wheezy. He was seriously ill and, for the first time in his life, Dennis felt vulnerable and tearful, even frightened. It was an emotional time and something he would never care to repeat. Or ever forgive.

Patrick sat on the bed and watched Lil as she slept. She looked so young and so tired, even in her deep sleep, that he felt the urge to wake her and reassure her that everything was going to be OK.

He looked around the room; it was spotless. Even the bed was relatively tidy because Lil very rarely moved once she had crashed out. He tiptoed from the room and snuck downstairs to the kitchen. As he waited for the kettle to boil, he pondered on the recent events.

The Williams brothers had caused a shifting in position for all the main players on their very limited stage. They were never going to be taken seriously again; in fact they were more or less liabilities. Their debts alone put them at the bottom of the scale as far as the customers they dealt with were concerned, and he would have to reassess the part they played in his organization. It was a difficult situation and he didn't relish having to sort it out, but in a way he was relieved, because he was going to have to push them out eventually anyway. They were not cost-effective any more and their useless grasp of any outside business was making them a laughing stock.

In his heart of hearts he knew that he should have given them a few crumbs from the drug dealing; Spider would have accepted it. But in all honesty, they were already getting on his nerves by that point. It wasn't Dave so much; he was a good guy. It was Dennis and the younger ones; they believed that they were the dog's gonads and they were anything but. They were thugs, common or garden thugs, the same kind you could see in any local pub around London.

They were fucking local heroes who would only be remembered because they could fight. Maybe they would get a sentence to add a bit of excitement to their reps, then spend the rest of their lives talking about the men they had mingled with while in prison. He had known this for a long time, and now he had the proof of it.

Patrick sipped at his tea, liberally laced with brandy, and sighing, he lit himself a Dunhill cigarette. The radio was on low and he could hear the strains of the Eagles and "Hotel California."

He glanced around the brand-new kitchen and felt his usual sense of pride in the home he had created with his Lil. It had everything that a woman could want; every labor-saving device on the market and the freezer and fridge were always laden with food. Like Lil, he needed to be surrounded with luxuries; too much food was preferable to not enough, something they had both experienced while growing up. His children had fresh fruit and veg on tap, they had juices and sweets; they wanted for nothing. They were good kids and he was proud of them.

As Patrick poured himself out another cup of tea, the kitchen door opened and he turned to see his eldest son standing there in his paja-

mas, his hair tousled and his tired eyes bright with pleasure at seeing his
father.

Patrick smiled at the boy. Getting up, he fetched another cup and as
Pat Junior went to get the cookies, they both pondered on how many
times they had done this before. Pat Junior lay on red alert at night, his
ears tuned for the sounds of his father's presence in the house. He was
up within seconds of hearing him come in.

When they sat down together, it was with a congenial atmosphere;
they were very alike and they both enjoyed the other's company. As always, Patrick waited for his son to sip at his tea, scoff a few cookies and
then start off the conversation.

It was a ritual now, their special time together, and they both knew it
was a memory they would keep all their lives.

"How's it going, son?"

Pat Junior shrugged. "You know, Dad, the usual."

As he said that, he pulled a paper bag from inside his pajama top. "It's
all there, Dad. I can go back next week as well if you want."

He was deadly earnest and his handsome, boyish face was alight with
expectation. A part of Patrick was proud of his son; the little jobs he gave
him were worthless in many respects but he knew the boy liked earning
his own few pounds. Another part of him was sorry that he had taken
to it so well. What he did was drop off a few bets at a friendly bookies;
they were bets that were not worth much money, but Patrick took them
personally because the men he dealt with were old and trusted mates.
They still expected his personal touch, even though he was a busy man,
but as most of them had helped his rise in one way or another, he gave
them the respect they saw as their due. It had been a bonus that the
bookie Patrick owned was within walking distance of his son's school
and he liked the way the boy had kept it secret from everyone. He had
the Brodie genes all right.

Patrick smiled, a smile that crinkled up his face and was a rare sight
outside of this house. "All there is it, son? You didn't have a dip?"

Pat Junior looked scandalized and was suddenly flustered as he said,
with total honesty, "I wouldn't, Dad, never . . ."

Patrick grinned again. "I was winding you up, son, don't take things so seriously."

He ruffled the boy's hair and pushed the cookie tin towards him once more. Taking out a chocolate cookie, Pat Junior dipped it in his tea.

"How's everything here?"

"The usual, Dad. Mum is very tired lately and the twins are hard work. But me and Lance do what we can. Nanny Annie is a pain in the you know where, but Mum can sort her out. I make sure the rubbish is put out and any errands are done."

This was all said with a matter of factness that made Patrick want to laugh, but he didn't because he knew his boy had a lot of dignity.

"What about school?"

Pat Junior was less forthcoming about that, as his father knew would be the case.

"No more fighting?"

"I wasn't fighting for me, was I? It was Lance I was defending. For all his bulk he can't really have a row and yet he talks a good fight, as you know."

Indignation was threaded through the words and, once more, Patrick was reminded of his son's total honesty.

Lance was a risktaker. He was a nice enough lad, but he had the weakness of the Brodie grandparents running through him like a stick of Southend rock.

"Did you talk with your brother about it?"

Pat Junior nodded. "Course I did, but he don't listen, does he? But he don't mean it, Dad, he just doesn't know when to shut up. I ironed them out anyway, they won't be going near him now."

Patrick looked at his little son and felt an urge to hug him close but he didn't; he knew the boy was trying to be a man and he knew that he had to treat him as such. It was a hard road to manhood and he wanted his boys to be well able for it when it finally arrived. Lance was going to need his older brother because he didn't have the cunning this little lad had in abundance. Pat Junior was his father's son and Patrick knew he had a worthy successor for his business.

"You been to Mass this week?"

"I am serving as an altar boy, Dad. I ain't had much choice."

Their quiet laughter was broken by a scream that was as terrifying as it was loud and they both sprang from their seats and ran upstairs. Kathleen was hysterical and her mother was trying to calm her down. Eileen was sitting up in bed wide-eyed and white-faced. Lance was at the doorway surveying the scene with his usual lack of interest.

"What the fuck is wrong with her, Lil?"

Lil was cuddling the crying child to her and shook her head.

"What did you see, Lance? You were first on the scene, so to speak."

Lance shrugged nonchalantly. "She was dreaming, I think."

Lance walked towards Kathleen but she shrank away from him. "Go away."

Kathleen slipped from her mother's arms and climbed into her sister's bed. Eileen automatically made room for her and the boys looked at each other and shrugged. This was not an unusual occurrence for the girls; they often slept in each other's arms, even though they went to bed separately. Everyone put it down to them being twins; they even talked to one another in their own language.

Calmer now, the girls snuggled down to sleep, although Kathleen still had the wary eyes of a frightened animal. The twins' hair was now all tight curls and a bronze color that enhanced the deep grey of their eyes. They had Patrick's mother's eyes but, unlike hers, the twins' eyes held only love and innocence. His mother had the hard eyes of a woman who had known too many men and lost too many dreams.

Now the drama was averted, Patrick kissed his daughters and led his sons back to their bedrooms. He could hear Lil talking to the girls, reassuring them, and he smiled once more. This house was better than a theatre; there was always a drama of some sort or another. Four kids guaranteed that much but, all in all, they were good kids and he was inordinately proud of them.

He winked at Pat Junior as he tucked him into his bed. Pat Junior's bedroom was messy; it had *Boy's Own* annuals and Airfix kits everywhere. A real boy's room, it was cluttered and smelled of football boots, Germolene ointment and potato chips. It had wallpaper that was covered in pictures of WW2 planes and tanks. Patrick loved this room; it was filled with everything he had never had as a child and he felt at the pinnacle of his success just breathing in the aroma.

He walked into Lance's room. Lance's fastidious ways made him smile. Unlike Pat's room, it was all neatly folded clothes and horror comics. Lance loved the occult and anything to do with vampires. His walls were covered with posters from Hammer Horror films: women with copious amounts of bosom on display being attacked by vampires or werewolves; Vincent Price grinned down from alongside Peter Cushing and Lon Chaney Jnr. The room smelled of Parma Violets and Bazooka Joe bubble gum. Lance had also had a fine collection of porn that his mother had found and confiscated. It was odd, but if it had been Pat Junior with the copies of *Penthouse*, he wouldn't have been so bothered but there was something wrong with Lance having it and he didn't know why. Kissing Lance's tousled hair, he closed the door quietly and went to the bedroom he shared with his wife.

Lil was already back in bed, her long hair spread across the pillows and her white breasts straining against her nightdress. She looked good enough to eat and Patrick fought down the urge to take her there and then. He knew she was not on top form and he was sorry for that in more ways than one.

As he lay beside Lil, he snuggled into her and she laughed at the erection pushing against her thigh.

"You are like those batteries they advertise on the telly. Everreadies!"

"You know me, girl. Shag a fence I would!"

Patrick grinned and grabbed at her playfully. Lil pushed him away, good-naturedly but firmly.

"I'm sorry, Patrick. I am just about cream crackered."

He yawned and kissed her gently. She knew he had a hard-on that was so rock-solid it could stop a speeding bus, but the fact that he didn't push it made her love him even more. She was bone-weary and hadn't been sleeping because she was worried about where he was. Now he was beside her and she could settle down and drift away in peace. If only men understood how vulnerable women felt when they were heavily pregnant, especially when it wasn't the blooming and exciting kind of pregnancy the first few had been. This one was bad enough to make sure this child would be the last. She had no intention of going through all this again.

"Night, darlin'. Sleep well."

Lil smiled in the darkness at his soft words; now that he was beside her, that was exactly what she was going to do.

Pat was thinking about a little redhead who had been giving him the come-on for a while now. He needed to slake his urge and she was just the girl to do it.

"Babe, I might be late again tomorrow night, OK?"

Lil was half-asleep. "What about the party, I thought we would start sorting that out?"

Patrick tutted at her and Lil realized she had annoyed him with her domestic chat. But it was her son's tenth birthday and she wanted it marked properly.

"Who are you fucking tutting at?"

She was wide awake now and Patrick could have kicked himself. He felt guilty enough as it was because he was already planning what he was going to do to the redhead.

"I wasn't tutting. I'm tired, that's all." He was trying to sound hurt to stop any kind of argument because now he really was dog-tired and his Lil could row for England when the fancy took her.

"I want you to help me make the boy's day a bit special, Pat. If that's too much for you, then you let me know and, as per usual, I will do it on me own." She was steaming now; she knew that he was wrong-footed and she was making the most of it. The sleep had left her faster than a bank robber in Barclays Bank.

"Look, Lil, for fuck's sake . . ."

She punched him none too gently in the shoulder. "No, *you* look, Patrick. I spend my days here with the kids while you swan around being the big fucking I am. And I want your eldest son's tenth birthday to be something to remember all his life. I never had one party, not fucking one, and you were all for it until tonight. Well, fuck you. If you have more important things to do, then do them."

She lay back down. Her breathing was heavy and his conscience was even heavier. He was wide awake now and she knew it.

"Please, Lil. I was just tired, that's all. You can do what you like for the boy; you know I'm useless at all that party stuff . . ."

Lil leaned up on her elbow and he could see her in the dim light from the lamppost outside their window. She was stunning in her anger; when she defended her kids she was like an Amazon to him. But at this moment in time she was being a pain in the fucking ring. He forced a smile as he said, with as much aplomb as he could muster, "You know the shit I have had to deal with this week . . ."

She turned away from him and sighed heavily; a calculated sigh that she knew would make him feel guiltier than ever. She knew what he was up to when he wasn't with her and tonight she didn't even care about that any more. If someone else was giving him his due, then good luck to them. At this moment in time all she wanted was a good night's sleep and for her son's party to go off with a bang. Anything else was not on her radar. He was beneath her notice but she was not going to let him off without a fight.

"Fuck you. Do you know what my life is like, Pat? Backache, a weak bladder and four kids who can't fucking sleep through the night without a bastard drama. On top of that, I have a husband who stays out all night on a regular basis and I am expected to believe that it's work even though I worked the clubs with him and I know the score better than he does. I just asked you a perfectly simple question, that is all. I wanted to know about *our* son's birthday, but I forgot that we ain't interesting enough for you any more, are we? Oh no, you are more interested in what you get up to, night after fucking night, while I stagnate here like a fucking pet monkey!"

Patrick would not have even attempted to interrupt or argue with her until she brought up about the clubs and now he was as angry as she was. Guilt was eating at him and he was determined to throw her off the scent. Attack was the best form of defense; his old man had proved the truth of that one.

"What are you trying to insinuate, Lil? That I am dipping my wick elsewhere?" It was the wrong thing to say and he knew it even as he was saying it.

She was out of the bed with the lamp on quicker than a pimp in a power cut.

"You said that, not me. What's the matter, your conscience playing you up, is it? I am here day in and day out with four kids and another one cooking inside me and you are like a fucking single bloke. You waltz in and out of your children's lives like a fucking ghost. All I ask is that you be here for one bastard night to sort out your son's birthday and you act like I am trying to pin you down for a court date. Well, *fuck you*, I will do it meself, as I do everything by meself lately."

In the lamplight she looked demonic and Patrick was sorry that the night had deteriorated into this. But he was also wondering if this was a good opportunity to go on the trot and hunt down his redhead. Lil was getting him going again; her anger made him want her all the more. He knew she had every right to confront him. He had been out a lot lately and he could have come home except he had been enjoying himself, but he had been sorting out a lot of aggravation too. Her condition made her cranky for the slightest reason and, not for the first time, he was going to exploit that. Looking at her now though, like a woman demented, he saw his chance. Climbing out of bed, Patrick started to get himself dressed. He was all subdued anger and righteous dignity. Every action was exaggerated and overdone.

It was an act and they both knew it. Patrick was wide awake and he had an itch that had to be scratched and his wife had just given him the perfect excuse to leave the house and get it scratched thoroughly by a little redhead with a pretty mouth.

"What do you think you are doing?"

It was a question she knew he had no intention of answering with any kind of truthfulness.

He sneered at her instead.

"What does it look like, Lil? You're the expert, you tell me."

He pulled on his socks and, slipping his feet into his shoes, he carried on in the same sarcastic tone.

"I am going back out because it is obvious to me that you ain't going to let me sleep tonight so I might as well be out on the fucking town. I might as well give you something to moan about."

Lil was nearly in tears, not because she was upset, but because her anger was overwhelming her.

"You are going to walk out because I asked you about your son's birthday and you think that is reason enough to go to your whore?"

Patrick's anger abated at her words. "What whore? I *ain't* got a bird, Lil, not a real one, and you know that. I take a flier now and again, but that is it."

He walked around the bed half dressed, running his hands through his hair in consternation, and, pulling her into his arms, said softly, "You are one fucking awkward bastard, Lil, when you are pregnant. I am tired of this. You know what has been happening lately with the Williams brothers."

He was looking into her eyes and his sensible head was telling him to stay home and make her happy, but his cock and his new-found energy were telling him to go out and have a good fuck. Get all the tension out of his body that only a faceless, uncomplicated fuck could do for a man.

Women didn't understand men and other women: it was nothing personal, it was about shagging, that was all. They were there for the taking, and you took. Simple as that; it wasn't rocket science. With other women you just *did* it. You didn't worry about them enjoying it too much and you didn't have to be nice to them before or after, though he was; you just bought them a few drinks and had a laugh. If you saw them again you smiled and that was just about the extent of the relationship. If they had delusions of grandeur, you put them in their place with a few choice words and a gentle hand on their backs as you walked them out the door. Now Patrick had the scent of other women in his nostrils and his wife was making him feel like a fucking intruder in his own home: a perfect recipe for him to justify going back out and not feeling too much remorse for his philandering.

"Look, Lil. Of course I want the boy to have a great day but, no matter what I say, you will decide it all in the end anyway. You want a row and I ain't going to let you have one."

Lily knew exactly what he was trying to do and the knowledge depressed her. She could indeed start a row in an empty house, he was right about that much. But she was right about him and his other life as well. He called them fliers, she called them the reason she couldn't sleep.

"Get back into bed."

She allowed him to tuck her in, fighting the urge to cry. She ached all over and she was tired and irritable. The twins would be up at six and she would have to be up with them no matter what she felt like. This was the edge he always had over her. She wondered what he would do if she fucked off one night and left him there wondering where she was, who she was with and when she would be back. That would never happen though, and they both knew it.

"Get a bit of sleep, Lil, you need it. I am only making you upset by being here and neither of us want that, do we?"

As Lil lay back against the pillows once more, she was amazed to see her husband finish dressing himself. She watched as he checked his pockets for his wallet and keys and then, kissing her lightly, he left the room, closing the door quietly behind him. She stretched out in the bed then and the sleep that had eluded her finally overcame her; this was a milestone in their marriage and she knew it. For the first time ever, she was glad he was gone from her. She knew he had come home the conquering hero and she had pissed all over the fireworks. The knowledge saddened her.

Chapter Nine

"What are you doing, boy?"

Pat Junior grinned as he poured the tea out and he basked in his mother's pretend annoyance. He loved it when she acted like he was still too young to do things for himself or for the others.

"Making the breakfast, Mum. Sit down and have a rest."

Lil laughed happily. "Have a rest, I only just got up!"

Since his birthday invitations had gone out and his cake had been ordered, Patrick Junior had been like a dog with six lampposts. He was a good kid anyway; he would go to the ends of the earth for her or his sisters and brother but, since the party had been organized and authenticated with handwritten invitations, he had been like something from a Hollywood film. He could not do enough for her. Her contretemps with his father had, as always, blown over. She blamed herself for it because she should have had the sense to keep her trap shut and her opinions to herself. She knew that her husband had more temptation before him than most men, and she knew that now and again, he was going to succumb. What he didn't need was her giving him the green light by nagging him out of the door.

She was sipping her tea and nibbling on the toast her son had made her, when she saw Lance's face. It was bruised and scratched. "What's wrong with your face, mate?"

Lance shrugged. His deep-blue eyes were, as always, devoid of any real emotion; at least that was how they looked to her. She hated herself for thinking it.

Pat stood behind his chair and she realized that his eyes were exactly the same as his brother's, except that she enjoyed looking into her older son's eyes.

"He had a fight at school, Mum."

Lil sighed. Her frustration at her youngest son's bored demeanor was putting her on edge.

"What are you, Pat? His fucking parrot? Let him answer for himself. He ain't deaf, is he?"

She was sorry for her words and her anger immediately; Pat Junior was crushed by what she had said and the way she had said it. He had always been the buffer between her and his brother and she loved that about him. She felt the usual pang of guilt about her reactions to her younger son and prayed once more that she might find it in her heart to love him like she did all the others. She played the part of the doting mother so well that she believed it herself at times. But seeing Lance bruised and scratched made her feel guiltier than ever because she had not noticed it the night before.

Pat Junior stood behind his brother with one hand on his shoulder, and the other hand shielding eyes that were filled with tears. His head sank on to his chest and Lil knew he was trying not to break down in front of his siblings. She pulled him into her arms.

"I'm sorry, darling. You know I ain't myself lately. You are such a good boy, Pat, and I depend on you, which is wrong." He hugged her tightly and she felt the solidness of his body; he was becoming a young man. Although Lance was bigger and heavier, he didn't have the tight muscles of Patrick Junior. Lance looked like the older brother but he didn't have Pat's sense or intellect.

"Now, Lance, come here."

Lil held out her free arm to her second son and felt his hesitation before he moved towards her. She hugged them both to her tightly and Lance squeezed her back as if his life depended on it.

"So, who hurt you, Lance? Tell me."

He stepped back from her and shrugged like he always did when questioned about anything he was the cause of.

"It wasn't his fault, Mum. It was the bigger lads; they pick on him because of his size."

Lil held up her hand to silence Pat Junior. He was always trying to keep the peace but she knew that Lance was the one causing fights; it was in his nature and the school had just about had enough of him. Lance was on his last warning, and he knew it.

"Who were you fighting, Lance? Tell me and I'll let it go. But if you lie to me, I'll be angry. Now, answer me truthfully. Were you fighting again?"

He nodded and she sighed. It was pointless going on about it; he never listened to her anyway.

"Have I got to go to the school?"

Patrick Junior shook his head. "It was outside of school, Mum, on our way home. Honest, it's all sorted, really."

Lil nodded and lit another cigarette. As long as she wasn't going to be dragged up to the school she didn't really care.

Pat Junior was subdued now and she wished she had left it. After all, Pat had always looked out for his brother and that was never going to change. She worried that Lance's big mouth and knack of picking fights would one day land his older brother in trouble that he couldn't handle. So far he had bailed him out regularly and with the minimum of fuss, but she knew that as they got older it would not be so easy for him. Patrick could call on a lot of friends if he needed to, but Lance didn't make friends; he only had Patrick. She instinctively knew that in the years to come, Pat Junior would still be clearing up after his little brother. Lance depended on him too much and she blamed herself for that.

She smiled at the boys then, to show she was over it all, and they smiled back.

It occurred to Pat that his mother had not attempted to dress his brother's wounds like other mothers would have done and, as always, he felt the burden of Lance falling on to his shoulders.

Dave was sitting in his mother's house waiting for Bernie to bring Dennis back from the hospital. He was still bad, by all accounts, but he was better than anyone had expected him to be. Dave had left him there for three weeks without once going to see him. At first he had left it because he was so upset. Then he had left it too long to go without having to explain his absence. Now though, he had to face him and sort this thing out once and for all. Bernie would be here with him any minute and he had made sure that they would be alone.

He was nervous, but he didn't regret what he had done any more. It had been on the cards, the pressure had got to them all and he had blown, simple as that. Dennis was such a handful he could start a fight in a monastery. It had been inevitable they would come head to head at some point.

Dave glanced around his mother's living room: the Yorkstone fireplace and shagpile carpet were stained and dilapidated and he was once more reminded of the money they had squandered without a second's thought. As Pat had once pointed out, he had helped them make it and he was not obliged to tell them how to spend it. But he had tried. He had warned Dave about the way he was spending, had told him that until you line your pockets properly, keep your money in your pockets. Never let anyone know what you've got, had been another one of his favorite sayings; once people were aware that they knew too much about you, they wouldn't be comfortable with you ever again.

How true those words had been, and how Dave wished he could turn back the clock. Hindsight was a wonderful thing. That was another of Brodie's sayings that he wished he had listened to.

Pat had more or less told him that he was still with the firm but not in the capacity he had been before. Now he was on the payroll, on a wage, and he knew he had to swallow that. The fact he had even contemplated trying to force his way into Patrick's and Spider's business arrangement was enough to see him six feet under so he was more than aware that he had been given a second chance.

He was not going to blow that. At least he had learned that valuable lesson and he had learned it well. Now he had to talk his brother down, and he was not relishing that at all.

Dave lit a cigarette and pulled on it for long moments, breathing the smoke deep into his lungs. The shaking of his hands was evident, even to him, and he willed himself to relax, but he had no idea what Dennis was going to be like when he walked through the door. With Dennis, the unexpected was the norm.

He heard a car pull up and stopped himself from leaping out of the chair and looking out of the window. He wanted Dennis to see him calm and controlled; it was important that he took the lead in the conversation and tried to salvage not only his brother's love and friendship, but also his position as head of the family. Dennis was strong enough to take that from him and he knew that better than anyone.

Vince had not forgotten, although he had forgiven. Dave had apologized profusely to him more than once and he was also on a promise to Patrick and Spider to keep Dennis on the straight and narrow for the foreseeable future. This first meeting was important inasmuch as he had to make Dennis understand that he was living on borrowed time until he could prove that he was not going to try to muscle in on anyone else's business.

He was aware that Dennis had not spoken to the police, who had questioned him in a perfunctory manner. Like him, they felt he had got his comeuppance at last and they would have known exactly what had gone down. They would have visited him because they had to, not because they wanted to solve any kind of crime. Dennis was hated by everyone in his orbit in one way or another.

Dennis had been the driving force behind every failed deal they had invested in, he had been the instigator, the front man, and he had been the one who had blamed everyone else around him when it had all gone tits up. Everyone, that is, except himself. He had been the same all his life; everything was always someone else's fault and he had always got away with it.

All their big dreams and it had come down to this. They were broke, humiliated and back where they started; on a weekly wage and having to prove themselves worthy of future advancement. His younger brothers had been cleaned out financially and he knew he should have put a stop to it long before it had got this far. Dave knew they had placed their trust in him and he was aware that they knew Dennis had been allowed to call the shots and that he had more or less taken over the family business and finances. And he had allowed it all to happen. He had listened to his brother's big talk and believed him when he insisted that they were shrewd enough and respected enough to overlook Brodie's and Spider's involvement in the drugs trade.

He could only put it down to madness on his part. He had no excuse for his behavior except greed. If it was anyone else in this position he would have found it laughable; somehow he didn't find any of this amusing in the least. Especially since he could hear Dennis cursing and shouting as he got out of the car and limped slowly up the gravel path.

This was, without a doubt, the hardest thing Dave had ever had to do, and he had done some harsh things in his time.

Dennis came into the room and, even though he had lost weight in the hospital, he was still larger than the average Williams brother. His face was harder than Dave remembered and his shaved head showed the scars where the scalp had been sewn back together. Dennis looked like someone who had been in a plane crash and Dave had to remind himself that he had inflicted all the damage: the deep head wounds and the swollen bruises around his eyes and face.

And the worst thing of all was that, if he was really honest with himself, he had enjoyed every second of it. In a strange way, he wished that he had finished the job; it would have made his life a lot easier. His nervousness had suddenly gone and he looked at his brother with a rueful grin and said quietly, "All right, bruv?"

Patrick was in his club, it was early evening and the girls were getting ready for the night's excitement. They were like a flock of chattering birds, their heavy make-up and skimpy clothes belying the stormy weather outside.

Patrick Brodie loved the West End when the days started to draw in. The tourists were long gone and even though the takings dropped off, he loved the feel of the real Soho. On nights like tonight he loved the clubs; when the girls were getting on with each other and not fighting over the least little thing. This club was the biggest of them all and he had bought it for a song, taking it as payment for a large gambling debt incurred by a man called Pierre Lamboutin. The French name had been an alias. Why he had chosen such a mouthful Patrick had no idea;

aliases were supposed to be plain and dowdy, not something that drew attention to the person involved. But as Pierre was now as dead as a dodo and the club was his and, unofficially, the best earner in Soho, Patrick didn't give a fuck. Keeping on top of the game was no mean feat, considering all the competition that was opening up around him. But he had taken Lil's advice and as he treated the girls relatively well they were loyal hookers and he knew they made a point of not selling out anyone on the premises.

The club was situated in Frith Street, busy enough for passing trade, but not so busy it attracted the walkabouts, otherwise known as the weekend warriors or window shoppers. Patrick only wanted clients who could spend a few pounds and would not tear the arse out of one drink while they watched the strippers all night and felt up a hostess in between acts. He made the men pay a stiff membership fee on the door, guaranteed to separate the men from the boys. It also guaranteed the customers a modicum of respectability; it was a real club with real membership and their credit cards said as much, if their wives got their hands on them. Lord's Gentlemen's Club was a byword in the West End and Patrick was proud of its reputation and glamorous decor. It was about as prestigious as a girlie club could be.

As Patrick sipped a brandy at the bar he saw one of the new girls walk into the foyer. She was a stunner: tall and slim with long shapely legs. But it was her hair that set her apart from the other girls. It was a deep, natural auburn and, hanging down her back, it was thick and glossy like something from a shampoo advert on TV. She smiled at him and he frowned. The only flaw was her teeth; they were crooked at the front and even though they were white, it marred the illusion of perfection. She had pale-blue eyes and heavily arched eyebrows that made her look like a film star. Patrick also happened to know that she could drink like a sailor and fuck like a train.

For the first time in years, Patrick was seeing someone on a regular basis and he knew that he was dicing with death because Lil might swallow a flier every now and then, but an actual girlfriend would cause ructions. She would walk, he knew that. She would never allow him to disrespect her with a serious girlfriend, a contender to her throne. Like most women, her biggest fear would be a child arriving, a son or daughter of his that would also be related to her own brood. It was unthinkable and he saw her point of view.

Every time he saw Laura Doyle he told himself it would be the last time and then he found himself making arrangements to see her again. The thing was, she had no real interest in him and he knew that; he was like a john to her. Why he found her so fascinating he had no idea, but he did. He had even put her up in one of his better flats so he could have her whenever the fancy took him, secure in the knowledge that she would not have any other men there.

Laura was nineteen years old and she was a working girl through choice. She liked the night life, she liked the money and she had no qualms about sleeping with even the ugliest man for a fixed fee. The life suited her down to the ground and she saw Brodie as a step up, if only for a short while. He would tire of her eventually, she was sure, but until then she would milk him for everything she could get. She had a certain cachet with the other girls because of the relationship and she used it to further her own ends. For example, she made sure the head girl only gave her monied men and she also made sure that she was given her due. In fact, some of the girls had decided that she was pushing it a bit and she was not averse to letting them think that.

Patrick Brodie could be her passport to riches if she used her head and she was quite happy to use him for her own ends. If she could keep him interested, she could keep herself on the top rung and that was important to her.

For some reason she interested him and she had a feeling it was her complete lack of interest in him as anything other than a fuck. Her coolness intrigued him and she was glad about that. She did enjoy the sex with him; he was expert at it and she was an expert in making men feel like they were King of the Kip.

He passed her a small package and she smiled again. He always slipped her a wrap of speed, knowing that it was the staple for the girls who worked the clubs. It was always good stuff, better than she could ever score on the street.

As they chatted he saw Spider and Cain going up to his office and he followed them a few minutes later, telling Laura that he would see her later that night. This was Patrick's way of telling her not to go out with any of her johns. He didn't mind that she slept with other men, it was her job after all. He was not about to be her second dick of the night though. He liked his fanny neat, tidy, tight and clean as a whistle. The latter being the main criterion as far as he was concerned.

He watched her as she sashayed to the meat seats and then he slipped upstairs to his meeting. His face was grim now and his demeanor that of a man expecting big trouble, and expecting it sooner rather than later.

Trevor Renton was a gambler, and he was one of a very rare breed; he made a good living from it. Whether it was cards, the horses or the dogs, he made a decent living for himself. He lost of course: horses were unpredictable and cards were dealt at random; you could only play the hand that was given to you. Trevor Renton could bluff though. He had once taken a massive pot on a pair of twos, unnerving his opponent by raising him larger and larger amounts and with his quiet confidence in what was, in effect, a crap hand. Lessons had been learned and he had made his reputation overnight. When he sat at a table for a game he was treated like visiting royalty and, if he lost, he lost with good grace and paid up what he owed without a murmur.

Tonight he was in a big game and he was very excited although his face betrayed nothing of his emotions. He had already had a couple of wins on the horses that afternoon and he was in the mood for a nice long night of poker. He loved the game, loved the feel of beating the odds and he loved the company of like-minded men. He also got a kick out of hearing the stories of other big games, even though he had heard them a hundred times before, and was often a character in the stories himself.

As Trevor settled himself into a chair, he took out his cigars, his car keys and his wallet; he had a marker in there for fifty grand owed him by the evening's hosts. Placing them all by his drink, he then removed his jacket, placed it carefully on a nearby sofa, loosened his tie and rolled up his shirtsleeves. He knew that as a regular winner he had to make sure that no one could ever accuse him of cheating, whether that was to his face or, worse, behind his back.

Some people were bad losers, especially when they bet with money they didn't really have. He could get credit anywhere; he was known for paying off his debts within hours of incurring them. Other men were not so sensible and tried to win back money they didn't have any more. They tried to recoup one loss by gambling on with borrowed money, money that would be repaid no matter what the circumstances. He watched them sweating with fear, drinking to calm their nerves, the alcohol that was supplied free of charge making their judgment worthless so that they started signing IOUs all over the place; trying to win back their lives and their family's lives. Then, at the end of the night, he saw their faces as the realization finally dawned on them that they had just lost everything they possessed. Everything they had worked for gone in a few hours.

Somewhere, a wife and children were unaware that life as they knew it was over, that they would soon be caught up in a world of debt collectors and midnight visitors. A nightmare of such enormity that the reverberations would be felt for years. People were not aware that gambling debts did not, by law, have to be paid. They were a gentlemen's agreement, like a handshake. That was why the collection was usually guaranteed only with the help of violence and intimidation. The men who gambled away their lives were in fact putting themselves in a situation they could never escape from. The debts *would* be paid, it was as simple as that. The money was given with a smile and recouped with a baseball bat.

Trevor had seen it so many times and it depressed him that these men didn't have any self-control or any self-respect. At forty-eight years old he had been around the tables for over thirty years and he was still unscathed. There was not a scar on him and he had never been in a fight over cards or bets. Trevor was a gentleman and he knew his name was enough to get him into any game he wanted. He also knew that the younger men sought him out to play against him, hoping to get themselves a reputation as having beaten him. If that happened, and it was very rare, he shook their hands and gave them pointers and advice, making them friends for life. He had no problem with winners; it was a game of chance after all. Anyone could win and that's what made every night so exciting for him. As he sat nursing his ginger ale and waiting for the other players to arrive and get settled in, he was more than ready for the night's play.

"He is already causing fucking ructions and he's only been out of the hospital for a few days."

Cain's voice was heavy with malice and Patrick listened quietly as he always did. He had found many years before that if you kept very quiet people filled in the silences themselves, offering more information than they had originally intended to give. It was a habit now and one he was glad he had cultivated.

"What has he done this time?"

While in hospital Dennis had attacked a doctor who was on his rounds and a porter who had not brought him the Scotch he had ordered. He had been as obnoxious as he always was and now he was out and about and determined to cause a ruckus. Dennis was making sure that people remembered just what he was capable of. Even though he was a laughing stock in some quarters, Brodie knew it would still be a brave man who had the nerve to laugh in his face.

"He has been round and collected rents that were already ours. It *seems* that Dave hasn't explained the new scheme of things to him and he still *seems* to think that he has some kind of fucking stranglehold over us lot. I have told my boys to go and request the money nicely. If he tips them bollocks then they are to slice him and dice him as they see fit."

Spider's voice was cold and brooked no argument. Well, he certainly wasn't going to get one from him. Dennis had been shouting his mouth off as usual; Patrick had been advised as to what Dennis had said about him, and it had not been what he would call complimentary. It was only a matter of time before someone shut him up permanently, so Patrick had decided to sit back and let someone else do any dirty work that was required. He knew that, in reality, Spider and Cain wanted his permission to out Dennis Williams and he was happy to oblige.

"Fair enough, what can I say? He is a cunt to himself."

Spider and Cain relaxed at Brodie's answer, it was what they had been hoping to hear. They knew that Dave was still part of Brodie's firm and that was fair enough, unless it encroached on them of course.

Patrick sipped at his drink and when the atmosphere was warmer, he said jovially, "Don't forget my boy's party. Bring the kids and everyone is welcome."

"Fucking hell, Pat. Ten, don't the time go fast?"

Patrick nodded sagely. "Wish I was ten again and knew what I know now, don't you?"

Spider laughed, his huge head going back on to his shoulders and reminding Patrick just how strong he was in all ways.

"When I was ten I had just started nicking fucking motors with me cousin Delroy. You remember him, Pat, he was shot in Kingston about three years ago. He finally went back to Jamaica and got wasted over a fucking bird."

Spider shook his head in abject disbelief. "A fucking bird. Only Del could die over a bit of pussy."

He looked at Cain and said with pride and amusement in his voice, "He could sniff out pussy like a fucking bloodhound and it was always sweet, at least that was what he said anyway."

"He never got shot. He wore his cock out, Spider, and died of exhaustion. He got a hard-on looking at Fanny Cradock; he would trump anything. We used to have to hide our grannies if he was coming round."

Cain and Spider were roaring with laughter, the earlier atmosphere was gone now, and they were all boys together once more.

Cain took a large gulp of his drink and, wiping his mouth with the back of his hand, he said craftily, "You can talk, Pat. What is this I hear about you and a certain flat-chested redhead? Love, is it?"

Patrick Brodie paled in front of the two men's eyes and the shock on his face was almost comical.

Cain realized immediately that he had said the wrong thing. Spider was looking at him with undisguised anger and Patrick was, for the first time ever, lost for words. Cain had just made himself look like a gossiping old woman, had alerted Brodie to the fact that he was being talked about and his name was being coupled with this girl, whoever she was.

Brodie was a family man and very protective of his wife and his children, everyone knew that.

Spider replenished their glasses while Patrick busied himself lighting a cigarette and gathering his thoughts.

Cain spread his arms out in supplication. "I was only joking, Pat. I didn't mean to cause offense."

Cain was remembering the stories he had heard about this man: the torture of people who tried to thwart him and the torture machinery he kept in a warehouse in Silvertown. Spider had said that he'd seen Patrick electrocute naked men, hard men, without blinking an eye. He'd heard them begging him as they smelled their own skin burning and he had watched as the current had marauded through their bodies and caused them to be thrown a foot in the air, their screams eventually muffled by the quick-setting cement Patrick had forced into their throats once he had heard enough to satisfy his curiosity. No one ever crossed him twice. That was why Dave was so terrified about Dennis and his loose-cannon status and this was why Cain wished he had kept his big mouth shut.

Patrick was an anomaly; he was quiet, he was devious and no one ever knew what he was thinking or what he would do next. He went to Mass with his children, he took Communion every week and he had never had a rep as a womanizer; womanizers always ended up shitting on their own doorsteps, that was a phrase Patrick Brodie had used over and over again. He was right as well, Cain and Spider knew that. In the end, womanizers destroyed their families, had to look for a new home, had to deal with the resentment from children and relatives, and ended up in the same position they had been in at the beginning. Another, younger, wife and kids the same age as their grandchildren, and when the novelty wore off they were always out on the prowl once more. Patrick Brodie had no time for those men and the devastation they wreaked because they had no family loyalty, no respect for their wives, the mothers of their children, or the children they had created with those wives.

The stories about him were whispered, all rumor and innuendo; no one could ever place him at the scene of any crime and no one ever would.

It was that simple.

Now Cain had opened his mouth and given Patrick Brodie something to think about; the girl was a liability and Cain had pointed that out to him.

"Relax, son, you just did me a favor. Is it big talk or just rumors at the moment? More to the point, who told you?"

Spider could hear the underlying threat in Patrick's voice and he wanted to launch his brother into outer space for his careless talk.

This was Patrick all over; he was fastidious in his ways and he was almost a prude where his sex life was concerned. But Spider knew that his biggest fear was one of the blokes in their employ telling his wife or girlfriend about the redhead and the news then echoing back to Lil. She was everything to him and he would rather die a thousand deaths than have her hurt in any way, shape or form.

The fact that he was being talked about because of Laura was a worry, but he was also aware that Dennis's mother was a friend of Annie's and Annie would give ten years of her life for a piece of information like this.

"Look, Pat, it was me who opened me trap. I saw you with the girl a few times and it's not like you, is it? You are usually beyond reproach and Cain just got carried away, that's all. You know, joking about Delroy, it was just guys together. We would never talk about it outside this room."

Patrick grinned then and Cain saw the coldness in his eyes that until then he had only heard about. He finally saw the Patrick Brodie he had only ever heard about and Cain was aware that he would never, ever like to incur the wrath of the man sitting so relaxed and quiet in the chair before him.

"I understand that, Spider. I am a cunt. I just need to know if it is common knowledge, that's all. If anyone else is talking about me, about my fucking private life."

The sentence ended on a shout and Patrick was out of the chair and across the room in seconds. Cain instinctively put his hands up to cover his face, expecting to be attacked.

Instead, Patrick was at the liquor cabinet and his whole demeanor changed in seconds as he laughed jovially, saying, "Fuck me, son. Relax and we can sort this out sooner rather than later."

Spider was staring at his brother and Patrick was staring at him as well and for a few moments, Cain wasn't sure which one of them he was more wary of.

Laura let herself into the flat in Bloomsbury at about two-fifteen; she had been chauffeured there by a guy called Clinton, who was Patrick's driver on occasion. She was being her usual imperious self and Clinton had been told to stop and get her some cigarettes, which he had paid for and she had then insisted that he drive slowly because she was spilling the drink she had brought with her from the club.

Clinton had followed her into the block of flats and she could hear his quiet breathing from behind her as she tried to get her head around what she was seeing. She was wired, speeding out of her nut, but she was still sober enough to realize that there was something radically wrong, even though it was a few seconds before what exactly that was sank in properly.

The flat was empty, not a piece of furniture or even a curtain remaining. It had been stripped bare of everything except for two cases and a woman's overnight bag, which were placed in the center of the living room.

Laura was still standing there, trying to get her bearings, when Clinton picked the bags up and walked back down the stairs with them.

"What the fuck is going on?" She was screaming at the retreating Clinton like a banshee because she was suddenly aware that her life in London was over. If Patrick Brodie wanted her gone, then she would have to go and that was that.

Laura was racking her brain for what she could have done wrong, what she might have done inadvertently to offend him and she could think of nothing. So she had thrown her weight about a bit, that was not something he would care about, surely? The tears were hot and salty on her creamy skin and she heard the sound of someone coming up the steps; she assumed it was Clinton coming back to remove her from the premises.

The place was devoid of anything to say she had ever been there and she wondered if this was the end of the line for her, was he going to make sure she disappeared? Was someone going to kill her? Terror rose up inside her like a wave and she felt the full force of her lifestyle as she understood what it could finally bring to her doorstep.

Clinton turned off the light and snapped, "Come on, we ain't got all fucking night."

Laura faced him, her tear-stained and terrified face making no impression on him at all.

"Please don't hurt me . . ." She sank down on to her knees, the fear making her legs weak and her heart beat so loud she could hear it in her ears like a drum.

Clinton was a small man; he had a face like an angel, as his mother was always pointing out, but he was slight in his build. He was just a driver and a gofer and that suited him down to the ground. Now though, he was finally understanding the buzz that fear could give to you. He was enjoying Laura's fear, enjoying seeing her brought down a peg or two. She was a whore with big expectations and Patrick had given him his orders and he would carry them out to the letter.

He stared at the girl for long moments as she sobbed and begged for her life.

"Please, Clinton, don't hurt me."

Laura was imploring him with every ounce of strength she had left, the snot was running from her nose and she could feel it hanging in long strands as she scrambled across the floor to him, begging him, her lovely blue eyes wide with terror, not to harm her.

"Get up, you stupid bitch. You've got a long journey ahead of you tonight. You're the new suck and fuck girl for a friend of Patrick's in Manchester."

Then he unzipped his trousers and said, with a northern accent, "Get your laughing gear round that, lass."

As Laura looked at him she saw the rest of her life in stunning detail and she realized just what she had let herself in for. The illusion of independence she had harbored all this time was just that, an illusion. She would be dependent on men like this for her daily bread until she was reduced to the streets and alleyways as age crept up on her, and her body gave out.

Clinton was choking her with his cock and she knew he was enjoying seeing her debased like this, was paying her back for all the slights, the sarcastic comments and the rudeness he had been forced to endure because she was fucking Patrick Brodie. His nails were digging into her scalp and he used her head for momentum, grabbing at the lovely hair that had always been her crowning glory. As he was coming in her mouth she heaved with the sudden taste of his salty, red-hot sperm.

Clinton left her lying on the floor, her tears silent now and he tidied himself up in seconds. Her bright-red lipstick was smothered all over his penis and his belly. He had enjoyed it so much that he could do it again and he decided that he would do it again. On the way to Manchester he would have her on her knees in the parking lot of a truck stop. He was going to make the most of the opportunity he had been presented with. He knew she was out of his league and he wouldn't pay for it even if he had the money. So this was too good an opportunity to miss.

"But why? What have I done for Pat to do this to me?" Laura's voice was low, she was broken and he knew it. More to the point, she knew it.

"You've outlived your usefulness, darling, and now you have to go."

He was laughing as he dragged her up off the floor by her hair and pushed her towards the front door, making her stumble with the force he used.

He locked up with her set of keys and placed them in his pocket. Then he walked her to the car, and, pushing her none too gently into the back, he slammed the door with a finality that told her she was off the radar, she was already yesterday's news.

Chapter Ten

Trevor Renton was tired, tired enough to leave the table, but he couldn't. He had seen off the two biggest wallets in the game with no trouble at all, more fool him, he realized now. The four other men at the table, none of whom were known to him, had played with seemingly unlimited amounts of money and were nothing more than ice-creams who he should have taken out of the game in the first two hands. They were nothing more than three mediocre players and a thieving hustler.

He had not bothered with them before because he had been too busy concentrating on the real gamers. But now he was convinced that they were on the scrounge, were after his pot; he had started with a fifty on tap and that had turned into a little over a hundred grand. He wondered if he was getting too trusting in his old age, but then again this had been a proper game. No one involved in the setup had been suspect and he had been assured that the players were good for any debts incurred. Now though, he was not so sure. He had a shit-detector that was telling him that he was about to be scalped and there was not a thing he could do about it. He was a sitting duck and, ironically, this crowd of fucking morons held all the fucking cards.

Not that he would say any of that out loud, of course. He had far too much intelligence to accuse anyone of cheating at this table, not without the back-up of at least a fucking platoon of Vietnam veterans or a large crowd of serial killers. He was aware of the fact that this really wasn't his table in any way. It wasn't on his turf, for a start, and there was no one left that he knew or trusted as he had taken them out of the game. He was in a quandary of fucking Homeric proportions; he knew he was going to be ripped off, and worst of all, by a crowd of cunts he had seen as so worthless he had not even listened to their fucking names. He was *far* too well known and *far* too respected to have to worry about things like this.

He was backed by some of the biggest names in criminal history; he went into the massive games with their money on him as bets, that was how good he was. He had assumed that this lot he was left with were just the usual bystanders you got in a big game. All hoping to have a bit of luck and when they lost their few pounds they'd sit back, swill the free booze and watch the real card players at work. And it *was* work to him and his ilk. This game should have been something these blokes would have wanted to tell their mates about, the big card game they were in. For once in their life they had sat with the best and that was usually enough for them. He had done this lot a fucking favor and a half, he had knocked out not just the daydreamers, but the real players as well. But no one, it seemed, was being encouraged to stay and watch the climax.

The other players had just been escorted out the door; he had come back from the toilet to see them leaving under duress. The alarm bells had started to ring then and he wondered what was to become of him this night. Players always stayed; they wanted to know where and more importantly with whom, their money would finally end up. It was the way you brought yourself down to earth after you left the table. Any addiction brought your dopamine levels up sky high, it was what made you stay there and play in the first place, it was also what kept you there afterwards. Just because you knew you had to leave the game didn't mean you couldn't enjoy it anyway. For most of the real players, watching a good game was the nearest thing to being back in your seat. For the addicted gamblers, not the real players like him and his colleagues, it was the dopamine their brains created that made them stay at the table when all they possessed was lost. It was the dopamine that kept them out all night and made them throw in car keys or their houses; that was what addiction was about.

For him and other professional card players it was about more than the thrill alone, it was about beating the odds and making a pile. It was about keeping your head when everyone around you was losing theirs. It was about winning, calmly and with dignity.

He had noticed the other players being ushered from the room but he had a poker face and no one knew that he was bothered or that he had figured them out. He smiled a small, knowing smile that he had perfected many years before and he sat back in his seat cursing himself for his honesty and trust.

The man with the large belly and the crooked smile who, he suddenly realized, was scheduled to win all his money, was grinning and mugging with such an undisguised expression of glee that even Helen Keller would have figured out that she was going to be ripped off.

The man waved him into his seat with a smile that made Trevor angrier than he had ever been in his life and said with barely disguised menace, "I hope you ain't fucking off as well, Trev. We want a chance to win our money back, eh, guys?" The other three laughed as if he had just told the funniest joke in recorded history. It wasn't in Trevor's nature to cause trouble. He lost with aplomb, a certain cachet, he made sure of that. It was part of his reputation, why people didn't mind sitting in with him and why he was well past this kind of scam.

Trevor had never once questioned another player's tactics or agenda since he had been in the big league. He had never caused a scene of any kind or been the catalyst for anything even resembling trouble. But he was going to cause trouble after this little lot. He was going to cause fucking murders when and if he finally walked away from here. So he smiled and yawned, and he decided that he was going to have to lose gracefully and give them his marker. He had been around long enough to know when he was being shafted and he had been shafted royally by this shower of shite.

He was unable to leave the game, he knew, because these so-called players, who, incidentally, looked like a parody of Dean Martin and the Rat Pack, had more or less told him that if he went home now they would not be too thrilled. There was no actual spoken threat but then there wouldn't be, would there?

He would lose to them if that was what they wanted; the money was nothing to him, he only ever wanted the *game*. The game was all that mattered to him and for a few seconds he toyed with the idea of wiping them out completely. Playing them for all they were fucking worth. Toughing it out and taking all their money, but he knew he was playing for his life. Mister fucking Agreeable was going to take his dough one way or another. Only his calm exterior and a big loss would guarantee that he would walk out of this place in one piece.

"What do you want, Trevor? Anything you need you just tell me, OK?" The young man who was serving the drinks was a handsome and, suddenly seriously nervous, little fucker.

Trevor guessed, rightly, that he had only just figured out the situation and was not happy about being witness to anything that might drag him into the world of violent retribution. He was eighteen, at most, and he was so naive he probably thought Debbie Harry was a natural blonde. Collar *and* cuffs.

Trevor grinned and shook his head as if he was happy as a clam. The three gooners and the ponce all ordered large drinks and that in itself told Trevor that he was dealing with fucking amateurs. He wanted to scream out at the top of his voice, "Have me over if you must, but don't fucking rub it in and make it so obvious. Have a bit of respect."

Trevor was more disappointed at the way they seemed to think he was such a cunt that they could just take him for a fool. He would have had more respect for them if they had just robbed him; an honest robbing would have been preferable to this barrage of insults and foolishness. They were making him feel like a fool. Any real card player worth their salt went off the drink once the real money was on the table for the simple reason you never knew what might be in it. Certain people got pissed off when they were being wiped out. The Faces were the worst of them all; they honestly believed that you were robbing their fucking wallets somehow.

Trevor had made a point of never playing Faces unless they had the proper in. He insisted on a guarantee that they were *real* players. Which meant, of course, that they were happy to lose their money. Most criminals, especially bank robbers, were *not* natural losers. It was the nature of that particular beast that they tended to *take* money, *not* give it away to some bloke with a smile and a better hand than they had. Some had even been known to come back later in the evening with a shotgun and a chip on their shoulder bigger than Mount fucking Rushmore demanding their money back, convinced they had been short-changed. You couldn't do a lot about that, you certainly didn't remind them that they had been in a *proper* game with serious gamblers, not playing poker in prison for fucking peanuts, nine times out of ten with people who had no intention of losing to them. Somehow, that conversation never seemed to come up.

No one accepted a drink. A real pro got up during a break and then watched the fucker being poured out. In his world the barman would have the fucking sense to open a *new* bottle in front of his face; it was accepted, expected and it stopped fights. He was being rolled by a herd of fucking imbeciles. Big imbeciles admittedly, but fucking drongos all the same. The real insult was that these fucking Keystone Cops thought he was buying into this fucking lunacy. Really believed that he had not caught on.

In all his years, Trevor had never, ever, been treated like this. Oh, he had seen the chancers and he had observed gooners in his time. When he had first come on the scene he had been offered fortunes to be one. He had refused; he wanted to win fair and square. Gooners were players who were ornaments until the final sting. There was never *a* gooner of course, in the singular, because a good card man would wipe them out in no time. Gooners worked together so that, like now, when he had knocked out the real players and the pot was a small fucking fortune, they would sit at the table and work together against him. He was expected to believe that they were better players than him, that his luck had gone on the trot faster than an ex-wife with a lottery win and an ex-paratrooper for company. He was so insulted that he was determined to make these cunts work for the jackpot. Then he would congratulate them and leave with dignity and a fucking raging hard-on for all their arses. The bar boy winked at him and he wondered if, on top of everything else, they all thought he was a pansy.

"Not long till me party." Pat Junior's voice was proud and filled with longing for the day to finally arrive.

Billy Boot, Pat's long-time friend and Lance's archenemy, was almost as excited as he was at the thought of the party. This was the party to end all parties as far as he was concerned and he was thrilled that Pat was going to be the lucky recipient of such a wondrous event. Everyone within earshot was straining to hear the conversation and all those invited had been bragging about it for ages, with the girls discussing their outfits at every opportunity. Lance kicked a football that had rolled near him back to the boys who were playing with it. He was good at sports and he kicked it with all his considerable strength, knowing that it would slam into one of the younger kids who were waiting patiently for its return.

He was spot on and the ball hit a seven-year-old lad on the side of his head. He was a hardy perennial though, who rubbed his ear furiously, forced away the tears that were filling his eyes and carried on with the game, even though his face was crumpling by the second with pain and cold.

"I bet that hurt him." Lance was laughing at the boy's predicament.

"Course it hurt him. You meant it to. It's freezing today so that must have really stung." Lance shrugged as if he had no idea what Billy was talking about before saying loudly, "You're right, it is cold, ain't it? Hope my old coat is warm enough for you, Bootsie."

The boys were in the school playground in their usual place by the school gates. The weather was icy cold, and their coats were buttoned up tightly against it. Patrick knew that they were better dressed than any of the others and he accepted that, appreciated it. He also understood why his mother passed their old clothes on to other kids in the school. It was her way of helping people out and it was accepted in their world.

Unlike Lance, he had never felt the urge to point that fact out. Now he could feel the heat of Billy's humiliation as if it was happening to himself.

Lance was sneering at Billy, taunting him as he always did and Billy Boot was not going to put up with much more of it. Lance had never understood when enough was enough; he always had to push everything and everyone to the extreme. He spent his whole life causing upset and hurting people without a thought for their feelings or their circumstances. They had both been to Billy's house and Pat knew that Lance had seen how hard up they were. Billy had six younger brothers and three older sisters and a father who was always in the pub. He battered Billy and his brothers regularly and, without a second's thought, Billy's sisters were also beaten, but generally only on a Friday or Saturday night when he came home from the pub looking for his wife. Even though he knew he wouldn't find his wife, and knowing exactly what she was up to, he would smack his daughters around instead.

Everyone knew, including her husband, that Billy's mother moon-lighted weekends around King's Cross. She had to, someone had to pay the bills. Billy's father would come home drunk, kick up a stink and then rob her of whatever money she had. She would put a few pennies in her bag and when he had taken that she would have a bath and tell the girls that, as always, the bulk of her earnings were with Lil Diamond. Patrick had been married to Lil for about a year when he heard one of the neighbors, a hard old bird who had buried her husband and three of her children during the Blitz, telling one of her cronies, "You know who that is, don't you? Lil Diamond's husband." He had been amused by the fact that in the Irish community women were always known by their maiden names.

It was Lil's reputation as a Brodie wife and a respectable woman that kept Billy's father from demanding all his wife's money from her.

Though Billy's mother and her extracurricular activities were never talked about openly, everyone knew about them; the teachers, the police who came when she was being battered and even the little kids around and about. But because she was also a great friend of Pat's and Lance's mother, no one said a word about it to her face. It was a strange set up. You could whore in the streets in front of your home, as long as you were doing it for your kids and, even more importantly, your kids had to look as if you were flogging your arse for their benefit. If the kids were still running round with their arses hanging out of their trousers, and you were seen to be doing all right yourself, then, and only then, were you treated like an outcast. So, if you had half a brain you sorted the kids out. Feeding and clothing your children was paramount to these women; all they were and all they did was for their families. It was the most important thing you could ever do.

Those who had a husband who provided were revered. If your old man had run off, or was a useless bastard, you did the best you could; robbed him while he slept off the drink on pay night or, like the abandoned women, you moonlighted. Some of the women who were alone for a while eventually acquired lodgers, and these lodgers were treated with respect and would act the part for years. It was all about how things *looked* to the neighbors, not about how they actually were.

If your kids were taken away, you were finished. Go on the game by all means; no one thought the worse of you for that. As no one signed on, the hooking was considered almost respectable, whereas going on welfare was considered outrageous. Once you went to the welfare department you invited the government into your whole life.

And if, God forbid, you let your kids go into care, which, since the sixties, had become everyone's biggest fear, you were out. You were dragged out of your home by your hair, battered, spat on and left with no option but to leave. Now there was a new breed arriving in the flats and houses: young women with babies and no husband in the frame at all. Girls who lived off welfare and had no shame, like it was their right. The dole was supposed to be an interim measure till you got another job but now it seemed, with the seventies, it was a fucking lifestyle! It shocked and annoyed the women who had never claimed a bean even when they were on their uppers. Now, by all accounts, girls were getting pregnant just to procure for themselves public housing and a few pounds off the State. These young hussies were shameless about it, and the older women were starting to be nervous because more than a few of these so-called unmarried mothers were daughters and nieces of people they knew.

The sixties were over, the seventies were more than halfway through, and these women who were scandalized were only young, yet most looked older than their husbands. It was a new age for them and, as they ran one woman out, another one arrived with a child and no wedding ring. They saw these girls have a child without a thought for the fellow involved and, in their hearts, they admired them for their independence and their guts, even while they blasted them for living off the taxpayers' money. Still, as long as they looked after their children, they were tolerated. If they didn't, they were taken to task like any of the others.

Billy and his siblings were more than aware of what their mother had to do when she went out on the weekend. Billy could not remember when or how he had found out about it, but he had seemed to know all his life. He hated his father and he loved his mother, although he loathed what she had to do to keep them clean, fed and with a roof over their heads.

Billy knew that his mother was respected for the way she kept her family and that Lil was great mates with her. This was how Billy came by Lance's old winter coat and other bits of his wardrobe.

Billy was sick of having to wear other people's clothes and sick of having to live with a drunken father and a whoring mother. One of his sisters was pregnant so she was going to be another one of those unmarried mothers, and he knew that once that was common knowledge, Lance would slaughter him for it.

"You can stick the coat up your arse . . ."

Billy's voice was heavy with shame and embarrassment. He forced the words out between his teeth and he felt so fucking full of hatred for himself and the whole world that Lance could feel it coming off him in waves. He was frightened of Billy for the first time ever; he knew that he was capable of hurting him this time.

Billy was clenching his fists ready to have a fight. He wanted a fight, he wanted to crack Lance's head open for every slight he had endured from him and for every fucking man his mum had serviced. He wanted to draw blood for every time his dad had beaten him or his brothers because he had drunk up all his money.

"Come on then, Lance. Let's have a fight, shall we?"

Billy could feel a great black hate that was finally bubbling up to the surface. He could kill a man now, let alone a boy.

Pat Junior, as always, stepped in and tried to keep the peace.

"Fuck off, Lance. That was out of order." He pushed his brother out of harm's way.

Lance grinned. "It was a joke, Pat, that's all. And he *is* wearing me coat. So what. I don't give a toss; he's welcome to it."

Billy was still white-faced and stiff with anger. He knew that Lance had meant for his words to be heard by all the other kids standing nearby and he also knew that he had achieved his objective. They were being stared at by the majority of their classmates. Billy knew that most of them were in the same boat as him; money was tight in their households too, but it was the principle of it. He knew Lance had wanted to show him up and he had achieved that. Billy wanted to rip Lance apart and he knew he was more than capable of doing just that, but he didn't want to fall out with Patrick because they were best mates. Lance, as usual, took advantage of that and now Billy was feeling the full force of Lance's beaming smile and his convincing act of being contrite. The black hate was gone now.

"You are going to have to develop a sense of humor at some point, Bill."

Lance was smiling again, that even-toothed, amiable smile that made him look like an innocent. Billy didn't answer him or even acknowledge the smile. Instead, he turned his back on him and spoke to Pat, but the words were for Lance's benefit and they all knew that.

"Your party is going to be the biggest event of the year for us lot, everyone is talking about it and you deserve it. The whole fucking thing is amazing. Is it true you've got a proper disco?"

He knew it was true. He knew more about the arrangements than Lance; Patrick Junior had discussed it with him at length. And Pat understood Billy's desire to push Lance out of their little circle. He did it himself at times but it was hard because Lance, as much as he was a pain, was still his brother.

Over the last few months, Patrick Junior had experienced a growth spurt and now he was taller and broader than his younger sibling. He knew that this annoyed Lance who had always used his size to his advantage at every opportunity. They were both big for their ages and Pat was growing at what his mother jokingly called an alarming rate. He was head and shoulders above his classmates and he was also finally towering over Lance. This had done wonders for his self-respect as he knew his father was proud of his increasing size. He had always been able to batter Lance when it came to a fight but there had recently been a real shifting of positions between them. Lance had always looked the stronger of the two but now that was not so evident. Their father had even pointed it out to them both. He had told Lance that he was big-boned like his paternal grandfather whereas his older brother had the same solid build as himself.

Pat Junior was his father's double all right; even he could see that. He was proud to be so like the man he loved and adored and he was determined to be just like him in every way possible when he grew up.

"It's a party, a kids' party and you lot act like it's some kind of fucking big event." Lance's voice was hard and the jealousy he was feeling was threatening to erupt. Pat Junior knew that Lance was finding it difficult to accept the fact that he was having a big party for his tenth birthday. Lance had always been jealous by nature and Patrick, who was untroubled by envy or greed, was unsure how to react to it most of the time. He knew that Lance would be having his own party when his tenth birthday came around but, like everything else, Lance wanted his to be first. Lance only saw Pat's party as something to top when his turn finally came. He was already planning his own party and thinking of ways to make sure it was ten times better than the party his brother was going to have.

Lance didn't understand that Pat's party would be merrier because all the people going actually liked his brother.

Lance didn't make friends easily, and Patrick Junior always looked out for him although he knew that Lance resented that.

Pat Junior understood how he felt to an extent; all his friends with younger brothers were in the same boat. Being the youngest was hard enough but Pat Junior knew that Lance was aware that his mother preferred him and that had to be hard to live with. Even *he* knew that his mum preferred him to Lance although she tried not to differentiate between them. But he also knew that Lance was the apple of Nanny Annie's eye and that she loved him enough for everyone.

But Lance was unhappy a lot of the time and Pat Junior was sorry about that. He wished he could make things better for him. Nanny Annie might be all over him like a rash but it was his mother poor Lance needed, and Pat Junior wished he could make that happen. His mum loved him, and he loved her, the twins were everyone's babies, even Lance was mad about them. But his mum only pretended that she loved Lance and it was awful to watch because she was actually fooling no one. Least of all poor Lance, who knew that all the pretense was for his benefit.

Billy was still waxing lyrical about the party when Father O'Donnell rang the bell that heralded the start of their school day.

Pat Junior and Billy walked in together and Lance, as always, hung back as if walking in with them was like admitting a defeat of some kind.

Mick Diamond was feeling rough. He was always telling people he had a cold coming on, but he didn't. The reason he was red-nosed and feverish was because he drank too much. He looked around the flat that Annie now lived in, thanks to her daughter's generosity, and wondered at the way life threw you a curve when you least expected it.

That Lil could have ended up like she had still amazed him and he wished he had been a proper father to her when he had the chance. Now he was at Annie's mercy and she still made him pay for every fucking slight or wound she felt he had inflicted on her during their marriage.

She was still his wife though and she permitted him access to her house and her body when the fancy took her. It didn't bother him; he could shag a fence with a few drinks inside his belly and, knowing him, he probably had at some point. He knew he had fucked some horrors in his time, drink did that to a man. Beer goggles they called it on the telly. He called them pub fucks but he never remembered until he was reminded of it by someone who had obviously not drunk as much as him. He took their word for it though, as he usually had a feeling that there might be a grain of truth somewhere. Some weren't bad either, it was a shame that he was so drunk they never registered. He only went back to their places because they had more drink, no other reason. He would go home with Larry Grayson if he had a drink for him.

The thought made him smile and Annie, as always, was quick to question him about it.

"What you got to laugh about?"

Mick smiled at *her* then.

"I was just thinking about those kids, Annie. That Lance is a case, ain't he?" He knew how to push her buttons and he pressed them to his own advantage on a daily basis.

"He is not happy about this party they are having for the boy. It's ridiculous spending all that money on a child." Her voice was both disgusted and full of admiration at the same time.

She loved telling her cronies about the arrangements, knowing that it was the talk of everyone around and about. But she was also genuinely shocked that so much money was being spent on a ten-year-old.

Mick understood the reasoning, though he didn't say that to Annie, of course. Lil had never had a real birthday in her life until she married Brodie. Not even a card or an acknowledgement most years. He didn't blame himself for that; she was, after all, nothing to do with him. But now he wondered why Annie had not attempted to mark the day for her only child. He would not have allowed it if she had, but he was not about to admit that to himself or anyone else.

Now he guessed that Brodie, who had been dragged up himself, and Lil were making sure that their children had all the things that they hadn't. Pat Junior's tenth birthday was being treated like some kind of milestone in the boy's life. Mick was going to the party though, he was determined on that. He still pretended to people that everything between him and the Brodies was hunky-dory and he knew he had to show his face there to keep up the illusion of family.

Annie assured him that he was invited, along with her. She had cleared it with Lil by all accounts. He was interested to see what it would be like. The kids were nice enough, even he had to admit that. Especially those girls, the twins. They were as sweet as candy and, although he would never admit it, he loved the way they smiled at him on the rare occasions he saw them.

Lil had done all right for herself, he had to give her credit where credit was due. He admired her for the way she had pulled herself up in the world and for the way she had tamed a wild man like Brodie. He remembered now that when she had started developing he had made a point of catching her in various states of undress and had felt her up a few times. Mick stopped his mind going any further, he was not going to go there today.

Lil had developed enough of a body to attract any red-blooded male but he had not thought back then that she would have known how to use it and keep a man interested in her for as long as she had. Four kids and one on the way and Brodie still acted like she was his first girlfriend.

"Are you listening to me?"

Mick Diamond was brought back to the present by his wife's strident voice.

"Course I am!"

"Well, what do you think then? I heard that Dennis Williams was on the warpath again. He is a nutter, him."

Mick nodded. "True, Annie, very true."

He watched her as she cooked him bacon and eggs. She was a good old stick was Annie, really. She was just a miserable bitch and he knew he had contributed to that over the years.

"How is Lil anyway?" Mick asked about her because he could not think of any other topic of conversation and he knew Annie was after a chat.

Annie smiled. A rare smile that made the years drop from her and softened her face so that she looked almost beautiful.

"She ain't a bad girl really, Mick. There's plenty worse than my Lil."

Mick was so flabbergasted at her words that he forgot to swallow and nearly choked himself in the process. As he coughed like a TB patient, Annie slapped his back for him and he was saved from saying anything that would have alerted his wife to the shock and absolute amazement her words had caused him.

Annie, though, was more than aware of the effect her words had had on her husband and she finished off the breakfast in silence.

She wasn't going to enlighten Mick about why she had changed her opinion of her daughter because he would only use it against her in some way. But the fact that Lil could still find it in her heart to make sure that her mother was solvent as she approached old age, despite her upbringing, had really affected her.

To know that someone cared about you was a new and wonderful feeling for Annie.

As Mick had battered her down and broken her spirit within months of their marriage, she had done the same thing to poor Lil, blaming her for the abortion that her own life had become.

Lance made up for a lot with her; she had seen that boy born and felt, for the first time in her life, what love could be. She had experienced the selfless love that a mother should feel for her children, though she had never felt it towards her own daughter.

When Lil had called her into the kitchen the day before and handed her the paperwork to her little flat, she had been speechless. Even more so because she knew that Lil would have had her work cut out convincing Patrick Brodie to give her a penny candy, let alone the roof over her head.

Lil had explained that it was in her name but that the solicitor had written up a contract that stated it was Annie's until her death and only then would it revert back to her daughter. This, she knew, was so that Mick Diamond didn't get a look in and she could understand that. He was capable of bumping her off if he thought he would get his mitts on a few quid.

When Annie arrived home she looked around her. For the first time in her life, she was secure, really secure, and she wondered at how lucky she was that her only child had her best interests at heart, despite everything. She had made herself a stiff drink and then she had found herself being bombarded with memories of every little thing she had done, or, if she was honest and more to the point, *not* done, for her daughter.

It was only now that she was finally understanding what other women had taken for granted. All you really had in the end was your kids. Rich, poor, beggar or king, the children you had were the only people who cared about you in the end.

The knowledge that she was set up for the rest of her life had also given Annie a confidence that she would never have thought she could possess.

Whatever else Annie might have thought about her daughter, she would always appreciate what she had done for her. Even more so because she had done it without any kind of fanfare whatsoever.

Mick Diamond watched the changing expressions on his wife's face and knew from long experience that something of moment had occurred. What that might be, he had no idea. He would have to bide his time and ferret it out of her gradually. He was a patient man, he could wait.

Whatever it was, it had to do with money. That was the only thing that brought a smile to this woman's face. Other than Lance, of course, but he didn't count.

Chapter Eleven

"No, fuck off. You are having a joke, I hope?"

Trevor didn't laugh as he didn't think it was actually expected of him. Pat Brodie's voice was high enough not just to sound surprised, but to also convey major disbelief.

"How much did they skank then?" Patrick was trying to keep his breathing normal and not let his anger get the better of him. When he was like this he was capable of anything and he needed to hear everything that had occurred so he would not go off half-cocked.

"Over a hundred grand and, have a guess what, I had to go and get the money for them. They knew I pay out quick and that is what they were banking on. I had to hand over my hard-earned poke to those fucking idiots without being able to say anything. If I had argued, they would have killed me without a second's thought."

The fear was still in Trevor's voice and Patrick knew that he was obviously still feeling the terror that only that kind of threat could bring. Death threats were bad enough but when you knew it was not just a threat but a real possibility, it could really fuck up your day. Especially when you also had to undergo open-wallet surgery or the threats would materialize in seconds.

Patrick was itching to make amends; the fact that Trevor was not just a mate but under his protection was well-known. Trevor paid him a decent chunk of change to make sure he could sit in any game and be safe and secure.

The cards were a hard game for people like Trevor. He was a one-off, a real player; he was the exception to the rule. Somehow, Trevor won more often than he lost. He was a nice bloke as well, a decent guy, in fact. Patrick had always liked him and, more to the point, respected his talent because he knew that only a few people were given such a gift. He had watched Trevor over the years and he could not express in words just how fucking amazing the man was with a deck of cards and a decent pot. But the bottom line was that Trevor was not a fighter. He was not a hard man and he didn't want to be. That was the whole idea of making a few pounds, you didn't have to be anything. You bought the safety you required and you got what you paid for. To have Trevor here now, in a terrible state, telling him that he had been fleeced by three baboons and a nancy boy, was so outrageous that Patrick wanted to rip someone's head off just for the hell of it.

"Did you know them? Do you know where they drink? Anything that might tell us who was the brains behind it."

Trevor nodded. "The big one I recognized. It took me a while to figure it out but I've seen him with young Dave Williams. He's been in the casino a few times. I think he was nervous of me because I kept staring at him; he was getting right testy."

"Dave Williams?"

Patrick just stopped himself from saying, "My Dave."

Trevor nodded. "I'm sure, Pat."

Pat stood up and looked at Trevor for long moments, his eyes darkening with his growing anger. Then he suddenly said, "The fucking two-faced cunt."

Patrick's answer and the way it was delivered was the single most shocking thing that Trevor had ever heard. Patrick Brodie was known as a hard case but no one knew what he was really capable of.

Pat was sensible enough to keep the real villainy out of the mouths of locals. He knew that gossip was what put most people behind bars. Gossip usually had a grain of truth in it and it always amazed him when men discussed their skulduggery in public; it was like asking for a tug from the cops. Being well known was a very good reason to keep your trap shut because everything about you was discussed, exaggerated and believed by everyone around you. It was human nature and the only way to keep safe was to keep quiet.

Patrick had done some bastard things over the years and very few people knew about them. If they were ever discussed and the story made its way back to him, he would be able to pinpoint the culprit in seconds. The only way you could keep on top of the game was to fucking keep quiet.

Dave was probably only the fall guy, it was obvious who the big man was. It was Dennis he should be going after. And not a moment too soon either. He had warned Dave what would happen if he stepped on his toes again and now it was time to dole out some retribution. He had held back because of Dave and the fact that he had always had time for him. Even after the last debacle he had tried not to go over the top.

Well, he was done with being nice and trying to honor a friendship that was well past its sell-by date. He was just about ready to cause serious damage and the recipient was going to be Dennis Williams. He was actually looking forward to it.

Jimmy Brick was a big lad and, like most big lads, he was used to people either trying to fight *him* or being convinced that he was going to hurt *them*. Although Jimmy *could* have a row when necessary, he much preferred *not* to, if he could avoid one.

Jimmy had a large head that was overlong, his chin was thick and angular and, coupled with his wide-spaced eyes, his protruding, thick eyebrows and his buzz cut, he was often called Frankenstein. Even his mum had mentioned the likeness on more than one occasion. The family joke was that when he had finally emerged from his poor mother, the size of his head, which had caused her such torment, was commented on by all the women helping with the delivery. His granny had apparently taken one look at the boy who had taken nearly forty-eight hours to come into the world and shrieked.

"For Christ's sake, shove the ugly bastard back in!"

The laughter this had always received was not so much hurtful any more, as it was expected. Jimmy was past caring; looks were never going to be his strong point, he had soon figured that much out. And as he had seen his baby pictures, he was the first to admit that his granny had got a point.

He had been a very ugly child and adolescence had not made him any better. He had appalling acne and, coupled with his protruding brows and his loose bottom lip, he had settled down to a life of tranquility. Jimmy had been his granny's favorite in the end and she had helped him come to terms with his looks by telling him that he had two choices: to hide away or to learn to accept the stares he got from people and remind himself that they couldn't help it. He *was* an ugly fucker and nothing was ever going to change that. Harsh as that was, he was glad of her and her common sense; he had learned to live with himself and he was more than aware that many so-called beauties would never achieve that. Good looks, his granny had always told him, were a curse. He had the chance to be loved for himself. No one had loved him yet, but he was confident that once he had cracked it and had some dough, that would come.

Women were willing to overlook a lot for a nice house and an easy life. He just hoped the kids did not get his big head and cause whoever he married the same pain he had caused his poor mother. She was still going on about it now, all these years later.

Jimmy smiled at the thought. He had a nice easy temperament that stood him in good stead with the people who finally bothered to get to know him properly; his features made him look ferocious and stopped most overtures of friendship in their tracks.

Jimmy Brick was a really nice guy and he knew that better than any-one else. He was happy enough in his way and he enjoyed his life and enjoyed his job. As he often wondered, how many people could say that?

As Jimmy walked into Patrick Brodie's office, he was smiling. Pat grinned at the guy he genuinely liked and who he also felt so very sorry for. He was one ugly bastard and that was being honest.

"All right, mate?"

Patrick nodded and said nonchalantly, "Sit down, mate. I have a proposition to put to you, Jimmy, me boy, and I want an answer soon as. OK?"

Jimmy nodded and, as he sat down, Patrick saw the way he hitched his trouser legs up so as not to crease them too much; he was so fastidious in his dress that it was almost sad to watch him. As Lil had once pointed out, Jimmy looked like the Missing Link. At the time, Pat had laughed, but the more he looked at the lad, the more he saw what she meant. Jimmy Brick was like a huge ape stuffed into an expensive suit. He was a lovely bloke, a decent bloke, but he was disturbing to look at for any length of time.

"What can I do for you, Mr. Brodie?" The voice was rich and deep, the only asset Jimmy possessed.

Patrick loved the way Jimmy always addressed him by his full title when work was being discussed. It was another of the things he liked about Jimmy Brick. He knew that Jimmy separated his work from his real life, which was something he did as well. It was a necessity in their game.

"Jimmy, mate, I want to offer you an in, a real in. Good money and a lot of hard work. What do you say?"

Patrick was pleased to see the boy blush with pleasure and he was more certain than ever that he had chosen the right candidate for the job.

Jimmy held open his arms but he was having difficulty in finding the words he needed to accept the position. His face, though, spoke volumes.

Patrick poured them both large Scotches and, placing the cut-glass tumbler in Jimmy's hand, he said happily, "To many years, mate."

Jimmy clinked his glass with gusto, nearly shattering them both, and reminding them of his extraordinary strength. He said shyly, "I am absolutely over the moon, Mr. Brodie. It is an honor to be allowed to work with a person such as yourself."

It was flowery, it was cheesy, but it was from the heart. Patrick Brodie shook his head and, laughing, he said *sotto voce*, "Enough of that poof talk. Anyone hears us and they might think we're a couple of shit-stabbers!"

Jimmy Brick laughed out loud then; his head was thrown back and the laugh was loud and expressive. Patrick decided he liked the sound of it. Jimmy was going to be an asset, he was sure of that.

"We have our first assignment tonight, mate. We are going to give Dennis Williams the fright of his fucking life."

Patrick saw that Jimmy was pleased about that and wondered if anyone, anywhere, had ever actually liked Dennis Williams.

"Shall I get me tool kit?"

Patrick grinned then and said happily, "What do you think?"

For all his big talk, Dennis Williams was not expecting Patrick Brodie to come looking for him personally. It was something he had not allowed for at any point, or even thought was a possibility. Consequently, when Patrick Brodie swooped on him and his brothers on their territory, in their own local pub, he was nonplussed, to say the least.

Patrick had crashed through the heavy wooden doors of the Mill House in Dagenham like an avenging angel. It was a Saturday night so it was packed with families. Children ran around in their best clothes playing kiss-chase and waiting for the band to play "Pennies from Heaven." This was the highlight of their evening, when the adults would throw their change on to the dance floor and the kids would scramble around collecting as much money as they could. Then the disco would commence and the lights would be dimmed and the parents would feel like they were out for the night at last, as the kids went outside where there was bright light and other kids' chatter to interest them.

The Mill House was a real social club. It had the atmosphere that guaranteed a good night out for families and couples alike. It was shabby in the light of day but, come the evening, it took on a magic all of its own. It smelled of potato chips, stale beer and a multitude of different perfumes. The tables shone with polish and huge tin ashtrays bore legends such as Marlboro Reds or Senior Service. The floor was wooden and scuffed but so shiny the children could start their night off by sliding from one end of it to the other until they would eventually be scolded by an adult. The boys would swagger away like little hard men and go outside into the evening air where they could swagger some more and swear their heads off to impress the girls. It was the beginning of the mating ritual, the first lesson in making a girl notice you and respect you. It was a timeless dance that had been enacted by their parents and grandparents before them. They learned to court while drinking Tizer and playing kiss-chase. Fingers would explore and hands would be allowed liberties and everyone was hot and flushed with this new knowledge that they had acquired.

It was a real family club, not really the kind of setting the Williams boys wanted and not the kind of place where the regulars wanted to see the numerous Williams brothers. Now, though, Dave Williams and his brothers used the Mill House as their base, mainly because they were not sure if they were really welcome in any of the pubs they had frequented for years.

The Williams boys were used to the Mill House now and they were pleased to discover that they were the only real Faces who used the place. They were at first an anomaly and, for the most part, their foray into a local club had been treated with a certain degree of excitement, until, that is, the novelty had worn off. Seeing the Williams brothers now and again was one thing. Having them there all the time, using the place as their office, was now starting to irritate a lot of the regulars. They were all right, but dangerous. The committee members, older men with families and jobs, were unable to stop the Williams lot from wheeling and dealing as and when they wanted to, yet they were desperate to put an end to the trade that seemed to bring in a lot of unsavory characters. The big fear, of course, was that the place would be raided and closed down by the police. No one had the nerve to discuss the worries of the family men and the fear for their kids with the Williams family because they were not what was commonly known as approachable, if the subject touched on them or their businesses in a derogatory way. In fact, they were distinctly cold and menacing. Dennis in particular, who, with his scarred face and head and his broken-toothed grin, could frighten a banshee, let alone anyone else. Dennis was a hard man and he didn't try to hide it. He reveled in his notoriety and it was this that was such a worry to most people. He was vicious when viciousness wasn't warranted or indeed needed.

Being a Face was all Dave wanted from life, all he had ever wanted. A Face was a Face was a Face, as old man Williams would say to them as kids. He had loved Faces, he basked in their reflected glory and lived for the glamor he tried to share in. Now they were Faces in their own right and they were well-known enough to be able to deal their drugs here and share their glamor with a few of the local bully-boys who, like their father before them, would talk about them with hushed tones and respect.

It was a long way from when he was Brodie's main boy and Dave had eventually come to terms with that; at least he let his brothers think so. He knew that Dennis was living on borrowed time. He had hoped that he could keep him away from Patrick and Spider long enough for them to calm down a bit. Maybe even give Dennis another chance. Dave sighed. He was on the powder again and he knew that it was only the speed making him believe that Dennis could walk away from all the shit he had created. He was going to have to answer for his stupidity at some point and the burning question was, when? They couldn't hide away here forever. He was in such a high state that he was actually getting the rushes again and everything was suddenly so real and bright he felt the urge to start dancing.

Dave went into the toilet and cut himself another line. If only they sold this stuff to the customers they would be rocking with him. They didn't though. It was cut to fuck by the time they sold it off. But it was a good buzz whatever and, as he snorted the amphetamine, he felt the burn inside his nose that told him it had been cut with strychnine at some point. Dave grinned and said to his reflection, "Bring back glucose, all is forgiven."

Dave was laughing like a hyena at his own joke and he folded his envelope up carefully before going back out to the club. As he shuffled out of the toilet and went back into the club, the noise hit him like a wall and he winced in pain. He saw a couple of his dealers at the bar and sighed.

They were now responsible for any dope that shot out of the Anglers, the old man's pub opposite the Mill House, and a few other little pubs around and about that Patrick and Spider wouldn't be interested in. The Volunteer pub on the Barking and Dagenham traffic circle was where they should be dealing, it was always kicking. The club there was called

Flanagan's Speakeasy and it was packed to capacity almost every night. But Spider had that one sewn up so they let it go.

Dave started chatting up a young girl with badly permed black hair, glitter on her cheekbones and a bright yellow satin jacket that didn't cover her huge breasts. He knew, without asking her, that she was into Marc Bolan. Well, she could be into the fucking Beam River if she wanted to. All he cared about was a fuck. Although whether he was capable of any kind of hard-on, he wasn't sure. It was worth a try though.

Dave was rocking, speeding out of his nut. He knew she was a little schoolgirl dressed up for her night out and that her father was probably watching them with fear in his heart and no way to protect his child. Dave was past caring these days. He was a nervous wreck; he just seemed to be waiting for the shit to hit the fan. He was burdened with the guilt of nearly killing his brother; the realization that he was capable of nearly murdering his own flesh and blood had been a revelation. The fact that he had enjoyed it, was sorry he had not finished the job, was what was making him so uneasy. Dennis was his brother and he loved him. Unfortunately, he was also a vain, temperamental and violent lunatic who would always bring trouble to their door. Dennis couldn't even help it, he just attracted trouble. In all honesty, a lot of the time he caused it, mainly because he loved the adrenaline rush it brought him. And the attention, he loved to be the center of attention, always for the wrong reasons. Dave loved his brother but hated him with a vengeance for all the trouble he had brought to his doorstep. Because it was always left to him to clear up the mess, he was always the fall guy. And now they had no real income any more, no security, because Patrick Brodie had aimed them out of it and so he should. Patrick had given him the opportunity to come back, but how could he? Dennis wouldn't last five minutes on his own, and as for his other brothers, he had seen more brains on a butcher's floor. Dennis was a fucking liability and that was something that would never change.

As Patrick and his boys crashed through the doors and into the club, Dave almost felt relieved that this was finally happening and would soon be over.

Dennis was so surprised that he just stood there open-mouthed and looking, as more than one person noted, stupid.

Patrick looked at Dennis with a frown and then he said with deep disgust and an underlying menace that was evident to everyone around them, "You had to be expecting me, Dennis, so what's with the fucking shocked face? Surely you didn't think I had forgotten about you?"

Patrick Brodie was talking to him and worse, was treating him, like he was a nothing, a no-neck, the shit on his shoes and Dennis knew that only a madman would be fool enough to try to salvage what was left of their reputation by answering him back. He was expected to keep his trap shut and he knew that anyone with half a brain would shut the fuck up, but was not sure how much brain he actually had left.

The people around the bar were thrilled to see Patrick Brodie in their little club; they were also secretly hoping that he might knock Dennis Williams on to his arse. The general consensus was that he was a big-mouthed jerk, though no one would say that to his face, of course. Dennis was under the mistaken impression that he was popular. Faces were, for the most part, Diamond Geezers; nice blokes who were approachable and friendly and who didn't feel the need to be a hard man twenty-four-seven. Whereas the Dennis Williamses of the world, although they might be afforded the same courtesy as other Faces, were not liked enough to command either loyalty or respect from anyone around them. At least not when there was a real, bona fide Face making them look like they were a fool. A plastic gangster was a term that had recently come into common usage and it now seemed a fitting description for Dennis Williams.

Dave went to Patrick and tried to salvage at least a shred of the friendship they had shared for so long. "Not in here, Pat, eh?"

Patrick almost sneered at his one-time friend. His thick dark hair was almost blue in the disco lights and his eyes were like slits as he looked Dave up and down with obvious distaste.

"I want my fucking money and I want it now."

Dave screwed his handsome face up into a frown of confused wonderment. It was a face that Patrick had seen him pull once too often in the past when they were questioning someone and not getting the answers they required.

"What is he on about, Den?"

Patrick was not surprised that Dave took his word over his brother's; if Dennis Williams was asked what he had for breakfast he would add a sausage. Lying came so easily to him that he couldn't distinguish between the truth and his bullshitting any more.

"Dennis, please."

The music had stopped and everyone was watching them closely. Patrick flicked his head at Dennis and Jimmy Brick walked over to him and, with a pretense of friendliness, he ushered him out of the club and into a waiting car. Dennis was like a little lamb. He knew when he was beaten and he was not going to cause himself any more pain than necessary.

Patrick walked out then, followed by his other two bodyguards and Dave. He turned at the doorway and said, "Go back, Dave. This is going to be fucking seriously painful and before you get all fucking nostalgic for your brother, remember this: he had a hundred grand off my mate earlier today and that was the straw that broke this fucking cunt's back, all right?" He was not sure why he was justifying hammering Dennis Williams, but he heard himself doing it anyway. He respected and liked Dave so he didn't want to give him false hopes or any lies.

"Don't kill him, Pat, please. Me mum would go off her head."

Patrick laughed then. "Your mum is so far off her fucking head, even Ozzy Osbourne talks sense in comparison to her. Now fuck off and leave me to sort this out once and for all."

As Patrick got into the car with Dennis and Jimmy, Dave heard him saying quietly and authoritatively, "Look, Den, my old nan used to say there are two tragedies in life. One is not getting what you want and the other is getting it. You are getting what you have been asking for, Dennis, and you are not getting what you want. Deal with it and fucking stop eyeballing me, you fucking ugly cunt."

Dennis was shaking with fear. Jimmy Brick was a torturer who was known to have no empathy with his victims and he was capable of inflicting horrific injuries without any kind of remorse at all. He had stripped a man of all the skin on his leg just to find out if he had slept with a known associate's wife. The guy was locked up and had heard a whisper; he had appealed to Jimmy to find out the truth of it so he could put his mind at rest. Jimmy had taken the man's skin off in long strips and when he had found out what he wanted, he had dumped the guy in a garbage can minus his skin, his ears and his scrotum. The worst thing of all, though, was that he had done that for a favor, not even for remuneration or to get a rep. It had been done as a favor, that's all.

Now, Dennis saw Jimmy staring at his scars and he knew, without a second's doubt, that he was already working out the best way to go about his night's work. He would open a few of the scars for maximum pain and add a few more for good measure.

Dennis suddenly felt the cold hand of fear that comes to all violent people. They were always the biggest cowards when it was their turn to play and Dennis Williams was already crying silently before they had even turned out of the parking lot and on to the A13. Dave stood in the doorway of the Mill House and watched the car until the taillights disappeared into the distance.

Spider was in the Beehive in Brixton waiting for Cain to pick him up and eyeing up a tall African girl with dark eyes and four-inch platforms.

She was smiling at him with the invitation he was used to being offered and with the same high-handedness that always attracted him to his women. But he had enough on his hands at the moment with his latest partner and the tantrums she could command at any time of the day or night. He put this one in the back of his mind for future reference, though it was worth giving her a smile anyway. You never knew what the future might bring.

Spider was on his fifth pint of Guinness when Cain came in and motioned for him to go outside. For the first time in years, he saw his brother looking worried and he followed him outside with trepidation. A lot was going on this night and he wondered what part they would have to play in it.

*　　*　　*

Dennis was lying on a concrete floor and he could feel the coldness and the dampness seeping into his bones. He had been lying there for what seemed a long time, though in reality it had only been about forty-five minutes. He was trussed up like a chicken, his hands were tied behind his back and his legs were tied at the knees, making it hard to get himself comfortable. He could smell oil and gasoline and the smells were not making him feel any better. He was not sure exactly where he was. It was too dark and he had been too frightened to really take any notice of where he was going; he had been told to look at the floor of the car and he had complied because he knew he was now relying on the friendship he had once had with Brodie to see him through till the morning.

His eyes were getting accustomed to the dimness and he looked around him with interest; he could see tires piled up, smell the rubber and the dirt. There were also a lot of packing crates that he guessed held either knocked-off gear or drugs and as he was now sobering up by the second he wondered whose garage he was now incarcerated in. He hoped it wasn't anyone he knew well; the shame would be unbearable. As would this whole episode if it became common knowledge.

This was going to be the humiliation of a lifetime and he knew, without a doubt, that he would have to suffer it if he was going to come out with his life. Dennis finally understood that he had crossed all the lines and that he was not hard enough to ever take on the big boys. It was too early in his career and he was not liked enough to expect any kind of back-up. Dave had warned him over and over again and had even tried to knock some sense into him but he had not believed that this night would ever really come.

The door opened and as the lights were switched on, he felt the burn behind his eyes and the sting of the tears that he knew were more about terror than anything else. He watched warily as Jimmy walked purposefully toward a large workbench with a vise on one end and an array of spray cans on the other. Dennis saw then that this was a working garage so that meant they only had a few hours until the place would be a hive of activity.

He wondered how long he would be on this floor and how much of his blood would be spilled on the sawdust that Jimmy was now sprinkling liberally all around him. He could hear the faint sounds of cars in the distance and knew he was most likely still in London.

As he watched Jimmy prepare himself for his night's work, he understood just how he had made other people feel over the years, and he understood that with Jimmy Brick this wasn't about being a hard man, it was just something he did when requested and something that he knew he did well.

Dennis could hear a kettle boiling in the background; he hoped that it wasn't going to be part of his punishment and he prayed that whatever happened he would be man enough to take it without begging or pleading. Even now, how he was perceived was still his main priority and he still believed that he had enough credibility left to be given an easy ride.

Then, when he saw Jimmy Brick taking out his chisels and his hammers, he lost it completely and it took Patrick and Jimmy ten minutes to finally gag him and stop the screaming.

They were laughing as they did this, which did nothing to allay the fears of Dennis Williams.

Chapter Twelve

Patrick was happy enough with the turn recent events had taken. Spider and Cain had been involved, as had a few of his other trusted personnel. It was a week since Dennis Williams had been given a serious talking-to and the general consensus was that he had asked for it and he had finally got it.

No one actually knew what that talking-to was supposed to be about, but speculation was rife, and that was exactly what Pat Brodie had counted on. People had a much better time when they were speculating and, eventually, a load of old jokes would turn into public opinion; someone would get drunk and pretend they had been in on it all, knew the real story, and that would be that.

If anyone had actually been told the extent of Dennis Williams's talking-to, it would have made more than a few so-called hard men wonder if they would be seeing their last meal in a sink or on the floor within minutes of the details being revealed.

So, speculation was rife and that was exactly what Brodie wanted.

As he sat in his office and waited for Dave Williams to come by, as requested, he hoped they could finally put this whole sorry business to bed. Patrick had learned one thing out of it all, that he had given Dave too much leeway over the years and that was a mistake he was not going to make twice in a lifetime.

Jimmy Brick was becoming one of the main players in his world and this was also being noted by the powers that be, and Jimmy was feeling the warmth of his newfound status. Birds in particular were lining up for his favors and he was still deciding which one he was going to honor with his cock.

Patrick made a point of knowing what his workforce were up to and now he knew all about Jimmy Brick and his lifestyle.

There were two contenders for the title of Jimmy Brick's bird. One was a small blonde with big tits and a bubbly personality; she loved the life, loved being in the spotlight and loved the attention Jimmy was showering on her. The other girl was quiet, mousy-haired but with a body that most women would pay a fortune to be in possession of. She was also a kind, generous individual who had a nice personality, a good vocabulary and was unfortunately in awe of villains. She was basically an also-ran even though she actually liked Jimmy. The former was going to win the competition; she was brash and she had made sure he would want her and all her body had to offer. She would regret it until the day she died.

The girl in question was unaware that once Jimmy had made his mind up, the relationship was going to be a lifetime membership, whether she wanted it or not. Like a *Reader's Digest* subscription, Jimmy was for life, but as yet, she was blissfully ignorant of that fact.

Jimmy was not a man to take himself or anyone else lightly and the few months that his chosen beau would enjoy, playing the devoted lover of the new main man, would soon seem like a high price to pay. The excitement of becoming Jimmy Brick's bird would eventually turn into years of misery, jealousy and heartache.

The fact that the girl suddenly wanted him, coinciding with his new-found status, would be offensive to Jimmy, even though he would happily use that power to get what he wanted. It was a recipe for disaster: not for Jimmy Brick, but for the girl in question. Trust would always be an issue, as would any kind of honesty, because she would learn to tell him only what he wanted to hear. His natural antagonism would ensure that no matter what happened, she would always be suspect because he would always know that it was only his reputation and his money that kept her beside him. She would eventually fantasize about him being nicked so she could finally walk away from him.

Jimmy was a one-woman man though, like all his predecessors, and that was as rare in their world as a straight judge or an honest bank robber. Once he chose her, there would be no going back for either of them. He would own her, it was as simple as that, no matter what she felt about it. Jimmy Brick would keep her on side to show her fidelity, prove she wanted to be with him whatever. If she walked away at any time, he would be seen as an ice-cream, a loser. He would never let that happen to him. All he had was his dignity, and he would hang on to that with every ounce of his considerable strength. If a child arrived, it would only cement their relationship because no one in their right mind would ever dare to take her on board after that. Even a thirty-sentence passed eventually. But it would be a while before the life-sentence the girlfriend had inadvertently taken on would be seen as absolute.

Pat Brodie was aware of all this; he had dealt with Jimmy Bricks all his life and he knew how to handle them. He was a dangerous little fuck, and he would need constant monitoring at all times. That was also par for the course where looney tunes like him were concerned. They had a terrible habit of killing people for all the wrong reasons, mainly their wives or their girlfriends, occasionally even a stranger who was stupid enough to confront them on a nice sunny afternoon.

That would always be Jimmy's Achilles heel: the destruction of a drunken customer in the pub or the loud-mouthed bastard in the restaurant who didn't realize what they were taking on. That would get him arrested if he wasn't careful; anger put so many people in jail, it was unbelievable.

The people Jimmy was paid to harm or remove from his orbit were a different ballgame: there was no emotion then; no room for anger or resentment. It was just a job, no more and no less. Brodie understood this man's mindset and he also knew how to utilize it for his own gain. It was, as he always said, the nature of the beast, and they were beasts, all of them. They just didn't know how to classify themselves.

Jimmy was a young man who needed guidance, who needed someone to keep him on the straight and narrow. Brodie was going to be that person and he was going to take care of him, not only as an asset to his business but as someone he could mold, could make into a second-in-command.

Pat Brodie had to run a business and so he needed nutcases but this time, as an added bonus, he was involved with someone he liked and respected. The boy had potential and balls, the two main ingredients for their kind of life.

Jimmy had taken Dennis out with a deliberately long and completely unnecessary violence that had been tightly controlled but obviously hugely enjoyable to the man himself. Pat had been impressed and disgusted all at the same time. But this was exactly what was needed. From now on, Jimmy Brick would be a byword for hate and despair, pain and terror. His rep would stop trouble before it began because no one would want to tangle with a fuckhead like Jimmy. Those who did would then see the error of their ways right quick. He was like a cancer, he would get you in the end. He was like a guarantee of calm because now he had started his reign of terror only a fucking lunatic would be stupid enough to take him on.

Patrick was in the market for a Jimmy Brick because Jimmy would earn his inflated wage by going down for him at some point. As long as no one could prove who ordered a beating or a murder, no one could ever knock on Pat's door, it was as simple as that. Jimmy was a good bloke but also his own personal fall guy if everything ever fell out of bed. Jimmy Brick was the new Dave Williams. Not that he would ever point that out, of course, he was too shrewd by half.

Smiling, Patrick poured himself a large brandy and, sipping it, he looked out of the grimy window at people going about their daily business in Soho.

He was pleased with himself, happy with his life and what it could bring him in the near future. He knew Jimmy had been a shrewd move on his part and he was happy to relax now and wait for him to bring in the money, the poke, the peace of mind. He had been the resident nutter for too long, it was time he took a back seat. He could relax and just make the odd appearance when it was deemed necessary. People had no idea of the war that was waged on a daily basis; of how keeping yourself on top took nearly all your time. Soho was a place where fortunes were made, and fortunes were lost on the turn of a card; or the chatter of a belligerent employee. Where people were expendable and life was of no real consequence.

"You are who you beat." That was said by the man he had shot here so many years ago and Brodie knew that had been a lesson well learned by the both of them.

He looked out the window again, enjoying the sights and the sounds as he always had. This was his second home and when he wasn't with Lil, this was the only other place he felt comfortable, felt as if he belonged.

Nothing in Soho was ever really kosher, and no one ever admitted to anything *ever*. Even people's names were just pretend, like the whole place was pretend. More so even than the theatres that abounded; the stories they acted out for their audiences night after night were not a patch on the real-life stories happening on the streets outside their doors.

Brodie sighed and wondered at a man like himself, someone who could see this place as anything other than a cesspool. It destroyed people on a regular basis, especially the women; their turnover was phenomenal in comparison with other places that dealt in flesh and pornography, like Shepherds Market. That was where the Soho girls were likely to end their days, or Notting Hill and, worst-case scenario, for the diseased or for the beaten and scarred, the dock areas, what was left of them anyway. But as a man this didn't really affect him so he could turn a blind eye, choose to ignore the price women paid so he could smoke his expensive cigars and pat himself on the back over his success. That was the secret of Soho and its patrons: as long as you kept your minions at arm's length and didn't dwell too much on the price that would be exacted by the customers, you could relax, relax and enjoy the spoils of a war that had never really been declared on the unsuspecting girls who saw Soho as some kind of refuge. At first, girls could lose themselves there; no one would find them if they were clever enough to keep their real identities a secret. But it was a vicious circle and, like any circle, it had no beginning and no end. The great job they had acquired, the independence they thought was so important, eventually turned out to be the worst things that could ever happen to them. It was a seductive life for young runaways. It seemed glamorous and exciting, money for old rope, money that was easily earned and easily spent because it was always going to be there the next day and the day after that and the day after that, until years had passed and they were caught in the never-ending cycle that was prostitution. Every year their johns became less well-heeled and every year their expectations were lowered. In the end they would be on the street hustling for enough money to keep them stoned and out of it enough to forget what their lives had become.

This was a dangerous game and it was an earner, but not for the women of course.

The only real winners were the men like him, the men who used the women they found on a daily basis and discarded them when they were not needed any more. Over the years the girls, at least most of them, had become like animals to him; he had no real feelings for them. How could he when they had no feelings for themselves?

It didn't do to dwell on anything for too long in his job, especially as he was long past caring these days and he made sure of that much at least. He only cared about his family; anyone else was just collateral damage, no more and no less.

He stared out of the window. Late afternoon was a favorite time for him in Soho, the streets were just getting busy with people who were expecting a good night out and who were either ignorant or uncaring about how that would eventually come about. The night drawing in also brought out all the locals. The staple of Soho evenings, the reason people congregated here night after night. It was a mixture of the young, the stupid, the used and the users. Then, of course, there were the people like him, without whom none of the former could ply their wares. Whatever anyone thought of him and his peers, they were the staple diet of Soho, they kept the place ticking over and kept the mystique that attracted the johns and the revelers.

Everyone loved a Face, a villain, and everyone liked to be associated with the glamor that villainy provided for them. The rich and famous were drawn to people like him, like moths to a flame. It was how it worked and he milked it for all it was worth. What else could he do?

This was one of the reasons he needed a Jimmy Brick. The clubs were frequented by Names these days; they were the meeting ground for the great and the good, and in reality they paid enough protection, and owned enough cops to ensure that their more exotic customers got a free pass and peace of mind. Now he had to sort out the final piece of the puzzle and, once that had been obtained, he could relax with the best of them.

He watched the strippers passing each other on the street as they made their way from club to club, calling out to each other, glad to see their counterparts as it made them feel less lonely and less afraid of what the night might bring. The scouts were already at work, trying to talk the customers into the strip bars or the hostess clubs, promising the earth and delivering nothing but the empty promise of good times to be had. The air was cold enough to make all their breath visible and the scantily dressed women upped their usual pace, hurrying into the warmth of their next club.

Patrick Brodie loved the West End, and he felt at home there.

He had no worries about losing his crown because he had earned it, fair and square, and he was respected and, more importantly, he was feared. He had made sure of that, and he was proud of it as well. Soho was a shithole to the majority of people. To him it was just a means to an end.

Lil, the love of his life, was cooking another baby and once she was delivered of it, she would be back to her usual self. His kids were smart, handsome and well-looked after. He had money all over the show, a beautiful home and he had what he had never believed was possible for a man brought up as he had been. He had happiness inside himself, real happiness, even if he didn't look like he did. Only Lil, his Lil, knew how happy he was and how much he cherished his life with her. Everything else was as nothing when measured against his family.

God had been good to him, he knew, and he thanked him every Sunday by paying his respects and enjoying the peace and tranquility that church seemed to bring him.

Life, he felt, was good.

"My party is going to be the best party ever and you can invite any of your friends, Lance."

Pat Junior was feeling magnanimous, even though his brother had been irritating him all day. He knew that he was being overly nice about Lance and his wicked tongue and though he had decided that he was just a really annoying little brother like any other, he understood his brother's unhappiness better than Lance did.

"Why would my friends want to go to your crappy party?"

Pat Junior shrugged at his brother's words. "Well, the offer is there if you want to ask anyone."

He stopped himself from saying, "if you have anyone to ask that is," but he knew it was pointless because he didn't get any kind of thrill from hurting his brother's feelings. He knew Lance had the burden of knowing that their mum didn't really have a lot of time for him, though she pretended to, and that his Nanny Annie had too much time for him, which he guessed was why his mum got so annoyed with his brother.

His nan seemed to take Lance over as soon as she stepped on to the premises and that suited him because Pat hated her, really hated her, though he had never admitted that to anyone out loud, of course. He knew his mum put up with her and the girls liked her because she was enamored with them like everyone else was. Twins did that, they made people take notice of them somehow. He adored his little sisters, and he understood why they made such an impression. But Lance was hard work and he felt for his brother even as he got angry with him.

So he sighed heavily, saying, "Well you can ask anyone you want, OK?"

Lance nodded, feeling bad now. He knew Pat Junior was at the end of his considerable patience so he smiled and, as always, it changed his whole face; he looked handsome and innocent. The way he would have looked all the time if he wasn't always on the look out for slights or what he saw as insults.

"Thanks, mate. I'll think about it, all right?"

Pat Junior nodded.

And then they both sat down and watched *Jackanory* together in what was, for once, almost a friendly silence.

Lil walked in and saw her two sons together and smiled at them. They were both so alike and even Lance seemed happy for a change. As she sat down herself and sipped at a cup of tea, she wished that she could feel this contentment more often. But it was so difficult for her because she knew she couldn't.

Lance was watching her warily from the corner of his eye and the guilt that she felt because of him rose up inside her as it always did and made her feel so bad about herself that she almost cried. She tried as hard as she could with him, but the urge to slap this child of hers was overwhelming.

She watched as Patrick Junior glanced at his brother and then slipped his hand into Lance's, all the while acting like there was no atmosphere in the room and there was nothing to be worried about. It was the way that Lance grabbed at his brother's hand as if he was saving him from drowning that was the worst thing of all. Because she knew that Patrick was, as usual, acting as a wall that kept her and her second son as far away from each other as was physically possible and she did nothing to stop him.

Lil appreciated her eldest son's help and loved him all the more because she knew he was doing it all for her; she knew that he had no real time for Lance either.

Like her husband with Dennis Williams, who had eventually worn out his welcome, her son had the same attitude with his brother. Unlike Dennis Williams though, Lance had the sense to keep on his brother's good side.

Lil was worried though. Dennis had nearly brought trouble to her door and even though Pat had handled it, she was still smarting from it. No matter what Pat said or, more to the point, didn't say, she had her mother to rely on where gossip was concerned.

The Williams brothers would always be trouble to them, she was convinced of that much at least.

Dave was nervous and he wondered what kind of reception he was going to get in Patrick's office. He hoped against hope that he would be alone, that he didn't have to talk to him with an audience of any kind. He felt Pat owed him that much at least but he couldn't demand it; his days of demanding anything were long gone.

The fact he was invited to the club was significant because he knew that if Pat Brodie was going to do anything to him it would not be where he could be seen or heard. He needed to know the score, not just for him, but for his brothers who were waiting for him to let them know if they were safe or not. The family had been divided and all he could do now was to try to iron out their differences as best he could. If that meant keeping his mouth shut then he was willing to do it like a professional hostess. Dave was more than aware that anything he was given now would be the dregs and he had to accept that and work his way back into Pat's good books. He had to try to salvage something of their working relationship so that his brothers and himself could at least earn a crust of some sort.

He was also worried about what had happened to Dennis. He knew Jimmy had been on board, so he knew that it wasn't going to be anything he wanted to hear, though he would listen to the gory details if necessary and accept it with as good a grace as he could.

At the end of the day, he had to keep reminding himself that, no matter what, he had to do what was best for the rest of the family, himself included. That the old days were dead and gone. He had to take what was offered with as much pride and dignity as he could muster, and eventually it would all blow over.

At least that is what he kept telling himself.

As he parked his car and walked slowly through the evening bustle that was Soho, he felt the sickness rising inside his chest. This had once been his stomping ground, had once been the epitome of everything he had ever wanted or indeed ever achieved but now the streets were cold and unfriendly and he didn't feel a part of it all any more.

The flashing neon lights and the garish posters with nude women and their strategically placed stars, were alien to him. Sex was on sale everywhere, but underlying that was the stench of pimps and the Brodies, all out to take whatever they wanted.

The smell of Chinese food mixed with pasta was sickening and the grey-skinned women who only seemed to come alive at night looked sinister; their make-up and cheap clothes suddenly showing him just how false the world he had inhabited for so long really was.

Soho was all top show and if you scratched the surface you were reminded that it was all built on lies and pretense; he had been part of that pretense once and now he was being forced on to the sidelines. It was a very cruel lesson and one he would remember all his life.

No one acknowledged his existence any more. There were no friendly waves or the humorous shouting he had become used to. He saw people deliberately turning away from him, as if he was diseased, and in a way he was. He was now an outsider looking in and it felt worse than anything he had ever experienced before in his life.

As Dave walked into the warmth of the club, he was left with no illusions about his status in the community where he had once been a leading player.

The head girl, Lynda Marks, looked him up and down with obvious distaste before saying archly, "I'll let him know you're here, shall I?"

Her whole demeanor told him just how far he had fallen and it was this more than anything that really hit him where it hurt.

If the hostesses felt they could talk down to you then you really were about as low as you could possibly get.

But he knew he had to take whatever was dealt him, because he had fucked up big time. It would be years before he was even accepted back into the lower echelons of the world he had come to see as his own; let alone be trusted. He had to make sure that Patrick Brodie understood that he was here today, cap in hand and with all the humility he could muster, in the hope that he could salvage at least something from this debacle. At least get a living for himself and his brothers. He needed to find out whether Dennis was alive or dead and if they at least had something left to bury or whether he had to tell his mother there were no remains to cry over, nothing tangible to grieve for. As he waited for his audience he was sweating with nerves and dry-mouthed with fear.

"Look at that pair of maggots!" Annie's voice was soft for once and, as was her wont these days, it was the sight of her twin granddaughters that was the cause of it.

"Lovely ain't they, Mum. I hope this one's a girl and all."

Lil put her hands under her large lump and lifted it carefully; this was the biggest she had ever been before and everyone assumed she was either carrying a boy or failing that, another set of twins.

She wanted another girl though. She liked the girls and since Lance's birth, she was frightened of another son, of having another boy that she would not be able to love.

The twins were lying side by side once more and talking their own language. It was fascinating to watch them. They were like mirror images of one another and unless you knew them really well, it was difficult to tell them apart.

Her mother's obvious love for them had melted even her heart and their relationship had been easier because of that, easier than it had been for a long time. Annie was always trying to build bridges and helping her out and she appreciated that. As Lil looked around her cluttered front room, she felt the tiredness and the excitement of the new baby acutely.

She only hoped that Patrick would be around for the birth. He was always interested in how she was feeling; he thought he could figure out the sex of the child by asking her questions and feeling her belly. He was like most men when it came down to it, he had no idea what it was like to have your body taken over for nine months yet he was convinced he was an expert. She gave birth and he took the kudos. As her mother said, men were about as much use as a chocolate teapot around a pregnant woman and she had to agree that, for once, she was right.

Annie had been a godsend lately, what with the party and the twins and Patrick being on the missing list so much. Her body was rebelling against this child for some reason and she would be glad to get it out into the open and finally have a proper gander at it. Only a girl could be the cause of her uncomfortable nights, even more uncomfortable days, and the reason for her constant backache and penchant for tears. Never before had she felt so low, or so high, while carrying a child. This one, she was sure, would be special.

As Lance lifted Eileen up and carried her to bed, she smiled slightly; he was good with his sisters, especially Eileen. The weirdness she felt when she was around him had to be her fault, had to be coming from her. Lance tried his hardest to make her love him but she knew that no matter what she did to assure him that was the truth, he knew in his heart that she was pretending.

It was just on eight and the club was still almost empty except for a few of the City boys who liked a drink, a flash of stripper flesh and a quick feel before they lumbered home to their wives. When Dave was finally taken into Patrick's office he was on the verge of tears, such was his nervousness.

Patrick sat at his desk drinking brandy: a good sign, and smoking one of his cigars: a very good sign. Patrick loved his Cuban smokes, everyone knew that, even though he only smoked them when he was in a club, never at home.

Dave smiled tremulously and saw the pity in Pat's eyes. He had fallen so far in the space of a few months and he felt it acutely, especially now that he had finally gained an appointment with the man who had not only taken out his brother, but had also been the cause of every good thing that had happened to them for many years.

Pat smiled at him sadly. "Want a drink, Dave?"

He nodded his assent with far too much enthusiasm and with far too much relief. It was embarrassing to watch, and Dave knew it would make his humiliation even harder to bear. This was the shape of things to come and he knew he would not be able to bear it.

Patrick was heartsore at the predicament his friend had found himself in. He had always liked the kid; he didn't have half the brain or half the gumption of his older brother but he had possessed enough heat to make Pat feel he was worth giving a chance to out of respect for his dead brother, Dicky.

He had only given him an in because of his brother and he had made a bad judgment. Now he was paying for it; they were all paying for it.

As he handed the boy a drink, Jimmy Brick was ushered into the small office and young Dave went white at the sight of him. Even his lips had gone white, so shocked was he to see him.

This annoyed Patrick. Dave should have expected something like this; he was hardly going to leave the meet between these two for months or years, was he? The fact that Dave had not expected it was another reason why he should have realized that the guy was a skank, a fucking waster. Dave should already have had his speech prepared and his sincere apology; should have understood the economics of their world. Instead, he was standing there like a fucking nonce.

Patrick looked at Dave and tried to convey this with a discreet shake of his head; praying that the boy finally caught on to what was expected of him. He had to either fight like fuck and make a stand over his brother's death or keep his mouth shut and forever be a gofer, a cunt.

Dave did nothing and Patrick was devastated, even though he had not expected anything different. The room was filled with tension and also disappointment and Jimmy's easy shrug called for the whole episode to be brought to an end.

Dave watched as Jimmy Brick was embraced by Brodie as if he was a long-lost brother. He knew then that he should have made the first move and embraced Jimmy Brick as if it was all just a silly mistake. He should have realized that Jimmy would now be the person who controlled what he earned and how much responsibility he would be allowed to take on in the future. He had fucked up once more and no one was sorrier than Patrick Brodie; he had tried to build a bridge between them but he had been too stupid to figure that out. Dave observed the solidarity these two men displayed so openly with a sad face and a slumped demeanor. He was already beaten and they didn't need to rub it in; that much was obvious to them all.

Jimmy's dead eyes were finally alive and Patrick realized that they were alive with malice. He was enjoying this little meeting and he understood that Dave was being taught a very valuable lesson and it was Jimmy's job to ram it home, hard and fast, so it would not easily be forgotten.

Once more, the Williams brothers had missed a golden opportunity.

Chapter Thirteen

"I mean it, don't fucking wind me up. I ain't giving you nix."

Dave and Tommy Williams were both at a point where murder was definitely an option. The man they were fighting with knew this but was not worried; at least, he was not as worried as he should have been. Both the Williams brothers were more than aware that he seemed almost uninterested. Colin Parker was an arsehole and they knew it. Till now, though, he had always been a nervous arsehole.

"Where the fuck is the money, Col? Just give it to us, eh." The uncertainty was in Dave's voice and Parker knew it. He snorted with contempt, his red face and unshaven cheeks making him look worse than ever. He was an ugly man anyway, his sneer just made him look even uglier.

"Can I ask you two something?" His voice was calm, as if interested in their answer.

Dave nodded, out of curiosity. "Course, what?"

Colin grinned and it was a sarcastic and brave action. Holding out his arms, he said slowly, "Do I look even remotely bothered? You don't scare me. You're fucking ice-creams, no more and no less."

He lit a joint with steady hands and when it was sparked up properly, he said with heavy sarcasm, "If your brother Dennis ain't with you then you can both fuck off. Let's face it, he was the scary one."

Colin Parker smiled then, a confident smile, one that was guaranteed to annoy. He was a small-time gambler who had a serious habit and, ergo, an even more serious debt. He was paying fuck all if he didn't have to.

Colin was a short, shaven-headed individual, stocky and strong. A founding member of the ICF, he was a bully boy who saw himself as above the common herd and as someone who could also look after himself if the fancy took him. He fought on the terraces every Saturday although that was often en masse. Alone, he could hold his own but he preferred to have a gang behind him. Safety in numbers was his usual credo, but these two didn't seem to be too much of a worry. Not after what he had heard on the streets; they were on their last legs. The Williams brothers had once been a force to be reckoned with, but not any more. These two were like Mutt and Jeff. About as hard as a nun with a water pistol.

He knew the Williams brothers were not the Faces they had once been and therefore he saw no reason to give them any money he could be using to his own advantage. A bet was a bet after all, and if he could delay payment, all the better. He wasn't averse to a little break in his payments to give him time to recoup his money or win back what he owed.

He grinned once more as he said, with conviction, "Up yours, cunts."

There was no respect in his voice and no fear. His attitude was becoming a regular occurrence lately and it hurt. Dave knew they were not going to get anything from this bloke without some serious threats and some serious violence. But Colin was a football fighter, he spent his Saturdays looking for trouble on the terraces. As a Boleyn boy, born and bred, he saw the North Bank as his stomping ground. Upton Park was his excuse to hurt people and gambling was his excuse to relax and take stock between games.

The Williams boys held no real threat as far as he was concerned, he knew they were yesterday's news and even when they had been on top, he had not felt any real kind of fear where they were concerned. He paid out for Brodie, no one else, and that had always been just before a serious reminder of his debt had been called for. This time, though, he owed the money to Cain and Spider. People he had less time for than even Dave and his brothers.

When he was betting with Patrick he was a prompt payer, never more than a few days over his deadline, and even then, a smile and a cheery wave as he settled his debt. Not any more. Now, it seemed, he owed a grand to someone he saw as nothing more than a greedy black bastard; like *he* was going to put himself out to serve that punk up with anything other than a fucking good hiding. Brodie should be ashamed of passing the betting monies over to the blacks.

If he didn't have such an important job on the terraces, sorting out the men from the boys, he would have been in the army. And now he had the added insult of being accosted by a couple of has-beens collecting his hard-earned dough for the blackies. What a fucking liberty.

It was outrageous and he decided to be offended. "Tell the coons I ain't giving them nothing, all right?"

Dave saw the futility of his new role and his younger brother, Tommy, was looking at him with an expression that said he was getting toward the end of his tether; that he was looking for some kind of guidance from him. Dave wished that he had brought Ricky along. Although he was the baby, he was far more game and wouldn't expect him to guide his every move.

He had nothing left to give him. He knew that Colin Parker was a nut job and he also knew that if he didn't bring the money back to Cain there would be ambulances arriving and that they wouldn't be for Parker, they would be for them. His confidence was shot and he was a bundle of nerves; his life was like a fucking soap opera these days. All aggravation and excess alcohol, it was all he could do these days to climb out of his pit in the morning. He knew that Colin Parker was just bluffing, no more and no less, but he also knew that Colin Parker had already sensed that his tactic had worked. He walked out of the flat in Leytonstone with his heart beating loud in his head and his stomach ready to vacate its contents at any moment.

He took deep breaths to calm himself as he waited for his brother to follow behind him. "Are you having a joke or what, Dave?" Tommy spoke quietly, aware that they would be listened to by anyone within earshot.

Dave shook his handsome head and said in a whisper, "It's all shit ain't it? It is all fucking, lousy shit. And me and you are the fucking fall guys, thanks to that cunt we called a brother . . ."

Tommy was fed up with Dave and his girly whining. His anger was phenomenal and his temper was at its height. He was not a man to be fucked with any more. Something had to be said and he was the person to say it. His disgust was evident, even to himself, and also to the brother he had always looked up to. But times were hard and they were changing by the minute, as Dave would soon find out.

"Look at you. Call yourself a man, a *Williams*? Will you fucking give it a fucking rest? We have to collect this poke or we are *fucked*. I am just about fed up with it all. Right? So can you just for once, *once*, concentrate on the job in hand. I don't want a fucking post-mortem on our lives and I don't want a fucking post-mortem on our cunt of a brother and his mistakes. I just want the money, that's all. And I want it now, Dave."

Dave nodded with complete understanding, but without any kind of belief or any kind of energy. He was finished and he knew it but, more to the point, Tommy knew it.

"I know. Course I know that. But you saw Colin, he is an angry little fucker. What are we supposed to do? I don't want to take him on. I don't want to *do* this any more."

And he didn't. Dave had lost the nerve that was needed to iron out enemies. He'd lost the want and the enjoyment that a good fight could bring. Dave was like a fucking no-neck; he was like the people they collared off. Dave had made the ultimate mistake; he had become the person they depended on for their livelihood.

Tommy closed his eyes and sighed, forcing himself to be calm enough to talk rationally.

"What we going to do, mate? How are we going to sort this out, eh? Please, Dave. Pull yourself together and we'll beat this fucker to a pulp and get on with our lives."

Tommy was irritated and Dave could see that.

"I don't know what to do, Tom. We need to get that money, iron him out as we would usually, but Colin is a mad cunt."

Tommy sighed heavily. He could hear and feel the fear in his older brother's voice, could feel the indecision and the nervousness inside him. On one level he understood his brother's careful consideration for the family, on another level his brother was getting on his tits. He'd had just about enough. He stared around him for a few moments, breathing in the evening air and calming himself down so he wouldn't lose it completely.

They were on the balcony that fronted the flats, the air stank of chip fat and stale cigarettes. All around them was the bustle of a council estate during the early evening. The young girls were dressed in their finery and hanging around waiting for the young men who would be their downfall. Dealers were out for their first foray of the night and old dears were on their way to bingo, knitted gloves and knitted hats the order of the day. Kids as young as three were still playing out in the front, their clothes filthy and their faces already hardened by the act of bringing themselves up.

It was a reminder of their own upbringing and Tommy was on the verge of tears, tears of anger and the humiliation they were on the receiving end of. Tommy was a lump as the local people would say. He was big and he could have a row and he was at the age when he was willing to make his mark, even though his older brothers were happy to sit back and become no-necks, nothings. He couldn't believe they would let the work of a lifetime go, just because they were wary of Brodie. Well, fuck Brodie and fuck the rest of them. He was determined to make his mark, no matter what, and he was going to fight for his right to earn in the highest echelons of their chosen profession once more.

"What the fuck are we going to do then?"

It was a statement and Dave could hear the challenge as well as the anger in his brother's voice. He knew he was finished in his brother's eyes. He only wished he could explain properly just how much trouble they were now in.

"Are you going to answer me, Dave? For fuck's sake, we were asked to collect and I am going to collect, with or without you."

Dave shook his head in distress. "No matter what we do, Tom, we won't get any real thanks for it. All we will get is grief from Colin Parker and his cronies."

Tommy stared into his brother's face and swallowed down the urge to bash him one.

"It's a fucking grand, that's all. It's peanuts to this wanker and we are hardly asking for the national debt, are we? And if we don't spank for this one we're on the skids; who the fuck will use us in the future? Why would they? We have to make some kind of fucking stand now, or we will be scratching in the dirt forever."

Dave knew he was right but he didn't ever want to have to face Jimmy Brick or Patrick Brodie again.

"Give him a week and we'll have a rethink. OK?"

Tommy shook his head in disgust and, hawking in his throat, he spat on to the concrete floor. Then he walked back into the flat and, picking up a kitchen chair, he crashed it over Colin Parker's head with all the strength that he could muster.

Colin was as amazed as Dave. He tried to crawl across the floor on his hands and knees, his head pouring blood and his mouth trying to bring forth some kind of warning, but all he could manage was a low animal grunt. Tommy Williams repeated the blows over and over again. The force of his anger and disappointment made him vicious and determined. Parker tried to crawl under the table but Tommy just kicked him over and over again, until he was spent and Colin was still, lifeless. Tommy stripped him of his jewelry and his wallet and walked outside once more.

He looked at his elder brother and said quietly, and with hatred, "Fuck you, Dave, and fuck Brodie."

He pocketed his spoils and walked away from his brother without a backward glance.

Dave watched him go, his heart heavy with the knowledge that he had been beaten and cowed, but with good reason. He knew what could happen if you pushed it too far and he was sorry that he had not explained that sufficiently to his little brothers.

*   *   *

Spider and Cain were in the club they frequented in Paddington. The usual customers gave them the salute they had come to expect and, walking through the main bar to the small offices behind, they greeted everyone with a smile and their usual cheesy grins.

The club was owned by them, though no one would ever be able to prove that. Even paying legitimate taxes was beyond them. They were also not about to be placed anywhere for any length of time by the cops. This was just another hang-out as far as anyone was concerned. Nothing to write home about and nothing could pin them down here.

In the back room, called the office for no other reason than they couldn't think of a better word for it, sat Jimmy Brick and Patrick Brodie. That Spider and Cain were surprised to see them was evident, but they both recovered from their surprise with an ease that made Patrick Brodie suspicious.

"Hey, how are you, man?" Spider, as always, was pleased to see his friend.

Patrick grinned. "Good, as always." He stood up and clasped his friend's hand tightly, telling him that he was still in the frame whatever happened.

Patrick sat down once more and stared at Cain with cold eyes. "And how are you, mate?" The question was loaded with malice and Patrick was pleased to see the flicker of fear that passed ever so briefly over Cain's handsome features. He had hit the mark as he had intended. He just hoped that would be enough to bring him in line.

But Cain recovered his equilibrium quickly and shrugged nonchalantly, saying with the arrogance of youth and inexperience, "Never better."

Spider saw the look exchanged between Jimmy and Patrick and his natural suspiciousness took hold.

"Glad to hear it." Patrick threw a bundle of money on to the table.

"What are you doing letting people like Colin Parker have credit?"

Spider's eyes widened slightly at the words. Other than that, no one would have guessed that he was rattled by Patrick's words. Patrick knew he was though, which is why he had said them in the first place.

"Did you know about this?"

Spider was expecting the question as he knew Patrick would have been expecting him to know it. He wouldn't have asked it otherwise. Brodie was not going to throw him a blind side, a curve, he wanted peace at all costs.

They were just play-acting, and Spider appreciated his friend's decency and his guarded pretense as he spoke to him. Spider was so annoyed that he could easily have bludgeoned his brother with anything that came to hand. Instead, he said, with an almost genuine honesty, "Please, Pat. You know I would never countenance anything like that."

Cain could hear the underlying annoyance in his older brother's voice but he was still too new to this game to realize that he was being flaked by the three main players in the room. His brother included.

Cain was unaware just how angry Patrick Brodie was with him, or that he had stepped on someone else's toes. He didn't yet understand that it was only because of his brother he was being given a Get Out Of Jail Free card.

Cain was shrewd enough to know that he had dropped a serious bollock and he was only interested in talking himself out of any kind of aggravation.

"Have I done a wrong 'un?"

Cain was being rude and he was over the top. He was without a brain cell if he honestly thought he was going to get away with any of it. He was standing by Patrick, his arms out in a gesture of supplication; his whole demeanor was telling them that he had been caught and he was willing to learn from his mistakes. But it was also a gesture that said he was biding his time, that he thought they were all dinosaurs, his brother included. He was under the mistaken apprehension that he was too clever to be caught, that no one really knew the score where he was concerned.

Spider laughed loudly and punched his brother with more might than he would normally.

"You let a fucking racist thug have credit?"

Cain shrugged arrogantly. "Who cares what he thinks? He wanted to carry on playing and now he owes us more money."

Patrick nodded at the cash he had thrown down on to the table. "He owes you nothing. There is two hundred for your trouble."

"But he still owes me a grand." It was said quickly, without thought for who he was addressing and with anger and disrespect.

Patrick looked at him with a cold and calculated contempt. "You get what I give you, boy."

The atmosphere was heavy with malice and Cain was surprised to find that his brother was obviously on the opposite side. For the first time ever, Cain was on his own and he didn't like it.

Spider was seriously angry. His dreadlocks were thick and wild and they seemed to take on a life of their own when he lost his temper.

Cain was quick to note that Patrick was not at all fazed, yet his brother was almost spitting feathers. He had never before experienced anything like this and he was not impressed. He was *earning*, that was supposed to be what they were all about, so why was he being singled out for it? He was being vilified for making a few quid off the skinheads he loathed? Taking the money off the scum was what they were all about, surely?

"It won't happen again, Pat. I will guarantee it." Spider spoke with respectful authority and this annoyed his younger brother even more. Spider was supposed to be someone; Spider and Patrick were supposed to be partners. Why was his brother acting like a fucking houseboy?

Patrick knew what was going through Cain's mind; he had expected it. The boy was young, eager and if what he had found out was true, which he suspected it was, then he was also in need of a swift kick up the jacksy.

"Oh, have a day off will you!"

The laughter in the room hurt more than anything else.

Patrick was shaking his head in utter disbelief. The boy was a fucking beauty. He was off his tree if he thought they were cunt enough to think he was some kind of businessman. Who in their right mind allowed people like Parker to have credit? Parker was a strictly cash-only gambler. If he was asked to say what he had for breakfast he would lie, add a sausage and then accuse someone of stealing it. He was also a member of the ICF and they were not an organization to meddle with. They were just out for the fight, nothing more and nothing less. Patrick had no intention of taking them out over a debt. He would have done it if he had to; that went without saying. But he had no intention of bringing any kind of notice on himself or on anyone in his organization because of something so trivial. If Cain thought he was going to make his mark by letting people like Parker scrounge a few pennies then he was either a retard or in need of a serious talking-to.

Either way, it was now in Spider's domain and he was happy to let him sort it out. If Spider screwed it up, he would step in without a second's thought. He saw Cain was still feeling the heat and he decided to put a block on him once and for all.

"You think this is out of order, don't you?"

Patrick and Spider could see that Cain was still annoyed and that he didn't see what the problem was. Like most youngsters, he had started a chain of events that could bring them all down and he couldn't see that fact. He was still too stupid to even ask *why* he was being singled out as he was. He was so fucking arrogant that he didn't even have the savvy to question his betters and learn something for the future.

Cain didn't answer him. His pride was hurt and his sensible head was finally telling him to keep his trap shut. The way Jimmy Brick was watching him was disconcerting, to say the least, and he decided he would be better off retreating on this occasion.

"You borrowed money to people who would see any kind of payment as anathema, especially to the likes of you. Tommy Williams ended up killing Colin Parker over a fucking grand. A *grand*. A fucking pittance and you were the cause of that death, boy. Parker's death could easily have led to us lot getting our fucking collars felt and for what, eh? A poxy grand? You lairy little cunt. We don't need anyone causing us that kind of aggro and the sooner you get your thick head around that, the better."

Patrick looked at the handsome young man before him and wished he could have dealt with him in an easier manner, but he couldn't. Cain had to learn the hard way about their world and he had been cushioned by Spider for too long. Now they were all on tenterhooks over a fucking ice-cream like Parker. Parker was, after all was said and done, a fucking civilian and when they died people tended to ask questions.

Spider shook his head in desperation. Cain was going to get the rol-licking of a lifetime and he was going to enjoy distributing it; the boy needed to understand about the boundaries and guidelines that made up their world. Now was as good a time as any for a lesson in reality.

Jimmy Brick was sorry he was not going to be called on to distribute his special brand of justice. He didn't like Cain, he never had, but Spider had been a personal hero of his since childhood. A diamond geezer, a legend in his own lunch-time. The man who had given him his first real job.

Now he saw Spider as nothing more than a man, someone who was frightened for his younger brother. Family was a fucking bind in their game, it was something to be used as a weapon. If a man stood alone, he was safe and he could be brave and honorable. As long as there was no one you cared for more than you cared for yourself, you had an edge. But families were a danger, families and children were the downfall of many a great man. Once you cared for someone, you had a chink in your armor; you had a fucking gaping big hole in your defenses that would be used against you without a second's thought. Jimmy knew that because he would do the same thing himself if it gained him what he wanted.

Spider was a touch, a fucking dynamo in Jimmy's eyes, but he would never be the same man again now that he had taken for his little brother. Mainly because his little brother was not worth his loyalty, was not worth Spider's deliberate disregard for the friendship that he and Brodie had enjoyed for so long. Cain was not going to let this go, he was too worried about how he was perceived by the people in his world.

That alone was always a cause for concern but Jimmy would sit it out, watch the main players and, when the time was right, he would decide what side he was on.

Until then, he would keep his own counsel.

But he knew one thing. This was not over, not by a long shot.

"Is she still here?" Patrick's voice was loud and Lil, despite her anger at her husband's usual greeting to her mother, desperately wanted to laugh.

Her mother had decided to take it in good spirit even though no one would believe he meant anything other than malice.

Annie sighed theatrically, her eyes rolling upwards and her bosom heaving, but she was masking a smile that was evident to anyone watching her.

The boys were amazed, as was their father. "You feeling all the ticket, girl?"

Annie giggled like a schoolgirl and Patrick didn't know whether to laugh at the old bird's antics or be afraid. She had changed so dramatically over the last few months that he wondered if his old granny's tales of changelings did actually have some credence.

Pushing Lil into the kitchen, he whispered, "She on fucking drugs, or what? I had just got used to her as an aggro merchant and now it's like she's a born-again Doris Day."

Lil was laughing out loud now and Patrick was glad. It had been a while since she had been this happy, this carefree, and he sometimes felt guilty because he knew she worried about him.

"How you feeling, girl?"

She shrugged. "Like shit. I tell you now, mate, I will be glad when I deliver this one. It's the hardest yet, and I ain't the type of person to make a drama out of nothing, as you know."

Patrick hugged her to him, acknowledging the truth of her words.

She did look ill. She looked so pale and wan that he was worried about her. He would rather have her than another child, not that he would voice that opinion out loud. But his Lil looked rough and she knew it. "Sit down and take the weight off, I'll get you something to eat."

Annie did not come out to the kitchen and he was grateful for that. Normally, she would have been bustling about like a demented cow and making him feel like a spare part in his own home. He was well able for her and they both knew that, but she still enjoyed giving him a hard time.

The new, improved Annie was like a thorn in his side; he'd actually preferred her when she was a vindictive old bitch, but he had a feeling this was not the time to mention that.

Instead, he helped his wife make a few sandwiches and a pot of tea. That it was after midnight didn't really register. Patrick was a man who expected his woman to do his bidding whenever it suited him and wherever he wanted it. He had arrived home as if it was the norm for her to be making him a snack and listening to his day's events when everyone else was tucked up in bed. But that suited Lil. As tired and as heavy as she felt, Patrick was still her priority and this was what her life was all about; this selfish man and the children they had created between them. Lil was grateful to him every day of her life for making her feel wanted, valued and needed. He had given her a life she could only have dreamed of and she would repay him for her happiness in any way she could.

Lil loved these times, when they were together and the world was asleep and she could have her husband to herself for a few moments. She felt the love coming from him, and knew that, no matter what, she was his real priority, as were the children.

As she buttered bread and washed the salad, Lil felt the child kick. It was a strong kick and it made her double over. Patrick grabbed her and laughed loudly.

As he held her in his arms, she looked up into his handsome face and he said happily, "Whoa, Lil. I felt that one meself, girl. Another Brodie for the pile, another one cooking and waiting to arrive into the world and take it by storm. We make good babies, Lil, the best. All our kids will be someone and will do something. We are truly blessed."

Patrick looked into her eyes and saw the dark circles beneath them, the hollowness of her cheeks and realized that she really was ill this time. That this child was taking it out of her and making her ill and he had not even noticed until now. She waited for him to arrive back most nights and he accepted her getting up and cooking, talking or scheming with him and suddenly he felt the guilt of a man who had no real understanding of the pressure he put on the people around him. As he held Lil, he was ashamed that he had only just noticed how thin she was, she was all baby this time. His life outside the house was more real to him at times than the petty dramas his wife was left to deal with on a daily basis. He finally appreciated just how much she actually did for him, making sure that any worries he encountered were in no way the result of anything that might have happened in his home. As he heard the front door close, he knew his mother-in-law had left quietly and he knew even that was down to his Lil. She knew how much the woman aggravated him just by breathing the same air as he did. He also understood that the woman he hated and vilified made his wife's life much easier by her presence and by the little things she did. Even though there was always a price to be paid.

As he hugged his wife again he felt the full force of her sex and her goodness: a combination he knew he was terrified of. Like most men of his generation he knew he had not really given her the respect she was due as the mother of his children or as the love of his life. She had run his clubs at one time and she had done it well, had been respected for her acumen and her shrewdness. Now, thanks to him, she was back to square one, just a housewife, the receptacle for his children and she had accepted that as she had accepted everything else in her life. With dignity and without any kind of argument. In fact, Patrick was now feeling like a Class A bastard; he had practically forgotten about her and about everything that was important while he was sorting out his problems. He was finally feeling a serious guilt and, worse than that, he was looking at a woman who was at the end of her tether but who was still trying to hide her real condition from him so he would not feel that he should be supporting her in any way.

He kissed Lil gently on her lips, her eyes and all over her face as she stood patiently, allowing him access to her as she always had in the past.

His Lil was the best of the best. She was a fighter and unless he looked closely, as he was now doing, she would tell him nothing of import about her, or his kids; she was always more interested in making sure he was without worries and that he was happy and content. But she looked terrible, and it was worrying him, because he couldn't say that without hurting her. All the times she had been pregnant before, she had been happy and healthy, and she had never once asked him for anything other than what he had been willing to offer her. And then he made sure he felt good about himself while he was doing it.

And the worst thing of all was, he had needed her tonight, more than ever, and it was only because of that he had seen just how much his chosen lifestyle had affected her and all those around her.

For the first time in years, he was seeing her life from her perspective, and it was not something he was proud of, or indeed something he wanted to dwell on. Instead, he sat her down on the nearest chair and made her relax while he waited on her for a change. But it was a double-edged sword; she knew it was an act on his part, and she pretended that he was doing it all for her.

To see Patrick looking at her with such sadness and such care was enough to make Lil want to smack him in the face. She hated that the fact that she was pregnant made Patrick see her as weak and needy, and it made her feel useless because he didn't see women as anything of value. Every time she was pregnant, Lil felt the enormity of what she could do, what she was capable of.

Yet this miracle of life was still treated by men as if it was nothing, even though they could never do it; they relied on the female of the species to produce for them. And they had to trust the person who was having the child for them because only the woman could be one hundred percent sure the child inside them was actually their man's. The man had to take their word for it and if the man in question had chosen someone they didn't entirely trust, then that was a poor lookout for them all. Men who had chosen unwisely often had to puff and pant and threaten, to convince themselves that the child they were giving their name to, and paying for, was actually a blood relative. Patrick Brodie, she knew, had never had to worry about that, ever. And so, even as her husband felt sorry for her, Lil knew that she would always have the upper hand because she had put him first and she had always respected his work and looked after his offspring.

Lil was always aware of her husband's thoughts and feelings but she was not going to let on about that now. Like any woman worth her salt, she would milk this for all it was worth. Loving him was one thing but accepting this kind of treatment was something else. She was annoyed with him and the way he had suddenly decided to make out that he understood her life and the way she was feeling. It was an insult, on the one hand, and something she treasured, on the other. Anyway, she was determined to keep her trap shut in case she caused a row, but at times like this she wished he wouldn't act the big I Am.

That Patrick had only just noticed how she was feeling annoyed her but she smiled and allowed him to pet her and love her. After all, he was only a man and, as her mother pointed out at every available opportunity, they couldn't feel their way out of the womb unless a woman was pushing for them. Everything they did from then on was either to get a woman or to keep a woman. In some cases, they tried to do both things at once. When all was said and done, women ruled the fucking world.

As Patrick smiled at her with his smug face and enveloped her once more in his strong arms, she was more convinced of that fact than ever before.

Chapter Fourteen

Spider was feeling the heat and he was not a happy bunny. Cain was starting to irritate him on an hourly basis. The boy was somehow under the mistaken impression that he was more on the ball than his older brother; he was at the stage in life where a few quid and someone else's hard work seemed to make him feel he was the winner of *Mastermind*: chosen subject, villainy and drug dealing. He was now of the inflated opinion that he could run everything from a bar stool and that his brother, who had been kind enough to pave his way into the world of riches and money, had suddenly acquired the intellect of a Millwall supporter. It was laughable, but worse than that, it was also making Spider very frightened. And that was making him even more frightened.

Life was hard enough as it was without his little brother suddenly developing a death wish. It was as if Cain really thought that he was the brains of the outfit. The young man he himself had schooled and who he had grafted for suddenly seemed to think that he was the alpha male, the dog's gonads.

Cain really thought that he was a fool who would not figure out what was going on right under his nose and that his treachery would go unnoticed and, more to the point, unpunished. It would be funny if it wasn't so tragic.

The Williams brothers were pariahs in their community and what did Cain decide to do? Make them his bosom buddies at the expense of all he had worked for, all he had tried to achieve. Cain was suddenly prepared to overlook him, was prepared to forget everything in a heartbeat. He had no thought for anyone except himself and the shit he had decided to hang around with. Jasper the Rasta was bad enough, he had been hanging with him for a while now but, coupled with the Williams boys, it was a catastrophe of fucking Olympian proportions.

And Cain was so dense that he actually thought that he, Spider, his older brother, the man who had taught him everything he knew, had no idea where his brother's nights were spent and, worse still, what he was doing while on the missing list.

Spider had the unenviable task of telling Patrick the full story, although he had a feeling he already knew all about it. There wasn't much Patrick didn't know about, and what there was didn't merit his attention.

The Williams brothers had offered Cain the earth on a plate, convinced him they were what he needed to succeed and Cain had swallowed it all like the fucking useless no-neck he had become. It was this that was annoying Spider the most: that his Cain, his brother, could be that fucking stupid. Like he could trust white boys. White boys who were now lower down the food chain than the whores they were attempting to pimp and weaker than the drugs they were attempting to peddle in his name, and more treacherous than Judas Iscariot himself.

Cain had always been vain and that must have been how the Williams boys had got into him; it was the only thing he could think of to blame. They must have talked crap for England to get him on their side.

The Williams brothers thought they were the new rude boys and, with Cain onside, they seemed to think they were getting away with it. Except that Cain was only accepted because of his association with Brodie and that, of course, was only because he himself had been onside with Patrick Brodie since day one.

Cain was using *his* largesse and *his* goodwill with Patrick to further his own ends. The Williams lot must think that they would be protected because of *his* connections and that he would make sure his brother would get away with his stupidity. The Williams brothers had taken him for a punk as well as Cain; they had assumed he would look out for his brother and, to an extent, they had been right about that. But now they had stepped over the line; they had made him out for a fool and that he would not accept.

As much as Spider loved Cain, he had a reputation to uphold and that rep had never included whores or bores, a saying of his father's that had been proved true over and over again. The Williams boys were already starting to bore him and he had never really had much time for them anyway. Cain had finally pushed him too far and he had to retaliate to make him see what he had done. Spider needed to try to salvage something from the mess that had dropped into his lap.

Spider was determined to see that the accident the Williams brothers were going to have came sooner rather than later but did not include his brother in any way, shape or form. Cain was a fool; something he had never believed would have been a possibility until now. But he would save Cain's arse for no other reason than how his behavior affected him; how he was perceived and how people judged him personally and professionally. Cain was not going to screw up all his hard work by making him look as if he had no fucking idea about what was going on in his own backyard.

In a short time, Cain had gone from someone he would trust with his life to someone he would not trust with his car keys. Quite a leap for two brothers who were proud of their filial affection and who had once believed that together they could rule the world. Their world at least. Spider was having to rethink everything about their relationship and their dealings and work out how best to limit any damage that might occur if Cain was cunt enough to completely disregard him and his teachings.

On top of everything else, his brother had broken the cardinal rule that he had drummed into him over and over again: *never* take your own products whether it was the women or the drugs. And, if what he had heard was true, ketamine and amphetamines were rife where the Williams brothers were concerned, and the brown was always on the table. They were complete wasters and, like all wasters, they had a habit of taking other people down with them. Cain was slipping further away from him with every day that passed by.

Spider would take his brother out in a heartbeat if he ever became a liability; he had always told Cain that. Spider had explained to him that the world they lived in did not allow for sentiment of any kind. Once you screwed up you were out, even if you were family. Trust was all they had to rely on, the only thing that stood between them and jail. Once that trust was broken, no one was safe and that included baby brothers who had been lucky to have family who looked out for them and employed them in the first place; even if they were too stupid to understand that. It meant that even blood would be wiped out without hesitation for the greater good, for the guarantee of equilibrium once more. It was nothing personal as such, it was just the way that their world worked.

The big picture had always been the only picture as far as Spider was concerned and if that meant taking out family then so be it.

"What are you on about?"

Lil came out into the hallway; her mother's voice was loud enough to alert her to trouble and she knew, without asking, that whatever it was, it had been caused by her second son. It was strange but she had been expecting something like this, someone on her doorstep with hate in their heart and profanities on their lips.

It was almost a relief, as if her wicked thoughts needed to be proved true once and for all by an innocent bystander so she could admit the feelings she had towards her son had some kind of basis, some kind of concrete foundation.

Lil knew Lance was trouble and she knew that because she always let her mother sort it out; she was colluding with him, letting him get away with it. By turning a blind eye she had brought this woman to her door and she knew it had to be really serious for her to come here in the first place. Most people wouldn't have had the guts.

Today though, Pat Junior's party was on the horizon and her belly was heavier than ever before, and when her mother's voice was finally expressing her anger at the grandchild she usually defended with all her considerable strength, Lil had finally had enough.

"What's going on?" Lil's voice was hard, the words delivered with unusual vehemence, and the woman on her doorstep, Janie Callahan, was reminded of exactly who she was dealing with.

This was Lil Brodie, the wife of the man everyone around and about revered and feared in equal measure. Lil was a star in her own right and

Janie liked her a lot, but today she knew she had to make some kind of a stand and that Lil was the person she needed to deal with, not her mother. Annie Diamond was a two-faced, disloyal loser who only had the ear of the street because of her connections, because of who her daughter was married to. And she milked that for all it was worth; she was a terror of a woman who used her daughter's name for her own ends. Well, it was going to stop now because Janie was not going to stand for it any more.

Everyone else was terrified about making any kind of complaint about the Brodie kids and this was because Annie protected them, no matter what they did. Especially the main culprit, Lance. Lance walked on water as far as Annie was concerned and he was aware of the power his name gave him. Lance was a bully and bullies needed to be reined in sooner rather than later.

Janie Callahan was like any mother worth her salt; she was willing to take on anyone to protect her kids and if that meant taking on Annie, then she was going to do just that.

If it meant taking on Lil, then she was willing to do that as well. But she knew in her heart that Lil was someone to be reasoned with, someone who had a bit of sense; at least she hoped that was the case.

Janie felt angry enough to take the lot of them on, even Patrick Brodie himself, if needs be. Her children needed to know that she was looking out for them and they needed to feel safe. Janie was determined to make sure that they were, no matter what the cost to her personally.

"Get in, Lil, you are not in any condition to deal with this."

Lil saw the confusion on her mother's wrinkled face and then she shoved her none too gently out of the way. That gesture was enough to quiet her.

Lil had always liked Janie and she wanted to know why she was on her doorstep reading them the riot act. It had to be serious because Patrick Brodie was a byword around the streets and she knew just how hard it must have been for Janie to come knocking on her door. She sighed deeply, wondering what her son had done to merit this kind of reaction.

"Get out of the way, Mother. Come in, Janie, love, and tell me what on earth the problem is." Lil's voice was calm and she stepped aside so that Janie could walk into her home; she needed to sort this out and she needed to know what had been the cause of the woman's upset. She wanted to know what that little fucker had been up to this time.

Lil was aware that she also had to make some sort of stand in front of her neighbors; it was how they lived and how they survived. So she stepped outside her front door and looked at the women in the street; they were all standing on their doorsteps waiting to see the outcome of this little drama while pretending they had no interest whatsoever. Lil stared at them all, one after the other, her eyes hard and her jaw clenched in anger. She knew how to play the game and she played it with a quiet contempt that was as insulting as it was threatening.

"Had your fucking look?" Her voice was harder than she intended but it had the desired effect. The women knew they had overstepped the mark and she knew they would be chary of repeating that mistake in the future.

Janie was now inside the house and, hearing Lil's angry voice, her earlier bravado was deserting her by the second.

Lil could feel the fear and the loathing coming off Janie Callahan in waves; she saw the widening of her eyes and the way she bit on her bottom lip. She knew that it had taken every ounce of courage Janie possessed to come and knock on this door. She knew that this was serious, that this was not about the usual childish arguments or the kids' pranks so prevalent in the street. Janie was on a mission and her mother's quietness was, in itself, enough to convince her that Lance was indeed the culprit and that, as she had thought earlier, he had been seriously out of order.

Lil was frightened of hearing what Lance had done, and yet she knew it was inevitable that she would be regaled about his latest misdemeanor.

"Make a cuppa, Mum."

She smiled at Janie and it took every ounce of courage that she possessed. Then she said quietly and with a friendliness she didn't actually feel any more, "Come through to the lounge, Janie, and let's sort this out, shall we?"

Janie nodded in relief but she saw the way Annie looked at her and knew she had just made herself an enemy for life.

Cain was out of his box and his smile was as phony as his annoyance was real. Leonard Barker was never happy at any time, but giving this young man the news that his brother was searching for him all over London was making him even more depressed than usual. Cain had to be some kind of fool; Leonard would give his eyeteeth to have someone on board with him like Spider. But Cain was so blitzed he just shrugged it off.

Leonard walked from the room; he had done his chore for the day and he wanted to distance himself from this man as fast as possible.

Having heard the bad news, the Williams brothers were scattering. They were suddenly off for the evening, leaving Cain alone even though they knew he was not fit to use the toilet without help. But that was the Williams boys all over, they seemed to enjoy taking this boy down with them. And Cain himself was galloping towards obscurity and censure as if it was the only thing he wanted in the world.

Leonard Barker was collecting glasses out the front of the bar when he saw Patrick Brodie slip through the door. There were a few regular customers at the bar and Leonard noticed how Patrick was being observed without anyone actually looking directly at him. He waved nonchalantly at no one in particular and everyone in there greeted him heartily. Leonard felt his heart sink down to his boots and wished that his boss wasn't such a lazy cunt so he would not have to be the person overlooking this pile of shit. He would be glad when Cain finally got his comeuppance.

Patrick nodded at him in a friendly way; no one would ever guess at his anger or his dismay that it had come to this. He opened his arms as if in supplication and Leonard Barker nodded almost imperceptibly towards the back room, knowing that Brodie would have all the information he needed before he would have even deigned to walk through the doorway. It was a game that had been played out over and over again for years and the only changes were the players in the little soap opera. This time, though, a renowned lunatic, Patrick Brodie, had seen fit to sort his problems out in public and Leonard knew it could go either way for him because of that. He would either be the villain of the piece or the knight in shining armor, depending on the outcome.

Leonard just wanted his wage in his back pocket and fuck the dramas that came and went with a depressing regularity. He was further dismayed to see two huge men come into the bar with baseball bats neatly wrapped in red insulating tape. When the dirty deed was done they could unwrap the tape and burn it, thereby leaving the bats in pristine condition for further use and any evidence as ash.

Two of the regulars at the bar drank up and walked out quickly without saying their usual good-humored goodbyes and this seemed to be the sign for a general exodus, as was expected. No one questioned anything; the atmosphere said enough and no one wanted to get caught up in the situation here, and who could blame them?

Patrick smiled then and Leonard poured him a large Scotch before shutting the bar flap and leaving the place himself. He would sit it out in the cold and wait for them to vacate the premises before going back inside. Brodie owned the bar, even though he didn't run it, and Leonard knew that Cain was about to find out just what owning something or, more to the point, someone really meant.

Leonard sat outside in his little Hillman Imp and rolled himself a cigarette; his hands were trembling and that annoyed him. He started up the car and pushed a cassette into his eight-track system. Elvis Presley's voice filled the void around him and he closed his eyes and wished to Christ that he too felt lonesome tonight.

"What's wrong then, Janie?"

Janie sighed heavily. Her earlier bravado had deserted her and she was perched on the edge of the sofa with a dry mouth and a heart that was beating so loud it was almost drowning out her own thoughts.

Lil was aware of the woman's discomfort and she smiled once more, feeling phony because a large part of her didn't want to hear what this poor woman had to say.

"Lance is bullying my kids, Lil. I can't sit back and let him, it's gone too far this time." It was out, it was said and the world had not come to an end.

"In what way?"

Lil was asking all the right questions, she knew, but the truth was that she could have written Janie's script for her. But what Janie answered was nothing like what she had expected and she had, as always where Lance was concerned, expected the worst. She was stunned as she listened to the woman talk.

"Eight stitches in the head and that was when Lance pushed her off the bus . . ."

Janie trailed off as she saw the shock on Lil's face. She had assumed that Lil had heard about it. It was the talk of the school; not that they were willing to do anything about it. But what could Janie do? This had to be resolved because her kids were in mortal fear of even leaving the house.

"Her? Did you say her?"

Janie nodded. Her long face was even more worried now as she realized that Lil really had no idea about what had happened and she had gone so white she looked on the verge of fainting. Lil's huge belly and swollen legs were suddenly all Janie could focus on and she saw that Lil Brodie was ill. She was also in a state of total shock at the news she had just imparted to her. She guessed that Annie made sure Lil didn't get any information until after she had edited it to her own satisfaction.

"My Lisa is only six and he pushed her off the bus; she landed in the road on her head and the hospital said she was lucky she wasn't hurt really badly. Lil, I don't want to put this in your lap; I can see you are ready to drop but I can't let this go on. Lance has tortured them and he mouths me off if I say anything. He effs and blinds at me. I don't want to cause any trouble for you . . . I don't want Patrick after me, but if that's what it takes . . . It's either this or I have to move and I ain't got the wherewithal to do that as I am sure you know . . . Me old man's banged up."

Janie's voice was breaking now with sheer relief that she had said it out loud. Lil looked awful and Janie was sorry for her because she could see the woman genuinely had no idea about any of it. If she had not seen her reaction with her own eyes she would never have believed it.

Lil was digesting everything she had just heard and was now trying to make some kind of sense of it. She was stiff with anger and humiliation; this woman honestly believed that she had known of her son's antics and that she had allowed those things to happen without any kind of redress. Did everyone else think that? Did they assume that she didn't care? Did people think she condoned his behavior?

She was mortified because she knew that it was her fault if people did think that about her because she had no interest in the boy or in what he did or didn't do. She had no trouble believing what the woman was telling her, and she knew that she should at least be trying to *justify* his behavior, make allowances for him, at least try to *defend* him, but she had no intention of doing anything like that. Instead, she jumped up and bellowed her son's name out with all the force she could muster.

The kids had shot into the bedrooms when she had shouted at her mother and as they trooped back downstairs now she could feel the heat of humiliation and shame wash over her face and neck. The child seemed to move inside her with a sickening wrench and she had trouble staying on her feet.

Pat Junior and the girls were in the hallway and Lance was behind them, his eyes wide and, as always, displaying an innocence she knew he had never really possessed. He was a devil in disguise and she flew at him with a speed that belied the heaviness of her aching body. All she wanted to do was hurt him to make him realize exactly what he did to others; she wanted him to feel the same emotions as his victims.

Lance tried to escape her wrath and she grabbed at his ankle as he attempted to run back up the stairs. She dragged him by his legs and his screams were loud and piercing but she ignored them. She pulled him into the front room and flung him on to the floor. He lay there panting in fright and she saw the terror in his eyes as she shrieked at him. Her mother was trying to calm her down and she grabbed the front of Annie's carefully buttoned cardigan and thrust her back out into the hallway, nearly knocking her over in the process. The children were all staring at her as if she had gone mad. She didn't feel like she had gone mad though, she felt as if she had finally woken up from a bad dream. She felt as if she was free at last.

Annie's voice was cajoling her now, she was trying to calm her down.

Instead it made her anger swell inside her like a canker that was about to burst.

"Lil, calm down, love. He wouldn't do anything like that. He's a little fucker, granted, but he wouldn't do that. They pick on him . . ."

Lil shook her head in despair at her mother's words and, placing her hands on her ample hips, she said with derision and contempt, "Oh, Mum, fuck off, will you? He could murder all the neighbors in broad daylight with an axe and you'd say they must have deserved it. That they must have done something to him."

"You going to take her word over mine then?"

Lil saw the hurt on her mother's face and the frown lines etched there so she looked old before her time and she actually felt pity for her. Annie was almost delusional where Lance was concerned; it was as if she saw a different boy to the one everyone else did. She held herself in check, knowing it was pointless talking to the woman before her, a woman she didn't even like most of the time, but who she had thought she needed.

"Take the kids upstairs, Mother, and don't fucking come down again until I tell you."

Annie was beside herself with grief for the boy she could see no wrong in.

"Nanny Annie, please, Nanny Annie, don't leave me with her . . ." Lance was choking on his sobs now and even with the tears running down his handsome face, the face that was so like his father's, and his pitiable crying, Lil still couldn't find it in her heart to feel any kind of pity for him.

He tried to bolt from the room then, to get away from her, and she grabbed him by the hair and dragged him back inside. Then, slamming the front room door closed, she untangled the arms that were now desperately trying to grip her around her waist to make her cuddle him and she laid into him with all the strength she possessed.

Her blows were heavy and carefully delivered. He curled into a ball on the floor so she grabbed him once more by his hair and, holding him upright, she gave him a beating that was as vicious as it was overdue. He was bleeding and she could smell the fear coming off him in waves but it just added to her anger and her need to teach him a lesson that would be remembered his whole life.

She could hear herself shouting at him and in her rage she couldn't even comprehend what she was saying to him: "You fucker, you bullying, wicked fucker . . ."

Lil was screaming the same words over and over again and Janie sat and watched the scene before her with an awe that she would say later was due to the fact that Lance was still denying any wrongdoing even after his mother had opened up his eyebrow. She would tell people in a hushed voice that Lil Brodie was like a maniac, that she had doled out a hiding many a man would have been loath to be on the wrong end of. She would tell anyone who asked her that Lil Brodie was a decent woman who had administered a beating to that little bastard to teach him the error of his ways. She had paid him out tenfold for her girl's injuries and without realizing it, Janie set out Lil's reputation as a battler once and for all.

Lil was crying now, a low groaning cry of despair and disappointment and long strings of snot were hanging from her nose as she knelt over the boy, and, forcing down the urge to crack his skull open with her clenched fist, she said to him, "I'm on to you, boy, and you will get this or worse every time you step out of line. You fucking bully, you rotten, stinking bully."

Lance stared up at the woman he alternately loved and hated and he said through his tears, "It wasn't me, Mum, it was Patrick . . . I swear . . . I swear to God . . ."

Lance was still lying to her, still trying to worm his way out of it. He had not a scrap of shame or pride inside him. Lil pulled his head up towards her face with a force so great that his teeth crashed together loudly enough to make Janie Callahan jump. Lance could feel her breath on his face once more as she bellowed at him.

"You liar, you are still fucking lying. Tell me the truth, you mad bastard, tell me the truth or I swear to God I'll fucking bury you!"

She was staring into his eyes and he knew then that she meant every word she said. She saw the lids of his eyes come down like blinds on a window and knew he was changing tack. The knowledge depressed her even as it worried her. He was such a strange child and now she had acknowledged that fact to herself and to Janie Callahan, she felt her fear of him evaporate.

"It was me. I'm sorry, Mum . . . I'm sorry . . . She was looking at me . . . She thinks she is better than us, she does."

The whine in Lance's voice, and his constant lying, was too much for her. What the hell had she bred? Where the hell did this child come from? Lil threw him away from her then as if the effort of touching him was anathema. Then, holding on to the arm of the sofa, she pulled herself up from the floor with difficulty and Janie quickly leapt up to help her. She had been silent as she had watched Lil take matters into her own hands. Before, she would have laid out money that Lil had been aware of her son's reign of terror; how wrong she had been. And how relieved she was now that her kids would finally be free of the little boy who looked like an angel but had the vocabulary of a sailor.

Lance was battered and bloody and Janie could feel no remorse for what had happened to him. Like his own mother, she felt only distaste and relief that he had finally got his comeuppance. She had enjoyed seeing him squirm and it bothered her that a young child could stir up such feelings inside her.

"Get out of my sight." He dragged himself up slowly and Lil could see that she had gone too far, that she had really hammered him, but she didn't care. There was a kink in Lance's nature and she was going to iron it out if it killed her.

When Lance was gone from the room, Lil sighed and, lighting a cigarette, she pulled on it deeply. Blowing out the smoke noisily, she said sadly, "I am so sorry, Janie. I knew nothing about it. Is the little one all right?"

Janie nodded. Taking the proffered cigarette, she lit it and said, "He could have killed her, Lil, and it was that which brought me round here. I don't want any trouble and you know that. But my kids are mortally afraid of him. Not a day goes by but he is at them . . ."

She was crying again now. The sympathy that was in Lil's eyes made her break down.

"Where was my Pat while all this was going on?" She was suddenly afraid that her eldest son was a part of it all.

Janie shrugged and wiped at her eyes with a grubby tissue, the cigarette stains on her fingers showing just how bad her nerves had become. Looking at her with the cigarette dangling from her lips and the tear-stained face that was blotchy and swollen, Lil saw her own life if she wasn't careful. Lance was capable of making her into the wretch she saw before her and she was determined not to let that happen.

"He puts a stop to him if he catches him. He's a good boy, Lil."

The words were like a balm to Lil and she sighed again, heavier this time, before bellowing once more at the top of her voice, "Don't you dare go up to him, Mother . . ."

She got out of the chair again and, as she walked from the room, Janie could hear Annie Diamond arguing with her in hushed tones.

Janie looked around her at the lovely home that Lance lived in and she wondered at a boy who had everything laid on a plate and who still was going to the bad. The carpet was new and reached all the walls, the furniture was expensive and comfortable, and even the ashtrays were colored glass, shaped like big blue fishes. A color TV stood in the corner and velvet curtains adorned the windows. It was like something from a magazine or a shop window. Yet she wouldn't trade places with poor Lil for all the money in the world.

"I mean it, Mum, you leave him to stew in his own juices."

Annie was agitated and upset. Lil was amazed at the way her mother felt for this child of hers, considering the woman had never once shown her so much as a scrap of affection while she had been growing up. No Christmases, no birthdays, nothing; it was as if she had not existed. Now she was willing to argue for a boy who had thrown a six-year-old child off a moving bus. As she pushed her mother none too gently down the stairs, she said in a deep whisper, "Fuck off home, Mother, and leave me to sort this out." Annie was beside herself as she said quickly, "You ain't going to tell Patrick, are you?"

Her voice was high with fear and Lil was aware that she was shaking with emotion; her mother, on whom she would have bet her last penny that no real emotion had ever existed inside her body.

"Fucking right, I am telling Patrick. That child needs sorting out once and for all and I am going to make it my business to see that happens."

Annie was shaking her head like a wet dog, and then she shrieked: "He was only being a boy. All kids do silly things, Lil. Please don't tell Pat about this. Pat will kill him; you're bad enough but Pat don't know his own strength . . ."

"*Go home*, Mother. Leave me and my family alone. And while we are talking about Pat, he will blame you for all this anyway, so make yourself scarce before he aims you out the door once and for all."

Lil went up the stairs then and looked in on Lance. He was lying on his bed sobbing and alone and she was reminded of how little he was really. But his plight still didn't move her in any way. He was looking at her now with his big blue eyes and she saw the cunning behind them and shivered. He was a vindictive little bugger and she wondered where he had gotten that from. It had to be from her mother. Annie could be cold, she knew, and she was going to make a point of curtailing the time she spent with him.

When this baby arrived, she was going to take control of the reins once more, and she was going to watch him like a hawk. She never wanted to hear another story about him and his hate-fuelled antics ever again. This all stopped today. She was determined to make Lance finally appreciate that all his actions had consequences.

Closing the door on the sobbing boy, she went into Pat's room where the wide-eyed girls were sitting on his bed holding hands tightly as Pat Junior read them a story.

"Is he all right, Mum?"

Lil nodded. She was unable to trust herself to speak to a boy who was worried about his brother even though all his troubles were self-inflicted and even though it would ultimately make his own life easier if he didn't have to look out for him constantly. Pat Junior's loyalty was astounding really, considering who he was wasting it on.

That her children had been frightened by her actions was evident in the quiet around her and the fact that the girls didn't run to her as usual for a hug; they just stared at her as if she was a stranger in their midst.

Going back downstairs, she made a cup of tea for her and Janie; and a friendship was born that day that would last the two women a lifetime.

If Lance had done nothing else in his short life, he had brought these two women together as friends.

Cain was watching warily as Patrick circled him holding a chair leg in his hands he had retrieved from the debris of the office. Cain had been beaten to within an inch of his life and he had put up a good fight; in fact, Patrick and his cohorts were secretly impressed. The place was a shambles but Cain was taking it like a man and that stood him in good stead with his protagonists. His defense had surprised them somewhat with its ferocity, after all the drugs he'd taken.

As Cain sat watching them through swollen eyes he waited for the next assault that he knew would be forthcoming sooner rather than later. The weight of the weapon in Patrick's hands was evident in the way he was handling it; it was cumbersome, and the straight edges could do a lot of damage to skull and bone. And even though Cain was out of the game in comparison to the three men around him, he was with it enough to know that he was still in for a rough night. He was running on pure adrenaline now, unsure of exactly what was going on; he had no idea why Brodie was even there. Cain was unable to function properly, he couldn't even remember what this was all about.

The ketamine was kicking in once more and he felt the sweat envelop his body. He could smell it, a dank staleness that, until his foray into the world of the drug user, as opposed to the drug dealer, would have made him feel physically ill. The tannic taste of blood was in his mouth and the cocktail of drugs in his system was making him feel invincible. He was once more of the opinion that he could fight his way out of the room. The ketamine, a powerful horse-tranquilizer, was once more rushing through his system and mixed with the amphetamines he had been snorting with it for the past eight hours, it was confusing him. His mind was raving once more and the paranoia was creeping up on him. The sweat was running down his face and blurring his already limited vision. He could see the men looking at him, could make out their features as if he was looking through water; they were talking to each other and he knew it was about him. But he couldn't understand what they were saying. They were cunting him though, he was convinced of that, taking him for a fool and they expected him to sit and take it?

Cain shook his head and laughed at their foolishness, that they thought he wouldn't punish them for their outrageous insults to him? That he would swallow this kind of treatment? He screamed and, using his considerable strength, he jumped up from the seat and launched himself at Patrick Brodie. He was almost feral and his teeth were bared as he attempted to bite his face, tear off an ear or rip off his nose. The attack was as fast as it was unexpected and Patrick brought the chair leg down on his head and body over and over again until he finally stopped trying to rise up from the floor. He lay there, a bloody mess, his mouth open as he gasped for breath while still attempting to mutter obscenities and threats at his attackers.

Patrick stared down at him in amazement and, pushing him on to his back, he placed the chair leg on a nearby desk. Then he lit himself a cigarette with a calmness that belied his real feelings.

Looking at the two men with him, he said quietly, "Out of his nut or what?"

The bigger of the two men shrugged. "That ketamine will do it every time, mate; sends them off their shopping trolleys."

Patrick nodded sagely and went out into the empty bar.

He took the drink offered him by Leonard who had slipped back into the club a few minutes before and he gulped at the whisky, enjoying the burn as it went down into his belly. The fire of it was giving him the jolt he needed.

Leonard replenished his glass immediately and then he poured out two lemonades for the others. He knew that, unless Patrick said otherwise, soft drinks were all that would be allowed to them.

They sipped their drinks and chatted amongst themselves in the carnage of the trashed club as if nothing was amiss.

"Is the jukebox still working?"

Pat knew that Leonard would have taken stock of everything that would need replacing in nanoseconds; he had done it enough times before and when he nodded, he said happily, "Stick on 'Hotel California' will you? I fucking love that record."

Leonard did as he was asked and then he set about cleaning up the place as best he could, joining in with the ribald conversation at the bar and explaining to any customers who came knocking that the place would be closed for a few days on account of it being redecorated.

No one questioned that this place was redecorated four or five times a year on average. Thanks to long opening hours, excessive alcohol consumption, betting, women, football and occasionally religion, all these were things that seemed to make men capable of murder.

It was still early evening and so Leonard was hopeful of getting an early night for a change. As he always said, one man's loss was another man's gain. He hoped his old woman had partaken of her weekly bath and hair wash, he was in the mood for a quick flash and a bacon sandwich.

Cain was conveniently forgotten. He had been ironed out, straightened and sorted.

Chapter Fifteen

Jasper Jessup was a tall, angular man who hailed from the Caribbean, though where exactly no one seemed to know, least of all him.

He was a user. He used everyone he came into contact with but he did it with such aplomb and such good humor that it was hard to take too much offense. People just dropped away from him and he was very good-natured about it, so people forgot his bad points and hailed him if they saw him around.

However, he was in the know with what was left of the Williams family and this was mainly because he could always be relied on to ferret out half-decent grass or a banger girl, aka someone who was up for it with anybody, anywhere, anytime; for a price of course. More importantly, he could also find out what was happening on the pavements of south London.

He had his phony Jamaican accent off to a tee and his tall, thin body had a certain elegance that, combined with his dreads, gave him the air of a proud man, of a trustworthy man. This had stood him in good stead for many years, plus, as an added bonus, he had a certain panache about him; a scruffiness that suited his rangy body and put people off their guard. On certain days, he took it upon himself to wear the Rasta colors and, like a walking flag of Ethiopia, he would wander around Brixton market like a king. He would hail everyone he saw while toking on a large joint, his gold teeth glinting in the sunlight. He was well known there; he was part of the local color. The younger men, especially, were drawn to him with his tales of urban strife and the battle of the black man. Of course, once they realized that he talked shit, borrowed money off them too often and smoked their weed faster than they could procure it, he was dropped as they gravitated towards the other males in their community, the proper role models. It was a natural progression, a rite of passage for the teens he attracted, who imagined that being seen with an older man like Jasper would be seen as a measure of their own burgeoning manhood. Until, of course, they saw him for the predator he really was.

They actually learned valuable lessons from him though: that hustlers came in all shapes and sizes and, also, that their mothers were usually right in their opinions of the people they suddenly wanted to spend their time with. He had ruffled more than a few maternal feathers over the years and he retreated when the time was right because he was too shrewd to ever push his luck too far. The lads just faded away and when he saw them around, he grinned and laughed with them, always the picture of friendly affability.

And such was Jasper's *easiness* that they didn't hold him using them against him. He was just Jasper and he was all right; good for a story and a laugh in the Beehive on a Friday night. He was a local character and people tolerated him even though he was like a cancer in the community; he wised up the police when he had to and again his easiness, his smoothness, was why no one had ever questioned the fact that he had never once been hauled in. He'd never even been held on suspicion, which was remarkable because the suspect law was designed so the police could pull you in just because they thought you *looked suspicious*. It was a bonus for the cops as they had a perfect excuse to run in anyone they liked, just for the hell of it. A young man could be standing at a bus stop waiting for a bus, and he could legally be arrested, searched, and charged with basically anything that happened to pop into the overactive imaginations of the arresting officers.

A good hiding was often on the cards as well; it was the police equivalent of in for a penny, in for a pound. From the West Midlands Crime Squad to the Met, the police had almost complete autonomy over anyone they took a shine to. As everyone in the know was aware, for every person framed for a crime, even if they were a known criminal who had broken the law on numerous occasions and could not be held to account because the police had no evidence, once they were set up it meant the real perpetrator of the crime was still at large.

Suspect law was a law that had been passed with full knowledge of how it *could*, and most certainly *would* be abused by a large majority of the police force. People like Jasper actually needed the suspect law to survive. All he had to do was *hint* at someone's involvement in a crime and the law guaranteed they were pulled in without any kind of evidence whatsoever. Jasper actually had a razor-sharp brain, which he tried to hide with his foolishness and his stupid talk. But he had been responsible for a lot of arrests and he was a predator of the worst kind, whether it was impressionable young girls or the grown men he used to fill his wallet. People were relaxed around him because he acted far more stoned than he actually was a lot of the time. People were *easy* around him and talked about things that were best kept private. Jasper listened and he learned a lot about everything; he found this useful in his every-day dealings with the world.

Spider had once pointed out to him that he was a professional Rasta and so the Bob Marley hat and the crooked smile Jasper wore had never fooled him. To Spider, Jasper was the kind of black man that gave the rest of them a bad name. He was a poster boy Rasta and his own authenticity was what had alerted Spider to the fact he was a fake. Spider was the one man Jasper was wary of because he saw him for what he really was and this bothered him.

Jasper had no regular income, legal or otherwise; he lived off his considerable wits and it was his knack of finding opportunities that had led him to the Williams brothers and his latest earner.

Jasper had ingratiated himself with Cain and had introduced him to the finer points of smoking, from a joint to a pipe. He had helped the Williams brothers get involved with Spider's little brother and he was proud of his part in bringing down the arrogant little shit. The Williams boys were a few coconuts short of a palm tree, as his mother used to say, but they were also emerging from their Brodie-imposed exile better than he would have given them credit for. Now that Cain was onside they were in a unique position because Spider would not let anything drastic happen to his little brother. At least that's what this crowd of goons believed, anyway. Jasper wasn't so sure; Spider had seen through him as if he was a pane of glass on their first meeting and not many people were that astute. Shame Spider hadn't used the same instinct with his little brother but then family had to really piss you off before you outed them.

The Williams family were close, as close as their kind could be anyway, and they were paying him well for his contribution to their cause. Now he was sitting there with them, fooling them all with his smiles, his gold teeth and his thick Jamaican accent, all the while planning how best he could exploit them or utilize the knowledge that he was gathering to his own advantage. They were loose-lipped and he knew everything about them.

He began to build another joint knowing that if Brodie was looking for Cain then their days were numbered. Spider would have to swallow and he had a feeling that once Brodie had heard all he had garnered over the last few weeks he would not be a happy bunny.

The last few weeks had been a revelation to him and, as the boys talked, he listened while building his spliff and singing "Exodus" in a low voice, sounding more like Marley than the man himself. The Williams boys were messing with him periodically, thinking he didn't realize it, and he took it with good humor as always. Let them think he was a fucking moron. He was only sorry this lot didn't appreciate how he was playing them. But they would eventually, when it was too late, of course.

As Jasper sipped his rum and smoked his spliff, he was grinning and laughing, while wondering how this shower of shit managed to find their own arseholes without a fucking detailed map, a compass and a torch.

"Calm down, Lil. Lance what?"

Lil sighed in exasperation as she tried to explain the situation to Patrick, but she knew he was having a lot more trouble than her believing it.

"He threw a six-year-old girl off a moving bus. She had to have eight stitches in her head and she was terrified out of her life."

She sighed heavily at the shock on his face, knowing it was mirrored in her own. "He has been bullying the family for years, the little fucker. I think you had better go and look at him and see what I've done to him before we talk any more, OK?"

There was something in her voice that alerted Patrick to the truth of what she was saying yet he didn't want to believe it.

"Lil, is this a wind up?" But he knew it wasn't. He knew she was serious.

"What do *you* think, Pat? That I thought I'd have a joke with you about something this serious? He nearly killed a little girl. Fucking funny, is it? It's a big joke, is it? Only I ain't laughing, am I?"

Patrick took the stairs two at a time and went into his son's room. Lance was asleep. He looked like the victim of a train crash; he was swollen and bruised all over, his cut eyebrow had scabbed over and none of the blood had been wiped away. He knew that Lil had left him there without seeing to him and this bothered him more than the beating the child had taken; it said a lot for her feelings. He felt anger welling up inside him; the boy looked so little, so frail, and with his body curled into a ball and his hands placed under his cheek, he looked like an angel. He put out a hand to touch him but stopped himself. The boy was better off asleep. He was battered like a Friday night cod as it was.

Lance was sleeping deeply, as if he had no cares in the world. Patrick had a feeling this would not be the first time this child of his would be taken to task in his life and it pained him to admit that to himself, but he had always been a realist. Lance was the product of his own two parents, and that, mixed with Lil's family tree, meant the boy didn't stand a chance. Selfish and greedy, Lance was everything Patrick despised; he seemed to have all the bad traits of his ancestors and none of the good ones. Lance's only saving grace was how he was with his little sisters. How protective Lance was of them gave Patrick hope for this boy's future.

He forced down the urge to give the boy another hiding. He was sorry, not because Lance was battered and bruised, but because he felt no pity for him. Lance's eyelids were flickering, he was dreaming. Patrick knew that any other child would have been awake, would have been far too upset to sleep. He stared down at his son, wondering what he had bred. He knew that at some time in the future this boy would be an asset in any criminal undertaking but that as a child he was an anomaly. He found his dislike of his child was growing by the second. He wanted to drag him from the bed and make him understand just what he had done, but he knew that if he touched him, he would not be responsible for his actions. He needed to calm down first. The boy had been spoiled by his granny since he had first drawn breath and she had played a big part in all this. He had to blame her for a part of it, otherwise he would go mad. Well, he was going to sort the vindictive old bitch out. He needed to blame someone for his son's twisted nature and she was the prime suspect as far as he was concerned. Listening to the boy's soft breathing he knew he had to get away from him, to leave this room and all it entailed.

He crept into the other kids' rooms; the girls, as always, were asleep in one bed, a mass of plump limbs and baby sweat. Their lovely, long blond hair was damp from their body heat and their rosy cheeks made his heart swell with love for them. They were good-looking children. All his kids were handsome and he was proud of them; at least he had been, until now. Kissing them lightly he went to his eldest boy's room and, opening the door, he saw he was awake as if waiting for him to come home. He guessed this was exactly what his son had been doing.

"All right, Dad?" Pat Junior smiled tremulously at his father.

Patrick sat on the edge of his bed and smiled back. "What happened, son?"

Patrick knew he would get the truth from him, Pat Junior was as honest as the day was long.

"Mum was really cross, she went mad."

Pat nodded. "I can see that, mate, but she had reason to be, by the sounds of it."

The boy reluctantly nodded in agreement; as always he was trying to look out for Lance.

"But he didn't mean it, Dad. He does bad things but he don't really mean to, he just doesn't think . . ."

Patrick loved this son of his; he knew that he was still trying to defend his brother even though Lance wasn't worth this loyalty. Lance had no loyalty or respect for anyone but himself.

"But he did hurt Maureen Callahan, Dad. I heard about it at school and I asked him about it. He denied it."

Patrick nodded once more, the shame washing over him and leaving him feeling dirty.

"But you knew it was true, didn't you?"

Pat Junior nodded again as his eyes searched his father's for a hint of approval about how he was handling the problems his brother seemed to bring him on a daily basis. He didn't want to say outright that he had believed it from the start and that nothing his brother did surprised him.

"You're a good boy, son. Now relax and I'll talk to your mother and get it sorted. This is a serious thing that Lance has done, you do understand that, don't you?"

"I know. I felt sick when I heard. She could have been killed."

Patrick shrugged, a nonchalant shrug that took all his willpower because he was going to lie and he knew it was important that his boy believed what he was going to say so he didn't feel any more guilt over his brother and his actions.

"This isn't your fault, mate. You couldn't have prevented this. Lance has a mind of his own and when I am finished with him he will wish he had never laid eyes on that girl or her family. This is not your problem, OK? You don't need to worry about this any more."

Patrick looked into the face so like his own and wished he didn't have to deal with all this now. He had enough on his plate without a fucking Looney Tunes for a son. His actions seemed so far-fetched that he had thought it would turn out to be exaggerated or a big mistake. Now he knew that Lance was capable of anything. He was the child everyone was frightened of. Lance was a coward and it was that which made Patrick so angry; he had somehow bred a coward who had been able to bully his way through life because he bore the name Brodie.

Now he had to make some kind of sense out of this for Lil's sake and for this boy here, who he knew would be Lance's buffer to the world, until even he couldn't take it any more. He stroked Pat Junior's hair, feeling the thickness of it. The fact his son hadn't answered him was enough to make him change the subject and try to bring some normality into this twilight world the boy seemed to have stumbled into. Violence was his game and now it had crept into his home. All the years he had feared it encroaching on his family and he was stunned to find that its arrival had been heralded by one of his own children. This wasn't a boyish prank, it was a cold-blooded act of hate and as a man who used his strength and intimidation to earn a living, that was a very frightening thought. Controlled violence was one thing, as long as it didn't involve civilians and it was kept in their world. But the more he thought of his son's act, the more he knew he needed to be home more often than he was. Lance needed to be watched over and taught right and wrong. He needed a strong hand to guide him into the future.

Patrick forced a smile and said in a cheerful whisper, "Looking forward to your party?"

Patrick Junior nodded but the pain and fear were still in his eyes and Patrick knew he couldn't do this now; he had too much on his mind. Now that Lance's actions had finally sunk in he needed time to digest and cogitate on what the outcome should be.

"Come on you, get to sleep. Let me sort this lot out, eh?"

The relief in the boy's eyes was evident; the problem had been taken away from him. Patrick felt guilt weighing on him heavily for leaving this child to shoulder so much of the burden in the household. He was going to have to get out of the game; delegate more of the day-to-day running of the businesses. He was getting past all the skulduggery that constituted his main graft, his earned wage. If the truth be told, he was finally getting fed up with it all.

The Williams brothers should have been taken out from the start and because of Spider and his low-life brother, he had left the situation for too long, all the while expecting Spider to sort it out. Well he hadn't, not in time for him anyway. He had let it go on and that had set off alarm bells. Spider had an Achilles heel, as they all did to an extent, but where

Patrick would take out a family member if the offense warranted it, Spider couldn't. Cain was on his last legs and so was Spider if he played up. He had given him ample opportunity to sort the angry little fucker out. If Cain had been his brother the Williams brothers would have been warned off long ago. Cain would then have had his displeasure at the association pointed out to him with such force that he would have broken off any kind of friendship *tout de suite*.

Then he came home to another fucking war. Life was a bastard, there was no two ways about it. This son of his, who he loved more than life itself, was already carrying the weight of his siblings on his shoulders and he knew that if anything should happen to him, the boy would be carrying the mantle for this family long before he was due.

"Go to sleep, son. I'll sort it all out. Stop worrying, OK?"

Patrick Junior nodded once more and in the half-light Patrick saw the tiredness that was etched on the boy's face. This child was already old before his time, he realized now. He saw himself in this boy and Pat Junior was emulating his own life in the way he tried to keep the peace with everyone. He had learned to be a diplomat at a young age as well and had spent his childhood sneaking around his parents, trying not to annoy them. They had walked away from him regularly and left him to fend for himself without a second's thought and that had been hard. Now his son was in a similar position, trying to keep his brother on track and trying to be the man of the house for his mother, for Lil, who was weak with pregnancy and unsure of what to do about Lance and his antics. He sat there until Pat dropped off. Then he smoothed his son's thick black hair away from his brow and sighed heavily.

He went back downstairs into the neat and tidy kitchen and saw that his wife, his lovely Lil, was still standing where he had left her.

"Look, Lil, you're right. Lance is definitely not all the ticket, but what can we do?"

She shrugged. "I don't know, Pat, that's just it. What the fuck do we do about him? I talked Janie Callahan down and she had the sense to keep the cops out of it, so everyone thinks the child fell but the point is, he nearly *killed* her and he was still denying it, the little fucker."

That Lil was at the end of her tether was evident. She was near to tears, and, holding her gently to his chest, he kissed her softly, smelling Vosene shampoo and the sweet aroma of her scent. She favored Blue Grass and it lingered on her skin. It reminded him that soon she would be brought to bed with another child and would be his lovely Lil once more. No more backache, no more restless nights and no more upset because he was going to sort this out for her and give her peace of mind back.

"I do try with him, but he is hard work, Patrick. He lies, he steals, he causes upset everywhere he goes. Now it turns out he is a bully and all. Bullying girls, fucking little kids . . . What must people think of us, eh? He's getting away with murder and he knows that he can because of you. This has to stop, Patrick. You have to sort him out . . . I can't do this any more."

She was sobbing now and for his Lil to cry meant she was more than just upset and he understood how she was feeling because he was having trouble keeping a lid on his own temper at the moment.

"Don't get upset, think of this new baby . . ."

She pushed him away from her then, with force; a force that surprised both of them.

"Oh fuck the baby, Patrick. We need to sort out that mad bastard first. Then we can make sure this one doesn't turn out to be a nutcase and all . . ."

Patrick had never heard her speak like that before and he understood how she felt about what Lance had done, but shouting at him was not going to change that. He swallowed down his annoyance once more.

"Calm down, Lil. Getting upset is not going to solve anything, is it?"

Lil clenched her fists in rage at his words, knowing he meant well, but unable to play his game this time. She didn't want platitudes, she wanted action and she wanted him to tell her that her feelings for her child were merited. That he would sort this all out and take the onus off her. She wanted him to take Lance in hand and make him right in the head, make him normal and make her love him. She wanted him to make the hatred she felt for her child go away.

Janie Callahan had brought her worst nightmare into her home; as soon as she had seen her on the doorstep, she had known that Lance had finally overstepped the mark. She had almost enjoyed it, beating him and making him pay for the way he made her feel, for the guilt that lay over her like a lead weight.

"You're telling me to calm down? You fucking kill me. You think a few choice words are going to sort this out?"

The incredulity in Lil's voice was apparent and Pat closed his eyes. He only wanted to calm her down, that was all.

"He is a fucking *moron* and you know it. There is a cunning in him, Pat, a hateful, deceitful cunning that runs through him. He has to be curbed, he has to be taken in hand, Patrick. You can do it for once, you can fucking well sort this one out. For once in your life you can do the honors where that bastard is concerned, because I have had it, I can't do this any more."

Patrick could smell whisky and it was a few moments before it dawned on him that she was drunk. She was half-cut and, as he looked around the kitchen, he saw the half-empty bottle of Bells. Grabbing her arms, he forced her on to a chair.

"Don't you dare push me like that . . ." Her voice was louder than she expected and she knew she was getting out of hand, that the drink was talking for her. But she had needed something to take the edge off the day, help her relax and make her sleep.

"I didn't push you, Lil, I just helped you to a seat before you keeled over. Now, for the last time, calm down for fuck's sake."

His annoyance was in his voice now and she heard it with a thrill of pleasure. He was reacting at last and showing some kind of real emotion.

"You have to send him away from here, send him to a boarding school or something. I want him out of this house and I mean it . . ."

Pat poured himself a drink, anything to stop himself from answering his wife. He needed to calm down and think before he spoke to her. She was not in any mood for chit-chat and he wanted her calm and lucid before he talked the problem through.

"There's a Jesuit school in Ireland. I was reading about it a while back in the church magazine and they take problem kids. It ain't cheap but who cares about that. The priest will know more about it; we can inquire tomorrow. Either way, he has to *go*, Pat. He has to go away because I won't be responsible for my actions if he stays around me."

Patrick had always known that Lil had not taken to Lance as she should have. But he had not realized that it was as bad as this. Her mother had taken the boy over and, truth be told, it was the only reason he had tolerated the old bitch, because he knew deep down that Lil had no affection for the boy. He had understood, because Lance had a similar effect on him. But he rationalized his feelings and blamed it on the way Annie had taken him over from the second he had been born. He knew the relationship between Lance and his mother-in-law wasn't healthy but with Patrick Junior being a handful and the twins arriving so quickly he had let it go. He had tried to cut the cord a few times over the years but Lil had always been the instigator of her mother and Lance being reunited.

"A Jesuit school, Lil? That's your answer, is it? Send him away?"

She nodded and stared at him defiantly, letting him know that she was deadly serious. Now this had happened, now it was all out in the open, she wanted it resolved once and for all. Knowing what her son was capable of was enough for her to know she didn't want him near her.

"He ain't going away, Lil. He might be a fucker but he is eight. Eight years old. He had no real understanding of what he was doing . . ."

"He knew exactly what he was doing to that child. A few days earlier he had blacked her eye and punched her to the ground . . ."

She was nodding now at the horror on his face. "Yeah, punched the poor little mare for no reason at all. He is a spiteful little shit and he ain't ever going to get the chance to fucking vent his rage on my girls . . ."

"Stop it, Lil; he loves the twins . . ."

This was too far now; as if the boy would harm his own sisters.

Lil laughed sadly. "You just don't get it, do you, Pat? Either he goes or I do . . ."

"Don't be so dramatic, you silly mare, that's the drink talking. And you should know better than to get pissed in your condition. And as for Lance, he is the product of your fucking mother, and her constant mollycoddling. I'll hammer the little git and when I have finished with him he won't fucking dare put a foot wrong. Now, stop talking out of your arse, and let's get to bed."

He had finally had enough. He was going to nip this lot in the bud. Lil needed a good night's sleep and then maybe she would see this lot in a different light.

"I am not going anywhere, Patrick Brodie, until you promise me that Lance, the unnatural little bastard, will be taken away from here. Away from my other kids. From this new baby especially. I can't look at him without wanting to harm him and that is me telling you the truth of it. I want him out of this fucking house and away from me and mine!"

As she spoke she saw Lance standing in the doorway looking at her with those calm blue eyes that had bothered her even when he had been a babe in arms. She retched then and only just made it to the sink before the whisky and the day's events finally got the better of her and she threw up. As she retched she could hear her husband's breathing in the silence of the kitchen and she knew then that he would not do anything that she had asked of him. Lance would be taken in hand by him and he would fool his father as he fooled everyone else.

Spider was in a dilemma. His mother was looking at the lifeless body of her son and he wasn't able to do anything to make it better.

Cain had been found in a Dumpster. The Dumpster was outside a house in Leytonstone; the people who had rented it had expected a few other things to be dumped in it alongside the rubbish they cleared from their garden. A naked black man with a screwdriver forced through his ear had not been on their list. The woman's screams had alerted the neighbors and she was being sedated by the duty doctor as Spider and his mother were in the mortuary identifying his brother's remains.

Spider knew Patrick was angry, but he had not expected anything like this.

As he looked at his little brother he felt the full weight of his grief and, as his mother began to keen like a trapped animal, he was brought back to reality.

He nodded at the policeman and then watched as his mother was led from the room by a nurse. Her weeping was loud in the hushed quietness.

The policeman was watching him warily but Spider expected that and he looked at his brother's bloodied remains impassively. The less the cops knew, the better. He had to be clever with this now if he was going to convince them it was a random attack and not gang-related. They were more than aware of his credentials, which is why they had come to him quickly and quietly. They wanted to see if this boy's death was going to have any far-reaching consequences.

Which of course it would.

But the police in question would be well looked after if and when forthcoming events warranted it.

As Spider looked down at Cain and saw the gaping hole in his ear where a screwdriver had been forced through it, he felt nothing except a coldness inside him.

He only hoped Cain had been unconscious when the fatal blow had been administered; the thought of him knowing what had been happening to him was something he would not be able to bear. Violence was a part of their world and he knew that, but to think of his little brother going through all that pain was more than he could stand.

"Do you have any idea who might have been responsible?"

The policeman's voice was low and respectful, as befitted Spider's standing in the community. Spider knew that anyone else would have been interrogated by now. The assumption being, he had to know who the culprit was.

Spider shook his head keeping his face impassive as usual and looking as innocent as a newborn baby. "He was well-liked, popular; this had to be some kind of mugging. I don't know what else it could be."

The policeman accepted his explanation without any kind of query whatsoever, as Spider knew that he would.

He left the room and made his way back to his mother and sisters. They were huddled together, all crying, smudged lipstick and grief. It was so raw it was almost tangible in the room. As he saw them hugging and trying to comfort one another he felt the futility of many a man before him when faced with the mortality of loved ones and, more frightening in his world, the realization of their own mortality.

Young people dying did that to a body; it was like a shock to the system for the people left behind. It proved how tenuous the link was between life and death and how final the latter was. It occurred to Spider that he would never hear his brother's voice again. Never hear his explanation for the night's events.

He cuddled his mother and three sisters in turn, taking their grief on as his own. As he drove them home a while later he swore that Brodie was behind Cain's death and that he would have to pay for this night's work.

A warning was one thing, but this was something else entirely. That his mother had to bury her child was outrageous and Brodie would know his feelings on that subject sooner rather than later.

It was all going wrong, everything was caving in on him and now he understood what the life he had chosen could be like when you were on the receiving end of someone else's fuck-up. Until now he had always been the one calling the shots, had been the top dog, but he was finding out what life could be like on the outside looking in and, for the first time, he felt pity for the Williams brothers and all their ilk.

Chapter Sixteen

Ricky Williams was pleased with himself. He was like the others in looks but now his older brothers were dead and the others were like nervous brides; he was suddenly the acknowledged genius of the family. Which didn't exactly say a lot for the intelligence of the others, though no one was arguing about that. As long as someone was taking on the mantle, which they saw as the blame, they were happy enough. As Brodie had always said, if the brothers had someone to do the thinking for them, they were an asset. If they attempted to think for themselves, it was all bound to fall apart. Ricky saw himself as the Brain of Britain. In fact, like many before him, he felt he had been a king-in-waiting. The others were looking to him now and wanting him to sort everything out. They were a crowd of useless cunts but they were all he had so he was lumbered with them. Dave, Tommy and the rest were an embarrassment to him these days. He felt it was his duty to bring the family back on top and make people respect them again. They had used Cain for their own ends and they had not achieved anything from that. They were running scared and it was up to him to get the ball rolling once more, to bring them back into the world they had once called their own.

It had taken the deaths of half his family for him to finally be seen as a leader by his brothers but he was willing to overlook that in the light of his newfound status.

Ricky, however, for all his plotting and ideas actually had a very short attention span. Unless it was for women that is. And he had no real vocabulary unless it pertained to the female body or the uses he had found for it and even that was speckled with profane language. He was also a man who prided himself on his ability to act on the spur of the moment. He saw an opportunity and was in there quicker than a pimp on a Vespa.

As he chatted up the dark-eyed girl in the rah-rah skirt and the heavy make-up, he was patting himself on the back. He had seen a chance and he had taken it. When his brothers heard what he had done, he would be hailed a hero, he was sure. Cain, he had decided, had been ready to serve them up to his brother and he had made sure that would never happen. Cain was a piece of shit and his use was over and done with. Ricky had been sensible enough to look out for the others, to look out for the family; a family that had been depleted over the last few years by the likes of Brodie and his sidekick Spider. As his dad used to say: what do you call a man with more money than you? A sworn fucking enemy, and he was right. Why be the breakers, the fucking back-up, the runts who collected the money for everyone else? It was ludicrous that his brothers had not figured that out long ago. Without people like them, no one could ply their trades; the heavies were the backbone of any shady business. Ricky was absolutely thrilled with himself and with his antics. He was on a roll and knew that he was going to make sure the Williams name was put back where it belonged.

Now though, he was going to celebrate with a shag and a curry, in that order. This girl with the crooked teeth and the heavy cyeliner was just what the doctor ordered. From her denim vest to her Union Jack clogs, she screamed easy lay and he should know, he had been perfecting the art of ferreting out girls like her since he had been at junior school. She was soapy but that didn't put him off; he wanted to fuck it not marry it. Even though he had acquired a reputation for predominantly shagging birds from the lower-end of the female food chain, he had no shame. If it had a pulse he was there. No matter how old the birds were, as long as they were passable on a dark night, he was game. He didn't want Miss World, he was happy enough with Miss Buy Me a Drink and I'll Drop Me Cacks.

It was all relative as far as he was concerned. He liked the thrill of a new hole and enjoyed the feel of different breasts and different bodies.

He didn't want perfection, he just wanted a bird who was as up for it as he was. A bird who had no illusions about what would be happening to her and didn't expect declarations of love before, during or after the momentous event. A fuck was a fuck as far as he was concerned and he liked to get in at least a couple on a daily basis. He searched out other women like other men searched for gold or holy grails. He just loved women's bodies, all shapes and all sizes.

As young Natalie smiled her acquiescence he felt the familiar rush that a new conquest always gave him. She had been about, he knew that; her eyes and the way that she knocked back her drinks told him that much. She was the type who had found out at an early age that men were really only after one thing and she had been supplying them with it ever since.

Leaving the pub with her, he was unaware of the man watching him from a black Beamer in the parking lot. It pulled out quietly behind him as he hit the main road, his radio blaring out and his head full of the night's coming attractions.

Annie was alone again and she didn't like it. Throughout her marriage she had dreamed of a life surrounded by people, a life filled with events and happenings that included her. Unfortunately, she had never learned the knack of actually *being* around other people. Her daughter had been the reason she had finally found companionship but even then it was only the children she wanted to see. One child more than the others but she couldn't help where her heart lay, the boy had captured it from the moment she had seen his face. She didn't admit that her daughter had the baby blues at the time; that she had used her daughter's postnatal depression to inveigle herself into all their lives. She saw herself as selflessly taking on her daughter's family and helping her Lil out when she was at her lowest ebb. It was only because of that that she was even tolerated. Even Annie's harshest critics, and they were legion around their streets, gave her that as her due; she had been there for her daughter when she had needed her.

She had made Lance her own and for the first time in years she had felt something akin to happiness. Now though, she was once more on the outside looking in, and her Lance was being victimized for a prank, a childish prank.

As Annie put the kettle on, she looked out of the window of her apartment, the home her daughter had provided for her. The grass outside was in need of a good cut and the other apartments around her were all lit up, their occupants going about their nightly routines. The flicker of televisions and the occasional sound of a dog barking broke the silence for her. Families were eating together, watching television together, being together.

She was on the verge of tears once more and taking her tea, she walked into her front room slowly. The room was over-furnished and over-polished. A heavy smell of beeswax and cigarettes permeated everything, even the wallpaper with its pink roses and a thin gold line as the background. Every surface was covered in photographs, mainly of Lance, though the twins were also in evidence. Lil and Pat Junior were in only one. Patrick Junior's Communion photo. It was on the mantelpiece, along with Lance's.

Annie stared at them now, wondering if her boy was all right and worried about Pat Brodie's reaction to his son's foolish prank. She could kick Janie Callahan's arse for the trouble she had caused her family. She missed the twins, their little voices prattling on and the happy faces that glowed with pleasure every time she turned up with a Wagon Wheel for each of them. She now understood just what a joy children could be and, if she was honest, in her darkest moments, she wished she had learned that secret many years before. Lil had been a burden to her from day one, had always been a burden, but now she was sorry she had not made a friend of her only child earlier. She missed the conversation and the noise that her daughter's house seemed to be filled with constantly. She missed the pranks, the kids' laughter and the endless cups of tea and cigarettes that were now a staple of her days. Lil was all right and it had taken her this long to admit that to herself. She was heartsorry now for all the years she had made her own life a misery, along with her daughter's.

Annie had been lonely before, but now it was like a physical ache inside her and not just for Lance. She was actually missing her daughter, missing her chatter and her easygoing ways. It had been a week since she had been to the house and it felt like a lifetime. How she had lived under that cloud for so long she had no idea any more; the years of sitting in the quiet and waiting for a man who had no real interest in her seemed ludicrous now. The waste of her life bothered her. That she had broken under the weight of her husband's disregard and had joined forces with him in his hate and his disappointments, had made them her own, and for no reason other than that she had only seen him as a way to regain respectability because she had been pregnant with Lil. Now the opinion of the neighbors meant nothing to her; girls had babies without a second's thought and no one really cared any more. It was a nine-day wonder and she had been lumbered with her old man to give her child a name. She had thought it was so important once and she had held a grudge against poor Lil because of it. She had lived in a vacuum with a man who had snatched her up because no other girl would have had him if they didn't have good reason and lived in a home devoid of life, laughter and peace of mind.

Her daughter's house, on the other hand, was inviting and warm and, most of all, happy. Until Lance's little mishap with the Callahan girl it seemed to her, with hindsight, that her life had been ideal. And in truth, it had been.

Now she was back where she started, alone and unwanted. Even her new friends were only really civil to her because of her daughter's name and now she might be on the outs they were avoiding her like the plague. When all this calmed down she was going to make an effort to be indispensable, amiable and approachable; she was lost without them and she didn't want to feel like this ever again.

The knock at the door made her jump. She wasn't a woman who had visitors; in fact, very few people had ever been inside this room. The urgency of the door knocker brought her hurrying into her hallway and, as she opened the door, she remembered that she should have checked who was behind it first.

"Look, Spider, I never touched Cain in that way. You are barking up the wrong tree, mate, if you think any different. I think we all know who the culprits are, don't we? You knew he was on the missing list and you did nothing about it so don't come the fucking concerned brother now."

Spider was quiet. He'd had to ask and he knew Patrick understood that and wouldn't hold it against him.

"He had a fucking good hiding and I admit that. You know it was long overdue. Fucking screwdrivers in the lughole though; that ain't my kind of retribution. That smacks to me of an opportunist, an amateur using whatever came to hand. He was a skaghead for fuck's sake so he could have been done over by any number of people. Even though you are his brother it wouldn't stop anyone taking what was rightfully theirs and you know it. Not to mention the fact that he was hanging out with the Williamses. We dropped him near your place. We knew he would make his way there whatever and as he was out of his fucking box on Special K and whiz, among other things. We felt that he needed a hand in that direction. He was not capable of finding his own cock, let alone your drum or even his own, come to that. He was wasted and he was well battered and, believe me, I felt like taking him out but, at the end of the day, we are hardly going to kill him and dump him in a skip, are we? I mean, give us some credence, for fuck's sake."

Patrick poured them both drinks but his anger and his obvious disdain were more than evident.

"His dealer, another fucking skaghead, any number of people could have ironed him out for any number of reasons and you know it. He was on the brown and you can't fucking trust anyone on that; they would sell out their own granny for a two-quid wrap. He was a good kid and he chose to fuck up but you have to sort your head out, Spider. Stop fucking overdramatizing everything. Cain got mullered; it's sad but a fact of life. Get over it, will you, or at least look for the real culprits."

Patrick was a big man and Spider had forgotten how Brodie could intimidate those around him without resorting to physical violence. It was this that had made him the top of his game and it was also what kept him there.

"I'm having the Williams lot tailed to see where they go and what they do. I would lay poke they were behind Cain's demise because he was too fucking close to them. That fucking Jasper is on his way over to give his opinion on the latest events and you can bet he is in on the fucking lot of it. But this is the Williams brothers' fucking swan song. I ain't fucking letting it go this time. They have really pissed me off and I will teach them a lesson they will never forget. You were the one who wanted me to go easy on them, remember, you and Cain. So don't fucking bring your shit to my door ever again unless you want it cleared up. You had your fucking chance and you did nothing and now you are finding out what happens when you let your emotions take over."

Patrick's anger was ripe and justified. He had tried to keep the peace, had given Spider time to sort his brother out and this was the upshot. He must be getting soft in his old age. Well, he was going to cause a fucking war over this little lot. He was going to set an example that would be noted and digested by everyone in their world. He loved Spider like a brother and that was where he had gone wrong. Watch your own arse; it made life much easier in the long run.

Spider watched the changing expressions on his friend's face and knew he was on the sidelines himself over his brother's foolishness and his delay in curbing it. He also knew that Patrick was having family trouble himself; his son's crime was common knowledge and, though most people were of the opinion that he was out of order and in need of a good hiding, there was also a general consensus that he would make a great enforcer one day. If he had that kind of viciousness in him now, what would he be like in ten or fifteen years? He was a born heavy according to the powers that be and his rep was already being established. The little girl in question had already become an older boy in the retelling of the tale. All stories got stretched in the telling and this one was no exception. So Lance was already a known quantity to the men his father moved among. They saw him as a chip off the old block, as someone to watch out for in the future.

Spider had never liked the boy, though the other kids were lovely. He knew, as Patrick knew, that the boy had a screw loose somewhere. He was a weirdo and that was being nice about it. Cain, it seemed, had had the same defect, had suffered from the same selfishness, and it was this that was making it so hard for him now. Like Brodie he was of the opinion you cut out the cancer before it devoured you and yours but he had not wanted to do that to Cain. He had not been capable of harming him. He would have, eventually, he knew, but only when he had exhausted every other route first.

He knew his brother had met his death *because* of this man before him, if not by him, but he couldn't let that color his thinking. Patrick had only done what he should have done in the first place. What he should have done without thinking about it, uncaring of the fact that Cain was his brother and his best friend. He had loved that boy as if he was his own child and that had been his downfall; he knew that now and he accepted his stupidity. He had let his brother's bad behavior carry on without even attempting to curb it and now he was reaping what he had inadvertently sowed. It would never happen again, he was sure of that.

Now they were in a worse situation and it was all down to him. Cain was dead and gone but the world was still turning, the sun still rose and set and he still had a family to feed.

The Williams brothers were dead meat though, that much he could at least control. And he was going to make sure they were visited before the week was out. Spider believed in personal service and he was looking forward to taking them out one by one. But first he had to calm the waters with Brodie and ingratiate himself once more with the man who had given him everything he had in life and who had given it without a second's thought.

Spider had to salvage what he could from all this and he hoped that, at some point, that included his pride and the respect of this man who had given him more over the years than anyone else in the world.

Alan Palmer was a man who knew his own worth and, as the acknowledged front-runner in the world of the East End discotheque, he was more aware of what was happening in his nightclubs than anybody would have given him credit for. Alan was a big man, not heavy but solid, thick blond hair and icy-blue eyes; good-looking enough to warrant female interest with or without his loaded wallet. He had been dealing with Brodie for years; he knew that he would not be able to run his clubs without his express permission and he paid a fair price to guarantee that.

Alan Palmer had three brothers-in-law, all handy enough, all with decent credentials and all dependent on him for their livings. His brother had been murdered not too long ago by relatives of the young man sitting opposite him. He had Ricky Williams in his offices in Ilford offering him protection at a reduced rate and not one of his brothers-in-law were available to aim this punk out the door, so it looked like he was going to have to sort it out himself. For Alan, violence was a last resort, unlike his brother, who had seen it as a first resort. Now he was dead, so what did that tell you? Violence was also something to be used with the utmost discretion, especially in the entertainment business. This was something he had learned many moons ago and it had been an expensive, inconvenient and hard-taught lesson.

Alan smiled lazily, exposing his expensive teeth for the first time since Ricky had gatecrashed into his club.

"Are you on fucking drugs or what?"

His complete contempt for the man sitting opposite him was apparent in his every word and Ricky Williams was offended.

"Go on. Piss off home to your mother and don't ever strong it with me again."

Ricky sat it out, staring at Alan with a quiet intensity. "You should use your loaf, Alan. If we all band together, what the fuck is Brodie going to do, eh? I have half of south London on board and me and my brothers are going to take a piece of this place in the end. If you come on board with us now, you will be the fucking main man. The fucking number one."

Alan started laughing. But the boy's words were tempting, as Ricky had known they would be. Alan Palmer was a force to be reckoned with and that was a certified fact. Over the years he had gathered people to him, as any decent employer did; the fact most of his workforce were out on parole didn't bother him at all. He had a few good scams on the go and he also had a burning ambition but he knew that while Brodie drew breath he would never be challenged by anyone on his turf. If you worked for anyone, you inadvertently worked for Brodie; that had been established many years before. Patrick had sewn up all the main money-spinners and people like him depended on Brodie's goodwill and largesse to carry out their business dealings smoothly. Brodie guaranteed licenses and premises; without his say-so no one could work anything. It was a good arrangement in many ways because it meant that anyone could get a liquor license or a gaming certificate; anything they needed really, no matter what their past record might be.

In other ways, though, it was a bugbear; they had to keep on paying Brodie a hefty wad for as long as they were trading. Spider had been one of the main protagonists where Palmer's brother's death had been concerned; if needs be he could still take umbrage at his brother's demise or he might choose to accept it gracefully. He would wait and see what the outcome of this kid's ideas were before he decided what his reaction was going to be. Like any astute businessman, Alan Palmer was always open to negotiation with anyone who had a good business plan and something to offer him.

He knew Ricky Williams was on his last legs in many respects and he also knew that, like the rest of his family, dead or alive, he had the intelligence of a drunken wombat. All that aside though, it didn't mean he wasn't capable of at least one act of derring-do.

"Are you trying to tell me that you are capable of taking out Patrick Brodie?" This was said with a mixture of laughter and seriousness that wasn't lost on Ricky. He was actually shocked at how quickly Alan Palmer had swallowed the bait.

"You know the position my family is in now, thanks to Brodie and that cunt Spider. If I could remove Brodie, would you be willing to settle with me and mine and let bygones be bygones?"

Alan knew that Patrick and Spider were probably going to wipe this man and his remaining brothers off the face of the earth, and so they should. The Williams brothers had been asking for it for a long time now. It was overdue, there was no doubt about that. But if, and it was a big if, this prat did the unthinkable then he would not be averse to taking over the reins so to speak.

He was well-respected and he was also in possession of a serious fortune, both of which would be mandatory if he was to step up a gear and take on the mantle of a serious firm. His pulse was quickening at the thought of it; he could take the whole place over with the minimum of fuss. There was no one to stop him and, after Brodie, he was the next best thing.

Old Jimmy Brick would soon see where his expertise would be best employed and he would make him an offer he wouldn't turn down. It would mean recruiting the rest of Brodie's workforce of course, but that would not be such a hardship. Patrick had always surrounded himself with the best and he had been champing at the bit for a long time.

"You're off your fucking tree, Ricky. If you say things like that to the wrong people you could find yourself in a lot of trouble. Patrick won't be impressed, I can tell you, and you ain't exactly flavor of the month with him, are you? Cain's death has fucked you lot once and for all. Patrick is one thing but Spider is a fucking handful and you think you could take them both out then?"

He was laughing, but Ricky knew what Alan was saying to him. He was willing to do whatever was necessary to keep the Williams family safe. Ricky knew he wasn't cute enough to run anything himself; he needed someone else to do that for him but if he took out Brodie and Spider then his rep would be secured and Alan Palmer and his cronies would see him and his brothers right.

"Watch this fucking space, Alan. You just watch."

Ricky was laughing loudly, almost on the verge of hysteria, and Alan Palmer shook his head in disbelief, while making plans in case the mad bastard actually achieved his objective.

"He ain't going away, Lil, and that's that."

The finality in her husband's voice depressed her, but she knew that nothing she said would change his mind. Lil was a realist and where her husband was concerned she was sensible enough to know that further arguing would be pointless.

"You leave him to me, all right? I will sort the fucker out in future."

He had been as good as his word, she would give him that much. Lance had not left his room except to go to school since the day it had all blown up. Patrick had given him a stern talking-to and another good hiding to boot.

Lance was shrewd though; he was telling them all what they wanted to hear and, even though he looked contrite, she knew in her heart of hearts that he was anything but. It was just talk to him, it meant nothing. She had often secretly wondered over the years if he copied Patrick's behavior and his emotional responses because he seemed genuine enough to everyone else, but she knew, somehow she just knew, it was all an act.

Sighing, she went back to making more sausage rolls for the birthday party that she wished she had never agreed to now. Everyone around was chipping in and helping her; making sandwiches, cakes, tarts and quiches. She was providing the ingredients of course, but the way people had rallied around pleased her. Since Janie's visit she had taken on a new lease of life; she was back in the real world again and it felt good. Even with the baby dragging her down and Lance's aberration, she was feeling lighter somehow. Her mother's presence had always hung over the house like a shroud but now, though they spoke on the phone, her absence was like a breath of fresh air. People came round more, stayed longer and there was laughter and joking. Lil had forgotten how her mother managed to dampen everything with a few choice words. Now she was reminded of how different the house could be and even the stab of guilt she felt occasionally because she was relishing having the house and her children to herself wasn't enough for her to bring her mother back into the fold. She knew her mother would stay away until Lil told her otherwise. Patrick was blamed though the words were not said outright, just implied. Lance was confined to his room so she didn't have to deal with him too much either. Like her mother, he put a damper on everything. Somehow just his being in a room caused upset and, as bad as she felt about admitting it, she was still enjoying the holiday from the pair of them.

Janie arrived and they chatted together amiably as they made even more food. Covering the plates of sandwiches with tinfoil they placed them on the worktops ready for Patrick Junior's birthday party.

The boy himself was watching the preparations with barely contained excitement. He was going to be ten and he felt the enormity of his party as if it was a living thing. His friends, schoolmates, family and neighbors would all be there. It was unlike any party he had enjoyed before. He not only had a disco but proper food, and adults were invited as well as children. It was a big responsibility he knew and he was nervous about it all. The drink his father had bought was sitting in the hallway in large cardboard boxes. There was alcohol for the grown-ups and every kind of soft drink imaginable for the children. Just looking at it all made his heart race.

Patrick Junior's only worry was Lance. His mother and father were adamant that he was not going to attend the party as part of his punishment. He knew they were doing the right thing but at the same time Lance was going to miss out on something that would be remembered for the rest of their lives. Patrick Junior knew that he would not enjoy the day as fully because Lance wasn't there. Lance was a pain and he had done something really wrong, really dangerous, but he was still his brother and he would like him at his party so that in years to come they could discuss it without any bad feeling. To Pat Junior the party was the biggest thing that had ever happened to him in his life and he wanted to share the excitement with Lance. He knew that the party would be the main topic of conversation for weeks to come at school and around abouts. Lance would feel it acutely if he couldn't join in and that worried Pat Junior. He didn't want to have to stop talking about it because his brother had missed out, even if it was his own fault. Lance managed to ruin everything without even trying.

Even though Pat Junior felt sorry for Lance, a small part of him was also relieved that he wouldn't be able to show off in front of everyone, and he couldn't denigrate it if he wasn't in attendance; he put down everything that pertained to his older brother. Patrick Junior still had enough heart to feel sorrow for his brother's plight though. He knew Lance was in bits over his father's decision to keep him in his room, and although Pat knew that his punishment was for his own good and that missing the event would make him think seriously about what he had done, Patrick Junior instinctively knew that as bad as Lance was, missing the party would cause more problems in the long run than it would ever solve.

Ricky Williams was nervous and his brothers were all worried about the next few days as well. Looking around the room at them, Ricky wondered how he was going to keep them in line once his plans were put into place.

Dave, Bernie and Tommy were quiet as he told them what he had done and what he was planning, and Ricky knew that they looked at him with a new respect. They now saw him as the man *he* knew he had always been. All he wanted now was the chance to show everyone in their circle of friends his acumen and his strength of purpose.

Ricky looked over the bar and caught the eye of a dark-haired girl in a frilly shirt and, motioning with his hands, ordered more lagers. As she walked to the bar with her hands full of dirty glasses he watched her intently. She wasn't a great beauty but she had a nice plump arse and he liked that in a woman. She was a bit battered around the edges and older than he had first thought, but she had a nice smile. A wide-open smile that made her look friendly and approachable. He decided he liked her enough to present her with his secret weapon at some point in the near future. Her wink as she poured the pints convinced him he was on to a winner and, as always, his quest for other women took precedence over everything else.

They were in a pub in Kent. Until they were once more welcome visitors in London they had decided that their best course of action was to lie low for a while. Especially since Cain's unfortunate little accident. Ricky decided that he liked Kent, the garden of England. He liked the skirt, the pubs and the way the locals left them to their own devices. In fact, he was so enamored of the county that he decided there and then to buy a place there at some point in the future.

It felt good to relax properly for once, to just sit in a pub without having to watch the door, observe who was already there and buy drinks for a crowd of people he didn't even like, if truth be told. The easiness of the regulars here told him that this was a straight pub, a real pub, where people really did come just for a few beers and a bit of a chat. Ricky had forgotten how good that could feel but he was also aware of how good it could feel to be in a pub and know you could show off without fear or favor and where people fell over one another to get you a drink. Where you chose the music and the clientele and where you proved to yourself that you were somebody, that you counted.

Not long now and that would be his life once again. As the woman brought over the lagers he gave her a blinding smile and a big tip. Ricky was a great believer in laying down the groundwork first, that way you always got the result you wanted; her ready smile told him he was already halfway into her drawers. Life, he decided, was good. And from tomorrow it could only get better.

Chapter Seventeen

Jimmy Brick had the hump but no one looking at him would have known that. He had his smiley face on today, on account of it being the kid's birthday party.

He knew, however, that even a kid's party could turn pear-shaped in their world; alcoholic beverages and short tempers were often enough to start a world war.

His niece's christening, for example, had led to a murder and a life sentence for his brother-in-law, who had not been invited due to his habit of clumping her one when the fancy took him. He had been outed from the place they had once shared by himself and a few others, and had taken it in pretty good part. Until Ursula, his sister, had kissed her new bloke in the back garden of the marital home; cue said brother-in-law scaling fence, the shooting, the screaming of the female relatives and the rest of the Sunday sitting in the police station as they took statements.

No, Jimmy didn't trust even the most innocent of parties or the most innocent of guests. Everyone was capable of a tear-up given the correct set of circumstances; he was convinced of that much. He was determined to make sure that Pat Junior's party was fight-free.

The hall looked fantastic, all banners and balloons. The food was weighing down the large trestle tables and the aroma was killing him. Egg and cress got to him every time and he swiped a few and munched them quickly. The bar was now set up and the DJ, an obvious moron, was ready to rock and roll. Jimmy supervised the placing of the tables and chairs, had a quick smoke outside the church hall and then, finally, he relaxed. The kid was lucky to have a party like this at ten years old; he had not had anything even close to this for his twenty-first. He was a nice kid though, young Pat Junior. He was a sturdy little fucker and he looked like his old man. Was like the spit out of his mouth, as his mother used to say. The other one, that Lance, was a strange guy and no mistake. He was a head case and there was nothing wrong with that, but Patrick had made a point of keeping him away from the day's celebrations to teach him a lesson. Give him ten years though and he'd be a force to be reckoned with. Missing a party wouldn't be the highlight of his life's disappointments, he would lay money on that much. That Lance was a maniac waiting to blossom and, when he did, God help anyone who got in his way.

Lil was listening to her mother with half an ear. As she brushed Kathleen's hair she marveled at its softness; in matching cream party dresses the twins looked gorgeous. When they were dressed up, their likeness was somehow even more pronounced although Eileen had darker eyes but, unless you really looked, it wasn't that noticeable.

"When I answered the door and saw your man standing there I nearly had a heart attack."

Annie was pleased to see she finally had her daughter's attention.

"What, Pat came round yours? That's a turn up for the books."

Annie nodded with what she hoped was a winsome look. She so desperately wanted to get back into her daughter's good books that she was willing to try anything. She had never felt so lonely in her life as she had the last week or so.

"What did he say?"

Annie smiled slightly and her heavily wrinkled eyes reminded Lil of just how much her mother had missed them all. She seemed to have aged dramatically and, as Lil looked at her, she felt her mother's need of her and her family.

"He just said that Lance was going to be punished and that I would be better off keeping away for a while so you two could sort him out in private."

Lil was skeptical about that but she didn't voice her thoughts.

Annie was not going to tell her daughter that Patrick Brodie had read her the riot act; had threatened her with total banishment if she indulged Lance any more or treated any of the other children differently from him. He had told her outright that he didn't like her and she was only going to be brought back into the fold if she kept on the right side of him. One false move and she was toast, was how he had so nicely put it.

She had readily agreed; she would walk over hot coals if that's what it would take to get herself back into the bosom of her family. She had stopped herself from going near Lance today, acting as if she wasn't bothered whether she saw him or not. She wasn't fooling anyone, she knew, but at least they could see she was trying. As Lil pulled Eileen on to her lap to brush her hair through and put it into bunches like her sister's, Annie thought that she would die from happiness. Kathleen walked over to her and put her arms up for a cuddle without any coercion from her at all.

"Nanny."

Annie smiled in delight at the child's words.

"Nutty Nanny Annie."

Lil could have happily beaten her husband to death for teaching the girls to say that and as she waited for her mother to make a scathing remark she was surprised to see that she was laughing with Kathleen. Really laughing with her and it was such an unusual sight she felt her eyes fill with tears. Her hormones must be on overdrive because she was very tearful lately; the least little thing could set her off. Since Lance had hurt that girl, she had been on a knife-edge and though she knew her pregnancy was the main reason for her mood changes, her son's actions still gave her sleepless nights.

Eileen was laughing as well now and Lil hugged her daughter to her, thanking God for the twins, as she did on a daily basis. They were little angels and she knew that though every woman thought their kids were beautiful, hers really were. Not just to her, but to complete strangers. People always remarked on them when she took them out; they were such happy children and so friendly and contented that they made a stir wherever they went. And if they had melted Annie Diamond's heart then they had to be special, because in all her life she had never managed to elicit so much as a smile from her mother and at times that still grieved her.

Pat Junior walked into the room in his new clothes and Lil watched his handsome face as he picked up both his sisters in his arms and chatted to them in a funny voice. In his black Farah trousers and a white Ben Sherman shirt, he looked so grown up she was speechless for a moment. She suddenly saw the young man who was beginning to emerge and she was reminded once more that children were only on loan to you. Before you knew it, they were grown up and getting ready to fly the nest. She so wanted them to feel loved, and wanted them to feel that she had given them a happy childhood. She wanted them to have everything she had never had in her own childhood.

Annie saw her daughter's face and wished she had some gem of wisdom to share with her on this big occasion, but she couldn't remember Lil's tenth birthday, or any of her birthdays, for that matter. They had never celebrated anything and how she regretted that now, for letting her husband rule her, rule them both. She conveniently forgot that she had let him and had become like him. That she had resented the child that had forced her into marriage with him. Annie sighed. You lived and learned and she had been lucky enough to be given a second chance with this daughter of hers and she was grateful for that much.

She wondered if Lil was thinking the same as her as she looked at her eldest grandson, nearly prostrate with excitement at the thought of his party, and thanking his mother over and over again for all the work she had put into it. She couldn't help wondering if this was reminding her daughter of her own empty birthdays and her own childhood, as it was reminding her.

Annie heard the front door open and Patrick Brodie's loud voice as he called out for the birthday boy. Annie was still nervous of him and as she made her way out to the hall and admired Patrick Junior's new bike, she reminded herself she was still on probation as far as her daughter's husband was concerned.

He winked at her and she smiled at him with obvious relief. He grabbed his wife in his arms and said happily to Patrick Junior, "Ten, eh, son. You'll be eye to eye with me soon. My old man stopped giving me the belt the day I hit eye level. I lamped him one and told him that next time I'd do it when he was asleep and he never tried to beat me again."

Pat Junior loved it when his father told him stories about his own childhood. As he caressed his new racing bike, he asked him seriously, "Did he really hit you with a belt, Dad?"

"He fucking hammered me with anything that came to hand. Miserable old bastard he was. Still is, for all I know. But the belt hurt, I can tell you."

Pat Junior looked at his mother then. "Did Nanny Annie ever hit you, Mum?"

It was said in jest but he immediately regretted asking because the humor went and she answered flatly, "Come on, let's get sorted. Make sure you brush your hair for the photograph, OK?"

Pat Junior nodded and he saw his grandmother's face had turned scarlet. He felt the sudden urge to grab his mother in his arms and comfort her, even though he wasn't sure why. His father got there first, though. He watched with sad eyes as his father kissed his mother gently on the lips before saying quietly, "I love you, Lily Brodie, and don't you ever forget that."

Pat Junior felt the urge to cry then and his mother, sensing her son's discomfort, pulled him into her heavy belly and kissing him on the top of his head, she laughed.

"What a bleeding crowd we are, near to tears on the best day of your life!"

Pat Junior felt his father's hand on his shoulder and, embraced by both his parents, he wished that the moment would never end. He felt so safe, so protected and loved that he knew he would carry the memory of this moment all his life.

Dave, Bernie and Tommy Williams were drunk. They had been out on it since the morning and now it was early afternoon they were rocking. As they stood at the bar laughing loudly, they were aware of the looks they were getting from the regulars.

They had not been in this pub for a while and they knew that their sudden appearance would have already been reported back to base camp.

It was the day of the big party and anyone who was anyone would be going to the church hall laden down with presents and good-natured bonhomie.

They knew they were safe enough. Pat Brodie wouldn't be doing a lot today and they had kept a low profile for long enough. Now, though, they were all tanked up enough to face young Ricky and his perfectly understandable anger at their need to always be drunk. They would meet up with him eventually, when it suited them, nearer the time. The Blind Beggar public house was packed, as it was most Saturday lunchtimes. The clientele was an assorted mix of market traders, local shop owners, a few goons and a sprinkling of smalltime Faces.

There had been a time when the name Williams would have afforded them a warm welcome here; free drinks, a decent spot at the bar and the respect their name used to command. Now they were basically being tolerated.

With the drink, mixed with the speed that was coursing through their veins, they felt the cold-shoulder treatment afforded them far more acutely than it actually warranted. They were aware of how far they had sunk and, today more than usual, it really galled them. Seeing people who had once broken their necks for a glimpse of them, who had drunk with them, basking in their little bit of reflected glory, now ignoring them so deliberately and, worse still, as far as they were concerned, believing that they could get away with such cuntish behavior, psyched the three brothers up for what they knew they were going to have to do. Young Ricky was right; he was a shrewdie and no mistake. He knew the ins and outs of the cat's arse where Brodie and Spider was concerned and he had the edge on his brothers because he not only retained information, he also had the ability to put it to good use. He was a rising star all right and this shower of shit would soon realize that and mend their ways. Ricky was right; they had to do something spectacular, something audacious to get their name back where it belonged.

Tommy stared across the bar at a good-looking boy in his middle twenties. He was what they would term a lump, meaning he was bigger than the average, and could take pretty good care of himself. Tommy knew him slightly through Cain and smiling at him, he called out a greeting in a friendly manner; he would come in handy one day, he was sure. The man, a young up-and-coming Face who went by the name of Digger Trent, puffed out his thick lips in derision and shook his head slowly and deliberately, before turning his back on them. With that little gesture, he managed to convey his utter contempt for the brothers more acutely than if he had made fools of them loudly in public.

Tommy saw the width of the lad's shoulders, they were further emphasized by his custom leather jacket. Digger had thick dark hair, it was well cut and lay in perfect layers; he was a good-looking fellow and he knew it. He was also at the age where he wanted to progress in his chosen profession; he was collecting debts as well as working a few doors and he had no intention of letting himself be associated with a band of muppets like the Williams lot. He was confident enough in his local to feel perfectly at ease mugging off the ice-creams at the bar. They were a handful but he was confident he could take them if necessary. In fact, working over known associates was the quickest way to make a reputation for yourself. These men were still hard enough to be chary of, but on the plus side, they were not really affiliated with anyone important any more. Digger was debating whether or not to confront them and see what occurred.

A crony of his, Louie Blackman, was not so confident and he kept a wary eye on the Williams brothers as he sipped his pint of Fosters. He was older than Digger and he knew that the Williams brothers might have fucked up over the last few years, and might well be classed as a joke, but together they were still a fucking formidable force. And when Tommy walked across to where they were standing by the jukebox and he saw the glint of his glass, he stepped away as quickly as possible.

Tommy shoved his pint glass into Digger's face with all the strength he possessed. Digger had not known anything about it until the glass crunched into his cheek and eye; he was still standing with his back to the Williams brothers and Tommy had the edge because Digger had not had time to even lift his arms for protection, let alone to defend himself.

He dropped to his knees like a stone and Tommy commenced stabbing him over and over again with the remains of the pint glass he had used to blind him with.

The blood was spurting everywhere and Tommy's face and obvious anger served to keep anyone there from butting in or trying to stop him. His Pringle sweater was already soaked with Digger's blood and when he was finally spent, the good-looking young man was a bloody lump lying unconscious at his feet.

Tommy spat on him, the hatred and contempt on his big moon face keeping everyone at a safe distance. Bernie was giving everyone the evil eye, his fists raised threateningly. Dave had a large knife in his hand and he was brandishing it with a theatrical laugh. No one was going to step in and face that mad bastard; he looked almost maniacal as he moved about with a flourish, pointing the heavy blade at anyone who caught his eye.

The barmaid, a thin woman with saggy breasts and badly bleached hair, broke the silence as she said loudly and belligerently, "Oh, fucking great. Just what I fucking needed. Get your arse in gear and fuck off home. I'll get an ambulance on the go, and they'll call Old Bill."

Tommy grinned at her and she pursed her lips in annoyance. Pointing at the door she shouted in her deep voice, "Well go on, fuck off before the cops arrive. And don't fucking come back until you have the money to replace my carpet. Look at it, the fucking thing's ruined . . ."

She was still ranting and raving at him as he left the hushed bar with his brothers in tow, laughing and joking. Tommy walked to his car without a thought for how he must have looked; he was soaked with blood. The adrenaline was pumping now and, alongside the speed, he was rocking, he was up for anything.

"Did you see that bloke's fucking face when I had finished with him?"

Dave grinned and Bernie answered him with mock sarcasm.

"No, I was standing there with me eyes closed. 'Course I fucking saw it. Now get the fucking motor going so we can fuck off out of it. We have a lot to do today and Ricky will be wondering where we are. The last thing we need is a fucking tug by Lily Law."

"Not one of them skanks will put us in the frame, they ain't got the fucking bottle."

Wheelspinning on to the Whitechapel Road they drove off at speed to meet with Ricky so they could all sort out the bit of business he had arranged, and be home in time for dinner.

"What's the time, babe?"

Lil had just finished getting herself ready when she heard her husband's voice.

She laughed loudly. "Time you bought a watch."

It was just on five and she was finally ready to go. The kids were wound up like watch springs. Usually, it took so long to get them all ready, especially the twins, that she never had enough time to sort herself out. Today, though, she was determined to look her best and, even with her lump, her reflection told her that she did.

As she walked down the stairs, she saw Patrick's face and, smiling at him, she saw as always the longing for her in his warm blue eyes. Whatever people said about her husband, he had made her so happy.

Lil laughed once more when he wolf-whistled at her and Annie saw the deep love they had between them. As always, it made her feel like an outsider. Even Pat Junior and the twins were quiet as they watched their parents embrace each other.

The depth of her daughter's devotion to the man she had married and his utter and complete love for his wife never ceased to amaze Annie. That *her* Lil, *her* daughter, could command that much love from a fine piece of manhood like Patrick Brodie made her feel a jealousy that she hid well, but which ate at her at times like this.

Her own marriage had been devoid of anything remotely resembling love. She had got caught out and she had married the first man who had wanted her. She had spent her whole life without ever having a man hug her, make love to her with passion, or even just chat to her about her day.

That her Lil, the bastard child conceived during a one-night stand where Annie had lost not only her virginity but her pride as well, was capable of having a life that most women could only dream about, was almost impossible for her to believe. It was so unfair, life was so bloody unfair. Her feelings for her daughter swung between pride and hate and she wished that it wasn't so. She prayed for her yearnings to subside and for peace of mind. But the knowledge that her life had been so barren ate away at her. Annie still felt the urge inside her that only a man could satisfy. She still dreamed of being in love and of someone loving her back and she knew it was never going to happen. The nearest she had ever got to true love was with the birth of Lance and, even though she had strong feelings for the others, he was the boy she had always needed, he *wanted* her.

"Get the camera, Annie, and take a photo of me and my best girls and my number one son. Then we'd best get our arses in gear and deliver me boy to his party."

As Patrick spoke, Annie hurried to get the camera from the kitchen. When she came back with it she saw Lance standing at the top of the stairs in his pajamas and he called out to his brother softly, "Have a good party, Pat. Happy birthday."

Patrick walked up the stairs to his brother and the twins followed behind him as they always did. Lil was tempted for just a few seconds to let him go to the party; he looked so young and so vulnerable it was hard to believe he was capable of harming a fly, let alone another human being. But she reminded herself that he was an accomplished actor and liar and if they allowed even one chink to appear in their armor he would walk all over them for the rest of his days.

The two boys hugged and even Patrick felt moved by their closeness. They *were* close those two; Pat Junior was the only person other than the twins that Lance genuinely seemed to care about. It was obvious the boys had a bond of sorts, whatever might have happened in the past. Annie thought he adored her, but she would learn the hard way that Lance, his own son, was a mutant, a quirk of nature. He had too much Brodie in him; it grieved him to admit that but the truth was the truth.

Annie stood quietly in her finery and let her eyes drink in the first sight of her grandson in what seemed like months, though it was only a matter of days. She wished they would allow him to go tonight, wished he could join in with the rest of his family and friends. Although she would not say this out loud, she felt this was a cruel and unusual punishment for the child, and he was, when all was said and done, just a child. They seemed to forget that and she resented the fact she had no status in the family to argue his case for him, dispute his punishment.

There was a knock on the front door and Annie opened it wide. Must be the driver Pat had arranged. He could take the picture of them and she would be in it as well.

Jimmy Brick was getting anxious; the hall was filling with people and presents, the DJ kept playing Slade for two fifteen-year-olds dressed as twenty-year-olds, and the buffet was being eyed by a bunch of teenage degenerates with cropped hair and painfully new trousers. The tables were nearly all taken now and people were busy with drinks and snacks and were settling down for the night's entertainment. The parish priest was wandering around like a junkie with a welfare check and the bar staff, like the priest, were already half-pissed.

Most of the *real* guests had arrived and these were seated near Patrick and Lil's table, as arranged. He had a few blokes moving through the place, watching out for the first hint of trouble and under strict instructions not to harm anyone physically until they had been removed from the premises. Once they hit the parking lot, however, it was open season but, until then, it was arm up the back and smiling faces if that was at all possible.

The Palmers were there, their kids all getting ready to slide across the wooden dance floor in their brand-new white socks and the degenerates Jimmy had been keeping his beady eyes on had already whipped a plate of sandwiches and a bowl of trifle from the buffet table. He hoped they were not thinking of coming back for seconds in the not too distant future because he was not in the mood for polite conversation.

Things like this could be treacherous if they were not policed properly, and he was making sure that this party went off with the minimum of fuss and the maximum of enjoyment.

The lights were dimmed; Spider and his girlfriend were chatting with the Brewsters, a large family from south London who were into pornography: books and videos of course. Lenny Brewster, an old mate of

Patrick's from childhood, was telling filthy jokes at the top of his voice and, like Spider, he was watching the door. Jimmy glanced at his watch and realized that it was nearly six o'clock. Patrick was cutting it close, but that was his prerogative of course. They were only down the road and they were probably being waylaid by well-wishers.

The birthday cake was a work of art; it was a large, iced confection that was a replica of Wembley Stadium and the grass looked real from a distance. The baker said, off the record of course so as not to offend anyone, that if he never saw green icing again until the next St. Paddy's Day, it would be too soon.

Jimmy Brick was pleased with the turnout and he knew that Pat would be as well; every invitation sent out had been eagerly accepted and Faces and civilians were mixing together easily. The atmosphere was already buzzing with talk and laughter and, since he had delivered a few choice threats to the DJ, decent music. It had a real party feel to it and he was glad that Patrick and his family would be walking in to so much friendliness and camaraderie. He could feel himself relaxing now; he had done his job and once the main man arrived, he could cut himself a bit of slack.

There was also a nice little bird he had his eye on; she was wearing a deep-green chiffon dress and her high heels showed off her slim ankles to their greatest advantage. She had a decent pair of tits on her but he was a leg man and always would be. She had given him a saucy little wink earlier and, on closer inspection, he had observed that she wouldn't frighten anyone on a dark night. All in all, he had a feeling this was going to be a good party for everyone concerned once the guest of honor arrived.

Annie saw the man at Lil's front door and for a split second she wondered if she was imagining things, but when he shoved past her and she saw three other men come bundling into the hallway behind him, she realized that her first impression had been correct.

The first man was covered in blood and she heard Lil scream out as she was knocked flying. Then she saw that the men had knives and saw them start stabbing Patrick. He was trying to fight back, was attempting to stay on his feet, but they had the advantage; there were four of them and he couldn't take them all on at once. As he lashed out they were laughing at him. Then she saw the blood that was suddenly everywhere and she fainted.

Pat Junior and Lance watched the gruesome spectacle while holding their little sisters in their arms, pushing the twins' faces into their shoulders to try to spare them the sight of the carnage below. Pat Junior saw his father shouting and threatening the men; the men he recognized as the Williams brothers. He could hear the men yelling obscenities at his father and the squelching noise as the knives were plunged into his father's head and chest over and over again. Patrick was on his knees now and attempting to crawl away. The boys watched in shocked disbelief as Ricky Williams kicked him in the guts with all the force he could muster, lifting him bodily off the floor. Then, pushing Kathleen into Lance's arms, Pat Junior shouted at him to take them in the bedroom and stay there. Running down the stairs he threw himself on to the nearest of the men, his new shirt already stained with blood and skin. They were still hacking at his father and now laughing at his childish attempts to stop them.

Pat Junior saw his mother on the floor, saw her fear and terror and he felt so useless but he didn't know how to make it all stop. The biggest of the men threw him bodily against the wall and the pain shot through him. Lying on the floor he saw what was left of his father's face and he knew then that his father was dead, knew that the slashing and stabbing was just overkill, was for these men's own enjoyment. He knew that the blood and the laughter would never leave him, knew his life would never be the same again.

Pushing through them, Pat Junior flung himself across his father's bloody carcass. Tommy Williams had the knife raised again ready to plunge it into Brodie's face once more, when Dave stayed his hand. Dave suddenly saw the terrified child lying across his father's body and the enormity of what they had done crashed into his head with the force of a sledgehammer.

"Stop, stop it. You nearly fucking stabbed the kid, you mad cunt."

Dave's voice seemed to be the catalyst for them to stop and they were now silent, their ragged breathing loud in the quietness. Pat Junior was wracked with sobs and he heard himself crying and calling out "Dad, Dad," over and over, even though he knew his father would never answer his call again.

Lil, lying in the doorway that led to the kitchen, had watched her husband die as she felt the baby inside her kicking as if trying to escape the madness around them. She kept attempting to pull herself up but she couldn't move; she was a ball of white-hot pain and it was a while before she realized her water had broken.

She saw Dave sitting on the stairs, his head in his hands as he stared down at what was left of her husband's body. He was unrecognizable as a man, they had literally hacked him to pieces. It was only then that she saw her son, her Pat, dripping with his father's blood and lying across his father's body with his little arms spreadeagled, trying to protect what was left of his father's carcass. It was like a nightmare and she was convinced that at any moment she would wake up and they would be going to the party as planned and none of this would have really happened.

But it had happened. Patrick had been butchered in front of her eyes and her son had been witness to it all and had tried to protect his father. It was his birthday, it was her little Pat Junior's birthday and he was drenched in his father's blood. His new, white shirt that he had been so proud of, his first Ben Sherman shirt, was now crimson and dripping his father's blood all over the hall floor. As Lil looked around her she saw the blood sprayed up the walls and on the staircase. She could hear Dave Williams heaving, watched him empty his stomach contents on to the floor. She knew it was all true, she knew that her husband, her soulmate, was really dead and she was about to deliver his child into the world and he would never see it. He would never hold his child. It was then that Lil started to scream and it was her screaming, the sheer animal ferocity of it, that seemed to snap the Williams brothers out of their combined stupor.

Pat Junior saw them leave the house as if they were going for a stroll. There was no sense of urgency, no fear of capture; they walked out quietly, closing the front door behind them gently, as if all their anger had been spent on his father, which of course it had.

Patrick Brodie Junior was still crying, only it was now a dry, tear-less sobbing. Getting up off his father's body he went to check on his mother. With her screams still resounding off the walls he finally managed to stop shaking long enough to call 999.

Chapter Eighteen

Spider walked out of the hospital with Jimmy Brick; both of them were still in shock. Lil, God help her, had given birth to another boy; that was all she needed now, another fucking kid. They had hung about and stayed with her because they had not known what else to do. When the driver had come in and told them what had happened they had thought it was some kind of macabre joke. When they had gone around there and seen the carnage for themselves, it had still been unbelievable.

Patrick's death had been such a shock that no one seemed to believe it was true. They were still unsure, although Spider had identified the body. But it had been unrecognizable as a human being, let alone Patrick. Cain's death had hit Spider hard but Patrick's death had hit him in more than just an emotional sense; it was the catalyst for a whole new set of problems.

As Jimmy and Spider stood in the cold air they looked at each other and neither knew what to say about the night's events. It was so unbelievable that Patrick Brodie had been taken out by the *Williams brothers*: that it had been well-planned and well-executed was outrageous enough but that it had been the Williamses behind it was staggering. It seemed Ricky Williams was a law unto himself and within hours of Brodie's death he had made himself busy. He had been ingratiating himself with Pat's main contenders and displaying an acumen and intelligence that had brought for him, if not the friendship he craved, the respect that was his due off the people who mattered. The police had made a point of investigating the event with as much fervor as they would a black-on-black killing, meaning they wouldn't break a sweat. Which told them that someone was already onside with the Williams brothers and that whoever it was had plenty of sway where it counted.

"Fucking outrageous. Killing Patrick Brodie like that." Jimmy's voice was loud and a couple of men smoking cigarettes nearby while waiting for a friend to get his head stitched looked over quickly and, seeing the men's demeanor, decided not to rattle anyone's cage. Jimmy looked bad enough with his scarred face and his obvious aggressiveness and the coon looked a handful and all, but the mention of Brodie and the night's events was enough to quiet even their natural belligerence. A brawl was one thing, certain death was something else entirely. They were strictly bully boys; a row in the pub, an arrest, and home in time for pub opening once again.

"Had your fucking look, you cunts?"

Jimmy wanted to vent his anger and these muppets looked good enough for his purpose. He was paranoid at the best of times but now he was convinced they were tailing him and he was not going to let any-one fool with him. Brodie's death had certainly fuelled his paranoia. For all he knew these were paid off and were waiting to jump him and take him out. In their fucking dreams.

Jimmy moved towards them and Spider grabbed his arm.

"What the fuck you doing? They ain't worth a wank."

Spider gestured to the men with his free hand, dismissing them with a wave. They did not need any more encouragement and hurried off into the shadows.

Jimmy shrugged Spider's restraining arm away, clenching his fists in anger.

"They mullered him, Jimmy." Spider shook his head. "He was com-pletely destroyed. I said it was him but all I recognized was his ring, you know, the black onyx one. But truth be told, it could have been a side of beef lying on that slab."

Jimmy nodded. He had seen Patrick lying in the hallway and he would never forget that sight. Poor Lil's terrified screaming and the wide-eyed children huddled together on the sofa. Poor Pat Junior covered in his dad's blood, his eyes red-rimmed from crying and still trying to protect his siblings. He knew the boy was terrified the Williams lot would come back. He wasn't a stupid kid, he knew the score, he knew he had been lucky to escape. He had been told how they had nearly stabbed him and he knew then that the boy would never feel safe again. It was a disgrace, a diabolical liberty.

And it had thrown him off course, that was the worst of it. Patrick had left Spider to deal with the Williams brothers and Cain and he had made a fucking serious mistake. That error had led to him being taken out by a family of morons; it was the equivalent of the Boy Scouts creaming the fucking Paratroopers.

He looked at Spider then as the reality finally kicked in.

"I ain't sucking *no one's* fucking cock, especially not a Williams' cock. They are scum, fucking Irish scum and they can expect a visit from me in the near future."

Jimmy Brick was beside himself now the actual events had sunk in. Him and Pat had made a nice niche for themselves and he had liked the man and respected him. That the brothers had the audacity to butcher the man in *his* home in front of his pregnant wife and his children was, to him, the act of animals. It wasn't the death so much; in their game you knew you were a target, but it was the way it had been executed, the way they had descended on him like a pack of fucking animals in full view of his kids. The twins were babies, little dots who Pat had doted on. The death had made a mockery of everything they held sacred; you didn't touch family, civilians or the elderly.

"Wait and see who is in the frame with them before you go making trouble for yourself." Spider's calm voice annoyed Jimmy, even though he knew the man was right. There was serious skulduggery surrounding this night's work and until he knew the score and who was involved, it was best to keep quiet.

They stood outside the hospital smoking cigarettes and both were quiet now, having said all that was needed. Both knew that everything was about to change, not just for them but for everyone in their circle. Patrick Brodie's demise was going to cause all sorts of upsets and all those who had been involved with him were now either suspects or enemies, depending on what they did or didn't know.

"My money's on the Palmers or the Brewsters. The Williams brothers had to have had a sponsor, they couldn't fucking find their cocks without a fucking guide dog. They are amateurs, fucking no-necks, cunts. Pat should have taken them out when he had the chance, you should know that better than anyone."

The barb hit home as Jimmy knew it would. Cain was a fucking no-neck and he had found his level with the Williams boys. "Show me the company you keep and I'll tell you what you are. My mum was a wise old bird and she said that to me many times over the years. Cain was a knob and you know it, but he had you on his side. This shower must have a fucking good backer, they couldn't fucking rob a fucking tuck shop without someone calling the shots. No, mate, they have to be doing this for someone in the know. Someone close to it all. Ricky Williams is the genius of the family and that just means he can tie his own shoelaces. Someone has courted this and used *them* for their own advantage. The question is, who?"

Spider shrugged. That was exactly what he had been thinking but, until he knew the score for sure, he was keeping his own counsel. Jimmy was sound as a pound normally, but until he knew who he was pinning his colors to, he would make a point of being non-committal. It was how you kept alive in their game and Spider was going to stay around for the long-term, even if it killed him. Careless talk cost lives and this could easily turn into a war with no one involved in it really sure of whose side they should be on.

This was a melon scratcher all right and as his brother's death was still raw and the Williams brothers doing the star turns in this little drama, he knew he would have to play it smart for the next few weeks. He was going to be shrewd and add to his crew, his all-black crew and, if nothing else, he was going to keep his businesses in south London and add to them as and when the opportunities arose. Spider knew that anything he had with Patrick was going to be taken away from him. This was what Pat's death was about. Gathering turf, taking what was Patrick's and using a scapegoat like Ricky to further their ends. The perpetrator of this heinous act was using the Williams brothers as a front so they could then harvest whatever they wanted.

Spider was on his own and Cain's death still hung over him like the Sword of Damocles. He was in a very precarious position; Cain had been in bed with the Williams brothers and that would not be forgotten. Now Spider needed to see what was going to happen to the business interests he had with Patrick. Nothing was ever on paper, nothing was ever straight and he knew that a lot of his private earners would now be up for grabs and there was nothing he could do about it. A lot of Pat's clubs had silent partners, investors who would now want to stake their claim and, without Patrick around, that would now become easy. Spider had no idea who had put money in and who had not and Pat's bookkeeping would require the Enigma code breakers to fucking work it out. He had never bothered with the books before because he had always trusted Patrick; he could be a cunt but he was an honest cunt and he was a good mate. The chances were that he was now fucked, well and truly fucked. It stung, it really stung, and he needed to think long and hard about his next move.

Lenny Brewster looked at Lil Brodie and felt a prickle of conscience; she was as thin as a rake and her black clothes seemed to accentuate that, as did the whiteness of her skin. She was still a looker though; her grief seemed to add a vulnerability to her that he found appealing. Once she had mourned for a reasonable length of time he thought he might have a crack at her. A few months down the line she would be missing the old one-eyed snake and the thought of shagging Brodie's old woman appealed to him. Brodie had treated her like a goddess and he knew she hadn't been mauled by anyone else; the thought of shagging her was a pleasant distraction. His wife knelt down to pray after receiving Holy Communion and he knelt beside her, looking pious with his head down as if in prayer. Lenny knew he was out of order but he was ready to take the lead and had put in place a few nice surprises for the Palmer crew. Now he felt he was entitled to anything or anyone that took his eye and tickled his fancy. Lenny had always been a force, a respected Face, and no one had realized, until now, just how big his empire had become. A genial man, he had a knack of putting people at ease. He had a repertoire of jokes that he told with skill and he was good company.

He had sat and waited for his turn and it had arrived sooner than he had expected. Now it was here he intended to make the most of it.

Lil sat in the church watching her husband's funeral and anyone could see she was not up to it. As she held her new baby in her arms she was causing not only the women's tears but also the men's discomfort.

She had been screwed, no doubt about that, and she knew there was nothing she could do about it. She was in bits but she also knew she had to play it smart to salvage anything for her boys. Patrick would be cursing them to hell if he was watching but there wasn't anything he could do about it from where he was; it was up to her now.

Any monies in the bank were of course hers; not that they kept much money in the bank. Not real money anyway; if you banked it you would eventually have to explain its existence to the taxman. Lil was also the beneficiary of any insurance policies Patrick might have taken out and she should get a one-off payment from the powers that be. She would then be expected to keep her head down. Lil was now an embarrassment because everyone knew she had been royally had over. She knew the ins and outs of the clubs, she had helped run them, but that knowledge would not do her any good now; she was old news and she knew it. With five kids and a dead husband Lil was without any kind of protection. Even in her grief she knew she had to stay strong for the kids; she had to get herself together and collect what was owing her. She also knew where Patrick had hidden some of the proceeds from the various bank robberies he had given permission for over the years. She was going to make a visit to his main yard, under cover of darkness, and see what was left. It galled Lil that her life as she knew it was over, that everything Pat had worked for had been in vain. She had seen the fur coat on Lenny's old woman, it had cost a bundle, and she had walked in the church like she owned the fucking place, waving at people and nodding. She was the new First Lady and she was loving it. Well, she hoped she had better luck in that capacity than she had had.

As Lil sat in the church she felt a strange calmness come over her; she was aware of how close her family had come to complete annihilation at the hands of Ricky Williams. She knew that Tommy would have killed Pat Junior without a second's thought and she thanked God for sparing him. She accepted the fact that all her husband's hard work, the clubs, the bookies, everything he had ever undertaken, was now under new management. She knew she couldn't dispute anything, she had no power any more. As she had looked at her children that morning, she knew that she had to accept her fate with good grace and try to pick up the remnants of her life. For their sakes.

Ricky Williams had come through for his family and they were riding high on it. People were once more civil to them, overeager in their quest to be allowed a few minutes of their precious time. Ricky had known he had to do something spectacular to get them back in the groove and he had achieved his objective with outstanding results. Palmer and Brewster had both given him a public welcome worthy of a World Cup winner. Ricky was now the undisputed head of the family; he had dragged them back to where they belonged. As he stood in the toilet of the bar in Bermondsey that Patrick Brodie had once called his own, he looked in the mirror and admired his good looks and his dapper new outfit. Ricky loved the new fashions, he loved the materials, and in his fitted velvet jacket and his boot-cut jeans he felt like a real tasty geezer. He loved that expression, especially when he believed it pertained to him. His euphoria was at its peak and as he sauntered back into the bar he saw his brothers, what was left of them anyway, waiting for him with smiles and drinks. Ricky downed a double brandy and, feeling the burn, he held the glass out for a refill knowing that the barmaid would not measure it, not for him; he would be given the bottle on the counter as a measure of his prestige.

He *fucking* loved it, loved being on top, loved having the pick of the girls and loved knowing he was being talked about in hushed tones; his escapades being related over pints of lager by people who were impressed with him, were in awe of him.

Ricky was almost strutting, so pleased was he that his plans had made it to fruition. The little sort he had acquired earlier in the day, an eighteen-year-old from Mile End with big tits and an even bigger mouth, was drunk as a skunk. He watched her trying to articulate the bollocks that passed as conversation in her world and knew that these short sharp shags were going to be a thing of the past now. He would still have a dabble, of course, but he decided that a decent-looking girl with a bit of sense about her would look much better on his arm now that he was a man of substance.

Tommy and Dave were swearing their heads off as they spoke with her and he knew that was what was bothering him. Dave, Tommy and Bernie were louts. With Patrick on board they had managed a living of sorts but none of them really had the concentration required for long-term skulduggery; they preferred to be ornamental as opposed to instrumental and that, again, suited him. Ricky liked being the alpha male, the doer, the instigator of events. He knew his guests had arrived by the cries of greeting he could hear coming from the front bar. He saw his brothers' brows darken; they were still nervous that they might be brought to task over Patrick Brodie. It seemed that the frenzy of their combined attack, which he now knew had been brought on by the drink and drugs consumed by them earlier on in the day, worried them. They felt that people were maybe not as pleased as they were making out. He was pissed off with them. They were like old women with their fucking stupidity; their absolute cuntishness seemed to cling to them like shit to a blanket. He watched as Alan Palmer walked over to him with his usual swagger and he held his arms out in a gesture of friendliness. Alan stopped in his tracks and held his hands up in front of him, saying loudly, "Fuck me, we ain't on a date," then, turning to the henchmen, who were as always half a step behind him, he called out, "He's trying to fucking shag me. I told you, didn't I? He'd fuck anything."

Ricky was laughing with everyone else but the avoidance of the friendly gesture was noted and filed away for future reference. He was annoyed to see his brothers laughing like drains as if it was the funniest thing they had ever heard in their lives. That's how fucking stupid they were, they couldn't see an insult even when it was in front of their fucking faces.

He had his work cut out with this lot all right and with Palmer and all, by the looks of things. He saw his little bird staggering to the toilet and, winking at one of the regulars, he gave him a twenty and told him to cab her. She was not going to add anything to this meet and he was sick of her.

They all ordered drinks and settled down to talk, but Ricky was not a happy potato. In fact he was about a hair's breadth away from stabbing Alan through the heart just for the fucking fun of it. He had been ignored and he knew it. But he controlled the urge to retaliate and, smiling easily, he chatted as if he had no worries in the world.

Lil was still tired from the birth and the trauma of that day. Shamus had weighed in at nearly ten pounds and, as she had remarked to her mother, it brought tears to your eyes did childbirth. He was a good baby but she was still not sleeping, even when her mother took over for her. She still had times when she believed Patrick was alive, that she had dreamed his horrific murder. Seeing him buried though had put it into perspective for her, he was gone all right and she had to try to keep herself going for the sake of the kids if nothing else. The luxury of grieving was not an option for her, she had to keep her wits about her and try to salvage something to secure their futures. There had been twenty grand in the bank accounts but she knew that was not a lot with five kids and a mother to support.

As she let herself into her husband's scrapyard she hoped that no one came bowling in. She knew the place was used for a lot more than collecting old scrap. The dogs were running free as always; the two Dobermans knew her well and she petted them as she walked to the Portakabins that passed as offices. As she let herself inside, the animals lay down and waited for her.

Lil opened the safe without even turning on the lights; she didn't need anyone seeing the place lit up. She had opened the safe and counted out wages or taken cash out for sundries more than enough times and, as the heavy metal door swung open, she felt a glimmer of excitement at what she was doing.

"I'm stealing back our own money, Pat."

She laughed as if he had been there to answer, to share the joke with her and appreciate the irony if nothing else. She was stealing back money that had been stolen in the first place; this was his cut from bank robberies, jewelry heists and wage snatches.

The safe was empty and she wasn't really surprised; it had been a long shot. She guessed it was one of the men who worked for him, feathering his own nest while he could. Pat's death must have put the wind up a lot of people, especially those who depended on him for their livelihood.

The tears stung her eyes and she blinked them away. She was at her wits' end; she was going to need a lot of money to raise five kids.

She sat on the floor of the office. Cold and damp, it had the feel of the grave. She knew that nothing was ever going to be all right again. The tears were once more threatening, but she forced them back. There was plenty of time for crying in the future; now she needed to make sure her kids were taken care of.

Lenny Brewster was filled with his own self-importance; he had been like a youngster since the death of Patrick Brodie. A born-again bastard was how his enemies would describe him, though not to his face. Now, looking at the Williams brothers and Palmer, all waiting to greet him and ingratiate themselves into his life, he knew he was finally settled; he had taken what was rightfully his.

Ricky was all smiles, nodding to his brothers to make sure they understood the importance of the man before them. Lenny noticed the gesture and knew that the boy had at least a working knowledge of how things worked in their world.

Ricky was already clicking his fingers for the barmaid, making sure a fresh bottle of Courvoisier Brandy was opened and that the ashtrays and bar surface were cleaned. He knew the importance of respect and he respected the man who had just entered the bar like a conquering hero. Lenny Brewster was a legend, more so because he had always kept his head down and had never been a man to eliminate enemies without just cause. He had gathered an army around him and had never once trod on anyone's toes. He was a gentleman, and he was respected because of that.

Ricky saw Alan Palmer hold his arms out in much the same way he had himself; this time, though, the gesture was appreciated and returned with fervor. It galled him but he knew it was still early days for the Williams brothers; they had made a statement but now they had to prove they were consistent. That had always been their problem in the past; they never kept anything up. They had been given chances over and over again and they had always fucked up. So he understood the men's reticence, he would have been the same in their shoes, but it still galled him. He was now the family's facilitator and should be respected for that alone, especially after what they had achieved for the men they were now meeting with.

Lenny was all good-humored laughter and his usual theatrical gestures. Alan Palmer, Ricky noticed, was nervous but then he had just hit the big time at last and that was something Ricky knew about. Palmer was already laughing at Lenny's jokes and as they raised their drinks in a salute, Ricky saw Lenny wink at Alan in a way that told him they had business between them already. He was confident that could only be good news for him and his brothers. As Ricky smiled and chatted he saw Tommy mutter something to Dave and Bernie. Then he pulled an envelope out of his pocket and, walking towards the men's toilets, he opened the paper package up and put his tongue in the contents to check its potency. He saw Lenny watching him and knew he was not making a good impression. Even though this was a safe bar, it was still not proper etiquette to blatantly advertise any kind of drug-taking when bosses were around. Unless they started the night off with it themselves and then it was different. This was a meet though and they should all be on top form; no one trusted the judgment of a speed freak or a coke-head. It was just commonsense really and Ricky knew that Lenny was up for a lot of things, but not the drugs. He expected it to be fed to his hookers; prostitutes needed the edge, everyone knew that. But he was not someone who partook of the Colombian marching powder himself. He was a drinker, pure and simple. Tommy had just made them all look like amateurs and he wished he had been more forceful when he had given his brothers their instructions on how they should behave. At times he felt like he was banging his head against a wall; this looked like amateur night in a public housing complex.

Alan smiled but he saw the entourage that had arrived with Lenny and he was surprised; there were five of them. He knew that Lenny was astute enough to always keep himself safe but all these goons for a friendly meet seemed like overkill and he suddenly felt intimidated. He knew Lenny was a fucking hard bastard and he also knew that *he* was outclassed and that it was probably his insecurity making him feel that way. But for his whole life he had relied on his instincts; any successful villain had to. It told them when they were sailing too close to the wind and when the police were getting too close for comfort. It was a self-defense mechanism and his was going into overdrive for some reason. This didn't feel right; he felt like an outsider, like a spare part. Like he was nothing. Alan swallowed down his drink and tried to concentrate on the Williams brothers and the deal that he had made with Brewster. His earlier bravado was deserting him and he wished he had arrived with a full complement of bodyguards; it would have made him feel a lot better.

The bar was slowly emptying and it was a while before anyone noticed that Ricky had gone to the toilet after Tommy and, after giving him a dressing down, had returned to the bar and found Lenny leaning in and talking to Palmer. It had suddenly occurred to Ricky that most of the clientele had gone. The only people left was a small crowd of men in the outer bar. They were large and they were all wearing sheepskins and they were talking quietly to each other. He knew they were tooled up but in this place that wasn't so unusual. Most people he knew had a baseball bat in their car, a gun in their house and a club of some description about their person. Knives and guns were an everyday item to these people but he knew that their heavy sheepskins were hiding the fact that they *were* tooled up. As Ricky walked back to the bar he knew in his heart what was coming.

Lenny watched Ricky as he approached and he smiled, then ordered another round of drinks. As Alan went to pick his drink up, Lenny shanked him quickly and neatly; he aimed for the liver and when Alan turned to face him, which was a natural reaction and expected, Lenny aimed once more, this time for the heart. Alan's bodyguards watched it all without any kind of emotion.

Ricky saw Tommy, Bernie and Dave finally cop on to what the night was really about. Lenny smiled at him, a friendly and open smile that belied the psychotic personality it had always camouflaged.

"You must have known the score, Ricky? You and Palmer had to have known I couldn't trust any of you? You wiped out Brodie and as much as I appreciate that, you took a fucking diabolical liberty. People like *you*, scruffs and fucking numbskulls, taking it on yourselves to wipe out someone like Brodie? You didn't honestly think that would go unpunished surely?"

Lenny started to laugh then, a sarcastic laugh, a laugh full of derision and triumph. Ricky knew that they were finished and he also knew that this was not going to be a good beating, no, a serious lesson was going to be taught here. The lesson was actually for the people who would hear about it, who would know that they had been lured to their deaths on a fucking fool's errand. He was sorry then. Sorry for their mother; she had buried enough children. Sorry for himself and for his brothers.

The barmaid had disappeared and Ricky hadn't even noticed. The bar itself was well decorated for the kind of establishment it was. The wall lights were throwing an eerie glow on Palmer's body and it was a second or two before they realized he was still alive. His breathing was ragged and loud, wet-sounding from the blood that was filling his lungs.

"Fucking hell, he has a strong constitution for a cunt."

Everyone laughed and Ricky saw that the men from the outer bar were now walking through to join them, taking off their heavy coats and making themselves comfortable. As they rolled up their shirtsleeves he knew this was going to be a long night.

"Here, Johnjo, come and sort these out, will you?"

The name was all that was needed to tell Ricky that they were going to be dispatched with the maximum of pain and torture. Johnjo Milligan was a name that denoted terror; he was one of a family of Irish pikeys who had a legendary reputation. Few people had met them; they kept a low profile and spent most of their time on the fairgrounds. They were used for a number of jobs, but mainly for torture. Johnjo was a handsome individual with a lilting Dublin accent. He had a way with the ladies and a way with the police. They could never place him anywhere because he had a network of relatives all willing to swear blind that he was with them when it was necessary.

"What are you doing this for, Lenny? We fucking opened the door for you, we made this happen. You can't fucking do this . . ."

Lenny was smiling again. Ricky saw his brothers' faces; they were looking at him to rectify this situation, to make everything all right.

"I can do what I want, young Ricky. Thanks to you and your brothers I am the only sweet left in the shop. Now I have to make a show of my disgust. *Show* people that I can't let scum like you run riot and take the law into your own hands. I have to *show* my contempt for your actions and for Patrick's death, which, by the way, was a fucking liberty. I can't let people think they can do that to a fucking ganger and get away with it, can I?"

"I think the expression you are looking for is, to make an example." Johnjo spoke with a quiet dignity that always put people off their guard on first encountering him. He was a huge man with thick black hair and a white-toothed smile that always caught ladies' eyes. But he had a quirk in his nature, he had no feelings for anyone outside his close-knit family circle. He would wound anyone for cash and it had made him a force in his own right. He never worried about any comebacks, there were too many Milligans about for that and they were all like him: loyal and easily insulted.

The Milligans were fighters, bare-knuckle and extreme. Johnjo had been an extreme champion since he was fifteen years old. He had fought all over the world and earned a fortune. Extreme fights meant the opponents could use anything they wanted to win the bout. From biting and scratching to using the stools they were supposed to sit on between rounds. Johnjo was one of a kind and his talents had been useful over the years; he was called in when a point needed to be made. It wasn't only his violence, it was his penchant for torturing his victims that was required, and the exorbitant price he charged for these services was what made people widen their eyes with respect. If you used Johnjo Milligan you meant fucking business, and no one in their right mind wanted him towering over them with a pair of pliers or a soldering iron.

"Now, Mr. Brewster, Mr. Palmer is still on the oxygen; would you like to do the honors or shall I?"

Lenny nodded, as always impressed with Johnjo's understatement of the facts and his quiet way of talking that was totally out of place considering the circumstances around him.

Alan was moaning in pain but his open eyes told the men around him that he was more than aware of what was happening. Lenny walked over to the snooker table and picked up a cue. It took five good blows to Alan's head before everyone was satisfied he was dead.

Alan's body was dragged to the doorway by a couple of Lenny's blokes. Unlike the Williams brothers, he was just being killed. In fairness he was a name in his own right and so he just needed to stop existing. The story was already being relayed everywhere that he had financed the Williams brothers to do the dirty on Brodie for his own ends. Lenny would come out of all this as the person who had avenged Pat's death and honored the man by taking out his murderers. He would be the hero of the hour and he would also get the fucking lot for himself. A win-win situation for him.

"Tie their hands and feet, but strip them first, please." Johnjo spoke to no one in particular, but his henchmen rushed to do as he asked. It didn't take long; the brothers put up a good fight but there were too many opponents. On the floor, with the dirty carpet scratching their bare skin and the stench of cigarettes and lager in their nostrils, the fight finally left them. Ricky looked up at Lenny and his cronies; he had already got Alan Palmer's firm safely on board and with the Williams brothers' departure he would be hailed as the fucking Messiah.

"You cunt, you fucking treacherous slag. Do your fucking worst; you can't even do the honors yourself, you fucking coward."

Ricky was screaming out at Brewster; he was determined to go out with at least some kind of dignity and he wouldn't beg for his life off this scum. He had taken a chance and it had not worked out, simple as that. He wasn't about to fucking cry over it. They were already dead men, all four brothers; it was just a matter of seeing how long it took for them to die.

Lenny Brewster kicked him in the face and shouted down to him,

"Shut the fuck up, you ponce. You slaughtered Brodie in front of his family. How the fuck could you believe that such a fucking outrageous act, such a fucking shameful display, would be tolerated by anyone, would be seen by anybody as fucking acceptable behavior? You stepped over the line, mate, and you are going to pay the price for your obscene act. Anyone with a family wants you lot dead; anyone with a scrap of decency wouldn't fucking countenance you in their company, you fucking scum."

Johnjo had taken his shirt off and his muscular body was a reminder to the brothers of his strength, and his calmness was a reminder of his reputation as a cold and ruthless torturer.

Johnjo signaled for Lenny to move away from the men on the floor.

"Get back now. You don't want to be too close to these fecking idiots when I start me shenanigans."

Everyone in the room laughed but there was an undercurrent of excitement as well. None of the men present had seen the Milligans at work before, but they had heard the stories about them. They had wondered at the truth of them sometimes as they were so extreme; even making allowances for natural exaggerations and the need to make a story interesting, the rumors had been outrageous.

Johnjo looked at Ricky with disgust and he swallowed down a large brandy before saying softly and sadly, "You never touch children, boy, never do anything in front of them; it's the eleventh commandment. The slaughter of Pat Brodie, a good friend of mine, by the way, in front of his kids will ensure I take a greater pleasure than usual in my work tonight."

Then he doused them in brandy, soaking their hair and skin. The others all sat down to watch the performance and Ricky and his brothers cursed them all to hell.

Then Ricky saw Johnjo's cousin, Toby, lighting a blowtorch and he felt the tears roll from his eyes. Within minutes he was doing the one thing he had not wanted to do; he was begging not for his life but for his brothers' deaths. He begged for them to be put out of their pain. But he was forced to watch them die slowly, screaming in agony, before the Milligans turned their attentions to him.

*   *   *

A month after Patrick's funeral, Lenny Brewster sent a message to Lil saying that he wanted to see her. She knew she had no choice but to do as he asked of her.

"How are you coping, Lil?" His voice was calm and had the right inflection of sorrow and the expression on his face was one of genuine sympathy.

Lil shrugged elegantly and Lenny noticed the hollows in her neck and the way her breasts were straining against the material of the dress she wore. Her hair was freshly washed and styled and her make-up was flawless. As Lil crossed her legs he felt the heat rise up inside him.

"I need money, Lenny, simple as that."

He knew then that she was on to him, that she knew how he was feeling and was willing to go along with it if necessary.

He had made a point of making sure certain rumors had reached her ears, and had seen to it that no one offered her any help; he had assured the general populace that he was taking care of everything. Lil was at her wits' end and he knew it and he would use it against her to get what he wanted.

"I need a job and I need it soon. I used to run the clubs for Patrick and I was good at it. He *relied* on me as I am sure you know."

Lil watched the changing expressions on Lenny's face and hated him with every ounce of her being but he had made sure she had no one and nowhere to turn to. He was the only game on the street and she knew she had to do whatever he wanted.

"Why would I want *you* working for me?"

He was belittling her and she swallowed down the urge to walk out on him, to tell him what she thought of him. But the boys needed shoes, the girls needed clothes and the new baby needed everything. She needed to put food on the table and pay her bills. No one, it seemed, was willing to help her and she knew that was because this man had made sure she was left hanging. Even Spider had abandoned her. Lenny was a hero for what he had done to the Williams brothers, but she knew he had an agenda and she now knew that she was a big part of that.

So Lil smiled her best smile and shrugged gently once more. "Because I am good at what I do and I would be an asset."

Lenny stood up from behind his desk and walked towards her casually; he was well-dressed as always but he was running to fat now and he had a paunch that was clearly evident, even in his custom suit.

Leaning on the edge of the desk, Lenny stood in front of her chair and grinned. "How far are you willing to go though? How much energy would you be willing to put in, I mean, if I *were* to give you a job?"

Lil gritted her teeth and took a deep breath before answering him. "As much as was needed, of course."

Lenny grinned then. He had her and he knew it.

Unzipping his trousers, he pulled out his cock and massaged it until it was erect; he looked at her stricken face and knew he had to have her no matter what, by force if necessary.

Lenny stared into her eyes and Lil saw the want there, and the need, and she knew this was an act of violence inasmuch as it was designed to bring her down, and to break her spirit. Through her, Lenny wanted to shame Patrick. He needed to dominate her because he had never had the guts to take on her husband himself.

She smiled then and he saw the whiteness of her teeth against the red slash of her lipstick. Then she was guiding him into her mouth and he couldn't believe the heat of her tongue as it snaked around him. He felt her pull on his skin as she sucked him into her mouth and then she was moving her head quickly back and forth. Immediately, he felt the release and the satisfaction of ejaculating into her mouth and the shock as she swallowed his semen. She slowed down the movement of her head, sucking him lightly now, and making his orgasm last longer, bringing him back to earth with a gentleness that only made it all the more exhilarating.

Lil had blown more than his cock and he was left breathless, leaning against his desk for support. His trousers were still unbuttoned and his flaccid member wet and cold in the cool of the February evening. Lenny opened his eyes and looked down at himself. His clothes were in disarray and his cock was hanging out like a wrinkled gherkin. Shame washed over him. He had bucked his hips like a teenager, ramming himself into her mouth with an urgency he had forgotten existed. As she smiled up at him he saw that her lipstick was smudged and her eyes were colder than a witch's tits.

"You just got yourself a job, Lil."

"Have I?"

"You can start in the Baron's Room on Monday."

Lenny was busy putting himself away and tidying up.

"Will I use the same office as I always did? Has anything changed?"

He turned to face her once more. His legs still felt weak and he could feel the contempt for him in her voice and he hated her for the effect she had on him.

"You won't need an office, Lil, not for what you'll be doing anyway."

She knew then that she had lowered herself for nothing. She swallowed back the anger and the hot tears of humiliation. Instead, she stood up and said, with as much dignity as she could muster, "Then you can stick your job up your arse."

She took a gulp of her brandy and, swilling it around her mouth noisily, she spat the lot back into the glass.

As she picked up her coat and started to put it on he felt the pull of her once more.

"Come on, Lil, can't you take a joke?"

She stared into his face once more and he saw the deep grey of her eyes and the fine bone structure that made her look like a sculpture and gave her the edge when men looked her way.

"I haven't had a lot to joke about lately, have I, if you remember rightly."

He was on her then and as he kissed her he could taste his own semen mixed with the brandy and the urgency inside was once more overtaking everything else. This time he took her properly. He took his time with her; laid her on the leather sofa in his office, undressed her and aroused her in every way he knew until eventually she opened her legs for him with the same urgency and excitement as he was feeling himself. As she moaned with enjoyment he knew that he would never feel like this again about any woman. She was wet and hot; she wanted him all right. As Lenny gazed down at her, Lil knew she had him. She didn't know for how long but she knew that she had crossed the line and used the only thing she had going for her. How long it would last, she didn't know, and what would happen when he finished with her was anyone's guess, but she had the job she wanted. She had also found out that she could perform the sex act with him and even fake enjoyment in it as long as she pretended he was her Patrick. As long as she closed her eyes and pretended to herself that it was Patrick touching and kissing her. Lil had fooled Lenny as she would fool many men in the years to come.

That night, as Lil lay in her cold bed, she prayed that the kids would be all right and that their life wouldn't be too hard from now on. Then she finally let go of the tears she had been holding back for so long.

Lenny Brewster was settled in as the new and improved overseer of London. He had taken out all the wild cards, and brought Spider in as his ally; south London was somewhere he knew he would have trouble controlling.

Lil started working in the club she had once owned and sleeping with a man who now owned her. The irony was not lost on any of them.

The seventies was the decade that saw the explosion of recreational drug use, the second generation of West Indians were now making their mark and the country was recovering from another recession and yet another ineffectual government. It was the era of punk rock and unemployment lines. It was the time for the new generation to make their mark and show their disdain for the shambles they had inherited from their parents.

Lenny Brewster and his ilk milked this for all it was worth. They made fortunes on the generation growing up and on the relaxing of most people's moral codes. It was boomtime in the criminal fraternities and everyone was happy with their lot.

For Lil Brodie and for her children, it heralded the end of her life as she knew it. The death of Patrick Brodie would shape his children's lives and not in the way he would have wanted.

Book Two

The fathers have eaten sour grapes,
And the children's teeth are set on edge

—EZEKIEL 18:2

"I don't want him," said Rabbit. "But it's always
useful to know where a friend-and-relation is,
whether you want him or whether you don't."

—A. A. MILNE (1882–1956),
THE HOUSE AT POOH CORNER

Chapter Nineteen

"Well, I am sorry you feel like that, Mrs. Brodie, but your son is being expelled for fighting. If you can't see anything wrong with that kind of behavior then this is a pointless conversation."

Lily Brodie gritted her teeth in suppressed anger. "My Shamus is not a hooligan, Mr. Benton, and you know it. He's only ten and the boy he was fighting with is nearly fifteen."

Mr. Benton felt sorry for this woman. She was a handsome-looking piece, no man could fail to notice that much, and her life had been hard and so had her children's. She had produced two children in the last ten years and he was not relishing their arrival at his school in the future. The Brodies were a byword for trouble in these parts and he was sick of them all.

"The boy Shamus was fighting with was trying to stop your son from bullying his little brother; the fact that Shamus hammered him speaks volumes. Shamus is a *big* lad, a *strong* lad and he is a lot of things, Mrs. Brodie, but a victim is not one of them."

"His eldest brother is home now and he'll watch out for him. After all, that's what older brothers do, isn't it, according to you?"

The man laughed then and the laugh was genuine.

"Oh well, that's all right then. His brother is home from prison at last and is going to put young Shamus on the straight and narrow. What a wonderful role model he'll make. This is Patrick you are talking about, the same Patrick who was the bane of my life."

The man's sarcasm was not lost on Lil, but she knew it was pointless arguing any longer. Shamus was out, simple as that. And this sanctimonious old bastard was getting on her nerves.

"Shamus was defending his brother too. They were taunting him about my Pat. He came home from prison this week, as you know, and they were teasing him over it. He just retaliated, that's all. The older boy should have known better than to try and interfere in his brother's dispute anyway. How the hell will that child ever learn right from wrong if his brother bails him out all the time? He needs to learn when to shut his trap and my Shamus did what any other boy would do in his shoes; he defended *his* family. But my family don't matter, do they? They don't count. Their father was murdered in front of them and no one allows for that, do they? Oh no, you only care that some shite has been bullied. Well, the boy had better get used to it because his brother won't be there to protect him forever."

Mr. Benton shook his head in utter disbelief at her words. He heard this kind of talk over and over again from parents who saw school as nothing more than a necessary evil, not a place of learning. Their idea of valuable information was not dates and facts, figures and problem-solving techniques; it was the law of the pavements. That this woman believed her son's tormentor deserved a serious beating was in itself more proof of the running battle he faced on a daily basis. Just trying to instill a modicum of decency in these children was impossible. Mr. Benton sighed in annoyance. "Well, it's all academic now, isn't it? I would appreciate it, Mrs. Brodie, if you don't allow Shamus to hang around the school gates or wander into the playgrounds. He is no longer welcome here in any capacity whatsoever."

Lil sat back in the chair and surveyed the little man opposite her, and he was little, in every way. From his puny body and his bony little hands, to his small-mindedness. He was the bane of people like her and he was too stupid to see that. He lived in a parallel universe, in a place where people talked nicely to one another and washed their cars every Saturday afternoon. A world where shirts were worn to work and carpets were vacuumed daily. A world where people like her and hers were seen as failures and beneath them; because they had to fight to exist on a daily basis and this man couldn't fight if his life depended on it. He wouldn't last five minutes on their estate and it was because of this mindset that he couldn't interest any of these children in what he had to offer them, in what he had to say.

Lil stood up then and, holding her back straight, she looked down at the man who had been the bane of her life for years.

"Mr. Benton, my son will not trouble you again, you have my word on that. But let me just say this before I leave; if you had any kind of teaching ability you wouldn't be working in a shithole like this, and I ask you to think about that tonight when you are driving home to your family. Like the pupils in this school, the teachers here are on the bottom rung of their ladder as well. So remember that when you look down your nose at someone because, like I said, if you had anything going for you, this is the last place you'd want to be."

As Lil walked from the office she felt the headache that had been troubling her all morning start to subside. Shamus was sitting on a scruffy old chair outside the headmaster's office and when he smiled at her with his usual crafty grin, she laughed weakly, "Come on, mate, let's get you home."

Shamus walked beside her; he was a good lad at heart and she knew that, but he was also a fighter and she knew that one day it would bring him real trouble.

"I am sorry, Mum."

She knew he meant it, every word of it; he always did. Until the next time, of course.

Lil hoped the boys were home; she was worried about them and what they might be getting up to. Lance was bad enough but with Pat Junior now back on the streets and hungry to earn some cash so he could give it to her with pride and feel he was taking care of his family once more, anything was possible.

She stopped at her local shop and got a packet of cigarettes and a bottle of vodka on credit. She needed a rest from her kids but she knew she wouldn't be getting one.

"Can I have a fag, Mum?"

Lil smacked Shamus hard across his face and she knew she had hurt him by his pained expression.

"Don't push me today, boy, all right? I am on the cusp of a violent episode thanks to you and that fucking school. Why couldn't you just once, fucking once, walk away from trouble?"

She sighed in desperation. This boy would be the death of her. "You ain't even worth arguing with, are you?"

Shamus shrugged then and she knew he was upset, but for once she didn't care.

All she wanted at this moment was a large drink and a few hours' sleep; she was shattered.

Paulie Braden was drunk and, as always when he was drunk, he loved the world. Picking up his cigarettes he swept a low bow to his friends and, laughing loudly with them, he staggered out of the pub doorway. Taking a few deep breaths he pointed himself in the general direction of home and attempted the short long walk with all good intentions. As he strolled along the road he heard a car pull up beside him and, with his usual good-natured smile, he stopped and waited for the men to get out and threaten him. This was a weekly occurrence and he knew that it would be over quickly and he could get on his way. The money he owed was not that large an amount and once he got his wages he would pay a bit off the interest and keep this lot off his back for another few weeks.

But as Paulie looked at the young man who was coming towards him, he was nonplussed, this was not the usual bloke. This young fella had a cross face and a mean look in his eye.

The baseball bat hit Paulie with such force that he was knocked into the road and a car had to swerve to avoid him. The drink he had imbibed had made him unsteady on his feet and as he fell to the ground, the young man brought the bat down heavily on to his shoulders. The pain was excruciating and when the bat was brought down over and over again, he finally understood he had pushed his luck too far. When he was finally dragged to the curb it was a few moments before he properly understood what was going to happen to him. Another young lad had now appeared and, grabbing his arm, he forced him to straighten it. Then he held it so Paulie's wrist was on the curb and his shoulder on the pavement; it was when he realized what was going to happen that he finally tried to fight. The boy smiled, then rabbit-punched him quickly in the face, immediately mashing his nose, and straightened his arm out once more. The first young man brought his booted foot down on to it heavily, smashing the elbow completely. Paulie Braden was in such agony he was screaming like a trapped rat and people stood there watching the little tableau with resigned expressions on their faces. A police car cruised by, slowed down so the officers could have a decent gander and then speeded up and disappeared around the corner.

"Please, son, please. I can't take this . . . I ain't got the money, I swear . . ."

"You got the fucking money to get pissed though, ain't you, you old cunt. Well, I ain't a person who can be mugged off, see I have what is known as a personality disorder. Straight up, it's a recognized illness. They explained that to me in clink after I bit a geezer's ear off because I thought he was taking the piss out of me. He had taken one of my bog rolls from my cell *without* my express permission so you can see my point of view, can't you? He was wiping his arse on what was essentially mine and what's mine is *mine, and I want it.*"

The man stamped on Paulie's gut then; he was aware that this was well over the top considering what the man owed but he had to start off as he meant to go on. This would guarantee a lot of debts being paid in the next few days; the word would soon spread and anyone who owed Mills would be pawning their wives' wedding rings and selling their firstborn sons, anything, to make sure that nothing like this happened to them.

Paulie vomited loudly, the bile and beer spraying out of his mouth then running into the gutter with his blood.

"You owed Jackie Mills two hundred quid. Well, I have bought the debt off him for a oner so you now owe me *three* hundred quid and I *want* it. Don't you dare fuck me about. If I don't get my money I will come looking for you again and next time I will not be so reasonable . . ." The sentence was left unfinished, the threat had been taken on board.

He lit a cigarette slowly and, dropping the match on to the man's hair, he smiled. "You've got three days." Whistling happily, the young men got into the car and drove away.

Annie Diamond was washing her underwear in the sink when she heard her daughter arrive back from the school.

"How'd it go?"

Lil walked into the kitchen and sighed. "How do you think? He's been outed, expelled."

Annie shrugged, her thin arms were plunged into a bowl of soapy water and a cigarette was dangling from her lips. Lil took the cigarette from her mother's mouth and puffed on it deeply.

"Look on the bright side, Lil. He can get a little job, bring in a few pennies."

"I suppose so, but I wish life wasn't always so fucking hard."

Annie didn't answer her. In the last few years they had all learned about hardship. In fact, she didn't know how Lil had coped with it all. Especially with the boys; they had changed overnight.

"Did Lenny send any money round?"

Annie nodded. "It's on the mantel, only a oner though. He is as tight as a duck's crack, him. Even the Queen comes to the opening of his wallet."

Lil laughed then, a laugh she didn't think she had in her. She poured herself a large vodka and she knew her mother was silently chastizing her for it. But she didn't give a toss, Annie Diamond was the least of her worries at the moment. Shamus had disappeared as usual and she swore under her breath. He was a little fucker and she hoped Patrick Junior would have a word with him and sort him out, now that he was finally home. Lance just seemed to make Shamus worse, but then he was good with the girls. For all his fuckery, he was good to his sisters. Especially Kathleen. She pushed Kathy from her mind, she had enough on her plate without thinking about her and all.

"Where are the boys?"

Annie was rinsing her underwear now and her hands were numb, the water was so cold. She shrugged once more.

"They went out this morning just after you, and I ain't seen them since."

Then she turned to her daughter and shouted at her, "Put some orange juice with that, will you; at least pretend you ain't got a drink problem."

Lil laughed once more.

"If this was the only problem I had, Mother, how fucking easy life would be."

The years had not been kind to Lenny Brewster and he knew that. He looked like he felt; over the hill and short of breath. As he wheezed with laughter at his own joke, the young girl with him wished he would just crash and burn so she could go home and have a cup of tea and a ham sandwich like normal people. Lenny wasn't going to let that happen though and she knew it. He wanted his money's worth and she was going to have to make sure he felt he had been more than amply compensated for his initial outlay. He was a fucking mean bastard, and not only with money; he was mean in every other way as well. He wouldn't give a bogie to a dying man, he'd sell it to him.

Still, she had managed to get a car out of him; leased, mind you, so once he outed her it would have to go back, but it was a start anyway.

The men in the pub with him were all ready for the usual day's drinking. Lenny was a cunt but he was willing to bankroll his cronies and make a day of it.

"Jackie Mills was in earlier and he reckons he has sold all his debts on."

Lenny opened his arms in a gesture of disinterest. "So what. Jackie Mills couldn't fucking pull in a family allowance book without my help. It's about time he realized he wasn't up to the job any more."

He motioned to the barman for more drinks. "Who's he sold them to? Fucking Jimmy Brick?"

Lenny looked at his old mate, Trevor Highgate, and saw he was nervous about answering. That meant he had to deliver some bad news. It had to be bad news, otherwise they would all be putting in their tenpence worth. Lenny stared around him at his little posse of mates and, burping loudly, he held a hand to his heavy stomach while exhaling noisily. "My guts are fucking killing me."

He took a few deep breaths then and, grimacing in pain, he snapped, "Well, come on then. Spit it out for fuck's sake. Who's the lucky man who is going to be the hero of the hour collecting fucking pension books and giros?"

Lenny was annoyed. Like Jackie Mills and his fucking debts were of any interest to him.

"It seems young Pat Brodie and his brother, Lance, have bought him out, like. I expect they want to raise their game, eh?" Trevor relaxed then. He had delivered the news and Lenny had not lost that phenomenal temper of his.

"The Brodie boys? You mean he has sold out to a pair of fucking kids? Better keep an eye on your pocket money; next thing you know they'll be round your house half-inching your racing bikes."

He was laughing then and that was all the more worrying because the men around him knew he was making a mistake if he thought the Brodie brothers were beneath his radar and of no consequence. They were big lads now and they were their father's sons.

And the fact Lenny had given their mother two more children to worry about should have told him they were not kids any more.

"Good fucking luck to them, they deserve a bit of good luck. Young Patrick is home from clink then, I take it?"

Everyone nodded, pleased he had taken the news so well. But they were all wondering why he didn't know the boy had been released. If anyone should have known, it was him, considering the circumstances.

"Bad business that. The boy was fucking well within his rights but you know what the courts are like . . ."

Lenny shrugged. "I couldn't help him, he had already fucked up by hammering a cop. Once that happens . . ."

They all grinned at the memory; it had been a nine-day wonder at the time and Pat had made a rep for himself overnight. He had taken out a cop with three punches and it had taken a paddy wagon full of them to take him in. He was a handful all right and so was that Lance, but young

Patrick was the one they watched out for. He had the same presence and the same demeanor as his father before him.

"Bad business all round. I wish I could have helped him more . . ."

But the fact of the matter was Lenny *could* have helped him but he had not even tried. He was half-brother to the children Lenny had with Lil and that was what had caused the initial spate of whispering. Lenny had lost a lot of his kudos over the boy's sentence; he had not even had a decent lawyer on his side. People thought he should have made himself busy and stopped the whole thing before it had even gone to trial. He could have done that but he had chosen not to. People were not impressed and Lenny knew that as well as they did. He had taken a few hard knocks over it.

He'd lost a lot of his street credibility into the bargain. This was a man who could orchestrate a deal for fucking murderers and drug dealers, who bought prison sentences for hard cash, brokered with judges and barristers and paid off the police and the Flying Squad. Sixty grand guaranteed a five-year sentence instead of a fifteen and these deals were only done *through* him. And yet he had tried to bullshit everyone that he couldn't help out young Patrick Brodie on a fucking assault charge. His liaison with Lil had stopped overnight and that alone had caused suspicion. There was something fishy about it and, as a wise man had said many moons before, even dogs had the sense not to shit in their own beds.

Spider was in his local pub drinking Guinness and watching the cricket match. It was a lovely day and he was relaxing with his eldest son. Spider's real name was Eustace and he had passed this name on to his oldest boy.

He was called Spider because he had been a Spiderman fanatic as a boy; he still had all the *Marvel* comics he had collected and had even added to them over the years. They were worth a small fortune now, to the right person of course. He would rather be called Spider than Eustace any day of the week. But it was the name of his father and his father's father before him so it had been Eustace for his firstborn as well.

His son was a big lad with a handsome profile and the smooth, burnished skin of a real Jamaican. He'd had the look of a fighter from birth; Pat Brodie had remarked that he looked like he would be capable of a row. As his maternal grandfather had been a boxer called Micky McMurray, known to all as Mac, Spider had given the nickname to his son. It had stuck and over the years it had been bastardized to Mackie as well as Mac, and it was now the name he answered to.

The lad was a good kid; he was big enough to make people think twice about fighting with him and he was intelligent enough to think twice before starting a fight himself. Spider was proud of him, as he was proud of all his children.

The door of the pub banged open and Spider saw two young men looking around. They both had dark hair and deep-blue eyes and, jumping up from his seat, he shouted across the crowded bar, "Hey, Brodies, over here."

Pat Junior rushed to him and they embraced for long moments. As Spider felt the strength of the boy and his happiness at his welcome, he forced down the urge to weep. These children had played on his mind over the years. Everything that their father had been, and everything he had worked for, had been taken from them in a single night. Pat Junior was like his father's clone; it was like looking at his old friend once more. He even had the same mannerisms.

Spider pushed the boy away from him and held him at arm's length as he drank in his presence. He didn't seem the worse for wear, he could look after himself he knew.

"You good?"

Pat nodded. "Yeah, you?"

Pat was suddenly a man and Spider watched as his son embraced him. He saw that Lance, as always, was on the sidelines watching everything but never joining in until he was asked to. Patrick Junior had to drag him over to them all and Spider hugged him, as was expected, but the feeling was different. Lance was stiff and unyielding and he knew that, unlike his brother, Lance wasn't bothered about seeing any of them. Spider sensed that Patrick knew that but ignored it.

Still, each to their own.

"The Windies thrashing us as usual?"

Spider and Mac grinned. "What do you think? You white boys might have invented the game but you can't fucking play it!"

Everyone laughed happily.

"It's good to see you, boys."

"And you Spider, and you."

Even Pat's voice was different; deeper, and he seemed to speak slower with more emphasis on his words. He was also heavier in his body; he looked like he had been working out but that was usual for someone straight out of prison, there was fuck all else to concentrate on. But it suited Pat; he was a big lad and his huge shoulders and forearms made for an intimidating picture. He had the Irish coloring: the dark shadow that needed shaving twice a day and the thick black hair and glittering eyes that were a deep blue and made women want him.

As they all sat down, Mac slipped a small package into Pat's hand. "Grade A grass, just what the doctor ordered."

"Ta. You look good mate, you fucking handsome bastard."

As the two young men hugged again, Spider was reminded of the years that had passed and was glad that his son and Pat's son had forged such a strong bond of friendship.

"You look like twins, do you know that?" Mac observed.

Lance and Patrick shrugged with indifference.

"We've been told that all our lives," said Pat. "Now, what do you want to drink?"

Spider was already out of his chair.

"No way. I'll get them in. You all right for money, Pat?"

Pat nodded and, pointing at Mac, he said quietly, "He's already weighed me out, Spider, don't worry."

Pat saw the look of shock on Spider's face at his words and laughed once more.

"I see. So you are sound for the moment then?"

"Yeah, rocking, mate. Thirsty though."

As Spider walked to the bar, Mac smiled. "You got the gig then I take it?"

Pat nodded. "Bought it first thing. Now we're going to go round and introduce ourselves to the regular punters and make sure they know that it's in their interest to pay promptly. I should have your dosh for you in a few weeks. I have some other things lined up, as well you know."

Mac grinned and shook his shaggy head. "You ain't got a fucking Scooby Doo, have you?"

Lance was watching him closely. "Ain't got a clue about what?"

Mac looked at Lance. He was like a watered-down version of his brother; he had the same features but they looked different on him, he looked half mad most of the time. His eyes had no sparkle, nothing to say what he was feeling.

Pat took his pint from the tray that Spider had just brought over to the table and, taking a deep drink, he sighed in satisfaction. He turned to his brother and said quietly, "What he means, Lance, is that the money was a gift but it was a lot of dough and I would feel better if I paid it back, you know."

Pat looked at Spider then and the big man shook his head. "You don't owe us anything."

Lance watched his brother's easy smile and wished he had his relaxed way with people. If it had been left to him, he would have taken the money. Snatched their hands off, in fact. They did owe him, they owed them all, but he didn't say that, of course.

"How was it in there?"

Patrick smiled, showing even white teeth. He was like a young Georgie Best and he even had the same innocent look about him, a look that belied the real nature underneath. "All right, met a few decent blokes and even more fucking tossers. But it was OK."

"Did you get what I sent in?"

"Yeah. Thanks, Spider, much appreciated and all. I was banged up with young Terry Mason, nice fella. Hard fucker for all his scrawniness; he's like a fucking terrier. He took a geezer's nose off in the dinner queue. Great big fucking scouser he was and Terry had a tear-up with him. Believe it or not it was over the last plate of tapioca."

They were all laughing now at his matter-of-fact voice and his understatement of the facts.

"There was fucking skin and blood flying everywhere. I jumped in when the scouser's mates decided he was getting mullered. It was the first night after sentencing and me and Terry had arrived there together, just in time for dinner. We won the day and shared the fucking tapioca between us. We were battered to fuck but we didn't give a toss. We were starving after sitting in that fucking van all day. Anyway, after that we sort of teamed up; you know how it is."

Pat stopped smiling suddenly and, looking into Spider's eyes, he said seriously, "I need some guns, sawn-offs, can you sort that for me?"

Spider nodded slowly. This was a different boy all right and he was sorry for that; even as he understood how and why the change had come about.

"Where's Kathy?"

Eileen sighed. She took her coat off and hung it on the banister and said with her usual, exaggerated sarcasm, "It's Friday, Mum. She's still in the library. You know she changes her books today and you know how long she takes so I left her there."

"You're a lairy little mare, do you know that?"

Lil was laughing; Eileen was a case and no mistake. She was as different to her twin sister as a bird was to a fish. Outgoing and friendly, she was the life and soul of any gathering. Her whole life was one big drama and she loved it; gravitating from laughter to tears in minutes or from anger to heartfelt apologies within seconds. There was never a dull moment when she was about.

"Lance will pick her up anyway, he normally does."

She walked into the front room and, throwing herself down on to the sofa, she yawned loudly. "I hate that school. It's like being banged up all day in a sauna."

She was speaking to no one in particular and no one bothered to answer her. She went to the local convent but on weekends she worked in a bookies nearby. She had worked there since her fourteenth birthday and could easily run the place. Lenny had at least done that much for the girls. Kathy worked there with her but she wasn't really any good at it. She had never been good with strangers. Eileen watched out for her and that was how it should be.

Kathy spent most of her work day in the back of the shop watching

TV and counting out the winnings. She then placed the money in an envelope, wrote the lucky gambler's name on it and placed it in the safe until it was collected.

At school she worked well and was a model pupil. Her twin looked out for her there as well, but even the teachers had remarked on her nervousness and her quietness. If it had not been for Eileen, Kathy would have been a complete loner. Eileen attracted people and had a network of friends and as Kathy was like an extension of her twin sister, it looked like she was the same. But she wasn't.

"How does she seem to you, Eileen?"

"Who, Kathy? The same as always. You'll never guess what she did today. She went out on her own and got some lunch!"

Lil didn't laugh with her daughter, she found it sad more than anything. That a beautiful young girl like her Kathy could be so nervous of the world worried her.

"Is it me, Eileen, or does she seem even quieter than usual?"

Eileen didn't know what to say so she sighed; one of the loud, heavy, what can I say, kind of sighs she was so good at.

"Give it a rest, Mum, you know what she's like. She ain't going to wake up one morning and be a disco-dancing party girl just because *you* want her to. Not everyone has to go clubbing and drinking to have a good time. She's just a quiet person, she prefers her books and her music, and that is *all right*, Mum."

Lil shook her head sadly. "It's not about that, and you know it. She isn't right. You and her should be out having a good time together and she seems to get quieter and quieter as each year passes. I just think she's wasting her life sitting in that bedroom on her own."

"And that's what I am trying to say to you, Mum. That is her prerogative. Kathy's always been quiet and into herself. She ain't silly, Mum, she is just really shy, that's all."

Lil looked at this gorgeous daughter of hers, with her thick hair and her carefully made-up face. It was like seeing herself at that age and she knew that she had not aged too badly, she still looked good. Though how that could be, considering the life she led, she didn't know. But she couldn't understand how Eileen couldn't see the emptiness in her sister's eyes, the nervousness that couldn't just be a byproduct of seeing her father killed. Kathleen was fey, according to her mother. She was a fairy child and those words had comforted Lil once, when she had been little, but not any more.

"How was school anyway?"

Eileen screwed up her face in disgust. "Leave it out, Mum, what kind of question is that?"

The front door banged open and her two youngest children burst into the hallway and as they rushed into the front room, Lil wondered at how different they were to the other five. Colleen had big brown eyes and thick, curly hair and was all long legs and missing teeth and her brother, Christopher, had dark blond hair and the same brown eyes as Colleen. But Christy, as he was called, at nine years old, was already big for his age. Like his brothers he was going to be strong and tall.

Colleen sat on her mother's lap and began to regale them all with her day's activities. She was a dear child who was always sunny-natured and always at odds with Christy, though they were as close as two people could be.

Lenny Brewster had given her these children, had wanted her to have these children for him and all to try to wipe Patrick Brodie from her mind. He had made her his and that had suited her at the time; with five kids and no real income, he had been a necessity. He had forced her to take him into her life. After Christy, he had more or less abandoned her; he had made his point and was ready to move on.

She had expected that but she had also expected him to take care of them, and he had not been as generous as he should have been towards her. But as much as she loathed him for his neglect and his indifference he had given her these two babies and, for that much alone, she would always be grateful.

Chapter Twenty

"All right, Lenny?"

Lance's voice was, as always, neutral. He was a strange lad and Lenny wondered about this lad's calm demeanor, as he had many times in the past. He didn't bother to turn around and face him even though that was an insult in their world. He was too busy counting up the boxes of wine he had acquired that morning from a young up-and-coming Face who, it seemed, had a natural talent for hijacking trucks. He also, it had turned out, had an aptitude far beyond his tender years for sniffing out quality gear to thieve. Definitely someone to keep an eye on for the future; if he didn't get arrested and a large sentence within eighteen months, he would consider bringing him on to the firm full time. Until then, he would buy anything of value for a fraction of its true worth and keep the boy onside with his protection.

"All right, son. What brings you here?"

He was expecting an answer and when none came he turned around slowly, one eyebrow raised, and an inquisitive look on his face.

"What's the matter, Lance? You lost the power of speech?"

Not for the first time, he felt a prickle of fear. Lance was staring at him with those dead eyes and he knew that the boy was definitely a few ampules short of an overdose.

"You owe my mother money, Lenny, and you know it. I am here to remind you that we ain't kids no more and you are taking the fucking piss."

Lenny bit on his bottom lip; his fat face was red and bloated and he looked like he wasn't capable of anything that could be construed as even remotely out of order. Lance, like most people who got to know Lenny well, knew that was his strength. As the years had gone on though and no one had stepped in to challenge his authority, Lenny had stopped pretending he was a nice guy. In fact, he was making the mistake a lot of men made when they finally reached the top of their professions; he had stopped caring what people thought about him. He thought he was above everyone around him and that he could disregard the opinions and the goodwill of the people who actually made it possible for him to pursue his ideals. Or, in Lenny's case, earn his daily crust.

"You a hard man now, Lance?"

The words were said with such disdain that Lance felt them as if they were a physical slap.

"You don't fucking scare me, Lenny. I am more than capable of taking you out, mate. Unlike you, I don't rely on other people to do my dirty work. I'd do it meself and you know that. I've done enough of it for you over the last few months."

Lenny knew the boy was flexing his muscles and he also knew it was because his older brother was home from prison with a decent rep and the hunger for money and recognition that could be the death knell of people like him if they weren't careful.

Once you got too settled, you made mistakes, and one of Lenny's biggest mistakes was underestimating the boy in front of him. Lance was a handful on his own but only if he thought he had someone bigger in his corner and, until Pat Junior's release, that person had been him. Now, though, blood would out, as it always did in these cases. And Pat and Lance were close, closer than most brothers were; probably because of the circumstances surrounding their father's death. The trauma had affected all the kids in one way or another.

Lil's love for her firstborn had been the bane of Lenny's life with her; it wasn't just that she loved the boy, it was because he knew Pat Junior was his father all over again. As long as Pat was breathing she would never be without the man she had adored.

Two children later and he was still no closer to her than he had been in the beginning. She had used him as he had used her and he could even have accepted that if only she had not made him feel second best.

Lenny had everything that Patrick Brodie had worked for, *owned*, except the one thing that really mattered. Lil Brodie had been the icing on the cake as far as he was concerned. Only, he had got her by default and he knew that and, eventually, she had known that. Once he had laid his mark on her he had not wanted Lil any more and had punished her with his complete indifference. He had used her as he used everyone, even though a part of him, a small part of him, knew that what he had done to her was wrong. That the people in his circle who he depended on had lost respect for him over his treatment of Patrick Brodie's widow.

Lil's boys had grown up and now they were a team and it was up to him how that problem would be dealt with in the future. As he looked at the boy in front of him he knew instinctively that every sneaky deal he had done and every lie he had ever told, especially those that had pertained to Brodie's death, were finally coming back to haunt him. He had let people think that he was the man who had taken it upon himself to avenge that terrible death, to see that justice had been done when in fact he had actually been instrumental in its execution. He had allowed it to happen so he could take what he saw as his by rights. The affair with Lil had been seen as her falling for him because he had been so good to her. Because she needed his protection. Not that his wife had seen it so romantically, of course. She now lived in Surrey with a banker called Wright who had a comb-over and enough money to assuage her feelings of inadequacy and provide her with everything she had ever wanted.

That Lenny had abandoned Lil with two extra kids was a nine-day wonder and was something he would never live down. Until now, that had not bothered him too much; seeing Lil brought low had given him a measure of satisfaction. It had been the ultimate slap in the face for Brodie and for her, because her children were more important to her than he would ever be. Lenny would never accept that from anyone.

"Look, Lance, I appreciate all you've done for me lately and I understand you not wanting your brother to find out about any of it and he won't. He wouldn't be as open-minded as us, now would he?"

He let his words sink in before continuing; his voice, as always, neutral. "I wouldn't grass you up, would I? Think about it, you're like family to me."

This was from a man who had let his wife take his children away with her and who had no real affection for them or for any of his other children come to that, Lil's included. He gave women kids for no other reason than to put his mark on them. He did it to make sure that they never forgot him, even though he was liable to forget about them at some point.

"What about me mum; you won't get away with shortchanging her now *he's* back on the scene."

It was the way Lance had expressed his brother's presence that alerted Lenny once more to Lance's feelings about his older brother. He loved him, that had never been in any doubt at all, but he also resented him because his mother had worshipped her eldest son since she had given birth to him. Whereas Lenny knew that this boy was not high on her list of favorites. In fact, she avoided him when possible.

Lance himself knew that she found him difficult to care for and that she had no real affection for him. He had been forced to rely on his grandmother's love.

"Pat will make sure you sort yourself out, Lenny. He has a habit of making people do what he wants."

Lenny forced down his anger at Lance's attitude and his anger, when he let it go, was legendary. "Why don't you let me worry about that, eh?"

Lance stared at him and once more Lenny Brewster was unnerved by the boy's complete lack of emotion. He was only there now because Pat was finally home and he would be making a song and dance about everything as usual. Pat thought he was top dog, always had. Now Lance was nervous because he had been working for Lenny on a regular basis and he was worried that his big brother wouldn't approve. Lance would also know that Pat Junior would have expected him to watch out for his mother's interests, at least. Patrick, he knew, would be after something for his younger siblings and that meant he would be around to see him at some point.

"Why don't you get home, Lance, and let me worry about the big man, eh?"

The sarcasm was evident, as was his complete disregard for anyone or anything he saw as interfering with his equilibrium.

Lance knew that Lenny had something over him with Pat's release from prison and that he would use his recent disloyalty against him without a second's thought.

As he walked out of the warehouse, Lance pushed over a pile of boxes, knocking them to the floor with such force that the bottles of wine they housed shattered on impact. The wine bled out from the cardboard boxes, snaking across the concrete floor and picking up dirt and grime in its wake before finally disappearing down the drains.

Lenny stood there for a few moments watching the liquid as it slowly ran its course and then he turned back to the job in hand and finished his inventory. Lance had pulled a few stunts that were not exactly kosher and he had been well paid for them, so Lenny was secure in the knowledge that Lance, for all his bravado, would not want these little indiscretions coming to light. But then neither would he, come to that. Which is why he had brought Lance in on them in the first place.

But Lenny Brewster knew that he might have to welcome home the prodigal son with open arms because, by the sound of it, that was what everyone else was going to do.

Lil was in the club and she wasn't happy at all. For the last few weeks she had gradually been getting more and more irritated with the way the girls she worked with were carrying on.

This was a straight hostess club, no more and no less; she had opened the club with her old man, for fuck's sake, and now she was having to deal with people who acted like she was an incompetent. Lenny's treatment of her meant that they thought she wasn't worth their respect any more. It was hard for her to keep any kind of order and to make the girls work the way they were supposed to without her resorting to threats and intimidation. She was aware that the girls had heard the

whispers about her. Within days of her offering them a job, the inso-
lence would be on their painted faces. Lenny's attitude would be common knowledge, making her job all the harder. But the hostess had not
been born who would get the better of her and they eventually found
that out the hard way.

Since Patrick had come home from prison she couldn't help being
reminded that she had once owned the bloody club and that now she
was reduced to running it. To add insult to injury, the new crop of
hostesses were under the mistaken impression that they knew it all. A
few months on the game and they were convinced they had some kind
of fucking second sight. They thought they knew everything that they
needed to know about the life and were now experienced enough to
lecture *her* on the correct way to get them earning.

The main culprit was a new girl called Ivana. She was probably thirty
though she swore she was twenty-two and she seemed to have a nega-
tive opinion about almost everything around her. She had ambitions
for herself and Lenny, that much was evident in the way she spoke to
Lil and the way she smiled as if she had some kind of authority over her
and the club itself.

Lil was not in the mood for her tonight and whereas she usually
listened politely to the girls' petty grumbles and let them get them off
their chests, tonight she couldn't be bothered. In fact, she was feeling positively aggressive. As Ivana walked purposefully towards her she
knew it was going to be another twenty minutes of pointless griping;
insinuations that Lil didn't know what she was doing and if she would
just listen to what she was being told she would learn something of
merit. The girl was a hooker and, when all was said and done, that was
the sum of her life experience. She had the hard eyes and the blank look
of a woman who had slept with too many men in too short a time. Lil
wasn't in the least bit interested in entering into any kind of dialogue
with her.

"What is wrong with you *now*, Ivana? Is the floor too near your fat
arse? The punters not tall enough? What?" Lil was blunt to the point of
rudeness, as she had intended to be.

Ivana opened her arms in a gesture of futility; her slim body was encased in a cream boob tube and a black leather miniskirt. Her long, blond hair was styled to perfection and her make-up was flawless.

Lil was generous enough to admit that the girl was absolutely lovely; far too good for this club. She should really have been on someone's books earning a fortune and flying all over the world meeting rich Arabs, secure in the knowledge that they would pay her exorbitant amounts for her body and her discretion. That way she would have at least had the opportunity to marry someone with a few pounds. A lot of older men were willing to buy the girls with marriage and make them respectable in the eyes of the world, if not in the eyes of their Soho counterparts. Instead, the silly bitch was here and arguing crap every night like some kind of fucking shop steward. Lil knew there was a hidden agenda, there always was. Girls like Ivana saw everyone as a mark eventually; they used everyone in their orbit through sheer force of habit.

"Look, Lil, I am only trying to make this a better place to work in; we could earn a lot more money, you included."

Loud music then filled the club as a stripper walked on to the small dance floor. She was a Soho veteran, in her thirties, and she had her act off pat. Three minutes of pure semi-naked pleasure and for the last ten seconds, total nudity. Of course it seemed much longer to the audience. Like everything in Soho, it was an elaborate charade. It promised the earth while actually delivering next to nothing. The stripper would go from club to club throughout the night, with her music tape and her costumes. She would earn a set amount for each strip and still be able to have an Equity card and class herself as an exotic dancer.

Lil knew Soho like the back of her hand and to have someone like this girl standing in front of her, hands on hips and a face like thunder, trying to educate her, was beyond belief. She grinned at the utter stupidity of the Ivanas of the world and, pushing her face close, she said loudly and with menace, "Look, sweetheart, you are a *brass*, right, pure and simple. I know you have a high opinion of yourself and what you think you can do but this is a *hostess* club. Therefore, I can't earn off you girls unless I have favorites, and they would then be obliged to give me money and this would be to make sure I seat them with the best customers, wouldn't it? But what about the other girls, the ones who are not as fresh as they once were; how will they react, do you think? Well, I'll tell you, shall I? They will *murder* you without a second's thought, darling. Now, I know you feel you are being exploited and that is probably because *you are*. So shut the fuck up, go back to the meat seats and let me get on with my job, eh?"

Lil was loud enough for anyone who was interested to hear what had been said. She was angry enough to make the girl think twice about arguing any more. Ivana looked as if she was about to cry. Instead, she walked back to her seat and Lil rolled her eyes at the ceiling, making the older girls laugh. They knew Lil could have a row if necessary and that Ivana could find herself on the receiving end of a well-aimed punch. Like Lil, they had seen better days and understood the value of youth in their chosen occupation.

Going up to her office, Lil poured herself another drink, and as she felt the vodka taking hold she closed her eyes tightly. She had seven children ranging in age from twenty to eight and she was no better off now than she had been ten years ago. She had no money, no real job and her son was just out of prison and already hiding guns in her house. One of her twin daughters was unable to talk to her about what was bothering her and something was definitely bothering her, she knew. Her youngest children had basically been abandoned by their father, who would not even take any of her calls. The worst thing of all was that she had a terrible feeling she was pregnant again. She had drunk more than was good for her and slept with an old friend, more for the companionship and to ease her loneliness than anything else. Now she was like a young girl; terrified she had been caught out.

Life seemed to make sure she had one kick in the teeth after another. Every time Lil thought life was going to get better for her and her family, she was proved wrong. Her eldest son was home again and she could rejoice about that much at least. But Lance was once more like his shadow and even though she hid her feelings well these days, she still wouldn't trust him as far as she could throw him.

Lil swallowed her drink down quickly and poured herself another; she had fifteen minutes before she did her weekly check on the girls for track marks. She had never ever allowed junkies to work her tables; they were aggressive, always in need of money and they aged before their time. They always tried to hustle the john for money too quickly and that caused problems for everyone, not just the hostesses. It was a hard job in its own way, making sure the club ran smoothly, and she had been doing it for years. She had a feeling that was what was bugging her. As she poured herself another drink, Lil heard Lenny's loud voice approaching her office and she knew then, without a shadow of a doubt, that she was truly cursed.

Patrick was trying to forget that his mother was working in a hostess club and to remember that he was out and needed to take care of his family. Kathy and Eileen were his biggest worry. Especially Kathleen; she was not right at all and the time away had emphasized to him just how strange she had become.

"Come on, Kathleen. What's wrong, mate? You seem so sad, darling."

She shook her head gently and Patrick knew he was not going to get anything from her. She had always been quiet but he didn't remember her as quiet as she was now. In fact, she hardly spoke unless spoken to and even then she seemed almost startled, as if she couldn't believe someone had actually spoken to her personally.

"I'm fine, Pat, really."

She sounded sincere enough but he was still worried about her. He changed tack so she wouldn't feel intimidated by his questions. "How's school? You doing all right?"

Kathleen nodded and he was struck again by just how much she looked like her twin, and yet when they stood side by side, she looked washed-out in comparison. Kathleen was like a cheaper version of her energetic and vivacious sister and it was because of her permanent sadness. She had a deep and abiding hurt that sat in the back of her deep-blue eyes and nothing seemed able to shift it. When Eileen was near her she seemed much more relaxed in herself and happier but when Eileen was out and about, Kathleen retreated back into herself and only Lance seemed able to get through to her.

She looked haunted and it bothered him and he couldn't understand why she was like it. Kathleen had been such a happy girl, such a chatty child. Could it really be because of what had happened all those years ago? He supposed it was possible Kathleen had understood more than they had realized.

Lance came into the room with three mugs of tea balanced precariously on a small tin tray. The tray made Patrick smile; it was one they had lifted from the local pub years before because he'd liked the two little Scottie dogs on it—one black, one white—advertising a blend of Scottish whisky. He had eaten his dinner off it while watching TV so many times and seeing it now brought back buried memories of his father.

He forced them away. The past was over now and it was pointless revisiting it; he had learned that much in prison. In prison you realized that things were happening on the outside and no matter how much you cared there was *nothing* you could do about them. You were in the world but you were not *part* of it any more. Problems were suddenly huge, even the smallest, and eventually you had to come to terms with your inability to deal with them, to deal with anything that was happening in the outside world. Because you couldn't be a part of it all any more, you had no way of making it all better. He still felt that way; he felt as if he was on the outside looking in. The twins had grown up since he had been gone and little Colleen, who had been a chatty four-year-old was now a chatty eight-year-old and he knew he had missed out on a large part of her life. Christopher was a diamond but again, he didn't really know him now. And Shamus had grown from a small boy to a bruiser expelled already from school. Four years was a long time in their little lives; it was a long time in his life too. Visits were not enough to keep anyone informed of what was really happening in the family and any problems were glossed over anyway so the person locked up wouldn't worry too much. Again, the attitude was why worry them when there was nothing they could do.

Patrick watched the kids go to bed tonight and knew that they had been going to bed without him for years and it hurt him. It upset him, like Kathleen upset him. He couldn't help wondering if he might have been able to help her if he had been around. Lance, it seemed, was the person she turned to. He was a great guy and he made sure he was always there for her if she needed him. Lance was a fucking star and he knew that without him the family would have disintegrated. Especially where Kathy was concerned. He drove her places and picked her up so she didn't have to worry about getting home alone. He sat in her room with her for hours when she was in one of her depressed moods. As odd as Lance could be, he was always there when he was needed. Patrick only wished he could have been there to take some of the burden from him.

Now he was home once more and he was going to see to it that they were all taken care of and would make sure that none of them ever went without again.

And as for Brewster, he was going to have a confrontation with him at some point. Sneaking around with sluts and his mother still having to work the club for him. Oh, he was biding his time all right and when he finally had what he wanted, he was going to make that bastard pay through the nose for his blatant neglect of his family. Lenny was going to realize, once and for all, that he had a mission in life and that mission was to take care of his family. Even the family Lenny had provided before deserting them. Patrick had gone away a boy and come back a man. He had experienced many things in stir and one of them was the need to take back control from people who believed they were your intellectual superior. Brewster was a cunt but he would bide his time before he forcibly pointed that fact out to him; he needed to see how the land was lying in that direction and wait until he was settled once more. It took a while to acclimatize to being on the outside and when he had figured out all the options he would take great pleasure in distributing his own brand of retribution.

As they sipped their tea, he saw Lance look at Kathleen with a frown. Patrick knew he was as worried about her as he was himself. After all, he had been left as the eldest and had been left to take care of them all. He looked around the room; it had hardly changed since he had left it years earlier. There was the same couch, the same TV, the same carpet, the same everything except it was more dilapidated. In fact, it looked like something from a documentary on poverty in the Western world. The whole place needed upgrading and refurnishing. It was like a flophouse. But then seven kids tended to do that to furniture; it took a battering on a daily basis. Most furniture wasn't really built for large families.

As Brewster was loaded with dough it didn't seem a lot to assume that some of it might have been thrown in his mother's direction. She had needed someone to protect them when his father had been murdered and he had understood her logic, even admired it. She had the sense to know they were in danger from the Williams brothers and whoever was pulling their strings. Brewster had been the obvious choice and it was the price they paid for the world they lived in.

Lenny had been all over Lil once and all over them as well; he had been the answer to their prayers after his father's death. Then one day he had just stopped coming around and his mother had been left with two more children and Patrick had been old enough by then to understand exactly what the bastard had done to her. He had taken on the mantle of breadwinner then and it had landed him in the poke. Now he was a grown man and he was not about to let anyone interfere with his family ever again. His mother had kept them together no matter what and he was determined to take the onus off her, to take the mantle of breadwinner on himself once more, as his father would have wanted him to, have expected him to. Now he had settled back in and had a working knowledge of what was going on around him, he could work out a proper plan of action at last.

"Hello, Lil." Lenny was smiling at her and Lil noticed that his teeth had become grey since they had last talked properly. From his red flushed face to the veins across his cheeks, he looked what he was now, a drinker. Lenny was old, he was like a parody of the man he had once been. Seeing Lenny like this was awful; for all that he had done to her, she didn't wish him any ill. She had learned a long time ago that bad things happened to people soon enough; they didn't need her wishing it on them. As her mum always said, what goes around, comes around. It seemed it had come around to Lenny sooner than any of them had thought. Lil smiled easily, not letting any of her pity or her nervousness come through. She looked cool and this pleased her. "To what do we owe this pleasure, then?"

Lenny shrugged; that annoying, heavy-shouldered shrug that gave the impression of complete indifference to whoever was talking to him at the time. She had seen him do that to so many people she had actually forgotten just how irritating he could be.

He was watching her and, he had to admit, she looked good considering her age and the fact she had birthed seven kids. But then, Lil had the kind of skin that most women would kill for, and he knew that firsthand, he had seen every inch of her.

"This is *my* club, Lil. I don't see how you can question me about coming in here, do you?"

As always, he was making a point, trying to remind her of things best left forgotten. He couldn't help himself; he had to hurt and wound, make people feel they were inferior to him. For once, Lil took the bait. After the night she'd had she was suddenly up for a row. Who did he think he was? Who did he think he was talking to?

"With respect, Len, this was actually *my* club long before it was ever yours, remember. My husband bought it many years ago and you just took it, didn't you, after he was murdered?"

Lenny was shocked at her words. Lil could have a row, he knew, but she had never brought up anything like that before. She'd never once alluded to how her husband's assets had been divvied up. He wondered now if she had ever mentioned any of those things to her sons. They were big men now and he knew they were at an age when they wanted to prove themselves. Lance was safe enough but now that Pat was home, he was getting fucking ambitious and so was this woman here, by all accounts. He would have to watch her; she was under the mistaken impression that she had something of value to say. Always a bad move where women were concerned.

"You talking to me, Lil?" He was, as always, on his dignity when he felt he was being undermined and insulted.

Lil grinned then, remembering just how awkward a bastard he could be. "Don't you want to know how the kids are, Lenny?"

Lenny loved the question in her voice, the utter disbelief that he didn't care about her wonderful kids. He had made sure she had her work cut out; two of them close together but, like all his paramours, once they had produced, he had no more interest in them.

Lenny smiled and she saw the lines on his face and the way his hair was thinning and she actually felt sorry for him. He had taken her at her lowest ebb, taken everything she had. Not just from her, but from her kids as well. Then he had given her a job in this place, the place she helped set up, and now he was loath to hand over a few pounds for the kids she had given him.

"You're a piece of work, Lenny. You have two gorgeous kids and you ain't got a fucking ounce of compassion for either of them, have you?"

Lenny shook his head and laughed again, the false laugh that he really believed made him seem sophisticated, a man of the world. "I couldn't give a flying fuck, Lil. They mean nothing to me, love. None of my kids do; the fact they arrived through a cunt speaks volumes, if you'll excuse the pun."

He was laughing again and Lil felt the hurt once more; when he dismissed the kids like that, she knew she was capable of really harming him. She could feel her hands clenching into fists. If some of his so-called mates heard him at times she knew they would not believe their ears. He could be so hateful and so vicious and the worst thing was, he enjoyed it.

"Well, assuming your mother gave birth to you, then it stands to reason that you traveled into the world through a *cunt* yourself so at least your kids have got one thing in common with you, eh?"

He was finally silent and she knew that just for once she had got the better of him. Her toughness had attracted him but it was always brought to the fore when anyone or anything threatened her children. She was like a wild animal in that respect and as she was now, proud and angry, he remembered her attraction. He had used her, he knew, but it had not been a hardship. She was faceable if you didn't crave youth.

There was a tap on the door then and Lil opened it quickly, her anger already subsiding because she knew it was pointless.

Ivana stood there with a smile that said she was expected.

Lenny peered at her. She really was a good-looking girl, full-breasted for all her skinniness, with thick blond hair that made her seem healthier than she probably was and she knew how to look at a man; to make him feel desired and wanted. But it was too professional for his liking, even though he had already given her a whirl and he knew she was worth keeping as a back-up bird. Hookers were good like that, they didn't expect anything from you; a few quid and a good time would suffice.

Lenny saw the look in Lil's eyes and enjoyed her discomfort; the reminder that she was not a spring chicken any more. That youth was all around her and he had access to it any time he wanted. He knew the best way to place his foot firmly on her neck was to make her feel old and unwanted.

"What do *you* want?" Lil's voice was dismissive and Ivana waited for Lenny to invite her in, to show Lil that she was someone to be reckoned with, someone of note.

Lenny watched it all with his usual closed expression and, being the contrary man he was, looked at Ivana with a puzzled frown and asked, "Well, you heard the woman, what *do* you want?"

Lil felt sorrow at the girl's flushed face and knew the humiliation she was feeling. She didn't enjoy it because she had been on the receiving end of it so many times herself.

Lenny walked to where she stood and went to shut the door in her face. "You want to sort those girls out, Lil. They are getting above their stations, if you ask me. What a fucking liberty, *brasses* thinking they are welcome in polite company."

"Oh why don't you fuck off, Lenny." Lil's voice was so loud and so protective that as Ivana walked away, she felt the first stirrings of gratitude and respect for the woman she had despised up until a few minutes ago.

"Why do you do it? Why do you have to destroy everyone you come in contact with?"

Lenny didn't answer her. She was asking him a genuine question and, for once in his life, he was considering giving her a genuine answer. He could see the disgust in her eyes, the dislike in her face and the anger in her body language. He observed it without feeling.

"That girl earns a fortune and, if she had half a brain, she'd go on the trot from here and get herself into a real club, the New Rockingham or the Pink Pussycat. Somewhere they would treat her with a bit of respect."

Lenny sighed. He was bored with it all now. "Who gives a fucking *toss*, Lil. Like I give a flying fuck about *her*. Now, tell me, how is young Patrick and when can I expect a visit from him? I have a bit of work to put his way."

Lil knew she had him then, knew that her boy was finally at an age when Lenny expected some kind of comeback for his behavior.

"You leave him alone; he don't need to be involved in your old crap. He's already sorting himself out a wage."

Lenny bit on his bottom lip, a sure sign he was aggravated. "I don't think you have quite grasped the concept of worker and boss, Lil. *You* don't have an opinion, do you? I *tell* you what to think and you bow down to my superior knowledge. Tell the boy to come and see me."

Lil shrugged, enjoying his discomfort. "What did you come here for, anyway, Lenny? You must have heard my Patrick was home. A phone call would have sufficed to ask how he was."

Lenny didn't answer her, amazed at the way she spoke to him and knowing the hold he had over her was loosening by the day. Now Pat was home he would take over as the man of her house and Lil no longer needed anything from anyone. He watched her as she lit a cigarette. Pulling on it heavily, she licked her lips slowly and blew the smoke into his face, making him want to cough.

Lenny flapped his hands to disperse it, reassuring himself that her son was on borrowed time; that he would open the fucker's head and then listen to her crying as her son followed his father into the great beyond. So Patrick had made a good impression in stir, had looked after himself and shown the world that he could take care of himself. Well, he wasn't going to let the little fucker get a foot in his front door. He was being heralded as his father's son; well, they all knew what had happened to him, didn't they? He had sat it out for years waiting until the time was right to take what he saw as rightfully his. He now possessed all that Brodie had owned, including his wife and his kids, and he was certainly not going to stand back and wait for the boy wonder to reclaim his father's inheritance.

He had also heard the whisper of the pavement, that people were waiting to see if Pat Junior had inherited his father's taste for revenge. He had used Lil and fucked her over as if she was nothing and he was reaping the benefits of Brodie's hard graft. People were remarking on that a lot, lately, knowing the boy was due home. So he needed the boy to be close to him for a while until he knew the score for himself. He had to show willing, at least until he decided how he was going to deal with the situation.

"I hear Patrick is buying debts?"

Lil nodded. "Doing all right and all; he's desperate to earn, as you can imagine. He met a few blokes inside who took to him, you know. Billy Farmer, all that crowd, his *father's* old mates. They've all helped him get an in and get close to an income. Spider and his lad are on the firm with him now and all."

She was threatening him and he knew it. "Oooh, giving up work soon, eh, Lil?" The sarcasm and barely controlled anger was once more to the fore.

"That is what he is aiming for, yeah. He is like his old man, my Pat, and he had his priorities right. Les Mulligan sent him over three grand this afternoon and gave him a few debts for nix so don't worry yourself, Lenny, we will survive."

Lil was telling him her boy had backup, that he was not a lad any more and that she knew what he was planning. He knew he had treated her badly but unfortunately he didn't care, he treated everyone badly in the end.

The smile he turned on Lil though was full-beam and, pouring them both a drink, he said in a friendly manner, "Tell Pat I have a place for him if he wants it."

Lil didn't answer him, she just wondered at a man who had so much nerve he was actually offering her son a job in what had once been his father's business; the man had no shame. But she knew her boy was not a fool and Lance was sensible enough to let Pat plan their next moves. Now she wanted her son, her Pat, to wipe this bastard off the pavement. He had tried to break her and he had nearly succeeded. But now she was well able for him, as were her boys. Lance included.

It was a man's world all right and she was sick of it.

Chapter Twenty-One

"Lance, will you relax for five minutes and talk to me."

The two brothers were alone and it was only now that Patrick had noticed how little they had to say to one another. It wasn't for want of trying on his side but Lance was so close-mouthed that it was almost impossible to get anything out of him. He spent most of his free time with Kathleen in his room where they sat for ages talking. He was her rock, even more so than her twin. He was always watching her, even when they were eating or watching TV. He looked out for her constantly.

Pat popped open the can of beer and took a noisy swig. As he settled back into the chair he smiled at his brother and Lance, for the first time since he had arrived home, smiled back. A real smile and Patrick was reminded of how he had been when they were kids.

Since their father had died, they had become very close, all of them had felt the need to be together, to look out for each other. He and Lance had taken the twins under their wings; Eileen had gravitated to him and Kathleen to Lance. They had watched out for them and made sure they were safe.

Since he had been away, Lance had been keeping everything on the go; at least that was what he had been told. It must have been hard, he knew.

"Will you fucking sit down? I've got little Johnny White coming round in a minute."

Lance dropped on to the seat beside him. "It's good to have you back, mate."

"It's good to be back. Now, tell me, has Brewster been double-cross-ing the old woman? Because this place is definitely fucking dilapidated. I hear he ain't done fuck all but Mother won't tell me nothing. So, come on, before Johnny arrives."

Lance looked into the eyes so like his own and yawned. "Look, you know what Lenny's like; I've been doing a bit of ducking and diving meself for him. I made sure we were all sorted. Now, what does Johnny want?"

Pat punched his brother in the arm. It was a sharp punch, a warning punch, and they both knew it. Patrick had always been the stronger of the two; Lance had been the one with the short temper, the bully. That had all changed though. After the murder, Lance had seemed to sink into himself. The bloodbath had made Pat stronger and poor Lance weaker. His bullying days were over and he concentrated his energy on Kathleen. Like him, she had become a different child overnight. She had become quiet, withdrawn and sickly; she had been like a little doll. All big eyes and fear.

"So, come on, bruv, what's little Johnny want?"

Pat grinned, the old grin; the conspirator was once more home. "We are going on a robbery this afternoon and Johnny is going to be the counter man. We need serious cash and it's the quickest way to earn a few quid. The post office has money delivered there at four forty-five every Friday; ready for the wages to be paid out to the local firms. There's only about thirty grand there but it'll do us nicely split three ways. It'll help us get the business on the road, see, and we can use it to buy more debts."

Lance shrugged but he was nervous inside. Unlike Patrick, he had a worry of getting his collar felt. Pat took everything in his stride but Lance wasn't like that. He couldn't stand to be put away, he knew it would send him off his head. He couldn't bear to leave his family, espe-cially Kathleen; he would die inside, so strong were his feelings towards them all. Even visiting Pat had caused him to hyperventilate. He had never liked being confined but he had never let that secret out to any-one; not even to his brother. Pat would have slaughtered him if he knew something like that. Lance knew the robbery would be a laugh though;

everything Pat did was a laugh, that was what he had missed so much while he had been away.

"What post office are we doing?"

"Barking High Street. It's the perfect place. The old dears leave the money on the floor; they don't safe it, because they know it will be picked up quickly. They have a cuppa and they don't even bother to put it out of sight. All we need do is let little Johnny do his party piece and we can be in and out in minutes."

Lance laughed. "How did you find out about that so quick?"

"Mrs. Doyle worked there; her son was banged up with me. I popped round there to give her a drink and she filled me in on the basics. I owed her Kevin a favor and I said I'd pay her off with a few quid. Fucking Brewster was supposed to see her all right and he didn't give the poor old bag a fucking groat! He's doing a nine for that ponce and I can tell you now, he is not a fucking happy bunny."

Lance laughed at his brother's cheery voice even though he knew Pat was annoyed about the situation. "The man's a cunt and a fucking vicious cunt at that."

"Has he really ignored the old woman?"

Lance nodded then. He realized Pat knew the score without even asking him anything.

"I've been doing a bit for him, like I said. But you know what he's like, all over you one minute and can't remember your fucking name the next."

Pat crushed his empty lager can and threw it expertly into the bin. "Well, I am going to remind him about Colleen and Christy."

Pat had an edge to him now and even though he was still young there was the hardness about him that only a segregation wing can hone. He had been put in solitary twice while away and, because of his fighting skills, he had been moved into the prison system earlier than he should have been. He was proud of that, Lance knew. Men who had been away a long time respected Patrick because he could not only have a serious row but he could also do his time with the minimum of fuss. He also had his father's creds and had made a point of ferreting out anyone who knew a story about him.

Pat was a realist; he knew that he had to get his head around his sentence and sit it out because the one thing that was guaranteed in prison was that the time passed, *eventually*.

"We have to get this gaff sorted for Mother and the kids and make sure she ain't got to work any more. She has grafted enough over the years and we need to sort her out soon as, don't you think?"

Lance nodded.

Pat watched his brother for long moments and wished he could climb inside his head, because he was a different boy to the one he had waved goodbye to at Chelmsford Crown Court all those years ago. Lance was even more nervous somehow. He seemed worried although he was still vicious. Pat had heard about his ravings even in prison; about when he lost it. Lance was a fucking headcase when he did go; that was their strength these days. Lance was capable of great anger and great violence but only when he was goaded beyond endurance.

Lance had suffered over his mother's indifference, Pat knew; she had kept It quiet over the years and had hidden it away but it was still there, lurking around, waiting to surface in the future. Pat could feel it coming off her sometimes and he knew that if he did, Lance had to feel it as well. Pat knew that the bus incident was always near the front of his mother's mind when she looked at Lance and he still bore the scars from her hiding all those years ago. But he had been a kid then and now he was a man. At least Pat hoped he was; he would soon find out anyway.

Pat leapt out of the chair, forcing the thoughts away.

"Want another beer, Lance?"

Pat walked into the kitchen and, opening the fridge, the anger hit him once more. His father had worked his arse off for them and Brewster had walked in and taken it from under their noses.

He had heard all about it in prison, had heard the stories and the rumors. He'd also found out about Lance's dealings with Lenny but he had planned to wait a while before he mentioned that to him. He'd been hoping against hope that Lance would mention it first, would confess his involvement in Lenny's scams. Pat had been as patient as he could with his brother and reminded himself that Lance had been left to shoulder the burden on his own and that he had done what he thought was right. And now he had. Each day Pat was gathering more and more information and the more he learned the more he felt in control of his life. In the meantime, he could feel his excitement about the plans for that afternoon building up inside him.

When little Johnny finally arrived, Lance was reminded of how small he actually was. He was just over five feet two in height and he had dark skin and deep-green eyes. His thick hair was tied back in a ponytail and he wore the usual con man's garb: leather jacket, jeans, officer boots and a baseball hat that would of course be replaced with a black wool hood once they hit the post office.

Johnny was carrying a dark-blue canvas bag that held three sawed-off shotguns and a German Luger that Pat had ordered as a set piece. He knew he needed protection and he was determined that he would have it. In fact, he already had a Saturday-night special that had been the property of his father. He had known where it was hidden, even as a kid, and he had kept it in perfect condition ever since. He had also kept its existence very quiet; like his father before him he lived by the old Irish adage, people only know what you tell them.

Carrying a piece was as inevitable to him now as was his thirst for revenge, not just for his father but for his mother as well. For the struggle her life had been to feed and clothe them and bring them up, especially after Brewster had moved in on them and then dumped them. His mother, who should have been left comfortable, who should have been taken care of with his father's graft, had been reduced to selling herself to make ends meet. The drink had become her daily sustenance and had even made Annie bearable. His mother had been hardened over the years but he was determined to make her life as easy as it would have been had his father lived to see them all grow.

Like Spider said, his father had been murdered by the Williams brothers all right but all his graft was gone, his kids had been robbed of what should have been theirs by rights and Brewster was finally being seen for the two-faced, no-neck bastard he really was. He would pay for his fucking treachery and, by making him pay, young Patrick Brodie knew that he might finally get some kind of peace.

He had had a long time to think, learn and plan. That was the only good thing about stir; it gave you plenty of free time to decide how best to go about your daily business once you were on the outside.

As they all got ready to go, he glanced at a photo of his father and felt the sting of tears; he had worshipped him and he had seen him brutally killed. But his legacy would always carry on, he would see to that himself.

"Colleen Brewster, you bloody liar!"

Colleen was laughing her head off and it was such a deep and hearty laugh that it infected all the girls around her. She was a card was Colleen and now her big brother was out of jail she was intelligent enough to feel the difference in the way they were treated by everyone around them. The local shopkeeper had given her candy as gifts; refusing her money as if she had never been asked to pay for anything before. The first time it had happened she had thought it was a joke, then the man had smiled craftily and said, "Give your brother me regards, won't you?"

It was then that she and Christy had understood the esteem her brother was held in. Her father was a Face, she knew, but no one tried to get around them for his benefit because everyone knew he didn't give a shit about them. All her friends at school were aware of their parents' gossip and knew that her brother was home. Lance had a reputation as a nutter and Pat was a nut as well. When Lance went, it was so over the top he scared anyone around him. But her big brother Pat was the one people seemed to be more chary of; seemed to find the more sinister of the two. Colleen knew, though, that Lance, who was good to her, was the madder; she had seen him flip and she never wanted to see it happen again. She had been literally terrified and she had caused it; she had made him lose his temper like that. He had dragged the man out of his house and beaten him in the street until he was unconscious. She had been playing a game of knock-down ginger and the man had told them off. She had cried and then told Lance, who just lost his mind. Colleen had learned a big lesson that day. At seven years old she had understood the strength of her brother's anger and the trouble that an unwise word could cause.

As chatty as she was and as much as she loved to laugh, she was wary of what she said now. At nearly nine, she was already a diplomat.

As she walked home from school with her friends they crossed over the road and, walking together, they passed the bookies in the high street. Her father, Lenny Brewster, was standing outside with a young girl. Colleen looked at him as she always did when she came across him. He looked through her, as he always did when he came across her. It bothered her that he was her old man and he had no interest in her but as she looked at him she was also glad; he had a screwed-up, angry face. His teeth were overly big for his mouth; she knew she had his mouth but she also knew that on her it looked different. The thick lips and slightly over-big teeth gave her a pout that would one day be her best feature. Colleen had been told she had a lovely smile ever since she could remember and she believed it, because she knew her laugh made others laugh along with her.

She was bold enough to make eye contact with her father and she knew he was as aware of her as she was of him. She was glad that her Patrick was home and that everyone was happy because of that. She was beginning to understand that now her father would have to answer to their Pat and she wondered what the upshot would eventually be.

She heard her older sisters calling out behind her and she turned to see them walking towards her with their long blond hair and their navy school uniforms. She waved at them happily. She loved the twins, they were like extra mothers to her and Christy. She hugged her sisters as always and then waved her friends goodbye at the bottom of her street. She was holding Kathy's hand as she always did, though she often felt as if she was looking after Kathy and not the other way around. Even as young as she was, she knew that Kathy was in need of looking after. So Colleen looked up at her older sister and smiled sweetly at her. Kathy smiled back and squeezed her hand gently but the sadness in her eyes made Colleen feel like crying.

Kathleen stopped and bent over, holding her belly. "You all right, mate?" Eileen's voice was concerned.

Kathleen nodded and smiled grimly. "I've got the shits again."

"Charming! You've had that all week. See the quack or the school nurse."

"I will, I'll go tomorrow."

Kathy looked down at her little sister and saw her watching her dad and his latest amour and, squeezing her hand gently, she said, "Ignore him, darling."

Colleen smiled up at her with her bright little smile and said gaily, "Sod him, I don't care about him."

But she did sometimes.

Little Johnny and the Brodie boys stood outside the post office for a few seconds as they pulled on their wool hoods. It was just getting dark and the rain that had been threatening was already coming down. They walked inside casually and gently shut the door behind them. Then, pulling the shotguns out from under their coats, they started the attack. Little Johnny jumped on the counter and slipped easily over the glass partition known in the trade as the bandit screen. His small stature was ideal for that job and he got offered a lot of work because of it. He was small and wiry and he had slipped over more bandit screens than he cared to remember; earning a good chunk of change into the bargain.

There was no one in the post office, which was good, as the last thing they needed was a have-a-go hero. Lance was still watching the door in case someone did decide to come in and buy a stamp. If anyone did come in, they would then be firmly walked away from the window and told in no uncertain terms to lie on the floor and shut the fuck up.

The two women who ran the place had been taking advantage of the quiet spell and were having a quiet cup of tea. The sight of the men and the guns they were brandishing terrified them and both were rooted to the spot for a few seconds.

Smiling through his hood, Patrick said, "Come on, girls; sit yourselves down. We only want the money, nothing else; you can keep your virginity."

The two women rushed through to the back of the shop and watched in shock and fascination as Johnny leapt over the counter.

"Go and fucking sit down. You move and I'll blow your fucking heads off."

Little Johnny's voice was loud and frightening. It was all an act, he had no intention of shooting anyone but it was a requisite action; it stopped people from doing something stupid. He threw the bundles of money over the bandit screen and they were placed into a large leather shopping bag. The money was sealed tightly into neat packages and had the address of the firm it was to be used by printed on it or the bank it had come from. As they were neatly packaged, that made the job so much easier. Robberies like this were often committed for what was called running money. For the boys it was a little bit of a bonus, some startup money to make sure that they could buy up a few more debts and make a few more deals. A few months down the line and they might be tempted to rob the place again. People always thought lightning didn't strike in the same place twice but it did.

It was starting to really rain now, perfect robbing weather, and the greyness of the day made it nice and dim inside the old-fashioned shop. Anyone passing would not be able to see what was going on inside.

It was over in under seven minutes, though the two women involved would believe it had lasted a lot longer than that because of their fear. They were outside, hoods off and guns well hidden without anyone even taking a second glance at them. The car started first time and they were gone before the call had even been put through to the police or the ladies had set off the alarm. Laughing their heads off they spun away from the curb and went to a friend's yard to dispose of the guns and then they sat it out for a few hours, chatting and drinking beer until Pat deemed it safe to go home.

Lance noticed that little Johnny was happy to let Pat be the main man and he knew that a lot of other people were going to feel like that towards him. Pat had a knack of making people do what he wanted; their father had been the same way. He knew Pat was going to shake their world up and make them a force to be reckoned with.

Annie watched as her daughter poured herself another drink. The drinks were being consumed earlier and getting larger by the month. Since

Patrick had come home she had eased off a little bit but Annie knew her daughter well enough to know that something was bothering her, something more than usual.

She still looked good, she would give her that. Lil was one of those people who, no matter what happened to them, still seemed to look well.

She wasn't slim exactly but then, as a woman got older, she looked better with a bit of weight on her. She still had the voluptuous look that attracted men to her and her hair was shiny and thick; well-cut and groomed, like the rest of her. But Lil had the vacant look of the heavy drinker; the empty eyes that seemed unable to see what was going on around her. She wasn't bloated or pale-looking like most heavy drinkers but she was gradually losing interest in her surroundings. She was only really happy when the kids were around her and yet she was leaving the brunt of the household chores to her mother. Not that Annie minded; she loved being here, being in the thick of them all.

"Come on, Lil, eat something."

"I ain't hungry, Mum, how many fucking times, eh?"

Annie sighed and swallowed down the retort that came quickly to her lips. Lil was capable of telling her to leave and she didn't want that to happen.

"Keep your hair on. Have you looked in on Kathleen? She is rough, bless her. I took her up a cup of tea and she was already asleep."

Lil nodded. "She's all right. I saw her earlier and she has a gyppy tummy, that's all. She went to the doctor tonight; she fit her in like. She took her prescription and crashed out. She'll be OK, Mum; a couple of days in bed should sort her out."

"She is a fucker for that kebab house on the high street, no wonder she has the shits."

Lil laughed with her mum; the drink was taking over now and giving her the lovely relaxed feeling she craved. It made her happy and it made her forget the abortion her life seemed to have become.

Annie sat opposite her; she had cooked the dinner for everyone and then washed up and tidied away. She did this because she knew her daughter would put up with her if she was useful. "What's the matter, Lil? You can tell me, love."

Lil sat back heavily in the chair. The kids were out of earshot so she decided to confide in her mother; she needed to get it off her chest anyway.

"Lenny turned up at the club last night, all sweetness and light, the ponce. But he was worried about Pat being home, I could feel it. I don't trust him, Mum. He can make you believe anything and we know that better than anyone, don't we? And I don't want my poor Pat being put in a position where he might be used or, even worse, set up." Lil shook her head at the foolishness of her words, knowing how they sounded when spoken out loud. But she knew Lenny Brewster better than anyone and she knew what he was capable of.

"Pat is a shrewd fucker, Lil. He knows the score, so stop worrying, girl. He's done his time, kept his head down and his arse up and he ain't silly, love."

Lil nodded her agreement. "I know all that, Mum. He is my son after all, but he is out to make a name to get a rep like his father's. He wants to make a niche for himself and I know that Lenny won't let that happen. Patrick's memory is still too fresh in everyone's mind, especially *his*. He could never compete with him and he knows it."

Annie didn't say anything. The truth of what her daughter had said was evident to anyone who knew the situation, who knew the score. Pat Junior was a hard little fucker and, she, for one, was looking forward to when he took back what was theirs; she was sick of making ends meet. She was sick of kowtowing to a son of a bitch like Lenny and she wanted her daughter to have some peace of mind at last. That was something she believed would only come with Lenny's demise and she prayed daily for that to happen.

She sat with her daughter and the sound of the rain drumming against the window panes was loud in the room. Annie loved this daughter of hers and she wanted to protect her in any way that she could. Grasping her hand, she squeezed it tightly as she said quietly, "Stop worrying, Lil. We'll be all right; the boys will look out for us."

Lil laughed then; a low, sad laugh that sounded empty and hollow. "Oh, Mum. I think I'm pregnant again."

Annie closed her eyes in distress and annoyance.

"You *are* joking!"

Lil shook her head sadly. "I wish I fucking was."

Annie realized she was being serious and knew that it was true. "Whose is it then?"

The loudness of her voice, and the anger she could barely disguise, hit a nerve and Lil stubbed out her cigarette in the ashtray as she shouted: "Who are you, Mother, the fucking police? Mind your own business for once."

Then she saw her mother's face and the realization of what had happened to her again finally hit home.

"Oh, Mum. What am I going to do?"

Annie stood up and went to put the kettle on. "Well, you better knock the drink on the head for a start. The child will be born with a fucking hangover and a lighted fag."

Lil didn't answer her, she just poured herself a large drink and lit another of her endless cigarettes. This was the last thing she needed in her life and, like everything else that had happened to her, there was nothing she could do about it.

Christy and Colleen were playing in the park nearby. It was a cement paradise for the kids who lived around the area. The walls that surrounded the small park were completely covered in graffiti, brightly colored and deliberately obscure. The people around and about had no idea that the messages meant something to the kids who frequented the area. The police and the parents of the children who used the park had no idea that it had any real meaning whatsoever. They just saw it as a necessary evil, something the kids did because they were bored. It actually meant a lot to the teenagers; it was the writings of the ICF and the inner-city firm gave all its members the information they needed to know about where a fight or a rally would be. Christy and Colleen knew that, even at their young age.

They were on the swings when they heard someone screaming nearby, in one of the high-rise flats. It wasn't unusual to hear screams In this housing project; in fact, it was more unusual if there was no noise whatsoever. The park was a place of dangerous proportions; it was a place where anything could happen, and frequently did. Murder was not unheard of and fighting was a daily occurrence. But for the kids it was a place to meet up and chat, listen to music or score anything that took their fancy. Even though Christy and Colleen weren't scoring yet, the dealer knew that at some point in the future they would be. It was how the projects worked, how the black economy survived and how the kids learned how to waste their lives at a very early age.

"Did you hear that, Col?"

Colleen nodded, her open face troubled. This wasn't the usual screaming from a couple who had drunk too much and were fighting. This was a different scream; it had an edge of fear running through it that communicated itself to anyone who heard it. Colleen and Christy saw people coming out of their flats and congregating on their balconies. After a while they all walked down the stairs and the children saw them going towards the refuse area: the underneath of the apartments where the big industrial-sized dumpsters were housed. They got up in perfect sync and holding hands, they followed the sounds of the night. There was definitely something exciting going on and they, like the kids following them, wanted first-hand knowledge of whatever had caused the adults to abandon their televisions and come outside their homes into the cold night air.

"All right, Mum. What you doing?"

Lil was ready for work, her hair and make-up were done and her clothes were ironed and much sexier than she would usually bother wearing. The boys had burst into the apartment and the evening air swept through the house, making Lil shiver. She really didn't want to go anywhere tonight if she could help it but she needed the money. After her run-in with Lenny she wasn't looking forward to seeing him again in the near future but she knew that was what was going to happen.

She felt her son's lips on her cheek. Pat had always been tactile; kissing her and hugging her. Lance, on the other hand, knew that physical contact with him would make her ill. She smiled slightly at him and bowed her head in a gesture that said she acknowledged his presence. Lance nodded back at her and put the leather shopping bag he was carrying on to the table. Then he opened it up and started removing the money inside it.

Patrick picked up three thousand pounds and gave it to his mother, dropping it in her lap as he said seriously, "Your days of working for that cunt are long gone, Mother. You do *not* go back there, right?"

It wasn't a request and Lil knew it. Picking up the money she stared at it for long moments and then she placed it back on the table.

"You been out robbing?"

Her voice was neutral, there was no accusation in it at all. She sounded matter of fact, as if she just wanted to clarify something, which of course she did.

"Mum, of course we've been out robbing. Use your loaf, woman! We are intending to do a lot more robbing in the future and all. So get with it and take the cash and tell Lenny Brewster he can shove his job . . ."

Lil nodded. She was smiling now and she said loudly, "Shove his job up his jacksy."

Patrick grinned again and Lil noticed Lance was smiling as well. She wondered how she had existed with him so near to her; his whole attitude, his stance and even his voice made her want to scream.

She put the money on to her lap and watched as Pat gave Annie a few hundred quid. She saw the old woman's thrilled expression and her relief that she had a few pennies in her purse and could have a spend-up in front of her neighbors. Annie Diamond would never change while she had a hole in her arse.

"Thanks, son." The gratitude was in her voice and in her eyes.

"Lance was with me, Mum, it was a joint effort."

They were laughing together then and she knew they had smoked some pot; the joint pun was the giveaway. She smiled at Lance and he busied himself getting beers out of the fridge, unable to look her in the eye.

Pat watched them both; he had been observing the way they danced around each other for years and he knew that it would never be any different. They lived under the same roof but they could have been on different planets for all the contact they actually had with one another.

Christopher and Colleen burst through the front door. They were both talking at once and neither was making any sense whatsoever until Patrick eventually hushed them both up.

"What the fuck are you on about? One at a time."

He pointed at Christopher then. "Tell us what is going on."

"There's Old Bill all over the show, all over the flats . . ."

"What for? What have you heard?" Lance's voice was high. He was frightened and it was apparent to everyone in the room, even the youngsters. Patrick knew his fear was that they had been snitched on by someone and that the cops were on their way to arrest them.

Colleen picked up a piece of cake and bit into it before saying, "They found a baby. A dead baby over in the flats. It was in the bin; someone heard a crying sound but by the time the police and that got there it was dead. Mrs. Jones said that it was because someone had emptied their rubbish down the chute and it had landed on the poor thing."

"Oh my God, how terrible." Lil was shocked to the core and Annie knew that if she was pregnant this occurrence would affect her more than usual. Dead babies or dumped babies were not that uncommon where they lived.

"Fucking hell. Are you sure that's the truth?"

Colleen and Christopher both nodded vigorously.

"We saw them carry it to the ambulance. It was only small and they had wrapped it in a white blanket." Colleen's dramatic nature was now to the fore and she was milking the fact that she was the center of attention, as always.

The boys were relieved. They had both thought for a few moments that the cops were after them and were going to raid the house.

"Well, that poor baby saved our bacon tonight. Lance thought it was the cops coming for us!"

Lance was annoyed then. "No I didn't. But by the same token, we both got the wind put up us."

Lil saw Kathleen walking slowly down the hallway.

"You all right, love?" Her voice was low and full of compassion for this daughter of hers who was so easily hurt and who would suffer for the rest of her life because of it.

"Did I hear you say that a baby was dead?" Everyone nodded.

"That's terrible! So bloody awful . . ."

Kathleen was crying but then she did cry all the time over the slightest thing. This time though her eyes were even sadder than usual and she was sobbing into a tartan tea towel she had picked up off the draining board. She sounded so distraught it was upsetting the younger kids just listening to her.

Lance went to her then. Turning her around, he placed his arm around her shoulders and walked her slowly back up to her room. He was talking softly to her and calming her down. Everyone breathed a sigh of relief when she disappeared from view.

Annie started putting her coat on then and Lil and the boys looked at each other in exasperation.

"Where you off to, Nan?" It was Colleen who, as always, asked the pertinent question.

"I said I would pop over to see Gladys. Might as well get it over with, you know what she's like."

They all grinned then, glad of the light relief.

"You get over there, Mum, in case you miss something."

Annie pursed her lips in anger but she didn't say anything. She knew that for all their talk they would be relying on her to find out what had really happened.

It was freezing outside and as Annie walked along the road towards the flats, she wondered at a young man like Patrick who had brought about such a change with his release from prison. He was going to make everyone sit up and take notice, she was sure. He had that kink in his nature that his father had possessed. She only hoped that it didn't turn out to be the death of him.

Chapter Twenty-Two

"Come on, Lil, let's be having you!"

Jimmy Brick's voice was as miserable as it had always been but seeing Lil had put a measure of pleasure in it that was hard to detect unless you knew the man very well.

Lil turned in her seat to face him and she saw immediately that the years had not been kind to him. After Patrick's murder he had been on the scene for a while and then he had just seemed to drop off the face of the world. No one seemed to see him or hear about him. He had just disappeared. He wasn't in the clink, she knew that much. It seemed he had sold up and moved on.

Jimmy looked what he was, an old bruiser; someone who was displaying all the characteristics of an old fighter. He could still hold his own and he certainly looked capable of causing a row on a whim.

Lil's face had lit up with pleasure and that pleased him no end. He had seen her from across the pub and he had recognized her immediately. Even though she was older she had not really changed that much. In fact, he was amazed at how little she had changed since the last time he had seen her. He pushed that from his mind. If Lil brought it up, he would discuss it. Otherwise he would leave well enough alone.

Life in Spain had finally got to Jimmy and he missed London more than he would ever have believed. He had ended up hating it out there. It was filled with has-beens, wannabes and snitches. He had been called back to England like many others, through missing the weather, the women and the opportunities it afforded men like him. As he sat in the Crown and Two Chairmen pub in Dean Street and looked at Lily Brodie the past seemed so recent and yet he knew that was only because the memories were so vivid. If he lived to be one hundred years old he knew that day would be as fresh then as it was now.

"Bloody hell, Jimmy. Long time no see."

Jimmy smiled. His balding head that he now shaved bald, rather than have the thinning hair on show, made him look old and yet his tanned skin and expensive clothes appealed to Lil and she told him that. "You look bloody well, Jimmy. Where have you been?"

Jimmy pulled up a chair and, as he sat beside her, he caught her distinctive scent; a mixture of Estée Lauder perfume and Revlon lipstick.

"You look good yourself, girl. I've been living in Spain. I'm over for a while and maybe back for good. I ain't made me mind up yet."

"I bet that's a lovely place to live."

Jimmy sat back in the uncomfortable wooden chair and surveyed her. Lil knew he was making a production of the look, but that was Jimmy. He had always had a soft spot for her.

"Spain is a glorified shithole, Lil. No one would live there permanently unless they were in serious danger of getting their collars felt. I suppose it's all right if you have a family or whatever, but on your Jack Jones it's no good."

She grinned and Jimmy noticed her even teeth. She had a lovely smile and the best of looks, as far as he was concerned.

"You couldn't settle anywhere else. You're a Londoner like me and we can't seem to settle elsewhere."

Jimmy laughed with her and then they were quiet. The atmosphere between them was heavy with unspoken thoughts, making them both feel shy, suddenly.

"Well, I am Hank Marvin, Lil. Fancy a bite to eat?"

"Why not? I just have to meet my boys and then we can shoot off."

Jimmy was getting them a drink when he saw the boys arrive. The eldest, Pat Junior, was the living image of his father and on first sight he felt his heart constrict with the shock. It was like looking at Patrick again; he had the same stance, the same walk, everything. The younger boy, Lance, was still a strange-looking fellow as far as he was concerned.

But he hid his feelings and as Lil introduced him, he felt the pull of them all. They were a family that had been devastated overnight but it was plain to him that they had pulled through it somehow.

Pat Junior sat down and, peering at the older man with interest, he said quietly, "I remember you, Jimmy. You were a great mate of my father and it's a pleasure to see you once again. He loved this pub, I know. When I was away I met a lot of his old cronies and heard all the stories about him. They spoke highly of you."

It was a simple statement but it began a friendship that was already obvious to both of them. Pat felt the older man's emotion at being reunited with his old friend's sons and Jimmy Brick was reminded of the man he had been close to for so many years.

Lil watched the exchange and she was pleased to see the way the two of them seemed to take to one another. She also saw that Lance, as usual, was quiet and keeping his own counsel. She felt the usual distaste at being in his company but tried to make sure he didn't realize it. Lance was someone she saw as an outsider. She couldn't help it and she had tried to suppress her feelings but she couldn't. He sat there and she felt nothing for him except a deep and abiding distaste.

Every time she saw Janie, she was reminded of just what this son of hers was capable of and, even though she knew it had been forgotten by most of the people she knew, she would never forget what he had done and she would never forgive him. The only saving grace he had was how he was with Kathleen. Although Lil loved her dearly, Kathleen irritated her if she was around her for too long. She wanted the girl to pull herself together and stop being such a weak and powerless individual but she knew that was something that would never come to pass. Kathleen was always going to be a weakling; it was in her nature and Lance had been the only one over the years who had the patience to spend time with her.

Lil sat back and waited for the men to finish chatting; they already looked as if they had been together for years and she took that as a good sign. Pat could do with a Jimmy Brick in his life and, like his father before him, he knew that as well as she did. She caught Lance staring at her and the good feeling disappeared as it always did when she had to acknowledge him in any way. She didn't voice her thoughts; she had learned to keep them hidden away but Lance knew how she felt and that knowledge pleased her. She didn't want him thinking they were ever going to bond; she knew that nothing in this world would ever make her love this boy.

Kathleen was sitting in the front room watching TV. She always watched Frank Spencer repeats and no one ever thought to change the channel. She laughed at his antics and it was a real laugh, a deep belly laugh that made everyone around her happy. Kathleen's nerves were bad and she had very little in her life that made her truly happy. As she watched Frank get caught on a skateboard and dragged behind a bus, she was roaring with laughter and Colleen and Christopher were also laughing. They were waiting for the program to end so they could turn over to Happy Days and the Fonz. But they were like the others: willing to forgo anything if it made Kathleen happy even for a few moments.

Eileen came into the room with a tray full of cups of tea and she saw that Kathleen's laughter was, once more, turning to tears. She swallowed down her irritation, feeling guilty for her annoyance at her sister's distress.

"Come on, Kath. Cheer up, love. You took your tablets?"

Patrick had taken Kathleen to a doctor in Harley Street and he had diagnosed her as a manic depressive, whatever that was. He had prescribed antidepressants and Kathleen was not happy about taking them. Only Lance seemed capable of getting her to swallow them. Once she had them she seemed spaced, admittedly, but at least she was happier. Eileen sat beside her twin and hugged her tightly.

"Come on, Kathleen. Stop this, will you? Drink your tea and take your pills. If you don't, I will be really upset. You take them for Lance but not for anyone else and when he gets in I want to be able to tell him that you took them for me without a row."

Kathleen didn't take her eyes off the TV but she swallowed the pills with the scalding hot tea and Eileen sighed with relief although Kathleen was still crying. The last few days she had been so low that they had nearly taken her back to the doctor again. But according to Pat, once the pills got in her system she would be much better. Well, Eileen hoped so. She was her twin and she hated to see her like this. She was so unhappy and, even worse than that, so uninterested in her life or the world around her.

She was a teenager and she was already like an old woman. Eileen, on the other hand, was full of life and enjoying every second with as much energy as she could muster.

She sighed once more and, picking up a small hand mirror and her tweezers, she set about tidying her eyebrows. She had her eye on a new boy at school and she was confident that she might just get him.

As much as she loved her sister, she was embarrassed by her at times. She had been off school for a few days and Eileen was ashamed to admit that she had actually enjoyed her absence. For the first time in ages she didn't have to watch her and take care of her, she could just go to school and be like the other kids. This thought made her ashamed and she smiled at her sister once more. She wished she had the patience of Lance; he seemed to know just what to do with her, no matter what her mood.

She knew Kathleen was her twin sister but she was past the stage where she put all her energy into her sibling. She wanted to be young and she wanted to enjoy her life and with Kathleen like she was, that was not an option.

Pat was outside the hostess club his mother had been working in for years and he was not impressed. It was scruffy, and not just the usual seedy scruffiness of Soho, all top show and dim lighting; this place was so dilapidated that it would be apparent even in darkness.

He watched as the doorman, a large black man, walked two men into the club. He observed that even the doorman was a scruffbag and that his suit had seen better days. He was going through the motions and that told Pat enough of what was going on around him. This was a front. The money this place earned was nothing compared to whatever else was going on here. The real business had to be a serious earner and his mother must have been aware of it at some level. He wouldn't press her on it though. He knew she was close-mouthed because she didn't want him and Brewster at loggerheads.

The bouncer came back out to the small foyer and recognized Pat. He knew who he was; Pat had established himself all over London. That this man knew him from the start was pleasing to him though. Either that, or someone had heralded his arrival, but he forced that thought away. Pat was on his own because Kathleen was on a mad half-hour and Lance had gone home to look after her.

Pat had phoned home earlier and got Eileen. He guessed Eileen wanted to go out and, knowing Lance would walk over hot coals for his little sister, she had probably exaggerated her symptoms so he would come home and take over. Pat grinned. Eileen was a shrewdie, bless her, and she had the right idea and all. Why have a dog and bark yourself? If you could get someone else to do it, why not?

"Can I help you, Mr. Brodie?" The man spoke with a quiet respect that Pat knew was genuine. Up close he saw that he wasn't that much older than he was himself. He was a good-looking boy; obviously of mixed-race parentage and obviously able to have an almighty row if the fancy took him.

"Where's Brewster?" It was a statement more than a question.

The doorman didn't move for a while; he was as still as a corpse as he made a decision that would affect the rest of his life. Glancing over his shoulder to make sure no one was eavesdropping, he said, "He ain't here but he will be back within the hour; he is meeting up with someone you know."

Patrick nodded slowly. "What's your name?"

The man held out a meaty fist. "Colin. Colin Butcher."

They shook hands and Pat felt the strength of him and the coolness of his palm. This was someone who would not easily be rattled and, once more, he wondered if this was a setup. He knew the different angles that were used in their business and in stir he had been taught all about them and how to deal with them, by the masters.

But his instinct told him that this boy was good and he decided to trust in it. After all, it had never let him down before.

"I think I'll wait then, if you don't mind?"

Colin smiled then and he looked a completely different man. He had a wide, open smile that was automatically guaranteed to make whoever was on the receiving end of it feel relaxed.

Pat knew then that this man would be an asset to any business. He had the right demeanor and the sense to keep quiet.

"Can I get you a drink?"

Patrick nodded. "I think I'll go through to the bar and wait there."

They walked in the club together and Pat felt comfortable with him. He also felt optimistic when he saw the full extent of the club's shabbiness. It was a dump, and dumps were always easier to reclaim than palaces. He suddenly remembered walking in here with his father and he noted that it had the same flock wallpaper on the walls and the same dark-grey carpet that he remembered. It smelled of cigarettes, cheap deodorant and desperation, and he decided that it smelled just like Brewster himself.

Ordering a large Scotch, Pat settled himself at the bar and looked the hostesses over. They were watching him warily and he knew they were wondering if he would be as big a shit to work for as Lenny Brewster. He hoped not.

Hookers bothered him. Not because of how they earned a living but because the very act that made them money was also the thing that stripped away their self-esteem and their enjoyment of ever being with a man. Once women resorted to the game they saw everyone around them as marks and this was what made them so unreliable in the long run. They had no loyalty to anyone, not even themselves.

Pat noted everything around him without even seeming to glance away from his drink. Another little trick he had taught himself in jail; unexpected eye contact could be the death of you and, in certain prisons, it often was. He had also learned patience and he stood now, completely relaxed and at ease with his surroundings, and waited for Brewster to return.

Spider was watching his son play snooker and he was also watching the time. He knew it was early yet and that Pat wouldn't be there for a long while, but he was nervous. Something he had not been for many a long year.

The boy was a grafter, no doubt about that. He was also a handful; he had heard great things about him in prison and he knew that now he was out and about he was determined to get what he saw as his due. Not just his due, but his mother's due as well. She had been royally used and it was common knowledge. Pat and Lance had been kids and had not understood the seriousness of what had happened but now they were men, and men had a habit of taking great pleasure in reaping revenge when they could.

Spider watched the people in the bar, most of them had had run-ins with Brewster; he had not made a point of keeping friends close. Yet it was friendships and families that were the backbone of their way of life. You needed people you could depend on and that you could trust. Loyalty was important, especially if anyone got their collar felt. Keeping your trap shut when questioned by the police and doing your time without a squeak was considered the correct way to behave. Brewster had so many enemies now that he would only need a phone booth for a meet with his most trusted friends and advisers.

He had approached Patrick through other people, not even having the nerve to do the dirty deed himself. It was common knowledge and no one who knew about it was impressed. Everyone was waiting though and no one was going to say a word until the two had met and an outcome was decided. Until then, it was a waiting game and the waiting should finally be over tonight.

Jimmy Brick and Lil were walking into the club just as Lenny emerged from his car. His driver always dropped him outside the doorway, in full sight of his doormen and his workforce. The club itself earned a bit of dough but it wasn't really anything to shout about. It was his office space and where he went to plan or execute his serious skulduggery.

Seeing Lil with Jimmy, he felt his usual anger rising to the surface.

"All right, Jimmy? Long time no see." His voice was louder than he intended and he knew he was overdoing the friendliness. Him and Jimmy had never really been mates; in fact they had only tolerated each other.

But he knew he had to make an effort; he had realized that his usual disinterested rudeness would not go down too well at the moment.

Young Pat, as he was being called by all and sundry, seemed to have the same force as his father; it seemed that people were drawn to him. They had a high regard for him and he was only twenty. It was a fucking diabolical liberty to expect him to meet up like he was some kind of fucking gofer. But he knew that he had to figure this out and make sure that he was at least *seen* to be doing the right thing.

Now, in the middle of it, he had Jimmy Brick looking at him like he was last night's one-night stand. Lil was watching him; she had lovely eyes and, in fairness, she was still a very shaggable woman. Although Lenny was often seen with young women, he was actually far happier with the grown-ups. He liked his women to have a bit about them; liked to take the woman from someone else if possible. It suited his strange sense of humor. There was nothing like shagging a rival's bird or, even better, a rival's old woman. It added to the excitement as far as he was concerned, and it also marked the spot, like a dog pissing on a street corner to mark his territory. It let everyone know he had been there and he had done that.

Once he had acquired them, used them and made his point, he discarded them without a second's thought. They were old news, so why would he keep them on board?

Now, though, as he followed a silent Jimmy into the club, he felt the urge to laugh. He had arranged a little reception for them all and he was looking forward to seeing their surprise when they realized what was coming their way.

Jimmy Brick was not happy about taking Lil in with him but he had no choice now; she was coming inside with him or without him.

As they walked up the rickety stairs towards the office, Lil was reminded of how many times she had made that journey over the years. Now it seemed that this club was once more going to play a part in her destiny and in the future of her children. She was surprised to find that she was shaking.

She kept thinking that Lance should have been there. That no matter what she thought of him privately, he should have been there with Pat to sort this out once and for all. It would always be remembered that he had not been present and she knew that, in years to come, it would cause problems.

Pat Junior was already inside; he was actually seated behind the old desk, the desk that she had bought one sunny afternoon from Camden Market with Patrick. Now it was scarred from years of hot cups of tea and unattended cigarettes. It was scratched and stained but it still held a certain charm for her. And she could see her husband behind it once more, in the guise of her eldest son. Never had he looked more like his namesake than he did now. He had the same cold look, the same easy manner and the same promise of violence if he didn't get what he wanted.

Lenny saw him sitting there and, keeping a lid on his anger, he said loudly, "I hope you'll jump in my grave as quick, son."

He went to the small bar and poured them drinks; he was amazed to find that his hands were shaking, visibly shaking, and he knew that the boy had the edge over him for the moment. He had received no answer to his jocular taunt and he understood, for the first time, just how precarious his position actually was. There were none of his aides in the room, no one seemed to have arrived as arranged. In fact, even Colin was absent and that in itself was a revelation because he was up for promotion. He had been earning his stripes for a while and now it seemed he was happy to retreat when the trouble arrived. Colin was not a fool, he had a decent enough shit-detector and Lenny was aware of that; he had a similar one himself. It had kept him out of trouble for many years. Until now that is. Lenny had a trump card though, cards even; he had kids with Lil and they were half Pat's blood as well. He was confident that Pat wouldn't do anything too outrageous to the man who had sired his younger siblings. Patrick was like his father; he saw himself as far too decent to do anything like that. It was a weakness and he would find that out before too long.

Lil had sat down on the chaise-longue kept in there in case anyone wanted forty winks or needed a breathing space if things got out of order in the club. Many a hostess had drunk a cup of tea and vented their spleen on that sofa; it was a way of diffusing a situation that could become very difficult if not handled properly. Hostesses were fighters and they loved to fight one another when the fancy took them; a slight seen where none was intended or drugs were consumed and then caused paranoia. Now though, it seemed it was to be the throne that Lil sat on as her son reclaimed his father's businesses.

Everyone was seated now and Lenny was left standing in his own office. He stared at them all with his usual aplomb; as if nothing bothered him, which, until tonight, it actually hadn't. He leaned nonchalantly against the bar; his handmade suit was crumpled and his eyes were red-rimmed from the drink he had consumed that afternoon. Even the good whisky he had poured for himself tasted bitter somehow.

Lenny kept glancing at the door, expecting someone to enter, even though he knew deep inside him that that was not going to happen. Patrick seemed to know what he was thinking because he said quietly, "No one's coming to your rescue, mate. I saw to that days ago."

Lenny Brewster shrugged. "Am I supposed to be scared or something?" His voice sounded much more confident than he actually felt.

"Come on, Lil, sort this boy out, will you?" His voice was deliberately scornful; he knew he had to make an impression and he also knew he was in big trouble. For the first time in years he was afraid, mortally afraid.

Lil didn't answer him. No one had expected her to. She got up though and, walking to her son, she kissed him on the cheek. Then she said heavily, "You can't talk your way out of this one, Lenny. You have to stand there and take what's coming to you."

Her voice was his undoing; that she was there to see all this, to see him brought so low, was more than he could bear. It had finally dawned on him that no one was going to come up, that no one was going to help him. He was surrounded by his enemies and that was through choice; he had only ever made enemies.

The girl he had been with earlier had slipped into the club itself and he knew then that even she had heard a whisper about what might happen. She had covered her bases all right, but that even a slut like her was in the know, devastated him.

Young Patrick was still sitting there quietly. His deep-blue eyes were expressionless and his body taut and young. Looking at him, Lenny knew that he couldn't compete. But he was far from finished and he wouldn't go down without a fight.

"I ain't fucking standing for this, boy. I ain't your father, letting meself be taken like a fucking rabid dog. Looking forward to your birthday this year, son?"

Lenny Brewster had never carried any kind of firearm; he knew that if you packed a weapon you were putting yourself up for a seven-year stretch on possession of firearms charges. He had thought he had been so clever, making sure everyone around him was packing, but now he wished he had one to hand so he could blow these bastards off the face of the earth without a second's thought.

Patrick was unmoved by his words, was not going to be goaded into anger. He was calm and collected. Lil could see her son's demeanor and, standing up quickly, she said, "I'll be downstairs when you want me. The girls will need a firm hand and the sooner I start, the better."

As Lil walked towards the doorway, Lenny, his anger as always a heartbeat away, pulled his arm back ready to take a swipe at her. As he did so, Patrick and Jimmy were up and ready for him. But it was Lil who retaliated first. She grabbed a whisky glass off the bar and, with all her strength, she smashed it into his face. As he felt the glass break, the slicing of his skin, he was so shocked he didn't even move. Putting up his hand, he held it to his cheek, feeling the skin flapping as it hung in chunks from his cheekbone. Bringing his hand away from his face, he stared down at the crimson blood and knew then that he was finished. It was over. Lil had finally got the last word and he appreciated the irony of it. He had spent his life using anyone and everyone around him and he had known his time would come; it was inevitable. He just hadn't thought it would be at the hands of the Brodies. He smiled sadly, feeling the pain now. As the cuts began to sting, he knew Lil had been entitled to that one blow at least. He had hurt her enough over the years.

Lil watched the blood seeping down his face; the bone was exposed and she was amazed that she didn't feel auseous. He looked awful and it didn't bother her. She had no feelings either way about the wounds she had inflicted on him.

The shirt Lenny wore was drenched in his blood and she looked at it and felt a measure of relief. He had tortured her and worse than that, he had ignored her children; his own flesh and blood. For that alone she wanted him to hurt. The years of his abuse and his hate was spurting out of her now.

"Fuck you, Lenny. Fuck you, you rotten bastard. You took my Pat from me and you fucking knew you had when you came creeping around my house. You used me and you fucking enjoyed it."

He watched her and then he laughed. "Course I didn't. Who the fuck would want you lot? Tell me that? A fucking washed-up has-been and her gaggle of kids. Your cunt's bigger than Dartford Tunnel, darling. You're a fucking joke to me, you always were."

Patrick walked over to Lenny then. Lenny saw the look in the boy's eyes as he goaded him once more. "Your mother's son, you are, eh? A tart, she was a fucking tart, boy. She flogged her fanny in this very club. It's a wonder she never fucked your Lance. Let's face it, he'd be up for it, wouldn't he? Weird ponce that he is. And what about the twins, eh, the loon and the lesbian? I wouldn't want to be part of the Brodie family for all the coke in fucking Colombia."

Lenny couldn't understand why no one was doing anything about what he was saying. They were just standing there as if he was invisible. Then he saw that Lil had put her hand up, that she was stopping them from retaliating. The fact they were willing to do as she asked amazed him. Women had no place in his world; they were less than nothing. In fact, he had never once been bothered about one in his life.

Now, he saw the power women could wield over their sons or their lovers and he was glad he had never been reduced to anything so fucking humiliating.

"What about Colleen and Christy? What about them, Lenny?"

He laughed. His face was really hurting now and he could feel the blood dripping on to the floor. It was surreal, the whole thing was surreal.

"What about them, Lil? They mean nothing to me, no more than you ever did."

It was said so nastily and with such malice and hatred that Lil couldn't listen to him any more.

"You took everything from me, Lenny, but it doesn't matter. None of it matters any more because if I got nothing else from you, I got those kids and they are worth the world."

She looked at him then and she saw the blood and the sweat and she also saw the fear. He was frightened out of his life and she knew he had always been frightened of something or someone. Even Patrick had been taken out by the Williams brothers; this man would never have had the guts to do it himself. He had been the catalyst for all her family's ills and yet he had also given her two children she adored.

Her fear of him was gone; she had marked him as he had bragged about marking her. He had seen his children as nothing more than chains to keep her bound to him and they had been doing exactly that for far too long. Her son was going to rectify everything that had happened to them and, at last, she was going to be free of this man and his hate.

"I'll see you two later."

Lil walked from the room then and she felt lighter than she had in years. People thought that violence solved nothing and they were right. But she also knew that sometimes rough justice was all that people like her had left.

Lenny watched her go. He had the demonic look of a maniac and he watched in fear as Jimmy Brick and Pat Brodie took heavy chains from their pockets and then wrapped them delicately around their knuckles. He knew he would die in agony and then only after a long beating.

"I am going to enjoy this, Lenny, you fucking piece of shit."

He laughed at them, he was on autopilot now. "And what will you tell your little brother and sister, Pat? That you murdered their dad? I bet that will go down a fucking bundle, won't it?"

"They won't give a shit. They think you're a twat anyway, Lenny; they don't even like you."

Patrick pulled the chain tight and gave him a hard belt; he made sure it landed on the wound his mother had already inflicted. He had learned that one in prison; if the person you were fighting had any kind of wound, worry it and keep at it and the pain would be much more intense. It was the psychological angle and all. Once a cut was there it was human nature to try to protect it from more harm.

"You are going to die, Lenny, and do you know, not *one* of your fucking blokes tried to stick up for you. Not one of them questioned what we were going to do to you."

Jimmy grinned then and Lenny knew he would be over the moon at his part tonight.

"You are one fucking wanker and you spent your life taking what you wanted. Well, now it's my turn."

Jimmy had the chain and he also had a Stanley knife and he opened up Lenny's belly with it.

Lenny felt the sting as it sliced into his skin and he saw Patrick Brodie watching the proceedings with a casual air. He knew that this was indeed his father's son. It was no more than he expected, and he hoped he would take all he had to come, like a man. Patrick Senior had, he knew. He had not once begged for his life and he had put up a fucking good fight and all.

When Patrick started to lay in to Lenny, Jimmy stepped back and watched it all with a quiet interest. He observed the younger man and knew he was going to be all right. Like his father, he had the right temperament for skulduggery and prison life.

Within minutes, Lenny Brewster was begging for mercy, but he didn't get any.

Lil could hear him screaming with pain, as could everyone in the club. No one mentioned anything though. The hostesses who were not occupied with customers sat on the meat seats smoking and drinking and acted like they couldn't hear anything.

Lily Brodie felt, for the first time in years, on top form once more. She felt the weight of Lenny's anger and his hatred dropping away from her. Even though the father of two of her children was being murdered, somehow it just didn't seem wrong to her. She turned up the music until the sound of the Stylistics drowned out Lenny Brewster's screams.

Lenny was begging for his life as they sang, "Betcha By Golly Wow." It seemed a fitting tribute as far as Lil was concerned. The girls were watching her carefully and she knew that they were not going to give her any trouble. They knew the score better than anyone.

As Lil stood behind the bar and surveyed her domain, she felt the rush of excitement course through her veins.

Then, picturing her Patrick in her mind's eye, she knew he would have been proud of his son, his firstborn.

Colin the doorman winked at her and she smiled then. Life could only get easier from now on and she had waited a long time for that to finally happen.

Lenny Brewster's body was never found. He had been put in the crusher of a scrapyard in south London, his coffin being the trunk of a Hillman Imp.

He had still been lucid as he was thrown into the trunk by Patrick and Jimmy. Patrick had been determined on that much and Jimmy had been happy enough to go along with it. The last thing Lenny had seen was the two men smiling down at him as they slammed the trunk shut. He had heard the sound of the crusher as it had been cranked up and he had felt the car being raised from the ground. As it swung in the air the car had felt like a metal prison and Lenny knew that no one would care that he had disappeared, that no one would even bother trying to find out what had happened to him.

The noise of the metal as it was crushed into a small cube masked the screams of the man inside as he felt the heavy crush-bars coming towards him. The car buckled and bent as he tried frantically to scratch his way out. The lifeforce was so strong that he was still attempting to escape as his head was gripped as in a vice, and his body dismantled with bloodcurdling ease. When the small cube finally passed through the machine and landed with a quiet thud on to the dirt floor, Jimmy saw Patrick hawk deeply in his throat and spit on it.

An hour later, Spider was surprised to see the two men come into his drinking club and he knew then that it was all over.

Chapter Twenty-Three

Kathleen was in bed and no one could get her up. She couldn't seem to get herself together. Lance, as always, was spending as much time as he could with her. He talked to her for hours in his low voice, calming her down and making it easier for everyone else in the house. Lil couldn't keep her patience with her daughter; considering everything *she* had to contend with on a daily basis, a teenage drama queen was not something she had much sympathy for. The doctor said she was depressed, but how could a girl that age be depressed? And about what, for fuck's sake? The price of make-up, the new fashions; it was hard to understand. But Lil still felt guilt over Kathleen and her inability to make everything all right for her. The doctor had pilled her up and left them to it.

Now she had all this shit to contend with and, Annie being Annie, was also in the frame. She was with the pair of them as often as they would allow her and, as good as Annie might be now, Lil still remembered how she had treated her all those years ago. She knew that her mother had caused a lot of the problems in her life. Probably in her kids' lives as well.

Lil was still getting over the night's events. Even though her heart was telling her it was wrong, she was relieved that Lenny Brewster was out of all their lives at last. He had been an enormous presence; even when he wasn't around, his personality and his hatefulness had hung over the house like a shroud. His absolute disregard for the children had hurt, not just her, but them too. Then, he would arrive out of the blue, and the anger in him would make everyone feel uneasy. Lenny had enjoyed the fear his presence created and she had hated herself for what she had put her family through. The kids had felt his indifference from an early age. Now they would not have to go through the trauma of knowing he was nearby and that his absence was a deliberate ploy to hurt them, even at their young age. Her Patrick, her boy, had saved them from him; he had done what should have been done many years before; he had wasted him. He had removed him from their lives like a cancer that had flourished, strangling the life out of everyone in its orbit.

Lil had been at her lowest ebb when Lenny had come to her and, although she had known he was not the best of men, she had believed he would at least care for them all. Taking on Brodie's family had made him look like he was a good man, a decent man. That he had seen them all right. But, like Patrick before him, he had seen *himself* all right without a thought for her or her kids. Even Patrick, the love of her life, had left her destitute. He could have made sure they were looked after, *should* have made sure they were looked after, and she had to admit to herself that he just had not bothered. She had not only lost her husband, the father of her children, she had also lost everything they had. She had ended up a prostitute to make ends meet. They had five children, *five*, and he had not even had a will of any description. He had not allowed for his death, for his children's futures. It still rankled, still hurt her when she thought about it. She had loved him like she had loved no other. He had been her world and while he was there, he had looked after her, she didn't dispute that. But what had gradually occurred to her over the years was that he hadn't seen her as a soulmate, as an equal. He had seen her as his *wife*.

But now that Lenny had been disposed of, she felt as if she had been given another chance at life. She refused to mourn Patrick or the life she had once enjoyed any more. Her boy was home and he was taking over, like his father before him, and she hoped against hope that he wouldn't double-cross her as well.

Lil walked up the stairs and popped her head into Kathleen's room. She was lying there, her face turned to the wall and her shoulders hunched under the covers. It was a nice room, the girls had always kept their room nice. Lil looked around her then, as if seeing it for the first time. It was clean but it was in desperate need of redecoration. Patrick had given her enough money to get the place taken care of and she was going to do just that. As she sat on her daughter's bed she felt her usual irritation at the girl's complete lack of anything even resembling a life. She hid it as best she could, for the most part, but seeing this beautiful girl with her whole life ahead of her just lying in bed for weeks on end made her so angry; she hated the waste of a life. Or of a youth that Kathleen was too *young* and *stupid* to realize would be over before she knew it.

As Kathleen opened her eyes and looked up at her mother, Lil saw the same loneliness there that she had seen in her own eyes all those years ago, and she couldn't understand it.

Kathleen had a whole network of people who cared for her, and yet she chose to waste her life away in a bedroom, and with a sadness that made her mother sick with guilt every day of her life.

Lily forced down the annoyance and said, with as much interest as she could muster, "You feeling better, love?"

Kathleen nodded, slowly as always, as if the movement of her head was a really complicated maneuver and the question she had been asked was verging on life or death.

Lil had to clench her fists to stop herself from physically dragging this child of hers from the bed and slinging her out on to the street to force her to join in with real life; whether she wanted to or not.

Lil took deep breaths. She periodically felt like this about her daughter and, when she did lose it, she was always stopped by the others and made to feel so bad about what she had done. But Kathleen seemed to enjoy her depression too much for her liking.

"Have you eaten?"

"I can't, Mum, I feel so bad." Her voice had a whine in it that once more spelled danger to Lil, and she nodded gently before turning to leave the room.

"Mum?" The voice was stronger now and Lil turned to face it.

"What, love?" She was trying her hardest to hide her irritation; her short temper was already on a low fuse.

Kathleen looked deep into her eyes and Lil saw the black circles and the grey skin that told her she really was unwell.

"I don't mean it, you know. I don't *want* to feel like this. I don't want to *be* like this, so unhappy and so tired all the time. I can't help it, Mum, I just can't help it."

Lil's anger dissolved then, and she felt the usual rush of guilt. She didn't know what to do for her baby girl who was hurting, and she didn't know what would make it better. She didn't know how to make the pain stop.

She sat on the bed and took Kathleen in her arms, feeling the softness of her as she hugged her tightly. "I know you don't mean it, Kath, I just wish you wasn't feeling bad in the first place."

As she tried to stroke her daughter and comfort her, Kathleen pulled away from her. "Don't you ever hate life, Mum?"

Lil smiled then, a tiny, tired smile, and she answered her honestly, but with an edge of sarcasm to her voice: "Every day of my life, darling, every day of my fucking life."

Sergeant Smith was tall; tall and thin and he had a bad case of psoriasis. He spent the best part of his days scratching himself and, as he sat with Pat and Lance, they both watched him in morbid fascination. He was like a monkey in a zoo, except he had brown hair and watery grey eyes. Patrick knew he had been on the roll for a while; he was close with them all, at least he thought he was, and he was happy enough to change allegiance when he deemed it necessary. Like now, with Brewster's timely disappearance.

Like all dirty cops, he was not to be trusted. If he was capable of selling out his workmates, his so-called colleagues, he was not to be trusted any more than you would a rabid dog or a pregnant whore. That was why the people they dealt with had to make sure they had some insurance. Something that could be dangled over their heads when a point needed to be made or someone needed to be reminded of *exactly* who they were and, more to the point, who they were dealing with. His name was Roland and few people were aware of that. Those who knew were not brave enough to use it. He was always called Smith.

As he sat with the Brodie boys he was happy to take his payoff and assure them that he was happy enough with the change of management that had recently occurred. Smith was a shrewdie; he had a bastard of a boss who, he made sure, was never, ever, in any kind of compromising situation.

Smith had been Pat's go-between since day one and he was quite content with that. They were paid well and were rarely asked to do anything of merit. That the day would eventually come, they were both sure but, until then, they were content to go with the flow.

"Tell Scanlon I want a meet with him and I want it soon."

Smith was suddenly unsure how to answer the young man before him; he had the look of the convict about him and that wasn't unusual seeing as how he was one. But he also had a hard edge to his voice that told the listener he was not about to take any nonsense.

"Scanlon never meets anyone." This was said with a hint of amazement; Smith looked as if he had never heard anything so ridiculous in his life.

Pat stood up and took the money off the desk and he saw Smith's eyes widen slightly at his actions. "You tell fucking Scanlon that if he don't meet with me, I am going to fucking go over his head, all right? You ain't the only dirty cop in the game."

He opened a drawer and dropped the package inside it. "No meet, no dough. Sorry, mate."

Smith sat there for a few seconds, unsure how to react. Then Lance dragged him up bodily from his seat and bellowed, "Well, fuck off then! Tell the skank to get his arse in gear."

He pushed him towards the door then and Smith left as quickly as was possible without looking like he was running away.

Lance and Pat laughed at his exit.

"What a cunt, Pat."

"He will come in handy, don't worry."

Pat stretched with tiredness, rubbing his rough hands across his face and eyes.

He had achieved most of what he had set out to do. In fact, he had found it much easier than he would have believed. He had taken back what had been theirs in the first place and now he had to convince certain people that they were working directly for him. Lenny had made the mistake of never giving anyone their due, not respecting their part in any skulduggery that came his way or bothering to acknowledge their existence. Not a mistake Pat intended to make. He knew it was going to be hard, but he had a good back-up.

Pat also wanted to find out where his father's money had gone; even Lenny had not known the whole of it, where that was concerned.

But Pat knew a lot more than anyone realized; he had listened and watched his father as a kid and he had also known a lot more about who had been involved in the main businesses than anyone realized, his mother included.

Pat had promised himself that he would make amends, not just for him, but for his whole family. Every time he had been humiliated by Brewster or his mother had slipped out and prostituted herself for a few quid, the urge for retribution had been overwhelming. His father had been murdered and he was going to pay back everyone involved for that.

Pat was going to track down his father's assets if it was the last thing he ever did on this earth. He had to make it all right, he had to make sure that his family were secure at last.

Pat knew he was capable of keeping the businesses going and he also knew that his rep was already in place through his sojourn in prison. He had to act normal now, had to make sure that he was trusted and respected by all the people he would be dealing with. Then he would bide his time and when he had all the information to hand, all fucking hell would be let loose.

Pat saw his father's last moments every day of his life and he was not going to let that go, no way. He missed his father and he had ferreted out so much information with friendly chats and well-thought-out questions that he knew more about his father's last few deals than anyone else, especially the people his father had been dealing with. He was a good lad and he knew that was what his reputation was based on. But he was his father's son and, one day, people would realize that.

"You all right, Pat?"

Lance had seen him staring into space. Ever since they were kids, Patrick had gone off into his own world; he just sat and stared at nothing.

Lance hated it, hated the fact that Pat was not on his wavelength. He watched Patrick close his eyes and then, taking a few deep breaths, he came back to the real world once more.

"You were fucking miles away."

Pat laughed. "If only you fucking knew the half of it."

They laughed together then. Lance was much happier, knowing that Lenny was gone and that his association with him was over was making him feel better and more secure by the hour.

Pat wouldn't understand his actions, he knew, but he had done what he could to keep all their heads above water. Pat had always made him feel inadequate; he had fucked up big time when they were kids, and he regretted that, had regretted it ever since. He had been a kid and he had not understood what he had done to that girl. If he saw her now he felt bad inside.

Pat was remembering the day his father died. His father's murder had made him understand at an early age what being dead really meant, had shown him how much blood the human body actually held. His father's blood had been everywhere; it was sprayed all over the walls and covered the floor. It had been everywhere and he could remember seeing pieces of his father's brain tissue on the floor beside his body that night. That sight had never left him, had never left any of them. It had changed all their lives; in seconds, all they knew and all they had believed in had disappeared. Pat remembered going to the hall the next day. The balloons and the bunting were still up and the food, laid out ready to eat and enjoy, was now dried-up and stale. The presents still piled up on a table. Patrick had never again celebrated a birthday.

Pat thought about how much he missed his times with his father; the evenings when he would talk him through life and his role in the family. His father had asked him to do errands for him; a bit of ducking and diving, and so he knew much more about what had been going on than anyone realized. He would bide his time and get the money back. Get the lot back and, when he did, he would slaughter the person involved and enjoy every second of it.

Everyone knew that he had taken out Brewster and he was pleased about that. He'd wanted Lenny's death to be a statement, not just for the people around abouts, but for the people he had met in prison too. He still had a few of them to prove his worth to and he knew this act would be enough. Lenny was already old news and Patrick wanted his name coupled with his forever. When people talked about Lenny dying they would talk about the young man who had been responsible for it happening.

It had started his legendary status off perfectly and it was almost a public service. It wasn't a murder, it was more a culling and Lenny was to be the first of many.

Jimmy Brick was in the Prospect of Whitby pub; he was having a drink with a few old mates and his reception had pleased him no end. As he saw the drinks being bought, and heard the jokes being told, he settled down and felt the relief once more at being part of the winning team. It seemed that his contribution to the recent events had put him in good stead once more with the people that were important.

"Hey, Jimmy, I hear that Brewster was well fucking gutted when he was taken out. Is that true?"

Jimmy grinned. A few beers short of a witness statement, he knew that the circumstances were probably common knowledge by now. In a joking voice that was just loud enough to be heard by the people surrounding him and a few of the eavesdroppers standing nearby, he said, "Well, when he realized that he was on the way out, he was completely *crushed*, I can tell you." Jimmy nodded his head in derision and knew that he had made a statement that would be remembered and repeated for a long time to come.

Everyone laughed again and Jimmy was aware that Spider was smiling with the others but not, in any way, committing himself. But then, Spider never had overcooked the turkey; he was far too shrewd and still was, by the looks of it. Jimmy knew how fragile villains' friendships could be; unless you were born and bred with someone, how the fuck could you really trust them? Jimmy's instinct was telling him that he couldn't trust Spider as far as he could throw him.

He also understood that Lance had absented himself from the main event and that told him that he was also someone to watch closer than a cop with stolen goods.

He drank his drink and he watched the people around him; he knew how to play the game and it was why he was still on the dance floor all these years later. Young Patrick Brodie was going to be his golden goose; it was like having Pat back in the team. Like his father, he had the spark, that little bit of extra something that made people listen to him and respect him. And he also had the violent streak that was so attractive in men of their ilk.

Jambo Delaney was a good-looking man. He had broad shoulders, a strong jaw and he walked with a straight-backed strut that made him very attractive to the opposite sex. He had been given the nickname Jambo, Swahili for hello, as a young man. Everyone wanted to say hello to him; he had that kind of face, that kind of demeanor about him. No one could not like him, it was impossible not to like him. He had no bad points really. Not only was he great company, he also fitted in with any crowd. But he could, when required, have a row too. A real row, a row that stopped errant husbands from forcing their opinions on him or trying to get a reaction of any kind.

Left alone, he was good company and well worth an evening's drinking with, but upset, he was a different kettle of fish. Once first blood had been drawn he would defend himself with such vigor and strength that the assailant would always retreat in haste. He was a man who would let the first punch go for free; anything over and above that and he was entitled to defend himself and defend himself he would.

Jambo was a nice guy, if a little lazy, and a little forgetful. Sometimes he didn't know who the husbands were talking about; he'd forgotten the women involved, even though they rarely forgot him. As far as he was concerned, they were an interlude, a good time and, in some cases, a means to an end. But he never meant to hurt anyone, wife or husband; he never set out to cause any heartbreak.

Jambo earned cash by being a bodyguard, debt collecting or talking his way into company. He was a womanizer and, like all womanizers, he never understood why women took him so seriously. What made them think he was going to treat them any different to any other woman he had been with? Why did they always think they were the one who would change him, make him settle down and want to be with in the same place for the rest of his life? His famous last words were always the same thing. The four Fs: he fucked them, he fed them, he fought with them and he fucked off when they got on his nerves.

He was sitting opposite Lil Brodie, a handsome woman with a fine brood of children and a healthy sexual appetite. He liked and respected Lil, with whom he had often had a few drinks and a little bit of bump and grind, but today he noticed that she looked a bit worse for wear.

He knew her son was home from jail and causing a bit of a stir on the streets and Jambo was suddenly feeling a little bit nervous. Errant husbands were one thing, sons, especially young Pat Brodie, were another thing entirely. Not that he wouldn't defend himself, but he liked the boy. He was a good kid and he had not had many breaks.

"Jambo, you're not going to like what I have to tell you, but I'm pregnant."

Jambo nodded slightly. He knew it was pointless asking her if she was sure; this was Lil and she would be more than sure before she would even think about discussing it. He was also not going to ask if it was definitely his, he had more sense than that.

Lil watched his face and felt bad for him; he was a nice bloke and he didn't deserve this really. But she knew she had to tell him anyway.

"You want it?"

He wasn't asking her anything except what did *she* want, and she loved him for that alone. There were no recriminations, no stepping back as if he had never been near her in his life, no stroppiness and no body language that said, as soon as you look away, I will be out the door so fast you will wonder if you had shagged an Olympic athlete.

He was calm and interested in what she wanted to do about the situation. She was grateful for that much at least.

"I ain't got a lot of choice, mate, I'm Catholic. If it's there then what can I do?"

She shrugged then and he smiled at her. He liked Lil, he really liked her attitude to life and love. She was calm about it and she was not demanding anything from him.

"What do you want from me?"

It was a fair question, she thought. A nice question really. She knew Jambo was a man who cherished his single state and she understood why he felt that way. She was of a similar disposition herself these days. A baby was the last thing she wanted, or needed, but the child was created now and there was nothing to do except love it as best she could.

If she disposed of it, Lil knew she would never know another happy day. Not that there had been many of them over the last few years. But in Lil's mind, a child didn't ask to be born and she had no right to remove it from her body just because it wasn't convenient. For all her lifestyle, the Catholic part of her kicked in with her hormones.

"Can I be honest, Jambo?"

He nodded slowly, but he was wary enough, she sensed that much.

"I'm only telling you because I thought you had a right to know. I don't want anything from you, mate, not really. No undying love, no special treatment, no money even. I just want you to do me a favor, one thing, and that's all I will ask of you."

"What's that then?"

Lil grabbed his hand and squeezed it tightly, and Jambo knew she was a woman on a mission and that if he had any sense, he would make sure she got what she was asking for.

"Just give the child the time of day, not every minute of your time, I know you can't do that. But just for once in my life, I want one of my kids to feel that someone other than their mother cares for them. That is all I want. No more than that, Jambo. Just a visit occasionally to let them see your face and know who you are."

Jambo nodded and he felt so sad for her then. He knew how hard Lil's life had been, knew how much her family meant to her and had even guessed how much she resented them at times as well. That was real life, though most people wouldn't admit that. Women were so unlucky; they were left in charge of a human being, sometimes a crowd of human beings, and they had to be seen as doing the best they could. They had to make sure that all these *people* were taken care of in every way.

No one ever allowed for them to be tired out, to feel abandoned or just be plain pissed off with what had befallen them and just because they had allowed a man to get too close. Because they had just followed their natural inclinations and produced, as nature had intended them to. Then they were left on their own, and the man leaving them was in the same condition he had arrived in, physically and mentally. The women they left behind though were now the grand owners of stretch marks and a screaming baby and their lives would never be the same again.

Jambo understood that, he knew what men were capable of. He was an expert in hurting people himself and an expert in keeping himself out of trouble. But now Lil was asking him for no more than his time; no marriage, no partnership and no undying love. She was just asking that one of her kids had some kind of father figure. He couldn't refuse her and it surprised him that he didn't want to refuse her. She deserved this much at least and she wasn't asking him for more than he was ever going to be able to give.

"If you think I will be any kind of a role model, Lil Brodie, you are mad. I will do what you want but you got to make sure that I ain't walking into any trouble, OK? Your boys are fighting for the top prize and I don't want them to feel they need to hurt me to prove a point, you know."

Lil smiled happily. "Do you want to know a secret, Jambo? My boys are still young enough to listen to what I say and even when they are old enough to bury me, I will still have a fucking say in *my* own life. Don't worry, OK, just give this child a chance, an *opportunity* to see that the man who fathered them is interested in them and still on the scene, and me and you will never fall out."

It was a threat and it wasn't a threat, Jambo knew that; like him, Lil spoke the words and let the listener decide what the meaning really was. He also knew that she was asking a lot from him, but he was already committed now, and also he was intrigued to see what the two of them had created. The color of the child was not a problem, he knew; the one thing he *was* sure of was that none of Lil's children would ever question their own flesh and blood.

The child would be a nine-day wonder, but he knew Lil wouldn't care about that at all. He was in a catch-22; he had, on the one hand, Pat Junior, a boy who was already talked about with reverence and, on the other, he had Lance, a thug who had already put the hard word on him in private about his relationship with his mother. But Jambo knew that Lance had only been doing what Brewster had told him to do. Lance had been Brewster's gofer, his errand boy, and he had fucked him off with a hate that told Jambo it was about more than Brewster's usual dog in the manger. It was too close to home for the boy; Lance wanted him gone for his own personal reasons. He kept that gem of wisdom to himself though; he was happy for Lil to do what she thought was right. He also knew that nothing he said would change her mind anyway. Once Lil made up her mind that was that.

"I am keeping this baby under wraps for a while; no one has noticed yet anyway. I am letting you know what I want from you if it goes full-term, that's all."

Jambo nodded once more.

"If that's what you want, Lil, then I am happy to go along with it as I already said. But I ain't promising you no more than what you asked, OK?"

Lil laughed then, a real hearty, loud and dirty laugh. "Oh, dream on. I wouldn't want you, darling, if your knob was dripping with diamonds and you farted perfume."

Now they were both laughing and Lil relaxed a little, happy she had for once done what she wanted and not waited to see what happened. This child would at least have a fighting chance in life, she was determined about that. And once the novelty of her situation wore off it would all work out somehow, she was sure. She had been through the worst that life could throw at anyone and she had survived. Older, harder and a little bit wiser but she was still managing to live through every day.

Now Patrick was home and he was trying to make amends for the past so she hoped that, sooner or later, life for this child inside her might just turn out to be easy.

Chapter Twenty-Four

"All right, Mum, let's sort this out, shall we?"

Patrick's voice was so reminiscent of his father's that it made Lil go cold. They were in the office of the club once more; it was different now, all fresh paint and cheap furniture. The club was the front for the other businesses, as always.

But it was once again Lil's domain and she knew it. She enjoyed the way she was now, back on top; it was like years ago, when this had been her world. Lenny Brewster had snatched it away from her, taken everything that she had that made her feel a part of something bigger than her. And now she had it back; her life back, her self-respect back and, most of all, she was once more working at something she loved.

It might be a small victory to most people, but to Lil, after the years with Lenny, it was equivalent to the Pulitzer Prize.

Lil knew that the girls understood how she felt; in fact they were happy for her, most of them anyway. That is, the ones who had bothered to get to know her and understood Lil's craving for some kind of recognition, and for her need to be a part of the world she inhabited and that she loved.

"Sort what out?"

Lil was smiling at Pat innocently and she saw *herself* in his eyes and in his anger, not his father. Pat had her short temper and her ability to keep it in check if it was necessary. He was a clever boy, no doubt about that, and she loved him with all her heart. But he was also her son and her business partner, whether he liked it or not. She was the one he had left to put things back on track again. She would be the one who made the money that would give them their way of life. The taxman could climb all over this place and find nothing that would be cause for concern. She was the straight one out of them and he respected that; he knew she would never double-cross her son. You could only ever trust your own, most of the time anyway.

Patrick grinned and his white teeth made him look even more handsome than usual. He had dark Irish looks; his eyes were the giveaway, deep blue, framed with thick lashes that a woman would fight to make her own. He had the square-cut jaw and thick black hair that seemed to have a life of its own. Pat also had the appetite for the drink and that bothered Lil, as did his disregard for anything he felt as beneath his interest. That had been his father's downfall, not that anyone else would see that, of course. Pat should have kept his own house in order, fuck everyone else's. If he had sorted the Williams brothers he would still be here now, and Spider knew that as well as she did.

"Are you pregnant, Mum?"

Lil stared into Pat's handsome face and suppressed the urge to slap his name out of the phone book. How dare the cheeky little fucker ask her that?

"Well, are you?" He was talking slowly now, as if she was stupid, as if she didn't understand what he was asking her.

"What has that got to do with you?" It was said with all the indifference she could muster and with all the bravado she possessed.

Pat sighed. "So it's true, then?"

Lil had been dreading this, but she was still surprised that Pat had noticed so quickly. He had girls, but no one ever lasted more than a few days, so he had not even lived through a girlfriend's or a wife's pregnancy. He was so cute, he had noticed hers. One part of her wanted to cry because of that, but she wouldn't, of course. Lil didn't know what to say to him. She felt guilty, as if she had done something wrong, and that was because she felt she had. It wasn't him, it was her. Once more, she was giving birth and once more she was having a child that would ultimately become this boy's responsibility, like the others had. But she could no more dispose of this baby than she could have disposed of any of the others. It was the eighties and there was no longer any stigma for women who had children without the benefit of a wedding ring.

"I am a grown woman and if I want to have a baby, I'll have one. You are not my keeper, Patrick. You are my son and you have no right to question me about anything."

Pat Junior looked into the eyes of the woman he loved more than he had ever loved anyone in his life and he shook his head in distress at her words. The anger she was displaying and the secrecy, the fact she was trying to conceal her condition from him and the other kids, hurt him. He didn't care what she did, why couldn't she see that? He loved her no matter what. This was the woman who had cared for him, loved him, visited him in prison and tried to fight his end all those years ago when his father had been murdered. This woman had given birth to two more children with Lenny Brewster because she had believed that they would give her and her kids some kind of security, because she had thought he would take care of her; thus enabling her to take care of them.

She had even sold herself for him and his brothers and sisters; why couldn't she see that all she had done had made him love her more, not less. Had made him look up to her, not down on her.

Pat walked over to her and, pulling her into his arms, he said sadly, "Oh, *Mum*, I just want to help you, darling, that's all. You can do what you like, I ain't going to judge you, am I? None of us would. I just don't want you coping on your own any more. You don't *have* to. I am here now and I will do whatever is needed, OK?"

Lil hugged him and felt the strength of him as he held her close and she knew he meant every word he said to her.

"Whose is it, Mum?"

She could hear the nervousness in his voice and realized that he thought she was pregnant by Lenny again. He couldn't even say his name out loud. It would be laughable if it wasn't so tragic. As if she would be that stupid! And yet once more she was reminded of how she was seen by her children. That this boy, her eldest son, could think that she would even *consider* sleeping with Lenny again after what he had done to them all was so insulting that she had to fight the urge to smack his face. She wanted to tear at his skin with her nails and make him hurt as he was making her hurt.

Did they really think she was so low, so base that she had been capable of coupling with Lenny again after everything he had done to her, to them?

She roughly pushed Pat away. Her anger was in check, but for how long, she couldn't say.

"You can't think this is Lenny's, surely?"

Lil's voice was low and colder than Pat had ever heard it before. He knew she had picked up on what had been in the back of his mind. He didn't answer her and it was his silence that told her all she needed to know.

"I would never ever have given him the time of day. How can you think that I would have been capable of something like that?"

Pat didn't know how to react to her, didn't know how to make things right. He knew he had been well off the mark. But he had had to ask her. Especially considering the events of the last few days.

"No one has said that, Mum. And I don't care what you've done . . ."

Lil sat back on the big leather chair that told anyone who came in that the occupier of that chair was the boss. That chair said that she was the boss of everyone and everything around her.

"*Done?* What I've *done?*" It was that word that hurt more than anything. It was like an assumption of her guilt or her stupidity. It made her feel responsible for something and she wasn't sure what.

"You cheeky little fucker, how dare you talk to me like that . . ."

Pat didn't speak; he knew she had to get it off her chest. He knew he had said the wrong thing and he understood her anger.

"I did what I could all my life to make things better for us. To make sure you and the others had some kind of fucking life outside of what was said about us, what was assumed about us, after your father's murder. I had to live through it and protect you lot into the bargain. Your father didn't even see us all right for a few bob, did you know that? We were left with *nothing*. It was like we never existed for him or anyone else, come to that, after he died. Do you realize that we could have been taken out?

If the Williams brothers had decided to finish us off, that would have been it. I had to fucking make sure we were safe and that meant Lenny. He took them out, for his own reasons, I admit, but he took them out all the same. We were seconds away from death, boy. Your father made no provision for us, fuck all. And now *you* have the fucking cheek to look down on me, to *judge* me. And you expect me to swallow an insult like that without attempting to dispute it in any way?"

"Look, Mum, I just want to help you, that's all. I don't give a fuck who the father is . . ."

"Well, you *should* and you should also have enough respect for me to ask me straight out and not fucking insinuate. That you could even contemplate that."

Patrick watched his mother's anger and hurt and knew that he could not do anything to stem the flow of her unhappiness. So he said what was on his mind and hoped that she would understand his worry about her and his annoyance at her silence over her predicament. He was shouting at her and that was something he had not planned on doing. He just wanted answers and he was going to get them from her. No matter what it took.

"Well, who is the culprit then, Mum? *You* tell me because I can't fucking put the finger on anyone. I just want to know the score, that's all. You are me mother and I feel a certain responsibility towards you, to all of you. I feel the need to take care of you because whoever the fucking bloke is, he ain't beating a path to your front door, is he? No one has seen you out with a geezer and there ain't even any gossip in this dump. So unless you enlighten us, how the fuck are we supposed to know anything? Were you going to wait until it was born or what?"

Lil didn't answer him. She just stared at him with those big eyes of hers and the guilt he felt was once more in the forefront of Pat's mind.

"Look. I didn't mean any of that. You can do what the fuck you like, you're me mum. But you have to let me know what's going on. I want to help, that's all. I want to make it easier for you. If the bloke needs a fucking talking-to then that is what he will get, believe me, Mother."

Lil's anger was gone and she could understand what was wrong with him. But how could she explain that she had been too embarrassed to tell them what had happened to her, that she was pregnant again at her age. Why was she always the one who was caught out? Even with them all grown up she was still stupid enough to get caught and, once more, it was by a man who had no interest in her really. Though in fairness to Jambo, he was willing to do as she asked. But that was only because of her sons; she assumed that was why, anyway. But they didn't need to know any of that, of course. Lance, whatever she thought of him, was always her biggest champion. Not that it made her feel anything towards him but she knew that anyone who said a word against her was dicing with death. Patrick, however, was more like her than he realized. He understood on some level that she was still a relatively young woman and she needed not just the sex, but the holding part. The aftermath, when she lay beside someone and pretended, just for a few minutes, that someone cared for her and was looking after her for once and not vice versa.

"I was sixteen when you were born, Patrick. Can you imagine that? I had five kids so fast I didn't even have time to realize how hard it was."

She laughed gently. "Then the other two, who I love more than anything. They were once more *given* to me, by a man who didn't really care about the consequences of his actions. He gave me two kids and it meant nothing to him. And now you have killed him." She laughed huskily at the incongruousness of her conversation, of the whole situation.

"All my children are fatherless and both fathers were murdered. Can't you see the irony in that? One day the youngsters are going to want to know what happened and they still won't give a fucking toss. Do you know how that makes me feel? Do you? All my life people have taken from me, taken whatever they wanted, you included. All you kids did and that's because that is what kids *do*. Kids just take."

Lil lit a cigarette and tried to relax herself enough to give this son of hers at least a modicum of peace of mind. To make what had happened to them at least mean something to him and to her as well, if she was honest.

"Now this baby wasn't planned, Pat. Its father was someone I *wanted*, someone who *wanted* me. No love story or big drama to report, just two people finding a little bit of happiness together. And now I am pregnant again and, being a Catholic, having the child and doing the best I can, once more, is the *only* solution for me. Just like I did with all of you and, be fair, I never had it easy, did I? I'm not saying this so that you will pity me. I am just stating facts, that's all. But I did the best I could."

Patrick shook his head, this time with exasperation. Lil could see the way he cared for her and she knew how lucky she was with them all, except Lance, but she didn't count him as hers. She saw him as her mother's.

"Oh, Mum. I have been so worried about you, that's all. I want you to be happy, you deserve to be happy."

"I don't want any trouble when the time comes. I will tell you everything, well almost everything, but don't hurt him or threaten him, none of you. I was just me when I was with him. Just Lil Diamond, not Patrick Brodie's wife or Lenny Brewster's bird or someone's mum. I was just me for once."

She smiled gently then. Her relief that the secret was out made her look almost girlish once more, wiping the lines of fear and worry away with each word she spoke.

"One last thing, son."

"What, Mum?"

Lil stared at him for long moments and he knew she was worried that he was going to lose any respect for her that he had. He waited for her to speak in case he said the wrong thing again. He knew that once he found out the culprit, he would sort the fucker out big time. In private and with a weapon, if needs be.

"What are you trying to tell me, Mum?"

"It's black, Patrick."

Lance was collecting a debt that had been owed for many years. It was a big debt, fifteen grand. Patrick had bought it for two thousand but only because the person who had borrowed the money in the first place had exhausted every avenue trying to get it repaid. It was now a debt for seventeen thousand as it was not just the original debt that needed to be paid in full but also the money laid out to purchase the debt in the first place. This was a good debt in more ways than one. It was a cheap debt to buy and so guaranteed a good return and it was also owed by a north London Face who needed to be brought down a peg or two.

Lance wanted to prove himself. He felt the need to show his brother that he could do things on his own and use his initiative and, more importantly, he didn't want Patrick having any dealings with Donny Barker unless he was present.

Lance knew his absence when Lenny was being outed was being whispered about; the gossip even said that he had been severely reprimanded. His absence had raised more than a few eyebrows, he knew. Kathleen and her problems were not really common knowledge; he knew that because he had made sure of it.

But there was still some talk about her though Lance always made sure the talkers realized their mistake. But Lance knew that he was not seen in the same light as his brother. He was determined to change that, he was determined to give his image a boost. He was going to make people respect him as they respected Patrick.

His brother had been lucky in so many ways; as the eldest, he had possessed the edge from birth. Their mother had always treated him with love whereas she had never once treated him with anything that even resembled love. Lance was convinced that everyone knew that she didn't care for him and that it was all pretend, that even now, she wouldn't speak directly to him if she could avoid it.

Lance loved Kathleen with the love he should have given to his mother if his mother had let him. Like him, Kathleen made his mother feel insecure, made her feel she had somehow fucked up, which of course she had. She thought she could pick and choose the children she wanted. Well, she couldn't.

His mother was the reason for everything bad that had happened to them all and she couldn't even admit it. So she dumped the blame on him and poor Kathleen. She was pregnant again; she produced children like other women shelled peas and with no shame or care for any of them, really. Another bastard would be produced by her and no one would be any the wiser as to who the father was. She didn't tell them anything, she didn't see it as any of their business. The girls, even his Kathleen, were all excited about it and acted like it was going to be some kind of joyous event. Yet not one of them had had the guts to mention it to her until she decided to tell them. Patrick wasn't even annoyed. He just wanted to know who the culprit was and if she was OK. No real bother about the fact she was knocked up once more, that another child would be produced and, knowing her, neglected. Patrick was so like her, he really didn't give a shit what people thought or how people perceived them as a family.

Well, one day she would see what she had done to them all, he would make sure of that. Lance knew so much about all of them and he never said a word but that could change, of course. If the need to open up presented itself he would not feel bad about it at all. It would not be the first time he had spilled the beans and he had a feeling it would not be the last.

Donny Barker walked out of his safe house then. Lance slipped out from the car he had stolen earlier that night and, walking over the road nonchalantly, he beat the older man to his vehicle. Donny was alone, a rare occurrence in his world, but, having seen Lance, he didn't feel any kind of fear. In fact, he smiled in recognition. Anyone observing them would have assumed that they were old mates or at least business associates of some description. But if they saw the look that was on Lance's face then they would realize that he wasn't smiling at all. In fact, he actually looked like most people's worst nightmare.

Eileen and the three younger kids were watching TV as usual. It was Saturday evening and they were all curled up on the sofa watching *The A-Team* and laughing at their antics.

Shamus, Colleen and Christy were used to being left to their own devices when their mother was working. It was strange, but they had known from an early age that without her out grafting, their lives would be a lot harder.

Unlike the others, who had been lucky enough to have a father who had been there at least some of the time for them, the three youngest had never had that kind of security.

And now Colleen and Christopher's father was out of their orbit, once and for all, they didn't really feel anything about him at all. Lenny

Brewster had not really been a part of their lives ever, so his death actually meant nothing to them. The rumors around and about were rife and they had heard a whisper now and again about him but, in actual fact, they were not bothered one way or the other. Eileen knew the score, she had already put two and two together for herself and, like her younger siblings, accepted it as part and parcel of their lives.

She still had the odd flashback to the night her father had been murdered; as young as she was, she still remembered some of it with stunning clarity. This was usually when she least expected it and usually when she really didn't need the reminder. Pat Junior had never celebrated a birthday since and it wasn't through want of trying either. Their mum had tried her hardest to make the day a celebration rather than the anniversary of their father's death. Now, though, none of them bothered. Patrick really didn't want the reminder and, as they had all got older, neither did any of them. Though they had always tried to make an effort for young Shamus's birthday, despite it coming so quickly after.

Eileen glanced at the clock. She would give it five minutes and then start getting herself ready to go out for the evening. At nearly fifteen years old she knew she looked much older. She also knew that if she didn't get out of this house on a regular basis, her twin sister's madness would infect her as well. She would never refer to Kathleen as mad in any way out loud but in her head she could think what she liked and she did. Frequently.

Kathleen was still confined to her bed and she was not eating anything of substance. For that matter, she was not even attempting to talk to anyone about what was wrong with her. Eileen was her twin and yet Kathleen still didn't trust her enough to talk to her about anything that was going on with her.

Eileen saw Colleen and Christopher whispering to each other, much the same as she had with Kathleen when they were younger.

"What are you two whispering about?"

Colleen laughed nervously. "Nothing much. We were just wondering if Lance was going to come home soon, that's all. Do you know when he'll be back?"

It was a fair question, Eileen knew. She knew they were both worried about Lance's return to the house.

She felt so sorry for him because everyone knew that their mum, the woman who had birthed them all, couldn't stand to be in the same room as him. It hurt him, she knew it did. She knew that it had to be the worst feeling in the world knowing that your own mother didn't care about you at all. Lance had known that for years and she had known about it since she could remember. Even these two had figured that much out.

"Lance is a grown man and he will come home when it suits him."

Eileen got up then and wandered from the room slowly. She was going out and the last thing she needed was anyone drawing attention to her; she was not silly, she knew that this family could blow up in a heartbeat.

Colleen and Christy waited until Eileen was out of earshot before they started laughing with Shamus. They knew where she was going and who she was going there with. It was strange that the other people in the house had no idea about her secret life.

But then again, she was fifteen in a few weeks and to them she was ancient and they knew that if they opened their mouths she would launch them into outer space without a second's thought.

Jimmy Brick and Spider were in a private club off the Caledonian Road. They were drinking Guinness and dancing warily around each other. Neither of them knew exactly how conversant the other one was with the current state of affairs. This was a very common dilemma for many people in the know.

Conversation could be very difficult because, unless you were part-nered with someone, or you had been briefed about a certain person, you could not talk freely to them without the fear of exposing informa-tion that could cause potential havoc. Spider and Jimmy went back a long way and so the situation was even more delicate than usual. Jimmy had been off the scene for many years and this was seen as cause for concern by Spider. Jimmy, for his part, knew that Spider had his own little firm and a respected firm at that. He also knew that his old pal was wary of him because of his prolonged absence. That was something he had not discussed with anyone, of course, and would not do so unless he felt the time was right.

So when Pat finally bowled in surrounded by his boys, young men like him who had done a bit of time and were willing to work for someone their own age who was going places, they were overly pleased to see him.

Spider watched Pat as he said hello to the right people, shook hands or patted the appropriate backs, and marveled once more at the boy's natural business acumen. Like his father he knew how to play the game. Only this young man had a hard edge to him that was apparent to anyone who had any dealings with him.

As he sat down, Pat looked tired but both the men could also see that he was more than able to hold his own if it should come to that at any point. His new guys, his new bodyguards, settled themselves nonchalantly around the bar. Spider saw immediately that they were in key positions so that if anything were to happen, they would be available to protect him within seconds. He was impressed; unless you knew the score, no one would have even realized what was going on. This told him that the boy was more protected and far more on the ball than anyone actually realized.

"All right, guys. Sorry I'm late, it's been a heavy day."

The two men didn't respond, they weren't expected to.

"Jimmy, I need you close; you must have guessed that was coming, mate?"

Jimmy smiled slightly but it was a smile that signified agreement as if he had indeed known what was going to happen all along.

Pat Junior smiled then and Spider saw the menace in him, the real menace, for the first time ever. He had known this boy from birth and now he watched him and he knew that he was a changed lad from the one he had seen grow up. This was a different man to the one who had come home from prison all smiles and group hugs. The man he had paid and whose own son had visited and seen all right.

Pat was now someone to be wary of, was someone who had no qualms about erasing the enemy, and the enemy, it seemed, was anyone who happened to disagree with him.

"I'm going to run everything as before. Brewster did a competent enough job but he did not bother to utilize all the different branches of the organization."

Pat looked at Jimmy again.

"You know that my father always had his finger on the pulse? Well, Lenny wouldn't let anyone in the firm get near to anyone else. Everything had to go through him and that's why it was so easy to take him out and buy up his so-called fucking workforce."

He stared at Jimmy then and it took a few seconds before Jimmy Brick realized that he was being dismissed. That Pat had said his piece and wanted him out of the frame until he needed him once more.

Spider saw the look of shock on Jimmy Brick's face and knew his earlier reservations were not without foundation. He also knew that Patrick Brodie Junior was a hard little fucker and he had no fear of anyone or anything.

Jimmy walked away from the table without a word but this was not something he was ever going to forget about. He was humiliated and he looked it.

Spider smiled at Pat and he smiled back at him with eyes that seemed to look through him as if he were a pane of glass.

Spider knew exactly what Pat wanted and he also knew that he was going to give it to him. This boy had the one thing going for him that everyone in their world dreamed of having: a self-belief that was as intimidating to the people around him as it was natural to the man himself. He saw the new crew with him and knew they were all young and up-and-coming. He knew that Patrick was the new kid on their particular block. He had made good friends in prison and he had utilized them with the precision of an army general.

This was a dangerous man, and the fact that he himself had not noticed just how dangerous he was, until now, bothered him more than he would care to admit.

His son, Mac, was as close to Pat as any brother could be, and Spider wondered if his boy understood just how precarious and how dangerous this young man's friendship could turn out to be.

*   *   *

Lil was doing what she had been asked to do by her son and, even though it wasn't hard work or even difficult work, she knew it was important work. For her son it was important and he needed someone he could trust with his life to do it. She was going through everything Lenny had used in his quest for world domination and she had to admit that, like her husband, he had no idea how to guarantee any of his main businesses. He had put them all into the hands of friends; a shrewd move in some ways but not in others. For example, none of them seemed conversant with how to make money from a club and that was easier than conning Social Security. It was a cash business, for fuck's sake, how could you not profit from that? And, also, as she knew to her detriment, if the person died the so-called mates who owned the premises on paper often developed a terrible case of amnesia. After all, they owned everything fair and square, didn't they? She should know, it had happened to her.

Lil was making notes on who to aim out the door and who she was going to put in their place. She had a natural head for business; even her husband had admitted that. But she had been born in the wrong era; women were not supposed to be earners and listened to or respected. Patrick, who trusted her judgment, had still not seen fit to give her the fucking time of day. She knew she should let it go, leave the past where it was, in the past. But, somehow, she never seemed able to forget about it.

She concentrated on the paperwork once more and, as always when her brain was occupied, she relaxed. She worked out what was what and unraveled Lenny's complicated system, a system that was so easy a child could have done it. She felt the rush again, the rush that was caused by sheer hard work and pregnancy. The club was quiet for the moment; early evening in Soho was not profitable for the hostesses and so she didn't expect them in. Any that did arrive early she would assume were hiding out from either pimps or dealers; often both. That or they were trying to earn money as quickly as possible to pay off said pimps or dealers. They were fools and she knew they would not realize that until it was far too late to do anything about it.

The life she led was not to everyone's taste, she knew, but her almost encyclopedic knowledge of the hostess clubs and their different earning potentials was something her son saw as an asset to him. She had started this club and she had worked this club, from both sides of the fence, and now she was determined to make it a really big earner.

As the clock struck seven-thirty she heard the door of her office open and when she saw Ivana creep into the room she wanted to scream. The girl was always trying to get her attention and she irritated her beyond measure.

"What can I do for you, Ivana?" She tried to make her voice light and friendly; after all, the girl earned them a small fortune in her own way.

"Can I ask you something in private, Lil?"

Lil nodded her head quickly, the urge to get rid of the girl all important now.

"Course. What is it?"

She expected the usual hostess crap: how they were going to leave for another club because they'd been offered more money and that they would take their regulars, etc. It was a common theme with hostesses. She also knew that a few of the girls met some of the men outside the club and she accepted and understood them doing that. Not that she would ever say that out loud, of course. The girls were not fools; if they met the man outside, he paid less for his action and was pounds in and the girls got more than usual for going on their own in the first place. As long as it wasn't too often and no one took her for a fool, Lil was quite willing to turn a blind eye. The weekend warriors were the ones who would suggest that to the girls and she wanted them out of the club anyway. Freeing up the table for moneyed customers was more important to her than the girl taking a quick one.

Ivana was still not talking and Lil was getting even more impatient with her than she did usually.

"Ivana, love, any chance you can descend to planet earth?"

The girl was definitely nervous and Lil wondered what she had done now. Lots of the girls found themselves in outrageous situations; that was the nature of the beast. Once they left the premises and went on their own they were at their most vulnerable. Most girls used a short-time hotel in Shaftesbury Avenue. It was only a few minutes' walk but they cabbed it because there was no law about soliciting on private property and, as long as they didn't hit the pavement with their john, they were safe as houses from the police. Once inside the hotel though it was a different thing altogether. The man could turn nasty, refuse to pay any extras and she had even seen working girls who had been robbed at knifepoint, gang-raped or just battered for no other reason than that they were there. It was a dangerous game all right. So, as Lil steeled herself for Ivana's little speech, when the girl finally plucked up the courage to talk, she was not expecting what she actually heard her say. For a few moments she thought she had to be imagining it.

"What did you say?"

Ivana licked her lips in an anxious manner and Lil was once more reminded of just how beautiful the girl was.

"Well, talk to me then, I ain't got all bloody day."

Ivana took a deep breath and then she repeated in a careful and controlled voice, "There is a dead body in the basement."

Lil sighed heavily.

Of course there was, why wasn't she surprised?

"Are you sure, Ivana?" She was convinced this one was a druggie; she knew she liked a drink.

"Of course I'm sure. I went down there to see if Patrick was about, you know."

Lil nodded. All the girls were after him; for more reasons than his boyish good looks.

"And I saw it, a dead person. I shut the door and then came straight up here. But Lil, someone else could go down there, you know. It needs to be locked or something."

Lil looked at the girl with new eyes. She wasn't even trying to score Brownie points, she was genuinely worried that someone might discover it and cause trouble.

Lil nodded and then she said nonchalantly, "Did you recognize them?"

Ivana shook her head vigorously. "No. It's some black bloke."

She saw Lil's skin blanch and she rushed to her. Lil could hear genuine concern in her voice.

"You OK, Lil?"

She sat back in the chair and forced herself to smile gently.

"Well, Ivana, thank you for bringing that to my attention."

Ivana looked into her eyes and Lil saw herself as a girl and she knew then that was why she irritated her.

"Look, Lil, I ain't told no one and I ain't going to, but don't treat me like a mug. I came up here to stop anything happening."

Lil nodded and Ivana saw the tiredness and the worry that was ingrained in this woman's face. She'd always wondered why Lil Brodie disliked her so much when she saw Lil Brodie as a role model.

"I know, love. I'll see you get something for this, OK?"

"I don't want anything, Lil. I just want to keep my job here. I *like* it. It *suits* me."

Lil was still feeling faint but managed to say jovially, "Course it does, darling. You're still brand new."

Chapter Twenty-Five

Detective Scanlon was not a happy bunny. In fact, he was fuming. When he had been summoned, and that was the only way he could describe it, he had wondered if the whole thing was a joke. He was not a man to be ordered around; in fact, he had an allergic reaction to anyone ordering him about or trying to tell him anything.

As he sat in his car outside the club in Soho and watched the people walking by, he felt the anger again. That this little shit was in a position to dictate to him was showing him just how much the world he knew had changed.

He had been earning a bribe of this kind since he had been on the beat. It had started off with him turning a blind eye. As the years had gone on, he had carried on taking money because he had got to a stage where he was dependent on it. He needed it to provide the things he now saw as his right.

It was only now that he had been summoned like a naughty school-boy, by a child no less, that what he had been doing finally hit him. At some point he had known that he would be called on to perform some task to justify the wages he had been pulling in all this time. It stood to reason. He had a feeling that the time to pay for it was now. And he didn't want to do it. But the man inside this building owned him and, because of that, he could feel the enormity of what he had been doing for so long.

He got out of the car and, waving off his sergeant, he walked through the drizzle into the warmth of the club. The brightness inside the foyer was too much for his eyes after sitting in the dimness outside plucking up his courage, and he could feel them watering. He coughed nervously as a young lady with small breasts, a tight dress and long permed hair dyed a suspect shade of red smiled at him in a friendly manner. She was sitting behind a polished counter and, perched on a high stool, she gave the impression of being far more important than she actually was. He saw the bouncer eyeing him and knew he was as aware of his name and his occupation as he was himself. The shame set in then and he asked the young lady for Patrick Brodie. The doorman motioned towards him with his head and he followed him through the club seeing the hostesses sitting smoking, waiting for the next customers to arrive. He walked across the dance floor where a stripper was bending over naked. She had just finished her act and was picking up her discarded clothes from the floor. She wasn't even pretty close up; in fact, she had certainly seen better days. The thick make-up that looked so glamorous under the lights was flaking off but she looked Scanlon over as if he was something she had found on the bottom of her shoe. She made him feel even more like the traitor he was. The whole place seemed to reek of decay and his eyes alighted on the men already seated around the dance floor. They had the look of men who paid for female company, from their ill-fitting suits to the scuffed and well-worn briefcases that would have been presents from the wives and children who had no idea where the men in their lives actually spent their leisure time.

A heavy rock tune blasted through the speakers heralding the next stripper and, as she brushed past him, he smelled the aroma of stale sweat and Murray mints.

They walked through to the back of the club and as they descended the stairs into the basement he felt physically sick. The bile was filling his mouth, burning him and he swallowed it down as best he could. His nerves were already shattered and when he finally reached the cement floor of the basement he knew that he had finally reached rock-bottom in more ways than one.

Pat Brodie was sitting at a small table drinking a brandy and he was surprised at just how masculine the boy actually was. Scanlon nodded slightly to him in greeting and was aware that he didn't get any kind of recognition in return. Pat Brodie just stared at him and then, after what seemed an age, he pointed to a pile of what Scanlon had thought was rags in the corner of the room.

"All yours, mate."

It was only on closer inspection that Scanlon realized it was a dead body.

"Stop being so silly, Kath. Get up and come out with me." Eileen could hear the anger in her own voice and she tried to calm herself down even as she felt the frustration that her sister caused her.

Kathleen was the image of her, it was like looking in the mirror except she didn't seem to have any life about her. She had been bad enough before but lately she was even worse. Her whole body seemed to have collapsed in on her and her eyes were black-rimmed. It was heartbreaking to look at her.

"I don't want to go, all right."

Eileen gritted her teeth and forced a smile on to her face, "Oh, come on, Kath. You'll enjoy it once you get there and there's a band on as well. It's called Flanagan's Speakeasy and everyone we know is gonna be there. And it's in Barking so we won't have to worry about the boys watching over us."

"I don't wanna go, right?"

"Well, you're going!"

Eileen stood up and grabbing the bedclothes she yanked them off her sister roughly. Kathleen sat up in the bed and attempted to pull the bedclothes back over her. She was almost having a tug of war with her sister and then Eileen noticed that Kathleen had seen herself in the dressing-table mirror. She dropped the bedding and stared at herself. Eileen watched her sister for a few seconds, wondering what she would do next. Her eyes were hooded and she peered at herself as if she had never seen herself before.

Then she leant forward and, dragging the covers back up, she turned on her side. With her back to her sister she pulled the covers over her shoulders again.

"Look, Kath, there's something wrong with you and I don't know how to help you. I love you as my sister and I want to see you get back to normal . . ."

Kathleen didn't answer her. The quiet in the room was heavy with unanswered questions.

"Tell me what is wrong with you. I'm your sister and if you can't talk to me, who can you talk to?"

Eileen's voice was full of the desperation her sister's condition caused inside her. She was frightened that this depression that was now a part of Kathleen's life and the fear of going out in the daylight was going to happen to her. They were twins and she was terrified that she was going to turn into her sister. No one seemed to care and everyone pretended it wasn't as bad as it really was.

"Please, Kath, talk to me . . ."

Kathleen leapt up, grabbed her sister around the throat and screamed into her face. "Will you fuck off? Just leave me alone and fuck off! On and on and on . . . It's like listening to a cracked record. We look alike and that's it, Eileen, we ain't got anything else in common. Now leave me alone before I fucking really hurt you . . ."

Kathleen pushed her sister away then and climbing back into the bed she pulled the covers over her once more and said quietly, "Close the door behind you."

Eileen walked from the room just as Lil was coming up the stairs.

"What's all the noise?"

Eileen burst into tears then. "She went mad, Mum. What is wrong with her? I was just trying to help her, that's all . . ." Eileen pushed herself into her mother's bosom.

Lil hugged her tightly. Kissing her hair, she said sadly, "She is a strange girl but I don't know what to do with her. The doctor came in the other week and he said it's depression, as you know. She takes the Valium and she sleeps. I don't know what else we can do for her."

"She needs help, Mum, more than she is getting . . ."

The bedroom door opened then and Kathleen stood in front of them. Her nightdress was stained with tea and Ribena and her feet were filthy, her toenails rimmed with dirt.

"What, Eileen, you want them to put me in the nuthouse, is that it?"

"What are you on about? I never said—"

"I ain't going nowhere. You try and put me away anywhere and I'll kill meself. I swear to God, I'll kill meself."

Lil went to her then and, shaking her head slowly, she said, "What are you on about? No one has said anything about putting you anywhere. But you ain't right, Kath, and if you can't see that then maybe you do need to go away somewhere."

Kathleen laughed at her words. "You make me die, all of you! Murdering lunatics all over the house and *I'm* the one with a problem . . ."

Eileen looked at her sister and then she slowly walked down the stairs. "Fuck her, Mum. Let her do what she wants."

At the bottom, she said loudly, "By the way, sis, if you ever get around to smelling yourself, you know there's a lock on the bathroom door, don't you?"

"She's got a point, Kathy, you look like a tramp."

Lil's voice was jocular, she was trying to lighten the situation as best she could.

Kathleen slammed her bedroom door and Eileen slammed the living-room door and Lil stood on the landing wondering which daughter she should go to first.

Donny Barker was a man of few words. He was also a man who, if upset, was liable to open a skull, a cheek or, in extreme cases, a stomach.

He was a violent lunatic and he had a reputation for double-crossing people. North London was a no-go area for anyone he had a grudge against. He liked football, fighting, curry and spending the day with his mum, in that order. He had no time for women and no time for men either. Donny was an anomaly to everyone around him; the only person he was even remotely nice to was his mum. She was a small, bird-like woman called Vera with a loud voice and a smoker's cough. Donny worshipped the ground she walked on and the feeling was mutual.

As he sat in his mum's row house, he looked at the photographs around him, at the doilies on the table and the crocheted chairbacks

and sighed with contentment. Lance Brodie was a weirdo. He had heard
that he was and, knowing the same thing was said about him behind his
back, he decided he almost liked him. He had also liked his approach
and he was impressed with his nervous demeanor. He could easily work
with him; he was sure of that much. Unlike his workforce he didn't look
at him as if he was odd. He had been thinking about Lance's proposition
for a long time and he decided he had no choice but to go along with it
all. For the time being at least.

"Who the hell is this?" Scanlon's voice was trembling with fear, as was
his whole body.

It was surreal. The whole of the evening seemed so unreal, it was like
a bad dream except that he knew he wasn't going to wake up at any time
in the near future. In fact, he knew this was going to be a new life.

"What's with asking all these questions? Who are you, the police?"

Everyone laughed.

Scanlon felt his bowels loosening and he knew that the old saying was
true, you could literally shit yourself.

"What do you want from me?"

Patrick sipped his brandy and waved the other men from the room.
Then he motioned Scanlon over to the table he was sitting at and said
coldly, "Sit down and shut the fuck up. Just listen. You ain't paid to ask
questions, you are paid to make sure I *ain't* asked any questions."

Scanlon sat down with relief; he wasn't sure how long his legs would
hold him up.

He was slumped in the chair and Patrick liked seeing this man brought
low; he had heard a lot about him over the years. He was a bully who
made a big song and dance about everything. He had been known to
brag about his criminal connections. Well, after tonight he would have
him in his back pocket for always.

Dirty cops could get away with a lot. Like any system, the cops tended
to look after their own. That stood to reason; Pat knew it wouldn't do
the public much good if they knew the extent of the corruption around
them. He also knew that disposing of a body was something even a bent
law couldn't walk away from, hence the evening's entertainment.

"His name's Jasper and he was asking for what he got, that's all you need to know. A long time ago he sold out someone very close to my father and because of that he met a very untimely end. That happens a lot to people who annoy me."

Scanlon didn't answer him; he wasn't sure what to say.

"He has been tortured, stabbed and shot. The shooting was just for a laugh, nothing more. He was well dead by then but I like the American approach, overkill, they have the right idea."

Scanlon was listening, but he was not taking in anything of relevance.

"I want you to take the body away with my blokes and I want you to dispose of it."

Scanlon knew he was expected to answer and he didn't know how to. What could he say to such an outrageous suggestion?

"A squad car can drive anywhere, right? So I want you to get one round the back of the club by midnight; I know you use them for your own benefit. They call them Scanlon's cab service, don't they? So I figured that you might call a cab and dispose of Jasper, the wandering Rastafarian, as he was known. Then, once you earn your crust, that is to get shot of him, me and you can feel we have a rapport of sorts."

Scanlon was snookered and he knew it. "You worked for my old man when you were first on the beat and I need you to help me track a few people down and also find out a few facts that are relevant to my own investigation. I need a bit of help from you and, once I get it, you can walk away as if none of this ever happened. If you decide to annoy me, I will annihilate you."

Scanlon didn't answer him. He could hear the music from upstairs and it was a record he had always liked. The sound of Gary Glitter's "My Gang" was resonating through his brain as he sat in the dimness of the basement nodding like an idiot.

"Well, get a move on, you prick, you need to order a cab."

Lance, as usual, was alone. He worked better alone and he was grateful to his brother for understanding that. He wandered Soho as always; he liked to walk the streets at night, watch the people around and see the different lives playing out. He walked around with complete anonymity; it was a knack he had, no one ever seemed to take any notice of him. It was one of the reasons he had been so aggressive as a child. Pat Junior always made his presence felt and people looked at him, listened to him and it was all effortless, completely natural to him. He envied him that, even as he was pleased that he himself could merge into any crowd and not be noticed. He had come full circle, he was back outside the club and he knew he was overdue for his meet.

As he walked into the club to meet Pat, he saw the doorman was chatting to the ugly redhead with the bad perm and the non-existent breasts.

"You fucking watching this door or what?"

Keith Munroe turned and saw Lance and he also saw one of their hawkers; a skinny Iranian with a cheap raincoat and a gap-toothed smile. With him were two Arabic-looking men and they were obviously very nervous at the turn the evening had taken.

The hawker shrugged at Lance, telling him he was not to blame, worried in case he was going to be bawled out as well.

Munroe walked towards them, all smiles and camaraderie. The hawker spoke to the men in Arabic and they nodded and smiled. Opening their wallets, they paid the entrance fee of ten pounds each in cash. Once the girl on reception had walked them through to the meat seats, Lance pounced.

"You fucking waster, you fucking ponce. You didn't even bother to clock their wallets, did you? How are they going to know how to bill them if they don't know what plastic they've got?"

Normally, as the entrance fee was being paid, the doorman would look inside the wallet to see what they had moneywise and cardwise. He would then write their financial situation down on a piece of paper, the receptionist would walk them to the seats and then pass the information on to the head girl as if it was nothing more than proof of payment.

This information was what decided their bill at the end of the night. It was the lifeblood of clubs like this, it gave everyone the edge. The hostess would be told the score and she would then have an idea how much to hustle them for. She would insist on the expensive champagne and order herself the gift-boxed cigarettes; these held fifty cigarettes and were the girls' staple of the night for their hostess fee. At least then, if the man was not flush enough for sex, they had got something from him.

Keith Munroe was embarrassed. He wasn't exactly scared of Lance, he had his creds. But at the end of a very long day the man was Pat's brother and he had fucked up in front of him and all for a bird who was anyone's for a few quid and a few drinks. He arranged his face into a semblance of a smile and, walking to the door, he said blandly, "Sorry, Lance. I was chasing pussy; *you* know what that's like."

Lance knew that was a barb aimed specifically at him and he took it on board and filed it away for future reference. He went through to the club itself and, as he walked, he looked at everyone and everything and was aware that no one made eye contact with him. Least of all the girls. He knew that if they were wary of him then he would be seen as having a problem. Whores slept with anyone, anyone who could pay them or, in certain situations, advance them in some way. They should have been all over him like a cheap suit, not avoiding him. He knew that and he hated it; they seemed to overlook him and he should have had his pick of them. He should have been their lucky fucking charm. The head girl nodded at him respectfully and he inclined his head slightly, acknowledging her. At least she gave him his due; she knew who was in the frame and who wasn't.

Lance noticed a table with an empty champagne bottle and a very pissed-off client. The hostess was sitting there with her arms crossed and she had a cigarette dangling from her lip. He stopped by the table.

"Everything all right?"

The man shook his head and Lance saw him sneer at the girl. She was very young with green eyes and badly cut blond hair. She was obviously a newey and even he felt sorry for her.

"What's the problem, sir?"

The man was feeling ambitious; he had on a grey pinstriped suit and his shirt was expensive though his watch wasn't. He had obviously drunk more of the champagne than the girl, that was part of her job, and he was about five seconds away from an argument.

"I asked you a question." The words were spoken respectfully but with authority.

"I want to leave and she won't come with me. What the fuck did I come here for if I am going home on my own?"

Lance looked at the girl and raised an eyebrow in inquiry.

"So? What's the problem?"

She was absolutely terrified and the john quickly picked up on that.

"Go on then, mouth almighty, fucking tell him."

Lance pointed a finger at him and it was enough to shut him up.

"Come on, what's wrong?"

Everyone was watching them and she knew it. The hostesses were all standing by the dance floor like a flock of exotic birds. This was something that could affect them all and they knew it.

Lance was not unaware of them but he was concentrating on the john and his arrogance. The man's disrespect was annoying him. The girl was only young and she was a bundle of nerves.

"I can't go out unless the man buys three bottles of champagne . . . He can't seem to understand that." She pointed at the table holding the ice bucket and the empty champagne bottle. The ice had melted so he knew it had been there a while.

Lance looked back at the man.

"If you are in a hurry sir, we can wrap the champagne and you can take it to the hotel with you. But the girl is right, it's three bottles or she stays where she is."

The man was just getting the courage up to jump on his high horse when he saw another man walking towards them. He was the double of the man he was speaking with and he suddenly realized that he was in deep trouble; that the man in front of him was not going to be in any way amenable.

"What's the problem, Lance?"

Pat's voice was friendly but the man sitting with the hostess could hear the underlying question there. He knew the man was being asked not to harm him in any way and he was being reminded that they were in public. He didn't know how he knew that, he just did. It was a learning curve, an introduction to the world he had chosen to frequent for easy sex and the feeling of being a player.

The girl was looking down at the table; there was no way she was going to look anyone in the eyes or engage them in idle conversation.

"This man is trying to stiff us. He wants this girl to go out with him and he doesn't want to pay for the champagne. I am just going to explain the situation to him, explain how the club works. I need to explain that we ain't a fucking charity for cheap cunts or fucking muppets."

Patrick knew that Lance was on one of his missions, this happened periodically. He got a bee in his bonnet and nothing would be right with him until he had taken out his anger on someone. This man was not unaware that his life was in danger if he argued back or disagreed with the man smiling at him in such a friendly way. So that was good at least. He just had to diffuse the situation and get Lance away.

"Pay the lady and pay her now."

The client looked from one brother to another then he took his wallet out quickly and looked at Patrick, saying loudly, "Of course, how much?" He said it as if stiffing her had never entered his mind.

"Forty quid. Now."

The client gave the two twenties to the girl and she walked away from the table as fast as she could without actually running.

"Now get up, pay the bill for your champagne; they take money and credit cards at the bar, and then my advice to you is to fuck off."

The customer did not need to be told twice. As he got up from his chair, Lance grabbed him by his shoulder and dragged him physically through the club, past the girls and out the front door. As he landed on the pavement, Lance kicked him with all his strength in the kidneys.

Back inside the club, Patrick shook his head in absolute wonderment. "You never manhandle a punter on the street. What are you trying to do, Lance, bring the cops in here? Straight cops who will bring us to the attention of all the wrong people? And what about his bill, eh? The bottle of champagne he drank, who's paying for that?"

Pat wiped a hand across his face and forced himself to calm down so he didn't cause any more trouble for them both.

Lance turned to the doorman then. He was still after a fight of some description and everyone watching was more than aware of that.

"*You* should have sorted that, *you* should have been in here and watching the tables."

Keith had just about had enough now. For all that Lance was a big part of this life, he was sick of being treated like a fucking no-neck.

"That is the head girl's job, Lance. I resent you trying to fucking make me look a cunt. You might be his brother but I take my fucking orders from him, not you."

Pat stepped between the two men and Lance knew that this was something he would have to place on the back burner. He'd wait until the time was right to finish it.

"Oi. Come on you two, what the fuck is all this about?"

Pat pushed Lance towards the stairs and walked close behind him as they went up to the office. He shut the door quietly and then he turned on his brother with more anger than Lance had ever seen before.

"What the *fuck* are you doing, Lance? You lost your fucking mind or what?"

"What are you on about? I was trying to make us some money; that cunt is always chatting up the hostesses and he ain't got the fucking sense to do that job."

Pat held up a hand in a gesture of silence.

"You do not tell anyone what to do unless I expressly say so, you hear me, Lance? I am the boss of this outfit and that fucking includes *you*. Keith's all right and the Munroes are a fucking good crew. If you cause a war with him they will all be out of sorts and at the moment I can't afford for that to happen. So shut the fuck up and stop trying to cause upset where there ain't none."

Lance didn't answer him, he just stood and stared. His face was, as always, expressionless unless it displayed anger or distaste.

Pat wondered at times if this man was even on the same planet as everyone else. Lance was his brother and he loved him but he was a loose cannon and, worse than that, he was devoid of anything even resembling human emotion. Except when it came to Kathleen, that is; she was the only person who he seemed to care about. It was his one saving grace and it had saved him a few times lately, if he only realized that.

"What happened with Donny?"

"Sweet as a nut. The money was paid in full, of course."

"Well, where is it then?"

Lance shrugged then, as if he was talking to a moron, someone without any intelligence whatsoever. It was all Pat could do not to murder his brother there and then.

"It's in the safe over there, of course."

Pat nodded. He knew that if Lance had access to the safe then he was snooping all over the place and he made a mental note to have the locks changed.

"Come on, Lil, eat something."

"I can't, Janie, I feel like shit on a stick."

They both laughed then.

"You look like shit and all."

"I feel a bit sick."

"Well, a baby will do that to you, Lil. I was as sick as a dog with all mine."

Janie sat beside Lil at the kitchen table and lit herself a cigarette.

"I bet you couldn't believe it, could you?"

Lil laughed and her face looked young again, but just for a moment.

"Just my luck, ain't it? Another bloody baby at my age."

"Look on the bright side, Lil. This one could be the baby for your old age. Years ago, if women had a late one, it was seen as a blessing. A child for your old age, a child to look after you and make sure you were all right."

Lil sighed once more.

"I can't see it being anything like that, Janie. Kids nowadays don't seem to have that kind of tolerance. It's all about them, not anyone else."

Janie shrugged. "Well, you ain't done bad with the last lot, they seem to have got their priorities right."

Lil didn't answer her. Instead she poured herself another cup of tea and, as she sipped it, she looked around the kitchen. It was looking much better than it had for years. There was a new fridge, a washing machine and even a dishwasher. Annie was thrilled about that. In fact, her mother enjoyed it more than she did. Her mother was in her element, they were back on top and she was making the most of it. She even went to bingo so she could lord it over her cronies. Women who didn't like her now spoke to her because her grandson was out and back on the street.

Pat was a good boy, not that she had thought that for a little while. Until she had seen Jasper's body for herself, she had really believed it had been poor Jambo down there.

There had been so much death lately and it was bothering her, even though she knew it was necessary for her family's survival. That was the legacy Pat had left to them, to his sons, to her even. His insistence on working alone and making himself the only person who knew anything of merit, had caused his downfall. People had banded together and taken him down; they could never have done it on their own. His children knew that. Patrick especially, with his prison talk and his determination to find out the truth. He was his father's son in more ways than one.

The boys were honorbound to take back what they saw as theirs by rights and who could blame them after the way they had been treated over the years. They'd had to watch others make a fortune on what should have been their inheritance. They had been made to feel like second-class citizens knowing how hard it was for her to put clothes on their backs and food on the table.

She felt so bad at times. She knew her boys, even Lance, were doing everything for her, were trying to make things right for her again. But they didn't know, either of them, that nothing could ever be right for her again. She also knew that was the excuse they used to justify their anger and their hate.

They might tell themselves it was for her but she knew, and deep down *they* both knew, it was for themselves really. She was just a good reason for the insanity of recent events. She also knew that she would defend them to the hilt, lie in a courtroom under oath and stand in front of them with a shotgun, if necessary. Although she hoped that it would never come to that. But it might, nothing would surprise her any more.

Her mother's mantra over the years had been that they were as God made them. But she was worried that they were as *she* had made them. Not deliberately, but with the choices she had made over the years, and the mistakes she had forced them to live through.

She had created them. Together with her mother, she had created two men who were as dangerous as they were enigmatic.

Even Ivana was caught up in their thrall. But like any woman who was foolish enough to get involved with them, she was on a losing streak. She wanted to warn Ivana, but she knew it was a pointless exercise and that she wouldn't listen to her. No more than *she* would have listened if someone had warned her about Patrick. Life had a habit of repeating itself.

Chapter Twenty-Six

Spider was listening to the men around him with interest. He knew they were all wondering why he had not attempted to do anything about Pat's hold over the West End. Spider was renowned for never discussing anything unless he wanted to, so no one thought it strange that he chose to overlook the heavy hints around him.

He looked at his boys; a lot of them were young, up-and-coming sharpies getting an education at his door. But he knew in his heart that at least one of them was in the pay of Brodie Junior, maybe even more than that. It wasn't anything he knew for a fact, it was more a natural progression. Young Pat was everywhere and there wasn't a scam on the go that he didn't have a hand in.

Spider knew Pat was backed by the best. The people he had been locked up with had seen his potential. Spider had seen it himself. Pat was such an astute businessman and knew exactly what was required; how to get the maximum for the minimum. He also had a rep that was even more respected than his father's.

None of that bothered him personally, it was the way he had come home and acted like his long-lost son, thanked him for his help over the years with the family and had then just disregarded him. Not in any way that he could jump on, could use against him; it was a more personal insult. He said all the right things but Spider knew that he didn't mean any of it. And yet his son and Patrick were as close as ever. Indeed he wondered at times if it was his son's friendship with Pat that was keeping him alive. Because Spider knew that if Patrick wanted him gone, then gone he would be.

Spider was a realist; he knew the score in this world and he also knew that everyone had a shelf-life, even Pat Junior. It was the law of the pavement. If a big sentence didn't get you, a bastard with a grudge would. People in their world rarely died in their beds; each generation was waiting to step into the next pair of boots and, from what he had heard, Pat had been offered them on a plate.

He watched as his son rolled a joint. He knew he had served up Jasper to Pat and he respected that. But what Spider didn't understand was why no one, even his own flesh and blood, thought it appropriate to tell him what was going on. He had heard it from one of his guys; like a gossip, he was having to ferret out information. Yet nothing had occurred for months, and everyone was relaxed, except for him. He knew that Pat was like his father; he would exact his revenge slowly. If it took years, that would suit him; he would wait until the person concerned was settled in their life and work and sure that they were safe and then he would take great pleasure in proving them wrong. That was the real power of revenge, taking it when the person concerned least expected it, and had the most to lose.

His son was a part of all that planning and yet he had never mentioned it to his own father. He felt like an outsider and was being treated like one into the bargain. The main earner for the younger boys was the dope; it was almost their only business and he knew it was the thing that interested them most. They were all stoned and they were getting on his nerves.

He saw Jimmy Brick come in and he waited a few minutes before joining him. The man was in the same boat as he was and, like him, he didn't know where the fuck he stood any more either. And, like him, he couldn't gather any information; it was almost as if they had been singled out for ostracism. They were getting closer by the week and it was not going unnoticed. They knew everything was reported back to the powers that be. How times had changed and it was hard admitting that you were past your prime, past your best, especially when you felt stronger than ever.

*   *   *

Lil was tired. The doctor was back once more for poor Kathleen and they were trying to get him to see her properly. When he went into the room, Kathleen acted so normal, so together even Lil wondered if she was imagining the rest of it. But she had talked the doctor into pretending to leave and then sneaking back up the stairs and listening outside the door of her bedroom so he could hear her talking to herself.

Lil knew he thought she was the nutter but she also knew that he had to make sure that what she said wasn't true. Kathleen had developed black eyes and bruised arms and they were not caused by anyone in the house. She had to be hurting herself. And, as much as it pained Lil to admit that, she knew it was true.

Kathleen didn't eat and she didn't sleep. She refused to leave the house and she refused any kind of company. Even Lance was hard-pushed to get inside the room and he was the only one who seemed able to get through to her. Pat was welcome occasionally and every so often Kathleen was chatty with her; it was seldom though and she did most of the talking. Lil's growing belly seemed to attract her. She was interested in the coming baby, as were Colleen and Christy, they couldn't wait for it to be born.

As the doctor stood quietly on the landing listening out for her beautiful, troubled daughter to begin talking to herself, Lil wondered at how a life could be so plagued with problems and worries. She prayed that this child would have an easier time of it than her other children, that it would know at least a modicum of peace. This was her last chance to get it right and she knew it. She was focusing all her energy on this baby and the three younger children. She only hoped she wasn't wasting her time.

She heard Kathleen's voice then. She heard her talking to no one, but over the last few months she had listened intently and she knew that Kathleen thought there were at least two people with her.

She didn't really understand the conversations but Kathleen seemed to get some sort of benefit from them. She seemed happier somehow and that was what was so terrible. Lil just didn't know what to do and if the doctor didn't sort it out soon she knew that Pat was going to force Kathleen into a mental hospital. He was of the opinion that she should have been carted off ages ago, but he also knew that Kathleen's biggest fear was *being* put away. Of being perceived as mentally ill.

She had such a strange take on life; sometimes she washed everything she possessed and yet she wouldn't put any of it in the wardrobe or chest of drawers. Everything was hung on doors or folded up on the bed; it had to be in plain sight. She was not yet fifteen, and she was already being written off.

The doctor had heard enough and as he walked quietly back down the stairs, Lil followed him, her heart sore because she knew what he was going to say.

Eileen was in the back of her boyfriend's van. It was a warm night and her latest boyfriend, a thirty-year-old docker with brown eyes and a penchant for schoolgirls, was trying to talk her out of her top. She was happy enough with the kissing but somehow this was going a bit too fast for her now. He had her bra unhooked and her top up and she was having difficulty controlling the situation. As she pushed his hands away once again, he grabbed her wrists and, grinning, he pinned her arms to her sides. She lay back in her seat and looked at him warily. She had met him in a pub in Essex a few weeks earlier. He was a grown man and he made her feel like an adult. He treated her like a woman and now she was finding out exactly what that entailed.

"Listen, lady, don't prick-tease. I ain't hearing the word 'no,' do you understand me?"

Eileen was trying to force him away from her, trying to bring her arms up from where he had pinned them to her sides and he was laughing at her, he thought she was funny.

"Please, Nick. Please, let me go."

He was watching her with interest; she was so young and so naive, just how he liked them. She was sweating with fear and he could see it glistening in the half-light. But he was not worried, she would give in, they always did. This was the excitement for him, the chase itself. She was so perfect, so innocent and her make-up just made her look younger, like a little girl dressing up in her mum's clothes. Her fear was making her pant and the sound was making him hard. A bead of sweat dripped from her chest and on to her belly; she was fighting to keep her modesty and attempting to pull down her top. But Nick Parks was an expert at this; he had popped more cherries than a fruit picker on speed.

"Please, Nick. I ain't done anything like this before."

She was trying to reason with him, to make him understand that she had got herself in a position that she wasn't able for and that she wasn't mature enough to handle. She actually believed that he would stop what he was doing and take her home.

He was lowering her seat and she could feel herself being forced backwards and she knew that once she was horizontal she was finished. His hand was groping her and his knee was trying to force her legs apart. She regretted wearing a denim two-piece; the skirt was so short and the cropped jacket hardly covered her breasts. She had felt like an adult when she had put it on but now she wanted to cry. She was frightened and his tongue was raspy from the cigarettes he smoked and the speed he had snorted all night. He tasted disgusting and her stomach was rebelling against him and what he was doing. He was covering her mouth with his so she couldn't even call out and she was pinned to the car seat, unable to even move her face away from him, let alone anything else. She could sense the urgency inside him and feel the hardness of him against her thigh. He was pulling her knickers down, exposing her to the night, and she was mortified. She used all her strength and tried to buck him off her. It just made him laugh more.

"Come on, little girl, you've been leading me on all night and I ain't going nowhere until I get what I want."

She was really crying now and Eileen knew that all the things her mother had told her were true; that most men just wanted one thing and when they got it they lost interest. She could feel the tears rolling down her face and Nick's knee was trying to force her legs apart when the van door opened.

Nick Parks looked behind him, ready to bawl someone out, when he felt himself being dragged bodily off the girl. He regarded himself as a reasonably hard nut and he took a swing at the man. It was only then that he saw there were two of them and that they were policemen.

Eileen jumped from the van as fast as she could and the young policemen saw she was trying to pull her clothes back into place.

"You all right, love?"

"Course she's fucking all right, we're courting."

The way Nick was talking about her made Eileen wish she had never left the house and had never gone to the pubs in Ilford and Barking. She regretted the rush she had been in to grow up and get away from her family and the house full of people who loved her and wanted the best for her.

She started crying then. "I want to go home . . . I just want to go home . . ."

Eileen was in a country lane somewhere and she had no cab fare. She was frightened that the policemen would leave her behind if she wasn't careful. The two policemen took pity on her, they could see the situation and they both wished they had a pound for every time they came across it. They'd never have to work again.

"What's your name, love?"

"Eileen. Eileen Brodie."

"Get in the fucking van, you silly bitch and stop fucking about."

Nick was trying to act like they were an item and he knew he was not being very convincing. But this child was making him look a fool. Another ten minutes and she'd have been popped and on her way home. He was still on the cusp and he wanted to do the dirty on her.

"Shut your trap and let the girl talk, will you?"

Nick was staring at her with a look of complete longing on his face and Eileen knew then how sneaky he could be.

"Come on, babe, you don't want to cause any trouble now, do you?"

He was the nice guy once more and his handsome face looked as if he had never had a bad thought. Eileen shook her head sadly.

"Can you take me home, please, or at least give me a lift to the train station?"

"Get in the car, love, we'll sort you out."

She climbed into the police car then and she hated the feel of it.

"You had better watch out in the future, mate. Jailbait can get you in a lot of trouble. Now piss off."

Nick drove off in his van and Eileen watched him go with tears running down her face. She didn't like all this growing-up lark, it was scary. Nick was the last in a long line of older men she seemed to gravitate to and she didn't know why. This was the first time that she had been frightened though. She had only ever teased them in the pub before this, giving them the talk and acting older than she was. Now she knew how dangerous that could be. The two policemen were young and friendly. The chattier of the two was called Andy and he offered her a lift home when his shift finished. She accepted his offer readily, just wanting to get away from this place and the situation she had got herself into.

Pat was in bed with Ivana and she was lying in his arms, her slim legs wrapped around him. She was so tiny and Pat liked that. He liked the feel of her; she was fragile in comparison to his roughness. She felt so minute and so soft, that holding her was almost like taking her. She made him feel good inside and made him want to protect her and he knew that she liked the feeling as much as he did.

But she was a hooker and hookers were not meant to be loved by anyone. It was hypocritical, he knew, considering his mother's background. But he also knew she would be the first person warning him against letting his feelings get the better of him.

Ivana snuggled into his body once more and he held her tightly to him. She could feel his heart beating and smell his aftershave.

"Is that your real name?"

She laughed. "Course not. No one is born with a name like that. It's a work name, an exotic name that makes me sound interesting. My actual name is Denise."

He laughed then and she laughed with him.

"You *are* joking?"

She was still laughing, no shame at her own words, just honest humor.

"I'm not. My name is Denise Jones, a boring and unattractive name for a girl who wanted to be interesting and beautiful." She was laughing at herself again, only this time it wasn't as convincing.

Patrick hugged her once more, tighter, and her little laugh made him feel sorry for her. She was a nice girl, a really nice girl. He sighed, she was addictive.

He got out of the bed and relit the joint they had left in the ashtray. The sweet aroma of the grass filled the room and he looked down on Ivana and saw her lying there with her hair all around her face and her milky white skin smooth and soft against the bed sheets.

"You all right?" Her voice was soft and Pat sat back on the bed and smiled down at her.

"Course I'm all right. How about you?" She didn't answer him, just smiled gently.

He knew she loved him. He knew she would hang around for years; he could marry, go to prison, anything and Ivana, as she liked to be called, would be there waiting for him. A constant in a world that was full of disappointments.

He felt sorry for her even as he wished he had met her as a civilian and not in a hostess club flashing her clout to whoever had the money. He knew that he would keep her on the side and he was ashamed that he wasn't man enough to take her as she was. But it was hard for a man when the woman they were with was well-known. Eventually, it would cause trouble. Eventually he would use it against her. That was the way the world worked. She was sensible enough to know that herself. He wouldn't have to explain himself to her, she would take whatever crumbs he threw her.

"I'd better get back to work, mate."

He nodded then and she saw the face that haunted her dreams and had grabbed her from the first time she had laid eyes on it. He had hit her like a bolt of lightning and the feeling had not decreased as it should have, it seemed to grow bigger by the day.

He dressed himself quickly and, kissing her gently on the brow, he left her.

Ivana lay there in the hotel room that was depressing now, with its scratched dressing table and dirty carpet, and she wondered what would be the outcome of this strange relationship they had.

The one thing she did know was that, no matter what happened, she would be there for him. She was caught up in him and needed him more than she had ever needed anyone or anything before in her life. She also knew that, without a doubt, he would break her heart.

Lance saw his little sister getting out of a car and he walked out of the house to see who had brought her home. He was surprised to see a young man in a police uniform driving an old Ford.

"What the fuck is going on?"

Eileen wished she was dead but she knew she had to defuse this situation before that luxury could be afforded to her.

"I got lost, Lance, and this man was kind enough to give me a lift home."

Lance bent down and looked into the car, peering in the window at the man in the driver's seat.

"Where did you get lost then?"

"I went to a party in Essex and lost me mates. I saw a police car and flagged it down."

The young man could feel her fear and it was communicating itself to him. This was a man who, he knew, instinctively, was definitely *not* someone to cross.

"Well, this ain't a fucking police car, or is it? Are the cop cars in Essex different to the ones everywhere else? Only I thought they were supposed to be instantly recognizable? Wasn't that the whole idea of them in the first place?"

"Excuse me, sir, but I was just finishing my shift and the young lady was obviously in a bind. I offered to drop her off rather than leave her alone at a train station."

Lance saw the logic of what the boy was saying and, with one of his lightning changes of mood, he smiled. This was something that was so rare it was more worrying to Eileen than his usual miserable demeanor.

"Thanks. You're right, of course. She is only young."

The young policeman could feel the terror coming off her in waves now and he was sorry he wasn't brave enough to stay around and see what the score was. He couldn't wait to get going, in fact. And, starting up the engine, he waved quickly before driving off in case this man decided he was not going to be so nice about it all.

Eileen looked at Lance for a few moments and she wondered how someone who looked so much like Patrick could not be called good-looking. On Patrick the same features were blindingly good-looking, on Lance they made him look like a psychopath.

"I know you don't want to hear it, Eileen, but I worry about you. You're a baby and there are men in the world who would take advantage of your youth and your inexperience."

For the first time ever, Eileen was grateful to him for his overbearing and protective attitude.

"Thanks, Lance. I know you're right and I know you're only trying to take care of me."

He was surprised at her answer, she knew. Normally, she would be causing murders, accusing him of all sorts and making a drama out of his concern.

"Is Nanny Annie in?"

Lance nodded and they walked amiably back into the house together.

"Bloody hell, wonders will never cease," Annie said in undisguised surprise as she saw them coming in together.

Eileen didn't bother to answer her. She walked through to the kitchen where her mother was making another one of her pots of tea.

"Fancy a cup, love?"

Eileen smiled and kissed her gently. "I love you, Mum."

Lil laughed then, a loud, knowing laugh. "Who hurt you, darling?"

She pulled her daughter into her arms and hugged her tightly.

"Come on. Who was it and where do they live?"

"Oh, Mum . . ." Eileen was crying now; her mother's astute observation at what had befallen her just made it all the more poignant.

"Sssh. Stop it, darling. Don't cry. Remember you have to kiss a lot of frogs before you find a prince."

Eileen suddenly felt her mother's body tense up and she made a low groan.

"The baby is on its way. I was having a cup of tea before I go off."

Eileen couldn't believe what she was hearing. "You're really in labor?"

Lil laughed again, that deep-throated chuckle that was her trademark.

"I'm having a baby, Eileen. It's not that hard, love. It is going to come out no matter what. In fact, I think it is nearer than I thought. I can feel it bearing down." Lil sat back in the chair once more and took a few deep breaths. "Phone the doctor, love. He must be sick of this fucking house. But, first, pour me out another cuppa. Lots of sugar, darling, for energy."

She bent double again and she knew the baby was well on its way now.

"Oh, Eileen, I forgot how much it fucking hurts, darling." She was still laughing when the child arrived twenty minutes later.

Pat was with Mac and they walked into the Eagle together. After ordering a couple of drinks, they made their way over to the corner and Pat smiled down at the man sitting there with his pint of Guinness. Then, pulling up a chair, he sat down easily.

"It's a boy. I thought you might want to know that."

Mac was standing behind Pat and Jambo was not sure what they expected from him so he just sat there and smiled gently as he always did.

"She OK, your mother?"

Pat nodded. He was looking at the man intently and he understood his mother's attraction to him. Jambo had a quietness about him that she must have found so refreshing after the other men in her life.

"Yeah. You know her, takes everything in her stride."

Jambo sipped his drink. "Not everything, boy, she feels a lot more than she lets on, you know."

Patrick didn't answer him. He didn't know what to say. Now he was here, he felt as if he was intruding on his mother's private life. She didn't have much of her own, much that wasn't about the kids or the family. Or the problems she had to deal with, and this man was her little bit of downtime, her escape from everything.

Pat had asked around about Jambo and knew his rep. Even though he wasn't the man he would have chosen for her, he hadn't heard anything detrimental about him.

"How big is the baby? She named it yet?" Jambo was surprised to find that he was genuinely interested.

"Eight pound and no name as yet."

Mackie was watching them closely and he decided they needed another drink. When he brought them back to the table he was not surprised to see the men chatting away together. He knew Jambo and he was all right. He liked his own company and women found him attractive; he was handsome in a masculine way. His skin was well-toned, not too dark, and he had the easy-going way that womanizers develop at an early age. But one thing in his favor was that he never promised anything he couldn't deliver.

Similar thoughts were going through Patrick's mind as he chatted with the man who had fathered the latest addition to his family. Jambo smiled at him and Patrick saw Lil's attraction to him. When he smiled, he looked like he had the world in his pocket.

"A boy, eh? But she's good, yeah? She is all right really, Lil?" He was genuinely concerned, both for Lil and the baby.

"She's fine. Why don't you come and see them? We can run you to the hospital. They took them in, just to be on the safe side, you know. She had it in the kitchen and gave my little sister a fright, I can tell you."

It wasn't a threat. Jambo knew that if he didn't want to go, no one was going to force him. But suddenly he wanted to go. He wanted to see this son of his. In fact, he felt proud and excited about him. If he was anything like this young man, he was going to be worth knowing. He liked Pat, he remembered him as a child and knew his father much better than any of them realized. It was how he had become friends with Lil in the first place.

"Eustace, why you not getting another drink, boy?"

Mac grinned. No one called him Eustace, most people didn't even realize it was his name.

"Wet the baby's head, yeah?"

Pat walked back to the bar again and wondered what it would be like to have a new brother at his age.

Lance was holding the baby and Lil watched him with a tired resignation. He seemed to be overwhelmed with the night's events. But then men always were, they were there at the conception and rarely there for the birth. Women, after the first baby, just got on with it. The miracle of life was actually just a fucking painful few hours when you came right down to it. The baby was the end result and that was all women were interested in.

For the first time in years, she was with Lance and they were alone and she didn't have the heart to push him away, or the inclination. She was exhausted.

Pat was over the moon. He was a good kid, they were all good kids. As she thought that, she glanced up at Lance and she still didn't feel she could include him in that statement.

"Give me the baby, will you?"

Lance smiled as he placed the bundle into her arms.

"He's a real bruiser, Mum. A real beauty."

Lil nodded. She wished her mother would come back from the canteen so she didn't have to make conversation with this huge man, a man who made her feel uneasy and inadequate.

The baby was looking up at her and she smiled with the pleasure of looking at him. He was handsome, and not just Mum handsome; she knew he would break some hearts before he was much older.

He started to cry, the high-pitched mewling of a new baby, the sound that she would hear through a hurricane and know it was her child. The crying caused the hormones to rampage through her tired body. She kissed him gently, smelling his newness and breathing in his very essence and enjoying his first few hours outside the womb. Already she felt like he had been there always, she felt as if she had never been without him and wondered how she could ever have coped without him. He was her baby, her last child, her redeemer.

Lance watched them together and the jealousy rose up inside him like a tidal wave. His mother had never looked at him like that. He knew she had never wanted him like she had wanted the others, that was clear to him. Watching her with the boy he felt the sheer loneliness of his life wash over him.

"I'd better get back to Kathleen. At least this has cheered her up a bit."

Lil nodded again. She felt all she ever did with Lance was make head movements or gestures, anything rather than talk to him for any length of time.

Kathleen had watched the birth with all the others and she had burst into tears; she was really affected by the power of it all. The little ones had been beside themselves with excitement. Even Shamus couldn't hide his pride at his new brother, though it wasn't cool to admit it. And she was so proud of them all, especially Eileen, bless her, who had more or less delivered her new brother.

The baby was mewling once more and, as Lil looked down at him, she knew the name she wanted. Looking at Lance, she said happily, "Shawn, his name is Shawn."

As she said that she saw Jambo walking towards her and she placed the boy into his arms without a word being spoken.

Patrick and Mackie were both laughing and cooing over the baby, and Lil felt happier than she had in years.

"It's Shawn. I've named him Shawn."

Jambo looked down at his son and felt a rush of love and protection. This boy was his flesh and blood.

Sitting on the bed beside Lil, he said happily, "You did good, Lil. You did really good."

Chapter Twenty-Seven

Shawn was a big child and he was also a happy child, everyone in his orbit doted on him. Even Kathleen, who had finally been diagnosed as schizophrenic, enjoyed his company. In fact, he seemed to cheer her up and made her forget her voices for a few moments. It was hard dealing with her condition but with the help of drugs she kept it pretty much under control. Other than her occasionally outlandish thoughts on the world in general, she was much better than she had been for a long time.

It made life easier for everyone when she was happy; everyone in the house felt her depression when it descended on her. In fact, it affected them all in different ways, even little Shawn felt the difference; he was quieter somehow, more clingy.

Annie was enamored of the boy and that was the most amazing thing as far as Lil was concerned. Lil knew her mother had a streak of racism running through her, as her husband had. The fact that Annie had not said a word was, to Lil, the most amazing thing of all. Shawn was not really black as such but he was dark enough so there would be no question of his parentage. His eyes alone were to die for, huge brown orbs, surrounded by long, silky black lashes. The girls were jealous of them, as they were of his coffee-colored skin and his soft musical voice. Shawn was adored, and he knew it.

A friendly child by nature, he seemed to attract people wherever he went. And Lil and the others couldn't imagine their lives without him in it. Even Patrick took him out in the car with him and Shawn loved it.

He loved cars and he loved his big brothers. Colleen and Christy took him to the park, Shamus taught him to swear and Eileen and Kathleen fought over who was going to put him to bed.

Lil had gone back to work three weeks after his birth and now, two years on, she ran all the clubs and oversaw the debts. Jambo was a regular visitor and they all liked him and accepted the way he wandered in and out of their lives at will.

Lil believed that Shawn's birth had been the catalyst for her luck turning. She knew it was stupid to even think it, but that was how it felt to her. Since his arrival, everything seemed to go smoothly for once. Everyone seemed to find a piece of happiness to call their own. He was her lucky charm, the child for her old age as Janie had once referred to him. All the bad things were behind them, she was convinced of that. In fact, she could go days without thinking of Patrick or Lenny. Somehow, when she thought of one she thought of the other. It tainted her memories of her husband and she knew she still harbored resentment at the way he had left them all with hardly a penny to call their own. She still found herself getting angry over it even though she knew it was completely irrational. The past was the past. It had happened and there was nothing she could do to change it.

Pat was in the office, as always, on a Monday night. Monday was when they worked out the debts, collected any rents owed and decided who was going to be where for the rest of the week. It was their busiest day and Lance was now sitting opposite his brother and waiting for the lecture he was sure would be arriving at any moment. It was boring. Pat thought he was some kind of fucking film star the way he carried on.

"Listen, Lance, you are starting to get on my fucking wick. Do you think I won't hear what you're doing?"

Pat was so annoyed it was all he could do not to lamp his brother there and then.

"What, what is it now, Pat? Did I breathe wrong, or what?"

The sarcasm was heavy and Pat sat back in the padded leather chair, forcing himself to relax.

"You beat up a fucking working man. He's got three fucking kids and you've nearly crippled him. How's he going to fucking earn a crust now? How are we gonna get our money? The money that is *so* important that you nearly crippled him for nine hundred quid. Nine hundred fucking quid and you beat him with a tire iron . . ."

Lance shrugged, as always, as if he had the weight of the world on his shoulders.

"He was two weeks late, what was I supposed to do?"

"You cunt. You knew he was on holiday, he's always had an account with us and his credit is fucking exemplary. He always pays on the nose, you fucking stupid, arrogant little shite."

Pat was out of the chair now and Lance flinched. Despite himself he was worried.

"Three fucking kids and a fucking life and you destroy it all without a fucking thought, you . . ."

Pat was hovering over him now and the urge to hammer him was so strong he could almost taste it.

"I ain't having it any more, Lance. This is your last chance and I mean it."

"It was an accident . . ."

Pat walked away from his brother and stared out of the window at the pavement below.

"Accident, my arse. You are on a fucking final warning, you vicious, vindictive *cunt.* How can I trust you now, eh? Even Spider and Mackie think you have gone too far this time. You're making enemies and your enemies eventually become mine."

Lance knew that this was serious. Normally Patrick went off on one and that was that. After all, their reputation for collecting money so quickly had been built on the fact he didn't take any prisoners. If the money didn't come to them at the designated time then the person was made to see the error of their ways. This was normally achieved with brute force and his unerring instinct for knowing what frightened the person involved the most, and using that knowledge without pity.

"This is too far, Lance. You have finally gone too far."

Pat was still on the verge of taking a tire iron to Lance himself. See how he liked being beaten over the head and back with a heavy object.

The thought of hammering him was so fucking tempting, just to vent this colossal anger. And all this over less than a grand in cash, it was laughable.

He knew Lance's strong points and he used them to his advantage, he admitted that. But this attack was a reminder of what he was dealing with on a daily basis. Lance was slowly becoming a liability and he didn't know how to rein him in without them falling out big time.

If he was honest, he was beginning to loathe the sight of Lance, and yet once they were outside of work, his brother was a different person. It was as if he was proving something all the time. But what that was, exactly, he had no idea.

Pat looked back at Lance. He was a strange guy, there was no doubt about that. From his ill-fitting suit to his scuffed brogues, he looked like Worzel Gummidge's little brother. Even his hair wasn't cut in any kind of style; he often needed a shave and he looked like he was a bit simple. But he wasn't. That was another one of his strengths: people believed he was a fucking retard and he wasn't. Lance was sharper than a samurai sword when he needed to be. He acted like a cretin and kept away from the pubs and the clubs, rarely venturing out unless it was to harm some-one. He was a fucking weirdo and he knew that something had to be done about it. Other than Kathleen and little Shawn, Lance had no care for anyone or anything and it bothered him.

"Just go, Lance. Fuck off out of my sight . . ."

Lance still sat there, his heavy body slumped in the chair and his sarcastic half-smile in evidence, as usual.

But Lance knew he had gone too far this time. Pat was distancing himself from him and he wasn't sure that he even realized what he was doing himself. They were spending less and less time together and it hurt him. Lance wanted to be his brother's best friend but it was impossible. Pat was happy to be friends with anyone and Lance couldn't be like that, no matter how hard he tried, and he had tried. He knew he made people uneasy. He knew that for some reason he didn't gel with anyone. He knew he looked odd and that made people uneasy and it wasn't deliberate, at least not at first.

Now he admitted that sometimes he used his personality to his own advantage. When he turned up on a doorstep at five in the morning with his smile and a blunt instrument, people tended to pay him what he asked without question. He was also asked by outsiders to collect particularly difficult debts on occasion and he was very well-paid for it. In fact, he had a reputation as the best collector in the city. He was admired for the simple reason he collected them alone; Pat had not been out collecting with him for a long time and he very rarely used anyone else. He had a few people he might ask to collect a small debt but not the big ones. Not the important ones. He preferred to collect those personally.

Why he had gone over the top this time he wasn't sure. In fact, he had known at the time that it was too much. But he had not cared, he had never liked the man. He was a clean-cut type with well-ironed shirts and a penchant for a bet now and again. He was a fucking drone, a fucking suit. He was nothing to him and why Pat was so upset about it all he couldn't really understand. But he was, and he had to show some remorse to make Pat think he was sorry about it.

"Look, Pat, he fucked me off . . ."

Pat turned on him again, shouting angrily, "Don't fucking *lie* to me. That bloke couldn't get the hump if he was Quasimodo. You were out of order *again*. This ain't the first time, is it? A few months ago you broke Jackie Tenant's fucking legs and he still can't work. You are the reason people have stopped betting with us, did you know that, eh? Punters are frightened you are going to turn up all guns blazing for a fucking drink, the equivalent of a fucking giro."

Pat poked a finger in his brother's face.

"You are costing *me* money, mate, and that is something I will *not* fucking allow. Once you start being a liability, you're out the door."

"Oh, have a day off, Pat . . . I was out of order, I admit. But at the end of the day we are fucking brothers and you're talking to me like I'm nothing."

Patrick could see the confusion in Lance's eyes and knew that he didn't really comprehend what he had done that was so wrong. He had always been like that; he pretended he was remorseful, but Pat knew he wasn't. It was like the girl on the bus all those years ago. He preyed on anyone weaker than himself; it was in his nature to do so.

"We are brothers and nothing can change that, but I will cut you off like a diseased limb if you cause anything like this again. People are talking about it. You might not have liked him but plenty of other people did, and you are bringing too much fucking interest on to us from the customers. It stops and it stops today, right?"

"Of course, Pat. I said I was sorry . . ."

"No, you're not, but all that shit aside, I am warning *you* to keep your temper in check."

Pat walked back to the window. His heart was beating so loud he could hear it and he knew that it was from anger and his disapproval of his brother's way of life.

"All right, Pat, I'm going and, once more, I'm sorry. I get carried away."

"Like when you were on the bus all those years ago? I ain't a mug, Lance, and don't treat me like one. You can go now and keep out of my face for a while until I calm down."

He had his back to his brother, knowing that he was still angry enough to actually strike him if he didn't leave him alone.

When Pat turned around, the office was empty; Lance had walked out without a sound as usual. He was good at that, was Lance. He knew it was the barb about the bus that had made him go. Lance hated that to be mentioned in any way. Pat knew he wondered if people still talked about it, remembered it. The girl he had thrown off the bus was the only person who seemed to have forgiven him; she came round with her mum and she always said hello to him. The world was full of strange things but that, he had to admit, was one of the strangest things he had ever come across.

Spider and Mackie were in a lock-up garage in Bethnal Green. The whole floor space was covered in black trash bags and the trash bags were full of cannabis. The smell was overpowering but, where they were, it only masked the smell of engine oil and overflowing trash cans.

As they waited for the buyers to arrive, they sat on a bench and smoked a joint together. It was a heavy smoke, all buds and no seeds. The first few hits gave them the spaced-out feeling that was the whole point of smoking dope in the first place. It was what dub reggae was for and why junk food was invented.

They were both aware of every noise, no matter how quiet, and they felt the heaviness that seemed to crawl all over their bodies while they waited.

"That's a good fucking draw, Dad."

Spider nodded in agreement. He was still taking short, quick puffs, determined to prolong the high for as long as possible.

"Too good to sell to this fucking crowd, anyway."

They both laughed then. Most of the dope they sold outside the community was not up to the standard they had come to expect.

"I love the quiet, don't you? It seems to seep into your skin and lets you become a part of it all."

Spider nodded once more; he knew exactly what the boy meant.

It was like becoming at one with the world. Unless someone interrupted that, of course, and then it was a different high altogether.

"You seen anything of Jimmy Brick lately?"

Spider shook his head again. It was a question he was being asked on a far too regular basis.

"Why you keep asking me that?"

Mac sighed. "Just interested, that's all. I know he's working with Pat. But I thought you were mates, that's all."

"We are, or perhaps I should say, were. Since he came back from Spain, he's not the same somehow. I don't know what it is, boy."

Mackie looked at his father then and he saw the heaviness of his dreads and the glittering of his dark eyes. He was well stoned.

"You didn't keep in touch then when he was away?"

"No. I didn't even know where he was, to be honest. After Patrick died, it was all fucked up you know. He didn't seem to have anything on paper, even my partnerships with him were fucking disputed. He was a shrewd man but he wasn't expecting to die, was he? So, like many a man before him, he was investing his money and living off the proceeds. With people like us, it's the equivalent to an overdraft. There was a lot of fucking doubting and fighting over it. Brewster won because he had the biggest crew behind him and, of course, he looked like he was avenging the death. A death that he had actually had a hand in arranging."

Mac listened to his father with interest.

"How come you wanted me back on the scene so suddenly?"

Spider was taken aback at the words. "What the fuck do you mean?"

"What I say. You had a new family, didn't you? You paid for us but you didn't really see much of me until I grew up. I used to wonder where you were, you know, wonder what you were doing. Is it because my mum was white?"

"What the fuck you on about, boy? All my kids are taken care of and you never went without anything that you needed. Your mother was the fucking bugbear there, her and her father, who, incidentally, hated me from the moment I knocked on his front door."

Spider was laughing again. It was the loud and boisterous laugh of the very stoned.

"Don't you tell yourself things that never happened, OK? You were my firstborn and I loved you from the moment I saw you."

"You've got three boys and we're all called Eustace. Don't you think that's fucking strange? Because, to be perfectly honest, Dad, I do."

Spider shrugged nonchalantly. "No, actually, I don't. Now stop this stupid fucking talk. I can hear a car outside, the dealers have arrived." He didn't say anything else to his son but the conversation had unsettled him.

Lil was with the kids watching a film and as Lance came in the room Annie jumped up, as always, to get him a drink of some description.

"What you watching?" He didn't ask anyone in particular, this was how he communicated when his mother was in the room with him.

Colleen, who was lying on the sofa with her legs across her mother's lap, answered him. "*An Officer and a Gentleman*. It's really good."

He sat down on one of the armchairs and Annie brought him in a glass of beer. He took it with a nod and Lil had to concentrate to block him out of her mind. Annie settled herself in the other armchair and Eileen and Lil were tangled up together on the sofa with Colleen. Christy was sprawled on the floor, his hands under his chin, and Shamus had a glass of shandy beside him.

"Is Kathleen all right?"

Once more, Lance was talking to the room in general and, once more, Colleen answered.

"She's upstairs talking to herself again."

Lil sat up and smacked Colleen's leg noisily.

"Don't say that about her!"

Eileen didn't take her eyes off the screen as she said quietly, "Why not? It's true. She was at it all last night, effing and blinding to the air as per usual. It gets on my nerves."

"She can't help it and you know that. So stop being so bloody nasty."

Lil sat up now, her nice evening ruined. "Why do you always fucking come in and cause upset, eh, Lance? Why can't you just leave us all alone for once?"

No one said a word. Christy was hunching his shoulders as if warding off a blow and Colleen had closed her eyes tightly.

Lil knew she shouldn't lose her temper so quickly but she couldn't help herself. When Lance asked about Kathleen she felt a note of accusation in his voice and she knew it was there, she wasn't imagining it. He was good at masking it but she knew him better than he knew himself.

"Did you see Pat's new flat?"

Lance didn't answer her as she knew he wouldn't.

"About time you got yourself somewhere and all. This place is getting too small now this lot are growing up and Kathleen needs a room to herself, as does Eileen."

There, she had finally said it out loud. The sooner he went, the better; she knew what had happened this week. She had been the one who had been left to tell Pat all about it.

"Leave him alone, Lil. Who'll look after Kathleen if he goes?"

Annie's voice was worried. Lance was the reason she got up in the morning and they all knew that in one way or another.

"Why don't you go and live with Nanny?"

This was from Christy, who was always trying to keep the peace. "She's in that flat all on her own and there's plenty of room there."

Lil could have kissed him, but she kept herself in check. Annie had been angling for this for a long time and now she knew that Lance had been put in a position where he had to make a stand of some kind.

He sipped his beer noisily and then he looked at his mother and said loudly, "I can't leave Kathleen. I'm the only one who can calm her down and you know it. I pay my way and if you want me out you'll have to throw me out."

Lance's voice was as cold and flat as always. No inflection at all, it was a monotonous voice that was like a loud scratch across a blackboard to Lil.

"Consider yourself thrown out then, Lance." The words were clipped and very determined.

Annie was pleased. She knew Lance would come to her, if only to be near Kathleen. He wasn't capable of living alone like Patrick. He couldn't even boil an egg for himself and, as Annie had waited on him hand and foot all his life, it didn't seem likely that was going to change at any time in the future. He didn't have girlfriends, so unless Lil pushed him out of the nest it was likely he would never have gone. He walked out of the room with Annie bustling after him, as always, and everyone breathed a collective sigh of relief.

"Can I really have his room, Mum?"

"Course you can, Eileen. Do me a favor and decorate it, will you? I'll pay and you can do it how you like, babe."

"What about when I need a room of me own?"

Lil looked at Colleen and saw the burgeoning breasts and the slim legs and Eileen seemed to notice her at the exact same time and she said, with false resignation, "I think you had better share with me and then Shamus can go in with Christy."

Colleen was thrilled at the prospect of sharing a bedroom with her big sister; she envisaged make-up and nail varnish, and Eileen envisaged someone who would sneak down and let her in if she had a late one.

Annie came back into the room. Her face was wearing its usual frown and Lil noticed that she was getting old. She seemed to be thinner suddenly and her skin was papery.

"That was a bit harsh, Lil."

Lil lit a cigarette.

"Look, Mum, you got what you wanted. I don't want him living here at thirty, do I? And the way things were going, that was a distinct possibility. We need the room and you know we do. Now, shut the fuck up and pour us both a nice drink. I have to go to the club later and I want a bath. It looks like the film is a fucking write-off, don't it?"

Ivana and Pat were sitting at the bar of the club. Most business was done from the premises now and Ivana was a useful addition to the club in more ways than one. She was quite happy to seat the girls and scam the customers and she did it very well with a nice smile and a friendly attitude. Even his mother had thawed towards her over the last couple of years. The more Ivana made herself useful, the more time Lil could spend with Shawn.

Pat smiled as he thought of the little boy. He really was a funny little kid, all happy smiles and friendliness. In their world that was more important than most people realized.

Pat glanced at his watch and said to Ivana, "Do me a favor and show that skank up, will you."

Scanlon was due any moment and he still disliked the man immensely but he was a necessary evil. To make sure he achieved his ultimate goal, he needed him.

Ivana ushered him in a few minutes later.

Scanlon was a different man to the one that had arrived there two years earlier. He was not as cocky but he was much more willing to work for his money. Now that he was actually out in the open, so to speak, he didn't suffer from such awful feelings of guilt any more.

As he sat down, he passed Pat a bundle of papers.

"Where did you get these?"

"From one of the vice blokes. To be honest, I think you should talk to him yourself."

Patrick stared at him for a few moments. "What, more money to be handed over to dirty cops? I'll be getting up a pension scheme for you all next."

Even Scanlon laughed at that and it changed his whole face. It was such an unusual thing to see him even remotely cheerful that Pat was struck dumb.

Scanlon shrugged. "I've got to admit that this is starting to interest me now. The more I find out, the more I want to know."

Pat understood that. He knew the man was a loner and, in reality, he was the perfect person to do his ferreting for him. He was naturally antisocial and he was also naturally nosy. It was a winning combination for Pat.

"Who is this vice bloke then? Can you bring him in to meet me?"

"I think so. He knew that what I'm doing is not on the up. But you'd be surprised how often this type of thing goes on. A lot of people want to see witness statements so they have the address of the witness and their account of whatever they saw. It's such a common thing now that there's a fixed price list."

Pat was scanning the papers before him and he got up and poured them both a stiff drink. Sitting down, he looked at the papers once more and said, "I was right, wasn't I?"

Scanlon nodded and took a large gulp of his brandy before saying, "It certainly looks that way."

Scanlon finished his drink in silence and Patrick was still sitting there staring into space when he left him.

Kathleen was sitting at the bedroom window where she sat and smoked for hours. The net curtains had lots of little burn holes from where she forgot what she was doing with the cigarette. As she talked to herself she would wave the cigarette around as if she was talking to real people.

Eileen was moving her stuff out and Kathleen looked happy enough about it, so Eileen didn't feel bad about it.

In fact, Kathleen seemed pleased. "Will you still sit with me though, when I want to go to sleep?"

Eileen grinned. "Course I will. If you get nervous I can still spend the night, can't I? I ain't going anywhere, only across the landing."

"Are you still seeing that bloke, Eileen?"

Eileen picked up a handful of sweaters from the drawer by her bed and, hushing her sister, she nodded.

Kathleen was giggling and Eileen shushed her again. Even though she knew Kathleen wouldn't say anything, she was still nervous that one of the younger kids might overhear and repeat what they heard.

Lance was packing, and she felt sorry for him, but another part of her was also glad he was leaving. At least her mother would be happier.

"Will you be all right, Kath, with Lance leaving?"

"Course I will. Nanny Annie will be happy, won't she?"

"I suppose. Mum left you a bar of chocolate in the fridge, do you want me to get it?"

"No, you eat it or give it to the little ones."

"You've got to eat, Kath, you're skin and bones."

Kathleen lit another cigarette and went back to gazing out of the window and Eileen knew that she wouldn't talk again for ages.

Not to any of them anyway. The low chattering started almost immediately and Eileen wondered, for the millionth time, why the murder of their father had affected Kathleen so much and not her.

She had overheard Janie telling someone years before that the twins, her and Kathleen, had tried to hug their father's body and had been covered in his blood. She didn't remember that. All she remembered was the crying and Lance sitting on the stairs in his underpants. And she wondered, at times, if she had imagined that.

Chapter Twenty-Eight

"Are you all right, Mum?"

Eileen's voice was soft and full of concern. Lil was off-color; she had been lying on the sofa for a couple of days and it wasn't like her at all.

"No. I feel tired again, I just feel really tired. I don't feel ill as such."

"Go to the doctor, for fuck's sake, Lil." Annie's voice was loud as she shouted through from the kitchen.

"I'll go tomorrow. You look nice, love."

Eileen looked stunning and, as she brushed her long hair, Lil was reminded of just how lovely the twins were. Even poor old Kathleen; she didn't wear make-up or dress herself in fashionable clothes but she was still a beauty.

As Lil moved her arm to pick up her cigarettes, she felt a pain under her arm. It was sharp and made her catch her breath.

"Ring Pat and tell him I am still out for the count, would you, darling?"

Colleen bounded into the room and said gaily, "I'll do it. Can I go to the Wimpy with Lance?"

"Course you can, love. Take Shawn if you like."

Hearing his name, Shawn opened his eyes and, yawning, he smiled up at the women in his life.

"Get him dressed for me, would you?"

Colleen picked the little boy up and walked from the room happily.

Pat came in then and, smiling at everyone, he said nonchalantly,

"You're going to see a bloke in Harley Street tomorrow, Mum. Might as well get you a full inspection, eh?"

"Don't be so fucking silly. I'm just tired, that's all."

Pat was kneeling down and giving little Shawn a packet of Jelly Tots as he said, in a firm voice that brooked no arguments, "You're going and that's that."

Lil lay back on the sofa once more, feeling worse than ever.

"What is it with you, Lance? What the fuck goes through your head?"

The two men were laughing as they walked up the driveway of a large house in Chigwell. The gates had been jimmied open by Lance with the aid of a set of bolt cutters. The driveway was graveled and their footsteps alerted the owner to their presence. He opened the front door with a baseball bat in one hand and a twelve-inch carving knife in the other.

"Oooh, that's not very friendly, is it?"

The man was grinning but the men knew he was frightened, the sweat rolling down his face told them that, plus the trembling of the hand that held the knife.

"Fuck off. You ain't coming in here."

"But that's just where you're wrong. We are coming in and we are removing certain objects; two of those said objects will be your bollocks if you don't get out of the way."

Lance pulled out a shotgun from underneath his raincoat; it was sawed-off and he cocked it over his knee. Then, holding it up to his chin, he sited it on the man's crotch.

"I think a sawed-off beats a knife any day of the week, don't you, Donny?"

Donny Barker nodded as if thinking the question over seriously, and he eventually answered in a game-show-host voice, "Without a doubt. Now, if you don't mind, we have chosen to forfeit the prizes and take the money."

The man was shaking his head. He was bald with small dark eyes and overlarge lips, and was not an attractive man at all. His wife, however, was a real looker, as he was wont to tell anyone who would listen.

Fortunately, his children looked like her side of the family. It was these children and that wife he was trying to protect.

"I ain't got the fucking money, how many times? I'll get it as soon as I can."

Lance advanced on him, still aiming the gun, and he walked the man back through his large entrance hall and into his kitchen.

It was a beautiful property and Lance and Donny were both pricing everything in their heads as they made their way to the kitchen with him.

"Put the weapons on the worktop, please, and step back towards the table."

The man did as he was asked, and Donny picked them up and studied them as if they were the most interesting things he had ever seen in his life.

"This knife is really sharp. You could do someone a real damage with this."

As he spoke, Donny smiled at Lance and he nodded his agreement.

"You could cut someone's eyes out or slice off a few fingers, anything really."

The man was white now and his eyes were on overdrive with nervous blinking. It was a reaction that Lance had seen many times over the years. He knew the man was thinking about how to get out of this, play for time, and then working out how to get the money required and get out of this once and for all. Lance also knew that he kept a small fortune in a safe, somewhere in this sprawling mansion that was hocked up to the hilt. The cars, everything in the place was rented or bought hot. He was like a lot of them he dealt with, all top show. Living far beyond their means and what for? That was the thing Lance had never understood. So a group of people he drank with knew he had a nice car and a nice home. It was a fucking con, all a con. Now he had borrowed his last fucking pound and they were not about to give him any kind of a pass.

"You owe me the money now, us. We bought the debt, see, and we are like the Mounties, we always get our man."

"Look, I can get you the money all right . . ."

Lance grinned. "Can you get it before your wife turns up with the kids? Your Bianca's ballet lesson should be over by now and it would be a shame if they were to walk into all this, eh?"

Donny nodded again. His ugly face was screwed up in mock concern.

"Poor little mares, coming in to all this. Good at ballet, is she?"

He ran a well-manicured nail down the knife blade. "Shame if she lost a toe or two, wouldn't it? I mean, toes are what help you balance, ain't they?"

He looked at the man then and saw his fear, his terror.

"You wouldn't. Not a kid, you can't hurt kids."

Lance answered him then. "I can. I'll fucking hurt anyone who owes me money. I take it personally, like an insult or a fucking prank. Now, where is your safe? Open it and pay us and we'll go. If you don't, I will slice up everyone in the house, even the new baby you're so proud of."

As he spoke, they all heard the front door opening and a loud voice saying, "Oi, have you seen the gates? They're wide open. You told me to keep them closed."

The wife walked into the kitchen and saw what was going on. She turned quickly, but not quickly enough. She was holding her baby boy, and her older daughter, who had just turned twelve, was still in the hall-way taking off her coat and boots. She looked up at the noise and she started crying when she saw the way her mother was flinching in fear, a man pulling her roughly back into the kitchen. The woman hunched over her baby. After seeing the gun she instinctively tried to shield the child from any shot that might be fired.

"Please, I don't want any trouble, we don't know anything, let us go . . ." Her voice was drenched with tears and she was stuttering with fright.

Her daughter ran to her, crying noisily, and that set the baby off. The noise was loud and Lance shouted above it. "Give me her, now."

Donny was as shocked as the parents of the child.

"I said, give me that kid, now."

"Leave it out, Lance, this don't warrant anything of that magnitude."

Lance stormed over to the little crowd and dragged the girl from her mother's arms.

The woman was now hysterical and Lance shouted at her. "Shut the fuck up or I'll shoot the lot of you, just for the peace and fucking quiet." He held the sobbing child in front of him and he pointed the gun at her head.

The child was quiet suddenly, as if she knew exactly how serious the situation was. The tears were rolling down her cheeks and yet not a sound emerged from her.

"All right, for fuck's sake, let her go. You fucking bastards. Let her go and I'll give you what you want."

Lance pushed the little girl away and she stumbled, her fear so acute she couldn't walk properly. Lance shouted at the sobbing woman, who was attempting to help her daughter up from the floor and hold on to her baby at the same time.

"Get out and shut the fucking door. Remember we can see you, so don't get clever. All right?"

The woman nodded and Donny could see she was on the verge of nervous collapse. The girl was almost in a trance and he knew fear could do that. He knew that the terror she had experienced would be there all her life.

"Well, fuck off then!"

She walked out of the kitchen towards their new conservatory, which was actually the reason her husband had gambled all his money away. As she passed him, she said angrily, "My mother was right about you. She said you'd end up in jail or being topped and now you've brought all this into my home."

She was pushed through the glass doors into the conservatory, and then Lance said, "I can always top her for you, as a sort of bonus for paying up. She sounds like a right fucking nag and those kids and that racket all day and night. I don't discriminate, I'll fucking shoot anyone." Lance waited for the man to tell them what they wanted to know.

Instead, he shook his head in exaggerated sorrow and said with a voice filled with regret, "Please, guys, give me a week. I just need a week, that's all. Then I'll have the money for you, I swear on my mother's eyesight."

Lance was angry now. That this man would still gamble his kids' lives was to him as unbelievable as it was disgusting.

"You *cunt*. You'd still fucking try and keep from paying a debt even though we threatened your *kids*? You know me and you know what I am capable of. You fucking lowdown, filthy piece of shit."

"Come on, Lance. You know I'm good for it, especially if you're collecting it."

"You bought tickets off Dodger Marks to go to Spain this Thursday. I own him, like I fucking own you now. I know everything about the people who owe me money. I put the word out and I gather information, so I know what I can ask for and what I can't before I even set foot near the mark in question. You think I believe that you were going to fucking pay me from fucking Benidorm? I would have turned up there, you fucking twat; there ain't nowhere you could go to escape me once I decide I want you."

Lance was shaking his head and laughing at the incongruity of this person's absolute stupidity.

"This is it now. You're a fucking enemy for life. If I see you around, I'll spank you and you'll regret cunting me off for the rest of your fucking days."

He pointed the gun at the man's feet and let off a shot. The noise in the kitchen was deafening and the blood and bone from the man's feet was everywhere. The man was staring down at the carnage of what had once been expensive shoes and was unable to believe what had just happened; the pain had not kicked in yet. It took a few minutes for that to happen. The shock of the event needed to wear off first before the brain realized what had occurred and then reacted appropriately.

Lance was like a maniac now. He was pointing the gun at the conservatory door, screaming with anger and hate.

"Go and get that baby, get that little girl. I'll fucking maim them and you'll remember your fucking disregard for their welfare all your life. I'll teach you a lesson for life. I'll fucking maim them so bad, you'll wish I'd killed them. And you, you'll wish I killed you and all."

Donny was in as much shock as the man they were shaking down. Lance was gone, completely gone. He had lost it, his eyes were glazed, his face was red with anger and he was spraying spittle everywhere as he spoke. He was completely and utterly off the game.

"You fucking heard me, Donny! Get the fucking kids in here again. I want to teach this cunt a lesson, teach him that you take care of your family and you don't offer them up."

The man was listening and, like Donny, he was in no doubt that Lance was capable of doing what he said, just to teach him a lesson, to prove a point.

He dropped on to his knees then. "Please, no. Please, Lance. I'll take you to the safe and give you everything; money, jewelry, whatever you want. But please, please stop this now."

Lance stared down at the man for long moments, and both him and Donny could see him physically trying to get his anger under control.

"Come on, Lance, let's get the money and split."

Donny's voice seemed to penetrate his brain but it was at least five minutes before he answered him. He was battling it out with himself and though both men had heard of his vicious temper, none had seen it at close quarters before. It was a definite learning curve for all concerned.

"All right."

He looked at the man on the floor. "Fucking get a move on, show me what I need."

The man had to drag himself from the kitchen; his feet and shins were like stumps of bloody meat and the blood was everywhere. He had to drag himself across the hallway and up the stairs to the galleried landing and Lance followed him while Donny watched the rest of the little family. By the time they entered the master bedroom, he had lost so much blood he was on the verge of passing out.

"The safe's behind that picture. The combination is 999999."

Lance grinned at the irony of it.

"The emergency services number and you'll be needing them. I reckon you'll need more than a corn plaster on those feet of yours."

Lance opened the safe quickly and, taking a carrier bag from his pocket, he emptied it of everything. It was more than the man owed but that was tough shit now.

He had done the one thing guaranteed to make Lance lose his temper for real.

He had tried to take him for a fool and he had tried it while his kids were in the vicinity.

He looked down at the man with hate and he said quietly, "You can either lose a limb now or I'll take one of your kids out."

The man was almost delirious with loss of blood and fear and Lance kicked him savagely in the face to try to bring him round. But all he managed to do was knock him unconscious and he was angry about it because he would have liked to know the answer to that question.

"Mum's been to the hospital for tests, Lance, have you heard?"

Lance nodded. Patrick sat opposite him and waited until Annie came into her little front room with the tea tray before continuing.

"Here you are, lads. Want a cookie? I've got some Bourbons in the cupboard I keep for me guests."

Pat shook his head.

"Sit down, Nan, I need to talk to you both."

Annie sat down, the serious tone of his voice told her all she needed to know. "Is it cancer?" Her voice was low, frightened and full of guilt.

Pat nodded sadly. "She goes in tomorrow. They are going to take her breast off and they think she's got a good chance if they do that."

He was not comfortable talking about women's things and he was still in shock that his mother, the strongest person he had known, was ill. Seriously ill, and her still relatively young, with young children. It was wrong, all wrong. Like she hadn't had enough to deal with in her life.

Lance sipped his tea, blowing on it noisily first. "She'll need help. Me and Nan will take Kathleen in here with us and that'll make a difference to the household. The others won't have to watch her then, will they?"

Patrick was surprised at this turn of events but the more he thought about it, the more sense it made. Lance seemed to understand his hesitation because he said loudly, "She worries about her and so she should. She's not the full ten bob, as we all know. But she also knows that I'll watch over her and whatever she thinks of me, she knows I have a special rapport with Kathleen and always have. Remember when we were kids and you would always watch Eileen and I always watched Kathleen. Mum will rest easier knowing the girls ain't got to watch over her and all. Little Shawn will be more than enough for them."

Annie nodded her agreement. "He's got a point, Pat. She worries about her more than the others."

Pat sipped his tea without answering her. He knew his granny and he knew that if Annie had Kathleen, it would take the onus off her having to look after the others. She would look good to everyone and she would come out of it all with Brownie points to spare, even though the bulk of the caring would be put on to himself and the girls.

Pat knew where Lance got his more suspect personality traits from. He loathed Annie at times, she was always after the main chance. But he didn't say that. He was trying to sort this out as best he could. If he didn't sort this out, he knew that no one else would. He also realized that Annie had not asked any details about the mastectomy or how her daughter was feeling. Or even what the visiting hours were in the hospital. She was seeing how this would play out for her in the future; she would be the center of attention with her cronies and have something to talk about. She was a user and she always would be.

But he didn't say a word to either of them and instead drank his tea as quickly as possible and excused himself from their company.

Both of them made him feel dirty and he hated being around them, especially when they were together. Annie Diamond had a lot to answer for, and his brother was just one of the things she had on her conscience.

"Have you seen Colleen?" There was something in Christy's voice that was so urgent it made all the others look at him.

"No, we thought she was with you."

"I ain't seen her all day. No one has seen her."

Eileen sighed heavily and looked at Lance who was helping her to bring a bed downstairs for their mother.

He rolled his eyes at her but she didn't bother to answer her little brother, they had too much going on at the moment. Their mum was getting back from the hospital later that afternoon and they thought it would be better if she was in the front room so she could recuperate with the kids around her and feel a part of the household.

It was six weeks since she had had the operation to remove her breast and a week since she had finished the radiotherapy. She looked ill and she was a shadow of her former self but she was a fighter, and that alone was enough to make her children believe she would get better. She just needed to rest now and get back on her feet. That was what they told themselves anyway. The thought of losing her was the biggest fear of all their lives. Since her illness had been diagnosed, they had been aware of just how much they depended on her.

"Well, I can't find her."

"Colleen is probably round her mate's, stop worrying."

Christy sat down on the sofa and sighed heavily, making Eileen laugh. He was such a drama king when the fancy took him.

"She'll turn up, she always does. Have you been to the library? She was saying about going there this morning."

"Her mates said she wasn't at school today."

Lance stopped what he was doing and turned to his little brother.

"What do you mean? Didn't you see her?"

Christy shook his head and said in exasperation, "That is what I am *trying* to tell you. I assumed she was with her mates. But they ain't seen her, no one has."

Eileen caught the inflection in his voice then and saw he was really worried about her. They were so close and she knew he wouldn't worry without cause.

"Didn't you see her at all today?"

He shook his head once more and his face showed them that he was fed up with repeating himself. "She don't walk to school with me any more, she hasn't for ages, she meets up with her mates and I meet up with mine. I don't always see her *in* school either. We're in different years, remember. But we *always* see each other on the way home; we meet up and walk the last part together and we talk about everything, you know."

He meant their mother's illness, but he didn't want to say that. Eileen understood his reticence, they all felt like that about it. Sometimes she was frightened to talk about it too much, it made it all the more real. Reminded them of what could happen and no one could contemplate her dying.

Her not being there any more.

"Have you tried all her mates?"

He nodded.

"Are you sure? There's no one she might have gone out with, run off with?"

He shook his head and then he stood up.

"I'm going out to have another look about but she never ran off before, and also, she knew Mum was coming home today. She was looking forward to it, so she wouldn't go anywhere, would she? Especially without telling someone? Use your heads."

He was annoyed that no one could see that this *wasn't* normal behavior for his sister, she was *always* reliable. He was the one who skipped out and who got in trouble. Not Colleen, she was a good girl, and he resented them trying to say different.

"Stay there, Christy." Eileen walked out to the hallway and picked up the phone. "I'm ringing Pat, see what he says."

Lance looked at his little brother and, sitting down beside him, he said gently, "You sure you don't know where she might have gone? Is there anyone you might have forgotten about?"

Christy didn't bother answering his older brother, he just shook his head despondently and sighed once more.

The policeman was looking at Patrick Brodie with interest and it wasn't because he was reporting a missing person. He had heard about the family and this was the first time he had ever seen one of them close up. They were a legend and this young PC felt as if he was in the presence of royalty. This encounter would be talked about for a long time to come.

"Are you a bit fucking dense? Go and get DI Broomfield, now!"

The young man didn't answer; the way Patrick Brodie was looking at him was scaring him and he knew that he should have taken more notice of what he was saying.

"Are you deaf as well as fucking stupid? Answer me!"

Patrick was yelling at him now. The anger was spilling out and he couldn't contain it, not when this prick was not interested in what he was trying to tell him.

The young man was already hyperventilating and, stepping away from the glass window that was supposed to protect him from the more violent members of the general public he said, with as much bravado as he could manage, "I will get a detective down here, sir."

Pat stood in the reception of the police station and held on to his temper as best he could. All around him were posters about burglars and stupid fucking photos of no one worth a shit and he had been expected to talk to a kid who he wouldn't trust to go down to the shops for him, let alone find a missing person. The place had the cop smell about it, cigarette smoke and lies. He hated them, hated what they stood for and what they meant to other people. He saw a different side to the police than most people and it certainly didn't endear them to him.

It was nearly midnight and Colleen was still nowhere to be seen. He was worried now, they all were. She wasn't the type of girl to go anywhere without telling someone first. Colleen was still a kid in many respects; she had never even had a sleepover at a friend's.

A familiar voice called out to him and he saw that the door leading into the station itself was open and Teddy Broomfield, an old crony of his dad's, was waving him through.

"Come on, son. Let's have a cup of tea and see what we can do, eh?"

Pat walked through the door, feeling better now that he was actually doing something constructive. He had everyone he knew out searching for her and no one had seen her or heard from her. She was missing. There was no way she would have missed her mum coming home from the hospital. He explained all that to Teddy, who agreed with him and who was obviously taking it far more seriously than the little shitbag he had spoken to earlier.

For some reason this just worried him more. It was as if now that he had reported her gone, it meant she really was missing and that she really did need to be found. That she couldn't get herself home, not without help. He was suddenly aware of how serious the whole fucking situation really was.

Lil knew within twenty-four hours that her daughter was never coming home. She didn't know how she knew that and she didn't say it to anyone else, she didn't voice her thoughts. But she knew. She knew that she would never hear Colleen's laugh again or chat to her, never hear her singing or practicing the recorder.

She just knew she was gone for good.

She knew that if she saw her again it would be to identify her body; there was no way that the girl had run off, left home as the police seemed so convinced of.

Lil had watched Eileen blame herself and her sons blame themselves and had seen neighbors and friends unable to find any more words of hope or comfort.

She cuddled her little boy and she lay on the bed and wondered at a God who could send this to her on top of everything else she had had to contend with over the years. She had refused to see her priest and she was never going to go back for Communion ever again.

Life goes on. That was a saying she had used so many times herself over the years. But this time she knew it was a load of old crap; her life didn't go on. Not really. She lived from day to day and she hid her heartbreak, her anger and her terror at what might have befallen her lovely daughter from everyone.

But in the night she lived through every nightmare a mother could imagine. Every terrible thing she had ever read in the newspapers or seen on a TV program was suddenly vivid and real to her, was feasible. Only she wasn't asleep when she saw these things, she was wide awake.

She wondered whether her baby girl was frightened, in pain, had been raped? Had she called for her mummy at any point? Had she needed her and she had not been there to answer that call?

There was nothing for them to hold on to, that was the worst of it. She seemed to have disappeared into thin air. No one knew where she could have gone or where she could be now. It was as if she had never existed, but they all knew she had. Her clothes were still in her wardrobe and her shoes were still in the cupboard under the stairs. Everything tangible, everything that proved she had ever lived here, in this house, was still in evidence. It was as if she had popped out and would soon be returning as usual. And they all felt that in different ways, she knew that; she watched them as they tried to understand what had happened.

None of them would ever be the same again and that was the thing Lil felt the most. The destruction of her family was so gradual, so complete and she saw it happening and she knew there was nothing she could do to stop it. She had started off hoping for a miracle, hoping Colleen would walk in the door and tell them it was a mistake. But eventually all she hoped for was a body, something to bury. Something to end the speculation that had been a part of her nights for so many years.

At least that way, if they could bury something, they might finally be able to mourn her, might finally find out exactly what had happened to her, and so understand why she had gone. Every Christmas, every birthday, was a reminder of what was missing, what was gone from them. It was the waiting that was the hardest, the waiting for news that could only break their hearts all over again.

Book Three

Non Omnis Moriar.
I shall not altogether die.

—HORACE (65 BC–8 BC)

I will fight for what I believe until I drop dead.
And that's what keeps you alive.

—BARBARA CASTLE (1910–2002)

Chapter Twenty-Nine

"You'll be forty in a few weeks."

Pat laughed. He was still good-looking but he had the same rugged-ness that his father had possessed. Lil had to admit that even though he was her son, he was a good-looking fucker, and he knew it and all.

"Well, Mother, I ain't having a party. We all know what happened at the last one."

Lil didn't laugh at that. All these years later it was still raw; she was still not over it. Patrick saw that then and went to her and, as he cuddled her, he said sadly, "I'm sorry, Mum. That was a bad joke."

She shrugged as always, as if she didn't really care but she did, he knew she did.

"It was a long time ago. It's in the past."

She carried on tallying up the set of books in front of her and Pat watched her for a while. She was a game old bird, no doubt about that, and he loved her. She was a mare but he loved her.

She was a legend in Soho and she made a point of living up to her reputation. He had gone on to bigger and better things over the years but his old mum, Old Lil Brodie, had taken the clubs and made them into goldmines.

She looked up at him over her expensive designer glasses and he laughed again. "You look like a glamorous granny."

"Oh, fuck off and pour me a brandy, will you?"

He poured them both a drink and Lil sat back in the heavily upholstered chair and, yawning, she said with feeling, "Have you talked to Lance yet?"

Pat had been dreading this but he knew he had to tell her. If he didn't she would only find out on her own. That was, of course, if she didn't know already and was waiting to see if he told her the truth. It wouldn't be the first time she had played that one on him.

He shook his head and she saw the thickness of his dark hair and how much grey was now peppering it. It suited him and she wondered at men; they seemed to age much better than women. The things that pointed out their advancing years were the same things that seemed to make them handsomer. It was one of nature's nastier tricks.

"I'm waiting for him to come in tonight; I left a message on his cell phone."

She knocked her drink back in one movement and held the glass out for more.

"Let me do it?"

Pat was biting his lip. He wanted to tell her to keep out of it but he knew he couldn't. You couldn't tell Lil Brodie anything she didn't want to hear. "Leave it with me, Mum. I've got it all under control."

Lil took the glass off him then and, sipping the brandy this time, she sat back once more and looked at him expectantly.

He sat opposite her. She was still an attractive woman and she looked after herself well. He knew she had indulged herself with a bit of nip and tuck. Nothing drastic, just the bags under her eyes and a bit of Botox, to freshen her up, as she put it.

She dressed well, tailored suits and designer handbags. And she liked scarves; expensive scarves that she draped around herself artistically. She kept her hair blond but cut short; an easy-to-manage style that suited her elfin features. He knew she still had good legs; he had seen younger men appreciate them and he knew she liked to show them off in her tailored skirts. For a woman who had given birth to eight children, she looked good.

She was thin though. After Colleen's disappearance she had never gained the weight back. She ate like a bird and he knew she didn't sleep enough. But then neither did he.

"Well, I want to be here when you talk to him."

Pat nodded his agreement. He knew she was not going to take "no" for an answer and he knew from years of experience that it was better to let her do what she wanted.

"But keep out of it, all right?"

She smiled. "Of course. What do you take me for?"

She saw his face as he raised his eyebrows and she said loudly, "Yeah, I know, a nosy old bag."

They were both laughing now and she yawned, wondering where the night's events would take them.

"Billy Boot is a good bloke and he done a lump, Pat. If he said something I would be inclined to believe him."

"Even over Lance?" He said it quietly, already knowing the answer she would give, but having to say it anyway.

"Especially over Lance."

She grinned and he saw the usual look on her face whenever Lance was mentioned or near her. It said that she only tolerated him and it was the truth, because she barely tolerated him at that.

She knew the conversation was over now and she relaxed back into her seat once more and surveyed her domain with relish. She loved the clubs, always had. Pat had taken back nearly everything that had been lost with his father's murder and she was happy to see them thriving and profitable. It seemed a fitting tribute to the man she had loved and lost all those years ago.

She also wanted to see what Lance had to say about Billy Boot's little bit of chatter and, as it concerned the clubs and some of the other business dealings they had, she was not only interested, she was also intrigued.

Eileen was locked in her bathroom; the new bathroom that had cost a small fortune and which had not given her any satisfaction at all. In fact, as she stood there, her hands gripping the sides of the basin and tears not far from her eyes, she wondered what the hell she had wanted it for in the first place.

"Eileen, will you open the fucking door!"

Her husband's voice was loud and threatening and she wished he would drop dead of a heart attack or crash his fucking car.

"Fuck off!"

"Oh, fuck you. I ain't poncing around any more."

She heard him walking away. He was such a noisy person; he clumped, he didn't walk anywhere, he clumped. He just stamped through life as if he had every right to be there, to interfere and bully everyone. She loathed him and she wondered at times how the fuck she had ever ended up married to him.

But she knew the answer to that; she just didn't like admitting it to herself. She heard the sound of his car starting up and the crunch as it left the drive and then, and only then, did she unlock the bathroom door and go downstairs.

She was desperate for a drink and she walked straight into the kitchen, dragging a stool from the breakfast bar over to the cupboard above the door that led into the utility room and she climbed up and opened it wide. It was empty. Not empty of everything, the cupboard actually housed the electrics for their swimming pool, but the bottle of vodka she had put there earlier in the day was gone.

Slamming the door shut she jumped down from the stool and shouted, "You fucking bastard! You fucking rotten shitbag!"

The shouting made her feel better, calmer inside herself. Then, picking up her car keys she left the house. Driving to the liquor store a few minutes later, she knew she was over the limit, she was driving too slow for a start and she realized she was already well on the way to complete oblivion.

She abandoned the Mercedes 220 outside the store and then, when she had purchased what she wanted, she walked back to her house happily. Dropping her car keys down a drain, she was laughing at what her husband would say about that when it dawned on her that the keys to the house were on the keyring as well. She broke into the house by smashing one of the windows in the back door. It wasn't the first time she had done it and she left the glass on the floor and the door wide open. Let him *really* have something to moan about, he was only happy when he had something to complain about. He was a miserable cunt and she was sick to death of him and his lectures and his fucking constant drone. It was like living with the prophet of doom. Pouring herself a large glass of whisky, she lit herself a cigarette and then cut herself a line of prime cocaine. Fuck it all, she decided. She was going to have a party.

"All right, Dad?"

Shawn was all smiles as Jambo walked across the pub to him.

"Yeah, son, you?"

Jambo had aged well; in fact, he didn't look much different now to twenty years previously. Pat put it down to him never really having a job or any kind of worries and Jambo secretly agreed with him.

Pat was good to him though, and he knew that after Colleen's disappearance and Lil's illness, the fact that he had been a constant presence had brought the boy around to his way of thinking. They got on well and they had a certain rapport that was unique and helped them to bond.

Poor Lil had never really gotten over Colleen, even Pat's murder had not taken so much out of her. He supposed it was because women, real women, once they birthed a child, could never imagine life without it. He didn't include Lance in that equation, he could understand her reservations about him. He felt the same way. Lance was not someone you liked, let alone loved. The boy made sure of that himself.

Now this boy, his boy, his Shawn, he was a credit to her. Lil had done a wonderful job with him. They all had. He was so loved and he was so happy all the time that he was a joy to be around.

"You get me a bit of puff?"

Shawn nodded. He had the same dreadlocks and the same smile as his father.

"Course I have. Don't I always?" He passed the grass over, green and fragrant, in an HSBC coin bag, with another big smile.

"It's prime. I got it for meself."

Jambo took it from him and slipped it into his coat pocket, then he sat back in his chair and waited for the boy to go and get the Guinness that was his staple diet these days.

Shawn got up and laughed once more.

"Look out for Christy, we've got to pick some stuff up before midnight."

Jambo nodded.

The two boys were exceptionally close and he was glad. He liked Christy, he was a good man. He had none of his father in him but a lot of his mother, thank God. He even had her temper and that had got him into trouble a few times over the years. But he was a grafter, a worker, like they all were.

Now the two of them were the Kings of the Puff and they were both expert at ferreting out the best grass going. A very handy occurrence for him, of course, as he had it on tap whenever he wanted it. He sipped his Guinness a few minutes later and watched Shawn as he looked over all the females in the bar. Shawn had a reputation as a ladies' man; they seemed to fall at his feet on a regular basis. He had the chat and the *easiness* that attracted a certain kind of woman. He was out for a good time and a good time was *all* he was after. He was his father's son all right, there was no doubt about that.

Lance was still angry. He was always angry and Annie was frightened of him when he was angry like he was now. He shouted, he raged and he took it out on her. Nothing she did was good enough and nothing she said could appease him in any way. As the years had gone on she had actually become nervous of him, nervous of his moods.

"Do you hear me?" He was leaning over her as she sat in the chair by the TV. She wanted to watch her program, she always watched her program, and if she missed it she was upset. But she knew she was not going to have any peace until he was spent.

"Of course I hear you, Lance, the whole fucking street can hear you!" The words seemed to do the trick. He stood up then and she saw how big he was. Over the years he had seemed to grow, taller and wider. He was overweight but it just made him look more intimidating. He didn't look happy fat, like most people with his build. He looked dangerous and she knew that he was.

She also knew that he tried to keep his indoor personality on a leash; he didn't want anyone to know how he treated her when they were alone. He bullied her, screamed at her and picked fault with everything she did for him. As she had got older and less agile, he saw her weakness as nothing more than an excuse not to do any work. He took it as a personal affront that she couldn't keep up with his demands on her time any more.

The only person he was even remotely civil to these days was Kathleen and she was as mad as a fucking brush. Not that she would ever say that out loud of course. At least she left the house these days. She only walked to her mother's, admittedly, but that in itself was a big step for someone whohad hardly left her bedroom for years. She took a cocktail of drugs that seemed to make her almost human and Annie was grateful for that much at least.

"Fucking summoning me, leaving *me* a message. Not, can you come in, Lance, but, get to the club by nine. Like I ain't got nothing better to fucking do! Like I have fuck all else in my life but pander to him!"

Annie didn't say anything. She wasn't meant to, she knew that much from years of experience. He just wanted someone to vent his anger on and that someone, unfortunately, was usually her. She tried to sneak a look at her program and she saw Gil Grissom from *CSI* talking away to the blonde woman she hated. But the sound was down and she couldn't make out a bloody word. But she didn't say anything or try to turn the sound up, Lance was aggravated enough as it was.

"All right, Lil?"

Ivana came into the office with a mug of coffee and, placing it on the desk, sat down and slipped off her high heels. As she twiddled her toes, she groaned with pleasure.

"I'm getting too old for these shoes and too old for all that standing around."

Lil laughed. "You'll still be going in twenty-five years like me."

"Oh, don't say that, Lil. I'm depressed enough as it is!"

They laughed together once more. It amazed Lil that there had been a time when she had really not liked this girl because now she loved her. Pat had kept her on a string for so many years and she had sat it out. Lil had eventually admired her and then found she liked her. Once she had gone away for a few weeks and Lil had then found that she actually *missed* her. Life was strange, it threw you a curve when you least expected it.

"Who's got the baby?"

The baby was twelve years old but she was still referred to as the baby by everyone.

"She's staying at Isabel's."

Lil relaxed then; Isabel was one of the hostesses who had married out of the job but still kept in contact with Ivana; they were close friends. Isabel was happy to babysit; she had three of her own anyway so young Georgia was actually a help. She loved bathing the kids, playing with them and reading them stories. She was so like Colleen it was frightening at times. Everyone had noticed it but no one had ever had the guts to mention it. But she was watched over by them all, and watched closely.

"Eileen was on the phone earlier. I couldn't make head nor tail out of what she was saying. But she was crying."

Lil shrugged, the trademark shrug that had seen her through all the trials and tribulations of her life, and said sadly, "It's the anniversary soon, Colleen, and then we've got poor Pat's birthday . . ."

Ivana nodded. "I know."

Ivana was still beautiful and looked much younger than she actually was. Her extreme thinness had turned to a pleasant plumpness after the baby had been born and she was still tiny, but not so gaunt looking. Pat was still with her and he was still out and about when the fancy took him. Lil was sorry about that but she kept out of it. Ivana seemed able to cope with it, so who was she to butt her nose in where it wasn't wanted? It grieved her though. She could see the sadness behind Ivana's eyes at times, and she wished she could do something to alleviate it.

"Forty, eh? How does it feel to have a forty-year-old son?"

Lil grinned then, her face screwed up in mock horror.

"Well, I've had fucking better days!"

Ivana was laughing with her when Pat walked into the office with Lance. The atmosphere was automatically charged; it was always the same when Lance was there. He seemed to bring upset with him wherever he went.

The air in the room was almost electric and Lil and Pat looked at each other warily as Ivana made herself scarce.

Lance had never once spoken to her directly and even though he had not said one word to her, she was more than aware of his opinion of her.

Paulie Brick walked into the house and looked around him warily. Eileen was capable of launching herself at him from a hiding place. She was a handful when she was drunk and, unfortunately, that was most of the time.

He regretted shouting at her earlier but she made him so angry at times that he could often strangle her without a second's thought. He walked through to the state-of-the-art kitchen and saw the glass everywhere. And on the granite work surface he noticed the remains of her cocaine and the screw top from the whisky bottle.

He sighed. He had noticed the car was gone but guessed she was in the house somewhere; she never seemed to stay out for any length of time. She preferred to stay home and get wasted. He wondered if the car was still in one piece and hoped that if she had crashed it, she wasn't hurt again. Last time she had been so out of it she had not even noticed a broken wrist.

He heard the faint sound of music and rushed upstairs to the master bedroom. She was lying on the bed. It had been left unmade for days and she was listening to Dionne Warwick; that meant she was even more depressed than usual.

As she sang "walk on by" to herself, she noticed her husband was in the room with her.

"Hello, darling, come and lie with me."

She was a good drunk now and he smiled at her tenderly. He loved her like no other and each day, as she attempted to destroy herself a little bit more, his heart broke.

He lay down beside her. Her hair needed a good wash, her clothes were crumpled, and her breath was atrocious. But when he looked into her eyes, he saw the guilt and the bewilderment that had attracted him in the first place. He had believed all those years ago that he could make her better. But he couldn't, no one could.

"Don't leave me, darling. Please don't ever leave me, will you? I'd die, see. I would, I'd just die without you . . ." She was slurring her words and he knew she would have no recollection of anything by the morning, but he held her tight and reassured her of his love and devotion.

"Don't you go and walk on by. I'd kill meself, I would. Do you think Colleen was walking somewhere, eh? Walking *by* someone . . ."

She was rambling now. He knew all the stages of her drunkenness; the next step was when she fell asleep, unconscious would be a more apt expression, and then he would lie there and watch her, wondering when this would all fucking end. He was tired of it, so bloody tired.

"I ain't got to answer to you or *her* for that matter."

"No one said you did, Lance. You want to walk away from this firm, then you go. No one's going to stop you and *her*, as you referred to our mother, has as much right to question you as I do."

Lance looked at his older brother with his usual disdain.

"I can work where I like and with whom I like."

Pat walked towards him then and, looking him in the eye, he said loudly, "But that's just it, Lance, you can't. You can't fucking go round with your mate Barker threatening people we are in partnership with. What kind of fucking stupidness is that? If they owe money to Barker then let him go and pull it in; you ain't got no fucking allegiance to that cunt. No one has; he's a standing joke, a byword for liars and thieves. He's one leg up from a fucking gas-meter bandit and it's a wonder he ain't out there kiting, he is such a fucking twonk!"

Lance ran his hands through his hair and laughed nastily. "He could fucking buy and sell you, mate."

Lil had heard enough and, getting up from her chair, she pushed Pat out of the way and bellowed, "How dare you! You're nothing but a fucking leech. If you think that by going around with that ponce and threatening people in their own homes with their kids there, that we will walk you out of that one, you can think again, boy. We've put the word out and if anyone wants to come back at you, they *can*. And you tell *Donny* from me, that if I ever see him again, I'll fucking dismantle him meself. And you know me, Lance. I am more than capable of doing that, if the fancy takes me."

"Oh, here we go, you telling me what to do as usual. You don't mind me breaking heads when it suits you two, do you?"

Lil started laughing then. Really laughing. A sad, almost heartbroken laugh that was as insulting to him as it was making the guilt inside him unbearable.

"Of course we don't mind *you* doing that, it's what we *pay* you for, it's what you do in this family. Let's face it, you don't do fuck all else."

Pat pulled her away and walked her back to her seat.

"Mum! Sit down and let's sort this out, shall we?"

Lil was not in the mood. Lance's complete disinterest in what they were trying to say to him had finished her. She wanted him out now and she was not bothered who got hurt by it, least of all Lance.

"Fuck him, Pat; if he thinks that he can do that without any kind of comeback, then let him go. Let him go and work with Donny Barker. Only he would be silly enough to fucking contemplate that. Everyone else gives him a wide berth but then most people do the same thing with *him*, don't they, Lance?"

Pat was annoyed now. His mother was making matters worse.

"Mum. Just shut up a minute, will you?"

She lit a cigarette, one of the few she smoked these days, and it was a sure sign of her agitation.

"No, I fucking won't shut up. I have wanted to say this for a long time. He takes us for fools and we let him. When I heard you had threatened the Chapmans in their own home for a few fucking grand, money that Donny had creamed off their boy, I was so ashamed and so fucking embarrassed that I nearly died. They didn't owe him a bean, their *boy* did and he owed a few hundred, that was all. Donny makes up half his debts and you, like the fucking div you are, go in there with him and do his dirty work. Half the debts he buys are not even valid. He fucking snows you and then he takes the piss out of you. Ask around. He thinks he is a big man because he has a fucking Brodie as a pet.

Well, Lance, you've been warned before and you ain't took a blind bit of notice. This time it's for real, this time I am going to sort you out once and for all. It's over."

Lance had never heard her like this before; she never spoke to him unless she had to. He had always used that against her, knowing that her guilt over him and the way she treated him had kept him in good stead all his life.

"Look at you. I remember when you hurt Janie's little girl, bless her heart. You were a fucking bully then and you're a fucking bully now. And it stops tonight, Lance. It finally fucking stops."

Lance was staring at his mother as if he had never seen her before. In all the years he had worked with his family, she had never said so much to him at one time. In fact, he couldn't remember ever having a conversation with her in his life. Pat could see the hurt his brother was experiencing; he knew that whatever had happened, he actually loved this woman who had never once given him a kind word.

"She don't mean that, Lance. She's annoyed, we both are . . ."

"Oi! Patrick Brodie, don't you dare talk for me. I am just about at the end of my patience with him, and *you*, come to that. I heard whispers about him years ago and I kept quiet. But not any more. I have to say this now while I still have the chance. My cancer is back and I will not go to my grave regretting that I didn't finally tell this fucking nutter what I really thought of him and his fucking carrying-on. I've left you nothing, Lance, not a brass razoo; so now you know. My mother took you the second you were born and you've been hers ever since because I *never* wanted you. Even as a baby you were fucking weird, *unnatural*. And, God forgive me, when my Colleen went missing I wished it had been you. I would have given my own life to swap her for you. I blamed you, for years I blamed you, Lance, and I don't know why. It was an instinct, a feeling I had, everything that went wrong I always felt that, somehow, it came back to you."

"Fucking hell, Mum, that's enough!"

Patrick was in such shock at her tirade that it was only after she had sat down and lit another cigarette that he remembered her saying her cancer was back. That was why she was smoking again and drinking brandy; it was her painkiller, always had been.

Lance was still staring at her. His face was devoid of any emotion. "You really hate me, don't you?" His voice was low and without any inflection whatsoever.

"Hate? I don't hate you, Lance. Hate is not a strong enough word for how I feel."

Patrick was appalled at his mother's words, yet he knew she had cause. Lance had always been an outsider and even as kids he had never really felt like a part of the family. He had been eaten up with anger and hate all his life.

Patrick had only protected him through guilt, the guilt he felt because his mother had loved him with a passion. All her kids had felt that love at some time but not Lance, and that had shaped his life. It was as if they had danced around each other for all those years and they were living a lie and everything that had happened to them was just leading up to this moment in time.

The door opened and Scanlon was standing there looking at them. The atmosphere in the room was heavy with hatred and belated honesty. It was almost physical, it felt almost as if it could be touched, it was so charged with emotion.

"What the fuck do *you* want?"

Scanlon took a deep breath and, looking at Lil Brodie, he said sadly, "They've found a body."

It was a few moments before Lil realized the enormity of what the man had said.

Chapter Thirty

Scanlon had finally arrived at the house. He had been dreading this, and yet he knew the news was better coming from him. They had waited up all night for him, and he knew that what he said and how he said it would be remembered for a long time to come. Patrick ushered him into the living room and he said hello to everyone as respectfully as he could. All the children were there, and he could feel the nervousness coming off everyone in the room.

Lil didn't waste any time on pleasantries. "Is it her?"

Scanlon nodded. "I am afraid so."

"You're sure?"

He nodded once again, his face full of genuine sorrow. "Her uniform was the marker, it was still more or less intact. Her schoolbag was also buried with her . . ."

Lil nodded as if she understood perfectly, when she didn't understand anything at all. Someone had buried her child somewhere, buried her school bag beside her and no one had known where she was until now.

"What happened to her? Do they know?"

Scanlon nodded once more, desperately sorry for the woman sitting on the large leather chair, who was hoping against hope that it was all a mistake and her daughter was alive somewhere, living a good life.

He looked at Patrick and Lance, sitting side by side on the sofa. They were both as shell-shocked as their mother. They were so alike, yet so different.

Patrick nodded towards the man, giving him permission to tell his mother what she wanted to know. Knowing she needed to hear the truth about her child more than ever now, no matter how bad it was, or how painful.

"She was beaten to death. There are three holes in her skull. It would have been quick though, the coroner says that any one of the blows would have been enough to render her unconscious."

Lil didn't answer him, she just sat and waited for him to continue.

"I am so sorry, Mrs. Brodie."

She knew he meant it, and being called Mrs. Brodie brought back memories of good times. Good times that had been destroyed first with her husband's murder, and then with her daughter's disappearance.

"Was she raped?" She had to know, even as she didn't want to know.

Scanlon sighed. "They don't think so. All her clothes were still intact; she was wrapped in plastic and that kept everything in pretty good condition. It seems more like a rage murder than anything else. No one knows *why* these things happen. Usually it's just a case of being in the wrong place at the wrong time."

Lil nodded again. Why, she didn't know. She didn't know what else to do, wasn't up on the protocol on how to deal with something like this.

"Any idea who did it?" Lance's voice was heavy with distress.

"Not yet." Scanlon stared at the floor once more.

"Where was she found?" Lil wanted to know the answer to her question, but she hoped against hope it wasn't somewhere they had looked. They had searched everywhere, over and over again, wondering if they had missed something. Hoping she might turn up there. Her fear now was that she had missed her child, had walked past her poor, broken little body. Had not seen her burial mound, not noticed a newly dug grave, had not realized they were walking over her last resting place.

"That is the strange thing about it. She was found buried in a garden in Chigwell."

Lance was staring at him as if he had just turned into Lana Turner before his eyes. "Chigwell?"

Scanlon nodded again, unable to do anything else. "The owners were having a pond dug, for Koi carp. The workmen came across the body late yesterday afternoon. I heard about it, and, after they had identi-

fied the body, I offered to tell you all about it. I explained that I knew
you . . ."

His voice trailed off. Pat knew that the man's cover was blown now,
that Scanlon had put himself on the line for them; to make this easier all
around. You found friends in the unlikeliest places.

"Thanks." It was such a small word for such an enormous thing, but
Pat couldn't say anything else. He was as dazed and traumatized as his
mother was.

"Fucking *Chigwell*. Why would she be there?" Lil was getting angry
now, the shock was wearing off and real life was once more creeping up
to overtake her.

Scanlon shook his head once more. "That is what we are trying to
find out, Mrs. Brodie."

Lil was nodding again, unable to think of anything to say, grateful
to this man for finally bringing news of her baby, of finally putting her
mind at rest. But resenting him, also, because now all hope was gone.

"Of course you are. Sorry, I wasn't thinking . . ." She started crying
then, a deep and heart-wrenching sobbing. Nearly twenty years of fear,
and questioning, and bewilderment, were now finally being set free. She
was still sobbing hours later and she wondered if she would ever stop.

Lance was also crying, and it was strange because it was he who went
to his mother's aid, not Patrick, and she let him hold her, let him comfort her, then she held on to him. For the first time in his life, his mother
was hugging him, and he was hugging her back as if his life depended
on it.

Spider and Jimmy Brick were both mulling over the news. Everyone had
heard about Colleen's body being found, and no one seemed to know
what to do about it. It didn't seem right somehow, ringing up, or going
to visit, until the family had finally taken it all in. It seemed intrusive. It
had been so long since she had disappeared, that it was almost as if she
had never been there in the first place.

Lil had once said to Spider that her only solace was, if Colleen was
dead, at least she knew that Pat would look after her. Care for her until
she could join them.

He had been surprised that she had not thought of the girl's father, had thought that in death he might have finally been redeemed. She was, after all, a church-goer, and she was a believer, as Pat had been. Lenny Brewster was not even to be trusted in death and, he had to admit, Lil was probably right about that.

"Poor Lil, eh? How do you cope with it? A husband murdered, and a child."

Spider poured them both more Scotch. Only whisky seemed appropriate today; it killed the pain somehow.

"You know, Spider, I always thought she had run off with someone, a boyfriend or such like."

Spider laughed then, a tired, sad laugh. "Not little Colleen, she was as green as the grass. She had a bit of life about her, I admit, but she and Christy were as close as two people could be. If that had been the case, he would have known."

Jimmy thought about what was said. "Yeah, I suppose you're right. But like Pat's death, it's never sat right with me, you know?"

Spider looked at the man he had known for so many years, and who had returned one day out of the blue. "Why did you go off, Jim? The truth now, let's be honest with one another."

Jimmy shrugged, his huge shoulders more noticeable in his expensive jacket. It occurred to Spider then that Jimmy had come back to them all a snappy dresser. Before Pat's death, Jimmy had been an average Joe; he had worked to live, now he lived to work. Liked good clothes, and nice cars.

"Honest, between me and you?"

Spider laughed once more. "Who the fuck am I going to tell, eh? We are old mates, and somewhere along the line we lost trust in each other, and it grieves me, Jim. All of a sudden, you were gone. One day you were gone, and that was that. You came back, and we were like strangers. Both unsure what had happened to us. To everyone around us."

Jimmy Brick knew the truth of Spider's words, and he was pleased that one of them had finally brought it out into the open.

"I didn't know who to trust any more, Spider. Patrick's death was so brutal, so fucking senseless, it threw me off kilter. I blamed you for a long time."

Spider was cross, as Jimmy knew he would be, but he had asked for the truth and finally got it. That child's death had made them all rethink their lives.

"Hey, you asked for the truth and you got it, don't fucking hold it against me now. You were protecting Cain, but you know you should have made sure the situation with the Williams brothers was taken care of. Patrick trusted you to do that; he would have sorted it immediately if it was one of his children. Let alone a brother."

"Do you still blame me?"

"It's been so long now, what does it matter? Nothing can bring him back, can it? I heard through the grapevine that young Pat ironed out Jasper, so he must have known the score. He is a shrewd man, like his father before him, but Patrick has something his father never had."

"And what's that then?"

Jimmy could hear the coldness that had crept into Spider's voice. "A taste for revenge."

Patrick had called and told them all there was more news about Colleen, so they were all waiting now with bated breath, and in Lil's case, a terror in her heart at what she was going to hear.

"Where's Lance?"

Patrick shrugged. "He said he was caught up in traffic, he won't be long."

Annie nodded. She was making tea while watching out for Kathleen as she chain-smoked her cigarettes and stared into space. She was capable of going on one of her wanders if not watched closely, and that's the last thing they needed on this day of all days.

Lil looked around her at everyone in the room. "You know, it's funny, but people have actually asked me what was worse, to have a husband murdered, or a child? And I couldn't answer that question. I *still* don't know the answer to that question . . . I always said that we didn't know if Colleen *had* been murdered, you know . . ."

She was panicking suddenly, and her voice was faltering; she felt the air rising up inside her body, hot and clammy. Stopping her from breathing.

When she opened her eyes, Scanlon was there, and everyone was looking down at her; she understood then that she had passed out. Never before in her life had she fainted.

"Come on, Mum, sit up, drink this."

She sat up with difficulty, and drank the brandy Eileen had poured for her. When she was feeling brighter, she looked at the policeman who had gone from enemy to friend in a few short days, and said, "Come on then, what have you got to tell us?"

Her voice was full of false determination. He knew she didn't really want to know; she needed to know. There was a big difference.

"Shouldn't we wait for Lance?"

"I don't think so. I need to talk now, get this over with."

Scanlon was so nervous, he had to tell them something so heinous, so fucking hateful, and he knew he had to do it. He knew he had to get this thing out, had to explain why that child had died. He was glad that Lance wasn't there, somehow it made this all easier.

"We traced the owners of the house back to a couple, now living in Spain. By the condition of the remains, and from the date she was reported missing, we sorted out who was living there on or around that time."

He sighed, and sipped the drink Patrick had poured for him, before continuing. "This is the strange thing, when the Spanish police went to their house to question them, the man broke down immediately and admitted everything."

No one spoke for a while.

"What was his name?"

This from Christy, who was already suspicious.

"Gardener. Sammy Gardener."

Lil sat up in her seat then, as did most of the people in the room. "Sammy Gardener, Ugly Sammy?"

Scanlon nodded again, hating himself for what he had to do, and knowing he had to do it.

"But why? He was friends with us, with Patrick, my *husband* Patrick. I knew his first wife. Sammy wasn't a killer . . ."

She was distressed, she didn't want Colleen to have been killed by someone they knew and trusted; it was worse somehow, worse than a stranger doing it. A stranger wouldn't have known how lovely she was, a stranger wouldn't have known how much they loved her. A stranger was just a nutter, and they were not someone you could focus on, could see as a real person.

"He said he had a reason for it . . ."

Patrick was watching him now, as were Shamus and Christy. The three of them all looked at one another, and they all seemed to know what Scanlon was going to say.

Eileen was crying now. The guilt that had been eating at her for so long was now once more to the forefront of her mind. "What reason could anyone have to hurt *Colleen*. She was a *little girl*, for Christ's sake, a bloody *little girl* . . . Ain't it enough me dad was murdered? Why was she murdered and all? What is fucking wrong with this family? What is this all about?"

Paulie pulled her into his arms then, and she buried her face in his chest, the tears were already falling. Eileen had thought about Colleen every day of her life, and it never got easier. Her guilt at Colleen's disappearance had eaten away at her for so long. Her mum had been so ill in the hospital, she had taken over as the woman of the house and she was supposed to have been looking after the kids. Watching out for them, caring for them, and she had lost her, had not even *missed* her until it was too late. Colleen had been taken and murdered, and Eileen was responsible for it, had been so busy with herself and pretending to be everyone's mother.

And she had not even *wondered* where she was. All the while she was being murdered, that poor little girl was being killed somewhere, and she had been more interested in how the house looked. Colleen had not even entered her mind. Eileen blamed herself for it, had always blamed herself.

Then when she had married Paulie, she had hoped to make everything better, but there had been no babies; the one time she had been pregnant she had lost it at five months, and there had been nothing since then. She had seen that as her punishment for losing Colleen, that God saw that she couldn't be trusted with a child.

The drinking had started after poor Colleen had gone missing. It had gradually escalated over the years until now she was an alcoholic and Paulie helped her keep her secret. Knew why she was like she was. Listened to her rambling on about Colleen, wishing there was something he could do to help her.

"Take her home, Paulie, will you?"

Eileen's secret was common knowledge to everyone, but until Paulie asked for help, they would let him sort it out, knowing he was good to her, loved her, and would one day see that his love and care was not enough to make her better.

Paulie Brick walked the sobbing woman from the room. Kathleen put her hand out to touch her as she passed her, and Eileen grabbed it tightly, saying, "I can't listen, in case they say it's my fault."

Paulie walked her out, and the silence was deafening until Shawn said, "Well, come on, what's this fucking reason then?"

Scanlon looked at the sea of faces around him and, taking a deep breath, he spoke once more: "Six weeks before Sammy snatched her, Lance and Donny Barker had gone to his house to collect a debt they had recently bought from an unknown party." He waited for some kind of reaction, but no one spoke. It was as if they were all in shock.

"Go on." It was Patrick who urged him on.

"Sammy's eldest daughter was held at gunpoint, and she was terrified. Only twelve at the time, he said she was absolutely in bits. He said that Lance had shot him in the feet with a sawed-off and that has been verified by the way, the shooting. He told the hospital he opened his front door, and someone had shot him cold. No one really bothered to pursue it, knowing it was obviously something and nothing. The usual falling out among thieves."

Scanlon looked around the room. "You all know the score. Anyway, he said that Bianca, his daughter, was never the same again. She couldn't eat or sleep. It really affected her. At one point she had the sawed-off aimed at her head. A month later, she cut her wrists. Killed herself."

No one spoke, they all seemed to be holding their breath.

"The girl killed herself? Over Lance?" This from Lil. "Why am I not fucking surprised?"

"That's why he ain't here, ain't it? He knew what you were going to say. Has he fucking packed up, Annie? Has he left?"

Patrick stared at the old woman and she was shaking her head in distress. "No, course not . . ."

"Fuck Lance for a minute, Pat. So what happened, Mr. Scanlon?" Lil was sitting up in the chair once more and her face quieted all of them.

"Sammy was distraught and went after Lance. He said he found Lance with Colleen that morning, watched them talking and, after Lance had said goodbye to Colleen, he went up to him and told him what had happened to his girl. He wanted Lance to at least acknowledge what he had done, but Lance just laughed at him and said she was better off away from him, that she was ugly and no one would ever have wanted her anyway. When Sammy pulled a weapon on him, Lance laughed, beat him up and drove off laughing. He said it was the final straw, he couldn't make any sense out of it all. He knew that Lance had no care or interest, had simply thought it was funny. Lance had found Bianca's death amusing. It drove him mad."

Scanlon sighed. "Sammy drove after Colleen then, to ask if she knew where Lance was going and she had said she didn't. Before he knew what he was doing, he had talked her into getting in the car, and he tried to explain about his daughter, thinking she might be able to make Lance understand what he had done. But Colleen got frightened and tried to get away and somehow, in the tussle, he killed her. He then drove back to his house and buried her in the garden. He waited, expecting to be caught, *wanting* to be caught, in fact. But no one ever put two and two together. He thought Lance would have been the one to bring it all out."

"That is fucking rubbish." Annie was shouting now.

"Donny Barker confirmed his story and he also confirmed that *Lance* had met him that day and bragged about seeing Sammy that morning and how he had laughed at him. He remembers it so vividly because it was the day *Colleen* went missing."

It was true. They all knew that, even Annie.

Lil couldn't believe what she was hearing, even though, in her heart, she knew it was true. Lance had bullied the man, as he always bullied everyone, and had finally sent someone over the edge at last.

Lil looked at her eldest son then. "I told you, didn't I? I said he had something to do with it. I knew it, I just knew it . . ."

No one spoke, it was as if a bomb had exploded among them.

"All right, Lance?"

Donny Barker was all nervous smiles and Lance walked to the bar in the corner of the room and poured himself a drink.

"Bit early for you, ain't it?"

Lance swallowed the brandy quickly and looked at his friend.

"Did you get the tickets for me?"

Donny nodded. "Course. The bloke is going to deliver them in a while. Why?"

Lance shook his head nonchalantly. "No reason. I just wondered, that's all. Did you get me money out?"

Donny poured himself a vodka and Coke and, adding ice and lemon, he sat on the edge of his desk and said quietly, "Is everything all right? What's this all about? All this fucking hurrying . . ."

Lance stood up and said in a loud voice, "You got my fucking money or what, Donny?"

Donny automatically leaned back; he could see the nervousness that would soon turn to violence. Lance was obviously in a state.

"Calm down, Lance, for fuck's sake. What is wrong with you?"

Lance sighed heavily, trying to control his temper and not doing a very good job of it.

"The money is all here, OK? The tickets are being delivered by Karen Hines. She booked them herself, OK? So fucking calm down."

Lance knew he was acting suspiciously but he was unable to relax. Once he had the cash and the tickets he would calm down.

"What are you going to Northern Ireland for, anyway? Hardly a fucking holiday destination, is it?"

"Who are you, Donny, the fucking holiday police?"

Donny laughed but he knew Lance would be taking a plane somewhere else from there. The question he wanted an answer to was where. He knew he had money, they all did, and he knew that if he was going on the lam then it meant he had an inkling that something was up.

Lance was a fucking leech and he knew that, had accepted that; his worry was whether it was something *he* should be worrying about.

Lil looked around her and saw her sons sitting there, all trying to understand what they had just heard.

Lance, the child she had never wanted, had never cared for, had destroyed everything that they had held dear. He had caused every person in the room heartbreak. Had ensured that not one of them had ever known a real day's peace and now, she knew, thanks to him, they never would.

And poor Patrick, he had tried to be a good brother, had tried to make up for her lack of warmth, her inability to love her own son by loving him enough for both of them. Christy was crying silently and Shamus was holding on to him, comforting him.

Colleen and Christy had been so close. The other kids had loved them, but they were the product of Patrick Brodie; he and Colleen had been Brewster's, a man who had not cared for them and had been the reason Patrick Brodie had died like he had. Together they had been strong, had always relied on each other for strength and love.

"Go home, all of you." Patrick sounded so calm and so normal that they all automatically did what he asked.

They knew what was going to happen, but no one said it, of course. "You OK, Mum?"

Lil smiled at them all; only her little Shawn would want to stay with her when Patrick said to go. He was a brave little fucker and she loved him, as she loved them all.

"I'm fine, darling, get yourselves off home and let us sort this out, eh?"

As they were leaving, she said quietly, "If anyone asks, we were together tonight, right?"

She glanced at Scanlon and he nodded.

"Good. Now get off home, all of you."

"I want to stay here, Mum, can I?"

Kathleen was looking at her with her usual sad eyes and Lil couldn't deny her.

"Course you can, darling, if that's what you want. All right with you, Mum?"

Annie nodded and Lil felt a moment's sorrow for her. Her baby, her boy, was finally unmasked for the shit he really was.

They all left without a further word, understanding the situation without needing to be told. As she watched them leave, Lil consoled herself that out of eight children, seven had turned out all right.

At least they knew when to leave.

"Mr. Scanlon?"

He didn't say a word, just left with the others.

Once they were alone, Lil finally broke down. "Take Kathleen upstairs, Mum. I need to talk to Patrick."

Annie stood in the room, her small body bristling with annoyance. "You can't believe that, Lil. Whatever Lance is . . ."

"Oh, fuck off, Annie. You know it's true as well I do. His absence alone should fucking tell you something." Pat's voice was angry and Annie knew that he had never had much time for her, but he was always respectful to her, as he was to everyone.

"Come on, Kathleen, let's get upstairs and put the TV on, eh?"

She was determined not to cause any more upset.

"Pat, can I tell you something?"

"Not now, Kathy, I have a lot of things to sort out, darling . . ."

His voice was sharper than he intended and Kathleen flinched at his tone.

He went to her and held her hands gently in his. "Later, eh? Me and you, we'll have a big conversation, but at the moment I have to do a few things. I need to find Lance . . ."

She smiled then. "I know. I want to tell you that he is going on holiday, ain't he, Nan?"

She looked at Annie expectantly.

"What you on about, you silly girl?"

Lil stood up then and Annie knew she had been found out, but she still couldn't tell them what they wanted to know. Lance was still her boy and he had promised to send for her when the time was right. He was everything to her, no matter what he had done.

"What the fuck is she on about, Mum?"

"Oh, Lil, you know what she's like. You can't listen to what she says. She's off her fucking tree half the time."

Kathleen sat down then and said, with more lucidity than anyone had ever given her credit for, "You helped him pack! You told him he had to go away. Like you always tell him what to do."

Kathleen looked at Lil. "I hate living there but no one stops them from making me stay there. I don't want to go into a mental home and they want to put me in one now, so she can go with him."

"No one's putting you in a mental home, Kathleen, I promise. Now tell us what is going on."

Pat was kneeling in front of Kathleen and she smiled at him sadly. "They will, Pat, they told me, and, if I go in a nuthouse, I'll die. I can't go in the nuthouse."

Annie sighed and tutted loudly. "Well, shut up then, you stupid girl . . ."

"Why don't you shut up, Mother? Come on, Kathleen, darling, tell us what is going on, yeah? I swear to you, darling, nothing will happen to you. You can stay here, you can always stay here, love, for as long as you like, but you never wanted to, did you?"

"I did, but I wasn't allowed to. But now Lance is going away and Nanny Annie is going with him when he is settled."

"She is talking out of her arse."

Annie was nervous and Kathleen saw that.

"I am not. I am not talking out of my arse and you can't say that to me any more. Lance is going away tonight and I don't have to be scared any more. She took my baby you know, Mum. Her and Lance."

"What baby, Kathleen?"

Lil's voice was quiet and Kathleen put her head down and started to cry.

Annie sighed heavily. "What fucking baby? There was no baby. Are you going to tell me you are listening to this fucking nutcase?"

Kathleen was out of her seat and, grabbing Annie by the neck, she screamed, "Don't you call me that. Don't you dare call me that. You took my baby away and you put it in the fucking bin."

She looked at Patrick and said angrily, "You were robbing the post office, remember? Lance told me that if you knew about the baby, you would put me away, no one would believe me. He gave it to her. And she put it in the bin, Pat, my little baby. I wasn't allowed to make any noise in case the police came and you all got arrested . . . Then Mum would have been cross and made me go away." She looked at Annie.

"Tell them, tell them. Now they are going and putting me in the nuthouse, that's what Lance said to me. The nuthouse, because you all hate me and don't care about me, but you do. Promise me you won't put me in the nuthouse, promise me! I don't like kissing Lance, Mum, and Nanny says I am telling lies but I'm not. Colleen knew, Colleen knew because she saw him. And Colleen went away. Lance made her go away."

She was crying now, sobbing.

"Fucking hell, Mum. Fucking hell. What the fuck is going on with this fucking family?"

Annie was standing with her hand over her mouth and Lil's blow knocked her to the floor.

"You bitch, you fucking evil bitch. You knew all along what he was like and you made me guilty about him. And you knew, you always knew . . ."

"Keep her here, Mum. Even if you have to fucking beat her brains out. Don't let her near a phone, don't let her warn him, right?" Patrick was shouting.

Lil nodded. "You go, mate, she ain't going nowhere."

Lil held her daughter in her arms as she saw Patrick walk from the room.

Lance was nervous, the small bar was filling up with people and Karen was still nowhere to be seen. The small bar was part of a private drinking club that was frequented by Donny's main workforce and some of the clientele were civilians who liked to feel they were on the borders of the criminal fraternity. It was a nice little place, men brought their girlfriends here, never their wives, and they knew they were safe enough from prying eyes. Donny prided himself on his business acumen; he had taken the bar in lieu of a debt. It had earned him ten times the original amount and also earned him the goodwill of many a Face who needed somewhere to rest a weary head without the police on their backs. He was watching the door with as much interest as Lance and he knew that this was going to be a hard old night, but he would survive it.

"How much longer is she going to take?"

Donny shrugged, his ugly face screwed up in irritation. "I don't know, she's doing us a fucking favor. Hang on and I'll ring her again." He walked away, dialing a number on his cell phone.

"You've rung her twice already. What is she, fucking thick?"

As he spoke, the door opened, and Lance knew then that Donny had sold him out. The man put his phone away and said sadly, "You're scum, Lance, and I always knew that, but this time you went too far." The bar was cleared within minutes of Patrick attacking Lance with a baseball bat. The police were called in when a passerby heard the screams. By then, Lance was unrecognizable as a human being.

Epilogue

"You all right, Mum?"

Lil sighed heavily and her laughter had a painful edge. "No, actually, I'm not, but you knew that, right?"

She was so jolly, so full of life, it was hard to believe she was dying. "Oh, Mum, what will we all do without you?"

Lil yawned. It was a deliberate ploy to annoy her sons.

"*You'll* all survive, *shit* floats, remember, just look after your sisters for me, OK? Especially Kathleen. She will always need to be cared for, and no matter how much she annoys you, or gets on your nerves, you remember me now, as I am, on me deathbed, asking you for this one favor, right?"

Christy laughed, and Patrick saw how much he looked like their mother, whereas he, on the other hand, was like his father, the spit of him apparently, as everyone seemed intent on reminding him at every available opportunity.

"Guilt is a great tool when you need something done."

Patrick grinned. "Deathbed promises are like pie crusts, meant to be broken."

Lil laughed feebly. "I mean it, boys, this isn't a joke. Eileen's got Paulie, but Kathleen has no one, remember that. Remember what she's been through."

"Mum, I'll take care of them all, don't worry."

Lil knew he would, but it didn't help her. She wasn't really happy about knowing her life was almost over, even though she was ready to go. But she knew she had to convince them; even though she was desperate to let it all go, was ready for the big sleep, she was still not sure that they were.

"I am ready, you know, ready to go. The pain is taking over now, and I need to know you are settled, happy in your own ways." They sighed together, and she could feel their pain as they were all feeling hers. She lay back on the pillows and watched them. She loved to see them together; they were close, all of them. Really close.

"Mum, we are as sweet as a nut, so stop worrying about us." Her Christy, her boy. Shawn, Shamus and Eileen. They all loved each other, in their own ways.

"Patrick, are you there, mate?"

"Course I am, Mum. What do you want?"

She sighed heavily, then she took his hand in hers, and he felt the weakness and the fragility of her. She was so ill, and so tiny it made him want to cry. She was as small as a child, the weight had dropped from her, not that she had ever been that big in the first place.

"Patrick, tell me the truth, yeah?"

"Oh, Mum, course I'll tell you the truth. What do you want to know?"

"What happened to Lance in the end? Did me mother claim him?" She looked at Ivana who she knew would tell her the truth even if Pat wouldn't. And she nodded almost imperceptibly.

"She took him, Mum, as far as we all know."

Eileen blew her lips out noisily in disgust. "Fucking old cow! She's only been asking if she can see you."

Everyone rolled their eyes in annoyance. Trust Eileen to open her big trap.

Lil smiled then, knowing what they were all thinking, and grateful to Eileen for being so honest. Lil looked like her old self, as she had looked years before, when they were small and she was still strong enough to care for them all.

"I'd like to see her one last time, on me own. I need to talk to her, make my peace before I go." She looked around the room at her children. Her hearts.

Jambo was there too, and she pulled him towards her, grabbing his hand and letting him know how pleased she was that he was there for her. "You made me so happy, you gave me my youngest child, and for that I will always be grateful. Me and you understood each other, didn't we?"

He nodded and she kissed his hand.

"Make them bring me mum, will you? I won't rest otherwise."

No one said a word, and she knew they wouldn't, had no intention of discussing it, so she changed the subject. "Have you heard any more about the court case, Pat?"

He shrugged. "They can't prove I done it; the evidence mysteriously got burned in that fire they had a while ago. Apparently, me and three drug dealers are all in the clear, no evidence, no fucking court case." Pat laughed heartily.

"Here, Mum, I also heard through the grapevine that the cocaine that was supposedly burned in the aforementioned fire had actually been *removed* beforehand. The British judicial system, eh, Mum? Best in the world, or so they say."

She laughed with him, knowing the score, as they all did. She knew that he was bluffing her; he was bailed out, whether or not he had a pass, a Get Out Of Jail Free Card, was another matter entirely.

But he would go away for Lance without a second's thought, and so he should. He was pretending that he was not worried, that Lance's murder had not been noticed. He had been on remand for a long time. It was only her imminent death that had got him out now. She knew that her illness had made the judge more lenient, that and his sister's murder. She supposed that, to outsiders, their lives must seem outrageous. The newspapers certainly seemed to think so. Rehashing her husband's death, and now making the most of poor Colleen's death, and of course Lance's. It was as if Patrick had already been found guilty of Lance's murder; the papers had already convicted him. Poor Pat, he had been on remand for so long, and now he was waiting for a court date, a court date that, thanks to the papers, would find him guilty.

His brother's death had been a cause for relief for everyone, if the truth was only known. Lance was the nightmare all mothers dreaded; he had been the terror that you couldn't see. In fact, Lance had been the evil you *couldn't* have foreseen. He was every mother's worst nightmare, and his granny's little soldier. To think her poor Kathy, her Kathleen, had been in fear of him all those years, when she had thought that his love of Kathy had been his saving grace, the one thing he had going for him, as far as she was concerned. His care of her had made them all believe that, somewhere inside him, a nice person was fighting to get out. Yet, her mother had made it easy for him, made it look normal.

Lily was still coming to terms with that, how someone who was so unstable was her own son; her own flesh and blood. That he could have been capable of something like that.

Pat's daughter came to sit beside her and Ivana stood behind her, with her hand on her shoulder. It was a lovely sight and Lil enjoyed seeing them. "You're a good girl, Ivana. If he had half a brain . . ."

They were all laughing then. Lil never let a moment go by without mentioning the two of them getting married.

The boys were all near her, and she waved them away from the bed, knowing she had a good while until she was actually on her way out. They didn't need to see that, they were still young enough *not* to understand that this would be them one day. They still believed life was long, that they had *ages* to go before they would need to make any arrangements for their own burials or their deaths.

She was actually looking forward to her death. Was ready, more than ready. But this constant pretense that she was not bothered about it was tiring. It was for her kids' benefit of course, it was them who weren't ready. She knew that they would be all right though. They were close, they would look out for one another, and she had to be content with that.

"Bring me mum to see me. I want to see her tomorrow."

"Are you sure?"

"Course I'm sure. I've got cancer, not fucking Alzheimer's. Do what I ask, will you?"

They all nodded in agreement and she wanted to cry for them. They left her a little while later, and she could finally let herself relax; the pain was so bad that she couldn't even breathe in peace. She took her morphine with a greediness that made her understand the junkies she had always hated, seen as weak. Their pain she knew was mental, hers was physical, and she just prayed for a good death, even though she was hanging on until she finally saw a priest. She knew that whatever had happened in the past, she would only pass properly with the Last Rites.

Death didn't scare her, she welcomed it. In fact, she felt that it was ordained somehow; it meant she could be with her daughter, her baby girl, her little Colleen.

Her Patrick would be waiting for her as well, she knew that. She didn't know how she knew that, why she was so convinced of it, but she was.

Death was a great leveler, it was something that no one could avoid. Money, power, nothing could stop it. *Death*. It was a law unto itself. It was something that you could only do alone. Beggars and kings, as her husband had pointed out, it happened to them all. She had read once that Elizabeth the First had said on her deathbed: "All my riches for but a moment in time."

Well, she didn't want any longer, she was happy to go now. She was happy to die, and to sleep finally without the pain and the burning that told her she was still in the land of the living. Her kids needed to be freed from her sick bed anyway, it wasn't fair on them. They needed to bury her so they could get on with their lives once more, without her illness taking over everything.

Once she died, they could live their own lives at last, and remember her as she *was*, strong and vibrant, looking out for them all, instead of seeing her as she was *now*, a tiny woman in constant pain, and wishing for death as she had once wished for life.

Kathleen would be all right, as would Eileen; in fact, they looked better already. Lance's death had frightened Eileen, stopped her drinking, made her realize that there was more to life than her bloody problems. And Kathleen was free of him, the bastard. Kathleen and Eileen were once more a duo, once more closer than close.

She could go now in peace, she had done all she could for them, and the last thing she could give them, the last thing she could do for them, was let them see a happy death. Their father's death had been so violent;

Patrick had been murdered with such hatred and so much blood. She wanted them to feel she had gone from them without any kind of fear or guilt whatsoever. They needed to say goodbye to her, and then go on with their lives. She understood now, that, as a parent, it was the most important thing you could give your children; you just wanted them to feel peace of mind.

She wanted the Last Rites now, even though she had not been to Mass for the longest time. This close to meeting her maker, she knew she wanted to see the priest, needed to make her last confession, receive her last Communion. The priest was due to come in the morning, she was looking forward to it.

God was good in his own way, he had given her the life she had lived, and she knew now, staring death in the face, that if she had been taught anything, it was that when all was said and done, life was for living, and no matter how bad that living might seem at the time, it was far better than the alternative.

Patrick came back into the room then, with her morphine, and she grabbed her son's hand tightly, saying, "Bring me my mother, bring her tonight, darling. I don't think I have as long as we thought."

"Are you sure, Mum, sure you want to see her?"

She sighed once more. "Oh, please, Pat, I can't go without seeing her, even you know that!"

He hugged her gently, knowing how painful her body was, knowing the cancer had crept everywhere, into her bones, and also knowing that she had let it happen. Knew that she had known for a long time that the cancer had returned, and she had decided to forego any treatment. Had kept it secret. She wanted to go, and he respected that, even as he hated her for it.

"Bring her, will you? I'm so tired, Patrick. Not of the cancer, but of the rest of it! I know you'll all survive without me, and I also know you'll look after the little ones. You're a good kid, Patrick, you were always my favorite. I trusted you, and I'm trusting you now. Bring me my mother, let me do this last thing before I go."

He was nearly in tears, and she said with a forcefulness she didn't know she had in her, "Oh, stop it, let me go in peace. I can't be sorry for you all, or I'll hang on, Pat, and, if I hang on, you lot will only re-member me dying, you won't remember me as I *was*. The things I *did* to make life easier for you will be forgotten, all you lot will remember is me dying, and that is not what I want."

"We don't want you to go. The doctor says you can still have chemo . . ."

"I *don't* want chemo, another few months or weeks, I just want to be *me* again, Patrick. Just *me* back in charge of my own life. I *want* to go, and you have to make sure it happens nicely, without anyone being hurt or worried. I'm ready to go, son, and I want to go while I am still lucid. I don't want my kids to remember me as nothing more than a bag of bones and a fucking rotten smell. I want them to remember me alive, so stop talking shite and bring me my mother. The only thing I need now is to talk to her, nothing more."

He nodded then. "OK, but I am staying with you, all right?"

"Of course! You can be there and you can earwig, just don't interfere."

He laughed again, a loud and boisterous laugh that she knew was as phony as Ivana's blond hair. "Oh, Mum . . ."

"Oh, son! Patrick, please, I am so tired, darling, just bring her, will you, and let me do this one last thing before I go, *please?*"

Annie was thrilled that her daughter wanted to see her. She had heard how ill she was and she wanted to make her peace with her. She was being ostracized by everyone, and she couldn't stand that; she needed the family around her and hoped that Lil would guarantee that hap-pened. Annie had completely wiped out Lance and what he had done, what she had caused, and what she had hidden. It was like none of it had ever happened.

Annie was now, as far as she was concerned, without stain.

As she walked into her daughter's bedroom, she could smell the can-cer, smell the hopelessness, and the medication that was keeping her daughter alive. She sat by the bed; she had not seen Lil for a while, and the change in her daughter was shocking. She was so thin, and her face, that lovely face, was all eyes and cheekbones. Her hair was still intact, but thinner, and up close she could see her daughter's scalp. It was cruel, upsetting to see her like that.

"Hello, Mum."

Annie, for the first time in her life, felt someone else's pain, saw her daughter's predicament, knew she was dying and knew she was lucky that she had this chance to make amends.

"Oh, Lil, how are you, love?"

For the first time in her life, Lil could hear genuine sorrow in her mother's voice. Knew that she really meant what she said. Actually cared that her daughter was so ill.

"I am all right, Mum. I am ready to go, *really I am*. I am glad my time is up. That's why I wanted to talk to you, why I asked Patrick to bring you here." She smiled at her eldest son as he sat down in the chair by the window.

Annie nodded. She was pleased at her daughter's request, relieved that she would see her before she died. She had prayed for this moment, and God had answered her prayers.

"Did you sort out Lance's funeral?"

Annie sighed once more. Bless her heart, Lil did care for him. At the end of the day, he had been her son, so she still wanted to make sure he was taken care of properly.

"I made sure he was buried properly, love, don't worry."

Lil laughed gently. "I am dying, Mum, do you realize that?"

Annie nodded, and grasped her daughter's hand.

"I wanted to talk to you before I went, before I go. I needed to say a few things so I can go in peace. Give my kids peace, you know."

"Oh, *Lily*. My girl . . ." Seeing her daughter dying made Annie realize what she would actually be losing, see what she would miss, understand how much Lil had been a part of her life.

No one had called her Lily in years and hearing it felt strange, felt wrong. "Mum, I have to tell you this, all right?"

Annie nodded, and Lil could see the relief in her eyes, feel the reassurance that she had been hoping for.

"I know, darling, but you don't need to tell me anything."

"Oh, but I do, Mum. I ain't got long, and that is not a problem. I am looking forward to the next step, the next life, you know. But I need to tell you how I feel before I go."

Lil took a sip of her drink; the straw in her glass was bright pink, and she sipped at it as if her life depended on it.

"I hope, Mum, that *you* die, screaming, of cancer. Alone and unaided, I pray that you are left to rot, and that you never lose the gift of consciousness. That you know exactly what is happening to you. I pray you never know a happy day again. That is my last wish on this earth. I wish *you* dead, but not until you finally realize that no one *wants* you, no one *cares* for you and I pray that you die alone and in agony, and no one finds your body until you're rotten, you're fucking putrid. Now, *fuck* off, and don't come near me or mine ever again."

Annie was devastated, and she looked down at her only child, her daughter. "You don't mean that, Lil, you can't mean that . . ."

"Oh, I mean it, Mum. I hope you never know another happy day. I pray that you sink lower and lower into your own fucking hatred. That's me prayer, and God *is* good, you know, he pays back debts without money. I might be dying of cancer, but you'll die of guilt and hate and no one will care. That will be your punishment, as it was Lance's. I hope *you* live for years and years, and no one comes near or by you. I hope you never know any kind of peace, or any kind of rest. I hate you so much it has to leave some kind of *mark* on you. Now, get *out*, and stay away from *me* and my *family*."

Annie was crying, her sobbing loud in the room.

"Get her out of here, would you, Pat, and make sure she never comes near me again?"

"Please, Lil, let me make amends, let me show you how much I regret everything . . ."

"If I needed a kidney or a bone-marrow transplant and you were the only person who could do that for me, I would rather die. I will wait for you, Mum. You'll hang on like the creaking door, and you'll die alone, with no one near you, and not one person who'll care. And that knowledge is what will make my death so much easier. My poor Kathleen was destroyed by you and Lance. That girl was tortured, and my little Colleen was served up, so you and Lance could play at grown-ups. But even when I die, and that won't be long, I'll still be standing at your shoulder; I'll make sure I am near enough to you, so you'll never know another happy day. My kids hate you, and that won't change, and I'll leave this world all the happier because I know you'll die alone."

"I loved *you*, Lil . . . Whatever you might think."

Lily Brodie looked at the woman who had borne her, who had given her life, and had then made sure that her life was unendurable, and then she looked at her son, her eldest son, and she said nastily, "Get her out, will you? I never want to see her again as long as I live."

She laughed then and said to Annie, "And that, Mother, is not long. But at least *I* will go with my family around me. I will die knowing I was loved, and if I never achieved anything else in life, I will always know that I had that much."

Janie Callahan was washing her friend, and she knew that Lil was dying painfully. As she washed her, making sure she was clean and tidy for any visitors, she knew that it would not be long before she would be gone.

"Thanks, Janie. I appreciate all you are doing for me."

Janie smiled at her and, sitting on the edge of her bed, she held on to her friend's hand as if her life depended on it. "I'll miss you, girl, and you know it. We go back so long. I loved you and I always will. You've been good to me. Whatever happened in the past, me and you have always been close. I hated Lance, and what he did to my girl, but I could never blame you, Lil. He was not a part of us, and you knew it, like I knew it."

"I'll miss you, too, Janie, and I don't want to leave my kids, but I must. Do me a favor, go home and enjoy the rest of your life . . ."

Janie was sad, so sad at the words, but Lil understood her reaction.

"Listen, life is short, even at its longest, it's short. I just want to be with my kids now, for the end. But I hope you'll always remember our friendship."

Janie went home, crying her eyes out for the life that was coming to an end, and for the woman she loved and admired.

*   *   *

Patrick was sitting beside Lil, as always. She felt him holding her hand, and she squeezed it as tightly as she could, but she knew he wouldn't feel it. She had no strength left, she was as weak as a kitten.

She was dying hard and, now it was really happening, she wasn't sure she wanted to go. The life force was a very powerful thing. She didn't want to leave them all, was frightened they would not cope without her.

"Patrick, always remember I loved the bones of you. Of all of you."

He kissed her hand gently. "I *know*, Mum, and I have loved you always. I still do, more than anyone or anything, we all do, darling."

"Get the priest in, Pat, I'm ready. I want to see my Colleen again, I want to hold her in my arms."

She closed her eyes then, and her children knew she was making herself ready for her maker.

She looked peaceful when the priest gave her the Last Rites, and she looked ready for the last journey.

They stood by her bed, and all watched her with fear and trepidation, because the woman who had been such a big part of their life was really going now, was leaving them. Jambo was holding one hand, and Patrick was holding the other. The twins, Shamus, Christy and Shawn, her children were all around the bed and the priest was still praying.

Then Lil Brodie opened her eyes and said happily: "Look at my Patrick, he's at the end of the bed, and he's calling me. He's calling me."

Then she was gone. It was so quick, too fast for such a momentous occasion. She just closed her eyes and left them.

Kathleen and Eileen were in bits and, as they cried, young Shawn said seriously, "I hope he did come for her, don't you? I hope he was there."

Patrick Brodie said sadly, "Oh, he was there, all right, and he was calling her, no doubt about that, they were closer than any two people I ever knew."

Shawn grinned then and, looking at his family standing around the bed, he said happily, "We're all *close*, Pat. Closer than most people, closer than even poor Mum ever realized."

Patrick laughed then.

"She *knew* that, mate. We are close *because* of her. She made sure of that. Now we have to live up to her expectations, look after each other; at the end of the day, we are all we've got."

"Do you think we'll survive her death, Pat?"

He looked at his brothers and sisters and saw them as his mother had seen them, all needing him and all needing each other.

"We fucking better, because she was the best thing that ever happened to any of us; she kept us together, and she made sure we were a family. Now all we have left is each other."

Christy looked at them all and said quietly, "Amen to that."